U1016326

彝族民间故事

张永祥　选编
汤茜　张立玉　译
［美］H.W.Lan　审校

国家出版基金项目
NATIONAL PUBLICATION FOUNDATION

“十三五”国家重点图书

中国南方民间文学典籍英译丛书

丛书主编　张立玉　丛书副主编　起国庆

FOLK STORIES OF THE YI NATIONALITY

出品单位：
中南民族大学南方少数民族文库翻译研究基地
云南省少数民族古籍整理出版规划办公室

WUHAN UNIVERSITY PRESS
武汉大学出版社

·汉英对照·

图书在版编目(CIP)数据

彝族民间故事:汉英对照/张永祥选编;汤茜,张立玉译.—武汉:武汉大学出版社,2021.11

中国南方民间文学典籍英译丛书/张立玉主编

“十三五”国家重点图书　2020年度国家出版基金资助项目

ISBN 978-7-307-22671-5

Ⅰ.彝…　Ⅱ.①张…　②汤…　③张…　Ⅲ.彝族—民间故事—作品集—中国—汉、英　Ⅳ.I277.3

中国版本图书馆CIP数据核字(2021)第214802号

责任编辑:郭　静　　责任校对:汪欣怡　　版式设计:韩闻锦

出版发行:**武汉大学出版社**　(430072　武昌　珞珈山)

(电子邮箱:cbs22@ whu.edu.cn　网址:www.wdp.whu.edu.cn)

印刷:湖北恒泰印务有限公司

开本:720×1000　1/16　印张:35.75　字数:431千字

版次:2021年11月第1版　2021年11月第1次印刷

ISBN 978-7-307-22671-5　定价:98.00元

版权所有,不得翻印;凡购我社的图书,如有质量问题,请与当地图书销售部门联系调换。

丛书编委会

学术顾问

王宏印　李正栓

主编

张立玉

副主编

起国庆

编委会成员（按姓氏笔画排列）

邓之宇　王向松　艾　芳　石定乐　龙江莉　刘　纯
陈兰芳　汤　茜　李克忠　杨　柳　杨筱奕　张立玉
张扬扬　张　瑛　和六花　依旺的　保俊萍　起国庆
陶开祥　鲁　钒　蔡　蔚　臧军娜

序

近年来，民族典籍英译捷报频传，硕果累累。韩家全教授等人的壮族系列经典翻译陆续出版，王宏印教授等人的系列民族典籍英译研究著作已经问世，李正栓教授等人的藏族格言诗英译著作不断在国内外出版，王维波教授等人的东北民族典籍英译著作纷纷付梓，李昌银教授等人的“云南少数民族经典作品英译文库”于2018年年底出版，其他民族典籍英译作品也在接踵而至。

近日，中南民族大学张立玉教授传来佳音：他们要出版“十三五”国家重点图书——“中国南方民间文学典籍英译丛书”。虽叫民间文学，其实基本上都是民族典籍。这一系列包括十本书，它们是《黑暗传》《哭嫁歌》《哈尼阿培聪坡坡》《彝族民间故事》《南方民间创世神话选集》《十二奴局》《召树屯》《娥并与桑洛》《金笛》《梅葛》。其中，好几本是云南少数民族的。只有一本是汉族典籍，即《黑暗传》。很有意思的是，这些典籍展示了不同民族的创世史诗或诸如此类的东西。

《黑暗传》以民间歌谣唱本形象地描述了盘古开天辟地结束混沌黑暗，人类起源及社会发展的历程，融合了盘古、女娲、伏羲、炎帝神农氏、黄帝轩辕氏等众多英雄人物在洪荒时代艰难创世的一系列神话传说。它被称为汉族首部创世史诗。《哈尼阿培聪坡坡》是一部完整地记载哈尼族历史沿革的长篇史诗，堪称哈尼族的“史记”，长5000余行，以现实主义手法记叙了哈尼族祖先在各个历史时期的迁徙情况，并对其迁徙各地的原因、路线、途程，各个迁居地的社会生活、生产、风习、宗教，以及与毗邻民族的关系等，均作了详细而生动的辑录，因而该作品不仅具有文学价值，而且具有重大的历史学、社会学及宗教学价值。《南方民间创世神话选集》包括一些创世神话，主要是关于世界起源和人类起源的神话。《十二奴局》是一部在哈尼族广泛流传的民间诗歌，它通过“哈尼”（传统歌）的形式在民间演唱，世代流传。“奴局”是哈尼语，相当于汉族著述中的“篇”、“章”或汉族曲艺中的曲目。“十二奴局”即十二路歌的意思。译著表现了远古哈尼先民奇特的想象，涉及天体自然、人类发展、哈尼历史、历法计算、四时季令、农事活动等各个方面的知识，完整地反映了哈尼先民对天地形成、人类起源、民族迁徙的认识，具有创世神话与英雄史诗的合集之性质，可以说是哈尼族最为重要的文学经典之一。《梅葛》是彝族的一部长篇史诗，流传在云南省楚雄州的姚安、大姚等彝族地区。“梅葛”本为一种彝族歌调的名称，由于人们采用这种调子来唱彝族的创世史，因而创世史诗被称为“梅葛”。

其余几本书展示了一些少数民族的风俗习惯、恋爱故事、斗争故事等。《哭嫁歌》是土家族文化典籍。土家族姑娘在出嫁时用歌声诉说自己在封建买办婚姻制度下的不幸命运。《哭嫁歌》是土家族姑娘演唱的一种抒情歌谣，富有诗韵和乐感，融哀、怨、喜和乐为一体，以婉转的曲调向世人展示土家人独特的“哭”文化。《彝族民间故事》是一部以流传于云南楚雄彝族自治州彝族人民中间的民间故事为主体，同时覆盖全省包括小凉山等彝族地区的民间故事集。这些故事丰富多彩，从中能看到民族民间故事的各种形态和生动、奇妙而颇具彝族民族特色的文化特征。《召树屯》是傣族民间长篇叙事诗，叙述了傣族佛教世俗典籍《贝叶经·召树屯》中一个古老的传说故事。这部叙事诗一直为傣族人民所传唱，历久不衰。《娥并与桑洛》是一部优美生动的叙事诗，一个凄美的爱情悲剧。《金笛》是一部苗族长篇叙事诗，富于变幻性和传奇性，尽情铺叙扎董丕冉与蒙诗彩奏的悲欢离合，热情赞颂他们在与魔虎的激烈斗争中所表现出来的坚贞不屈、英勇顽强的精神，许多情节含有浓郁的民族特色。

这些故事都很引人入胜，都很符合国家文化发展需求，向世人讲述中国故事，传播中华文化，并且讲述的是民族故事，充分体现了党和国家对各民族的关怀。

民族典籍英译是传播中国文化、文学和文明的重要途径，是中华文化“走出去”的重要组成部分，是国家战略，是提高文化“软实力”的重要方式，在文化交流和文明建设中起着不可或缺的作用，对提升中国国际话语权和构建中国对外话语体系以及对建设世界文学都有积极意义。

中国民族典籍使世界文化更加丰富多彩、绚丽多姿。我国各民族典籍中折射出的文化多样性极大地丰富了世界多元、特色鲜明的文化。人们对多样性形成全新的认识角度和思维方式，有助于开阔视野，丰富思考问题的角度，挖掘这些经典中的教育价值和文化价值，对世界其他民族都有指导和借鉴意义，并且有助于建设我国的文化自信。

民族典籍翻译与研究事业关乎国家的稳定统一，关乎民族关系的和谐发展，关乎世界多元文化的实现。在中国，民族典籍资源极为丰富，有待进一步挖掘、翻译，仍有许多少数民族典籍亟待拯救，民族典籍翻译与研究工作任重而道远，民族典籍翻译事业大有可为。

李正栓[①]

2019 年 7 月 19 日

① 李正栓，中国英汉语比较研究会典籍英译专业委员会常务副会长兼秘书长；中国中医药研究促进会传统文化翻译与国际传播专业委员会常务主任委员。

前　言

《彝族民间故事》是彝族的重要典籍，收录了流传于横断山脉地区彝族的民间故事，选取彝族具有民族特点和代表性的内容，以讲故事的形式再现彝族民众的历史记忆、现实生活、情感表达，彰显了彝族民众对社会的认识和人生的理解，是对彝族文化的重要传承。

首先，该典籍对于提高道德水平有重要的指导意义。比如书中记录搓日阿补和史拉俄特的孝悌之情、撒尼族弟弟和汉族哥哥的兄弟之义、阿米尼和阿达西的爱情之美等，宣扬真、善、美的内容比比皆是。其民族道德价值观念超越了时空的局限，至今仍有积极的指导意义。其次，该典籍对传承民族历史文化有重要的推动作用。彝族的民族民间文学历史上主要依靠非文字的口耳相传，其活在彝族人们的精神世界中，活在云南的部落里。该典籍就如一位彝族历史和文化的忠实记录者，通过挖掘和整理，使彝族的非物质文化遗产得以保留和传承。再次，该典籍有助于陶冶情操，提高艺术鉴赏水平。其中扣人心弦的故事讲述，形象、生动的语言表达等具有极高的艺术效果，能够提高审美，并在文学创作中起到借鉴作用。

中南民族大学外语学院张立玉院长致力于将南方少数民族典籍推向世界。在其领导下，编写团队着手选取《彝族民间故事》作为英译蓝本之一。

典籍英译需要丰富的跨学科知识，树立文化翻译观，以及采取合适的翻译手段。翻译过程中，在研究专家的帮助下，译者尽力将民族学和翻译学融会贯通地应用；同时，除了掌握两种语言外，译者还需了解目的语和源语的文化，充分考虑典籍中蕴含的文化因素以及读者的接受度；由于文化和语言差异，为了补足差异，正确的翻译策略也十分重要，译者将归化和异化策略及直译、意译相结合，力图使典籍的内涵和艺术风格有效地传递给目的语读者。

本书为汉英对照本，汉文版由云南人民出版社 2009 年出版，张永祥主编；英译由张立玉、汤茜主持完成，美国专家 H. W. Lan 教授审校。在此一并感谢翻译中各方的大力支持与帮助。

由于译者水平有限，对内容的理解和表达若有不当之处，敬请读者批评指正。

张立玉　汤茜

2019 年 7 月

目　　录

神祇与英雄

更资天神 ······ 4
人祖的由来 ······ 38
三兄弟 ······ 50
史拉俄特“买”父亲 ······ 72
搓日阿补征服女儿国 ······ 86
阿什色色和布阿诗嘎娓 ······ 138
阿鲁举热 ······ 160
南诏始祖细奴逻 ······ 190
阿乍利 ······ 210

我们的大地

火把节的传说 ······ 228
赛衣节的传说 ······ 286
牟定三月会的传说 ······ 304
摔跤的来历 ······ 310
尼施传彝文 ······ 316
三弦的来历 ······ 324
白车勒的故事 ······ 334

灵魂与人生

流浪孤女蛇娘 …… 346
红石岩 …… 388
小白龙和彝家女 …… 404
猎手和姑娘 …… 418
阿克和碧鸡姑娘 …… 430
神伞与宝葫芦 …… 440
阿勒喜和查尼诺 …… 462
虎子 …… 478
阿古与阿赊 …… 498
阿依利里 …… 524

Contents

Deities and Heroes

God of Gengzi …… 5
The Origin of Human Ancestor …… 39
The Three Brothers …… 51
Shilae'te "Bought" Father …… 73
Cuoriabu Conquered the Kingdom of Women …… 87
The Story of Ashisese and Buashigawei …… 139
Alujure …… 161
Xinuluo, The Ancestor of Nanzhao Kingdom …… 191
Azhali …… 211

Our Land

Legends of the Torch Festival …… 229
The Legend of the Saiyi Festival …… 287
The Legend of the Third Month Fair in Mouding …… 305
The Origin of Wrestling …… 311
Nishi Spread the Yi Language …… 317
The Origin of Sanxian …… 325
The Story of Baichele …… 335

Spirit and Life

Homeless Orphan Sheniang ········· 347
Red-stone Rock ········· 389
Little White Dragon and the Girl of Yi Nationality ········· 405
A Hunter and a Girl ········· 419
Ake and a Girl Called Biji ········· 431
The Magic Umbrella and the Precious Gourd ········· 441
Alexi and Chaninuo ········· 463
Huzi ········· 479
Agu and Ashe ········· 499
Ayilili ········· 525

神祇与英雄

Deities and Heroes

更资①天神

蒲依生更资

更资天神住在石姆岩哈的三重交天上②，他是天地万物的缔造者和主宰者。更资的母亲名叫蒲依③。

蒲依不是人，也不是神；她不是植物，也不是动物。

蒲依本来是一股气。在太古的时候，天地还没开辟前，头上没有天，没有星云雷雨；脚下没有地，没有生灵草木。宇宙间清浊二气搅缠在一起，天地像锅底一样，黑漆漆的，不透一丝光亮。蒲依便在浊气里形成，在清气里出生，然后自由自在地飘荡在清浊二气里。浊气是它的食物，清气是它的饮用水。它在浊云上睡觉，在清云里玩耍。这样过了九千九百九十年，气蒲依变成了云蒲依，有了云的形象。

---

① 更资：彝族各方言支系神话中，掌握天地万物的最高神王。又译为"策耿纪""恩梯古资""陈根子""格祖天神"等。

② 彝族先民认为，宇宙间共有人、鬼、神三界。石姆岩哈是神界。

③ 有一则神话说，天地万物都是蒲依生出来的。

God of Gengzi①

Puyi Gave Birth to Gengzi

God of Gengzi, creator and ruler of heaven and earth, lives in Shimuyanha, one of the triple realms of the universe②. His mother is Puyi③.

Puyi is neither human nor god, not plant or animal.

Originally, Puyi was a current of gas. In time antiquity, before earth and heaven were separated, there was no sky overhead, nor a star, cloud, thunder or rain; there was no ground beneath, nor any creature, grass or tree. In the universe, clear gas and foul gas were intertwined, and heaven and earth were like the bottom of a pan, in darkness, without a hint of light. Puyi, formed in the foul gas and born in the clear gas, wandered freely within, replying on foul gas for food and clear gas for water; Puyi slept on the foul cloud and relaxed itself in clear cloud. After 9,990 years, gas Puyi became cloud Puyi, forming an image of cloud.

---

① Gengzi: The supreme god and master of heaven and earth in all branches of the Yi legends. Also known as "Cegengji" "Entiguzi" "Chengenzi" "Gezu God" etc.

② The Yi people believe that there are three realms in the universe, namely the realm of human, the realm of ghost and the realm of deity. Shimuyanha is the realm of deity.

③ According to a myth, all things under heaven are born by Puyi.

这云蒲依长着螃蟹的脚，但它的脚是红云；蒲依长着鱼的鳞，但它的鳞是黑云；蒲依长着牛头马面，但它的面是白云；蒲依长着穿山甲的尾，但它的尾是花云；蒲依生长着猪身子，但它的身子是浓云。

到了第九千九百九十九年的头三年，云蒲依忽然感到心烦起来，喝清气不能解它的渴，吃浊气不能饱它的肚，在浊云上睡不着觉，在清云上没兴趣玩耍。因为定不下心来，它只好到处乱走，走着走着，便走到车云木吾嘎托的碑基木来了。碑基木有一棵玛支玛珂神树①，它的树干是一股扭结在一起的浊气，伸长在清气里，并在清气里分杈，变成繁茂的树枝。它的陈叶是浊云，它的嫩叶是清云。这棵树会唱风的歌、会唱水的歌。见了云蒲依，它就唱道：“蒲依飘过来，蒲依荡过来，是不是找伙伴，我就是伙伴；是不是找朋友，我就是朋友。”

① 这里的树，应当“树神”解。后文的牛羊猪马亦如此。故事原意中，这里的树是抽象的，并不代表实体。

The cloud Puyi had legs of a crab, but they were actually red clouds; it had fish scales, but they were black clouds; it had a face of ox-head and horse-face, but it was white cloud; it had a tail of a pangolin, but it was floral cloud; it had a body of a pig, but it was thick cloud.

One day in the first three years after 9999 years, cloud Puyi suddenly felt upset. It could no longer be satisfied with water from clear gas and food from foul gas, and could hardly fell asleep on the foul cloud and was not interested in relaxing on the clear cloud anymore. In this unsettled mood, it wandered about and came to Beijimu in Cheyunmuwugatuo. There was a sacred tree① named Mazhimake in Beijimu, whose trunk was foul gas kinked together, splitting and spreading to the clear gas, like branches with luxuriant foliage. Its mature leaves were foul clouds and its newly-grown leaves were clear clouds. This tree could sing songs of wind and water. When the sacred tree saw Puyi, it sang, "Flow here, Puyi; swing here, Puyi. Are you looking for a companion? I am your companion. Are you looking for a friend? I am your friend."

---

① The tree here should be explained as the "tree god", so are the cattle, sheep, pigs and horses mentioned later. According to the story, the tree here is abstract, not a concrete one.

蒲依听了，就朝玛支玛珂神树飘过去，先挂在它的树枝上玩了三天，又绕着树干飘了三天。在最后三天里，云蒲依觉得没有兴趣玩，它失望极了，于是不满地唱道：“玛支玛珂树，树梢光秃秃，树枝干巴巴，树干光溜溜，只能做我影子的伴，不能做我心中的伴。我不想和你做伴，我不和你玩。”唱完就要飘走。玛支玛珂树急了，伸出树枝抓住蒲依的裙裾，接着唱道：“蒲依不要飘，蒲依不要荡，你若是找心伴，我给你心伴，我做你心伴，蒲依莫飘走，把脸转回来。”

蒲依想飘飘不走，想荡荡不开，于是回过头来问：“玛支玛珂树，你别骗人好不好，你别哄人好不好，你在我的身外，我在你的身外，你怎么做我的心伴，你如何为我的心伴？”

玛支玛珂神树唱道：“你看我的枝干多粗壮，我要在上面开出三朵花，一朵是金灿灿的金花，一朵是银汪汪的银花，一朵是红艳艳的鸡冠花。只要你把三朵花采食了，我就到了你的心里，我就成了你的心伴。从此以后啊，你飘到天南，我伴你到天南，你荡到地北，我随你到地北，我到了你心里，时时陪伴你，永远不分离。”

After hearing this, Puyi flew to the sacred tree of Mazhimake, where Puyi hang on its branches and played for three days, and drifted around the tree for another three days. In the last three days, Puyi lost interest. In disappointment, Puyi sang, "Mazhimake, look at your bare treetop, dry branches and barren trunk; you can only be the companion of my shadow, not my heart. I don't want to be your companion, and I won't play with you anymore." When Puyi was about to leave, Mazhimake grabbed its dress with the branch hurriedly and sang, "Don't flow away and swing away, Puyi. If you look for a companion of heart, I am the one. I will be your companion of heart. Puyi, just don't flow away. Please turn around."

Being unable to flow away and swing away, Puyi turned back and asked, "Mazhimake, don't cheat on me, and don't coax me. You are outside my body and I am outside yours. How can you be my companion of heart? In what way?"

Mazhimake sang, "Look, my branches are growing stronger. There will be three flowers, one shinny golden flower, one argent silvery flower and one gorgeous cockscomb. Once you eat all the three flowers, I will get into your heart. Then, I am your companion of heart. I will accompany you wherever you go ever after, whether you flow to the north or to the south. In your heart, I will be with you at all times, and we will never be separated."

玛支玛珂神树说完，放开了蒲依的裙裾，把自己的枝干抖了三抖，抖得天摇地动，云团被撕裂，大气被搅乱。接着它又扭了扭树腰，扭得天地气云炸雷般“轰轰”直响。接着红光一闪，鸡冠花开出来了；金光一闪，金花开出来了；银光一亮，银花也开了出来。三朵花一开到树上，神树四周的云团变成了五光十色的锦衣，气流变成了千万条闪动腾舞的彩虹。蒲依的心晕晕醉醉，就像喝了酒，蒲依的眼迷迷离离，就像在做梦。于是她便把金花、银花和鸡冠花摘食了。

蒲依刚把仙花吞下，玛支玛珂神树就消失不见了。蒲依很着急，大声喊起来：“玛支玛珂神树，你到哪里去啦？”玛支玛珂神树在她的肚子里答道：“我在你的心里呢，我正在做你的心伴呢！”

蒲依一听，有点害怕，心慌起来了。她说：“你到我心里，真能做我的心伴吗？”玛支玛珂神树在她心里答道：“你如果想听歌，我就给你唱歌；你如果想说话，我就跟你说话；你如果想飞翔，我就帮助你飞翔。”

蒲依正想叫玛支玛珂唱歌，可是心里忽然像着了火，嗓子被烧得辣燥燥的。蒲依吓得哭了起来。她说：“啊呀不得了，心里烫烫的，脖子干干的，我想去喝水，我想去喝水。玛支玛珂，你救救我的命，告诉我水在何处。”

Mazhimake loosened its grip on Puyi's dress and shook its branches for three times, shaking the ground and heaven, thrashing air and cloud. Then, it twisted its wrist, making a clap of thunder between earth and heaven. Afterwards, there was a flash of red light and a cockscomb bloomed; then a flash of golden light, and a golden flower bloomed, which followed by a flash of silvery light, and a silvery flower bloomed. Once these three flowers bloomed, clouds around Mazhimake turned into beautiful clothes bright with different colors, and the airflow became a rainbow. Puyi felt dizzy, as if she was having wine. Her eyes blurred, as if she was having a dream. So she picked the golden flower, silvery flower and the cockscomb and ate them.

Once Puyi swallowed these immortal flowers, Mazhimake disappeared. Puyi exclaimed in anxiety, "Mazhimake, where are you?" Mazhimake replied in her belly, "I am in your heart. I am your companion of heart now!"

Puyi was afraid and nervous. She said, "Can you really be my companion of heart there?" Mazhimake replied, "If you want to listen to songs, then I'll sing for you; if you want to speak, I'll talk to you; if you want to fly, I will assist you."

Puyi was about to ack Mazhimake to sing a song, when she suddenly felt her heart was burning like fire, making her throat dry. Puyi was frightened to tears and said, "Oh, no. My heart is burning and my neck is dry. I want to have some water. I need it now. Mazhimake, save me. Tell me where I can find water."

玛支玛珂神树在蒲依的肚子里唱着答道："蒲依莫着急，蒲依莫心慌。展开你的翅，向西一直飘；启动你的身，向西一直荡。西方尼尔夺有一股神水，三天泛红波，三天泛绿波，三天泛黑波。你喝干神水，口渴自然消。"

蒲依听了后，急忙腾身飘起，一直向西赶去。尼尔夺的神水，看着像泉水，实际不是水，它是一股气，在空中流来流去。蒲依张开大嘴，把这股水全部喝干了。喝了尼尔夺神水后，蒲依心润润的，喉头甜甜的，心神果然宁静了。于是她又开始在浊气与清气之间荡来荡去地玩耍，和心里的玛支玛珂唱唱说说，日子过得非常快乐。

这样的日子过了三年，蒲依又开始不满足起来了。于是她拍着心口向玛支玛珂神树说："宇宙空荡荡，像个黑窟窿，我心虽有伴，但身却无伴，飞时不见影，玩时没对象，形单影孤独，无依又无靠，你还是出来，出来做伴吧。"

Mazhimake sang and replied in her belly, "Don't worry, Puyi; don't get panic, Puyi. Spread your wings and flow all the way to the west; set out and swing all the way to the east. There is immortal water in Nierduo in the west, which has red waves, then green waves and followed by black waves every three days. If you drink up this water, you will not feel thirsty anymore."

Therefore, Puyi set out and flew to the west hastily. The immortal water in Nierduo looked like spring water, which was actually a current of gas, flowing here and there in the air. Puyi opened her mouth widely and drank up. Afterwards, Puyi felt fresh inside out with peaceful mind. Then, Puyi began to swing and play between the foul gas and clear gas again, and chat and sing with Mazhimake, leading a joyous life.

After three years, Puyi became discontented again, so she patted her heart and said to Mazhimake, "The universe is hollow, like a black hole. Though I have a companion of heart, I have no companion of my body. There is nobody to play with. I am all alone and have no one to depend on. You'd better come out and be my companion."

玛支玛珂听了，唱道："我一进你心，就不能出来了，如果你要玩伴，我把你的心割一半，加上我的心一半，给你造个玩伴，让他出来跟你玩。"蒲依答应了。她忽然感到一阵撕心裂肺的剧疼，昏天黑地地挣扎了半天，等剧疼稍微减轻后，她生气地问："玛支玛珂神树，你是吃我的心呢，还是咬我的心？你再不住手，我就要死了。"玛支玛珂答道："我是在割你的心，我是在撕你的心，我要用你的心做你的伴。现在你蹲在浊云上，把尾巴翘一翘，我把你的伴丢出来。"蒲依依言蹲在浊云上，把尾巴翘了一翘，忽然有什么东西，从她的肚子里掉了出来，落在浊云上，哇呀哇呀地哭叫开了。蒲依吓了一大跳，把那东西拖起来一看，是个人模人样的小男孩。他长得胖乎乎的、嫩嫩的，张着嘴巴在蒲依的胸前乱拱，把蒲依拱得心痒痒的，神荡荡的，喜爱得头发昏。小男孩拱呀拱，什么也没拱到，便伸手踢脚，张开嘴哇呀哇呀哭起来。蒲依无论怎样也哄不住，急得跟着哭起来。她问玛支玛珂："我的心为什么哭，我怎么才能哄住他？"玛支玛珂在她心里答道："你把胸前的衣裳打开，我让你的血流到胸口上。你的心肝吃了你的血，才会不哭不闹变快乐。"蒲依依言把胸衣打开，胸前便鼓呀鼓，鼓起了一对乳房。小男孩吃了蒲依的奶，才安安静静地睡着了。

In reply, Mazhimake sang, "Once I enter into your heart, I can not come out. If you want a companion, I'll cut off half of your heart together with that of mine to make one for you to play with." Puyi agreed. Suddenly, she felt tearing pain inside and she struggled for quite a while. After her pain slightly soothed, Puyi questioned Mazhimake angrily, "Mazhimake, are you eating or biting my heart? You have to stop it now, or I'll be dead." Mazhimake replied, "I am cutting off your heart and tearing it apart, because I need it to make you a companion. Now squat on the foul cloud and hold up your tail. I will throw your companion out." Puyi did as Mazhimake told her. Suddenly, something dropped out from her belly and landed on the foul cloud, crying loudly, which startled Puyi. Puyi lifted it up and found that it was actually a baby boy, round and tender. The boy rubbed against Puyi's breasts with his mouth open. Puyi was itchy in heart, joyous in mind and dizzy in head because of the profound affection. The little boy rubbed again and again but got nothing. So he extended his arms, starting to kick feet and cry heavily. Not knowing how to comfort him, Puyi was tearfully upset. She asked Mazhimake, "Why is my heart crying? How can I soothe him?" Mazhimake replied in her heart, "Untie your clothes in front of your breast, and I'll let your blood flow there. Once your baby takes your blood, he will stop crying and be happy." Puyi followed. Then a pair of breasts swelled in the front of her body. The little boy drank Puyi's milk and slept peacefully.

从此以后，蒲依心里有了伴，身外也有了伴，这个伴是她的心，不会离她而去。她快乐极了，一天到晚抱着孩子，逗他哭，逗他笑，给他吃奶，哄他睡觉，并给他取了个名字叫"更"①。慢慢地，小男孩长大了，长成一个淘气可爱的大男孩。蒲依出门的时候，他拉着蒲依的衣角跟着跑，蒲依休息时，他就欢蹦乱跳在一边玩。掌管天地万物的主宰神更资，就这样出生、长大了。

神仙出世

更和蒲依妈妈一起，东飘西荡，玩了很久，慢慢地就感到日子过得乏味，不能满足了。有一天，他对母亲说："蒲依妈妈，宇宙间为什么除了气和云，什么也没有？我厌烦得很，我要新玩物。"蒲依听了，忙问肚里的玛支玛珂："玛支玛珂，我的心说厌烦气和云，要找新玩物，你说怎么办？"玛支玛珂说："我也没办法，不过你可以抽一股浊气上来，立在清气里，做成我当时的模样，让你的心去爬着玩吧。"蒲依听了，便去抽浊气。她先抽起两股浊气来，做成两棵杉树，然后问儿子："够了还是不够？"儿子摇摇头。蒲依又抽出两股浊气，做成两棵松树，又问儿子："这下够了吗？"儿子点点头，一天到晚就在四棵树上爬上爬下地玩。

① 更，是更资天神的本名。因为他是天地万物至高无上的主宰者，所以别人称呼他时，便加上一个"资"音，"资"意为"主宰者"或"掌管者"。"恩梯古资"就是"居住上界主宰万物的神更"之意。

Since then, Puyi had a companion both inside and outside. This companion was her heart, so he would never leave her. She became ecstatically happy. She hugged her child, tossing him with tears and laughter, breeding him with breast milk and coaxing him into sleep. Puyi named the child "Geng"①. Gradually, the child grew up and became a naughty and lovely boy. He followed her mother wherever she went, hanging onto her skirts; he played joyously by her mother's side when Puyi took a rest. Gengzi, the ruler of the universe was hereby born and growing up.

The Birth of Immortals

For a long time, Geng never left his mother's side, hanging out with her everywhere until one day he was bored about his life. He asked Puyi, "Mom, why is there only gas and cloud in the universe? Why isn't there anything else? I am so bored. I want to have some new toys to play with." Puyi hurriedly asked Mazhimake in her belly, "Mazhimake, my heart said that he is tired of gas and cloud, and want to have something new. What should I do?" "There's nothing I can do," Mazhimake replied, "but you can draw some foul gas and erect it up on the clear gas, making it something that looks like me. Then your heart could climb on it and play." Puyi did as told. She first drew two streams of foul gas and made them into two fir trees. She asked her son, "Is it enough?" Her son shook his head. Then, Puyi drew another two streams of foul gas and made them into two pine trees. She asked her son again, "Enough now?" Her son nodded and climbed up and down the four trees all day.

---

① Geng, the original name of the God of Gengzi. As the supreme ruler of heaven and earth, people added the sound of "zi" after the name of Geng when they called him, which means "ruler" or "controller". "Entiguzi" refers to "the God who lives in heaven and rules all things in the world".

更就这样快快乐乐地玩了很久。后来有一天，更正在树干上唱歌，忽然听见两棵杉树和两棵松树里，传出婴儿哇呀哇呀的哭叫声。更越听越奇怪，连忙跑去对蒲依说："妈妈呀妈妈，真是奇怪了。四棵树干，都学着我的声音在哭呢。"蒲依跟着儿子跑去一听，可不是嘛，四棵树干里都有婴儿的哭声，就和更小时候的哭声一模一样。于是蒲依用手爪去撕树干，刚撕开一个口，就跳出两个只有甑子①高的小人来，一个是男的，一个是女的。这样，四棵树各跳出两个小人，一共是四男四女。为了便于记认，蒲依便给他们每个取了一个名字。从第一棵杉树里跳出来的男孩叫儒热古达，女孩叫儒木力力；从第二棵杉树里跳出来的男孩叫阿呒书布，女孩叫术嫫却却；从第一棵松树里跳出来的男孩叫书热尔达，女孩叫书木吉吉；从第二棵松树里跳出来的男孩叫司热底尼，女孩叫妮木布布。这四对兄妹可不像更要食母乳才长大。他们是见风长，转眼就变成了四对高大健美的人。更很喜欢他们，便对他们说："我给你们做伴，你们和我玩耍，我们在一起生活，可以吗？"

① 译者注：甑子是一种古代炊具，主要用于蒸米饭，外部略像木桶。

These trees had kept Geng happy for a while. Until one day, when he was singing songs on the tree branch, he suddenly heard babies crying from the two fir trees and two pine trees. As the sound became clearer, Geng hurriedly went to his mother Puyi and said, "Mom, it is so strange. The four trees are mimicking my sound of crying." Puyi followed her son and found that there were really sound of crying of babies from the four trees, which were exactly the same as that of Geng's when he was little. So Puyi tore the tree branch apart. Upon tearing an opening, two babies, a boy and a girl as short as Zengzi①, jumped out. Likewise, two babies also jumped out from the other three trees respectively. So all together, there were four boys and four girls. For the convenience of recognition, Puyi gave the boy and girl from the first fir tree the name of Rureguda and Rumulili; and named those from the second fir tree Afushubu and Shumo-queque; For the boy and girl from the first pine tree, they were given the name of Shureerda and Shumujiji; while the boy from the second pine tree was named Siredini and the girl was called Nimububu. These four pairs of brothers and sisters did not need breast feeding like Gengzi. Instead, they grew with wind. So they grew up quickly and became tall and strong in a short time. Gengzi was fond of them enormously and said to them, "I will be your companion and we can play and live together. Alright?"

---

① Translator's note: Zengzi is an ancient rice steamer. Its exterior is like a wooden cask.

四对兄妹说：“我们很想和你玩耍，很想要你做伴，但你是气生的神，我们是树生的仙。仙只能做神的属民，不能做神的朋友，只能听神的使唤，不能做神的玩伴。”

更很失望地说：“我真不明白，为什么会这样？”四兄妹便又告诉他说：“因为你的父亲是玛支玛珂，他是先天的浊气精，你的魂是尼尔夺神水，那是先天的清气精，你的母亲呢，又是浊气和清气的精，所以你将是天地万物的主宰；而我们的母亲杉树和松树是你母亲抓起来的后天的浊气；我们的母亲是因为你在树上玩耍，才生我们的，所以我们不能和你平起平坐。”更听明白后，就说：“既然是这样，那我吩咐你们和我玩。”四兄妹只得和更一起玩。可他们对更唯唯诺诺，不能平起平坐。更玩得别扭，一点也痛快不起来，于是只好把四个男的封为四神，把四个女的封为四仙，把他们派去掌管宇宙八方。

The four pairs of brothers and sisters replied, "We want to play with you and be your companion, but you are the God born from gas and we are immortals born from trees. So immortals can only be the subordinates, not friends of the God; we can only follow the orders from the God, instead of being playing partners of the God."

Geng was disappointed. He said, "I can not understand, why is it so?" The four pairs of brothers and sisters told Geng, "Because your father is Mazhimake, the spirit of foul gas; your soul is the immortal water in Nierduo, the spirit of clear gas; your mother is the spirit of foul gas and clear gas, so you will be the master of heaven and earth. Our mother, the fir trees and pine trees, are foul gas drawn by your mother; we were born only because you were playing on these trees, so we cannot be on an equal footing." Having been told that, Geng said, "Alright, then I'd like to make a request to ask you guys to play with me." So the four pairs of brothers and sisters had to play with Geng. But they were a bunch of yes-men and they could not accept Geng as one of them. So Geng was awkward and unhappy. Therefore, he had to confer four immortals on the four boys and four fairies on the four girls. Afterwards, he assigned each of them to rule one of the eight districts of the universe.

打发走四神四仙后，更便缠着蒲依要个和自己一样的玩伴。蒲依没办法，只得拍着胸口对心里的玛支玛珂神树说："你把你的心和我的心再割一点下来，给更做个伙伴吧。"玛支玛珂神树说："心是不能再割了，我割一半肝试试。"接着蒲依昏天黑地地痛了一会儿，肚子里又掉出来一个人模人样的小男孩。蒲依给他取了个名字叫"阿尔"①，又开始哺养他，更也一天到晚兴高采烈地背着他玩。但不幸的是，这个名叫"阿尔"的小男孩，只能在浊气上行走，不能升到清气中去，而且无论怎么长也长不高，个头总是只有更的一半高。这时的更，已经成长为一个魁梧英俊的男子汉，个头就像大山，四肢如同杉树，捏一把浊气，可以把浊气捏成铁，揉一把白云，可以把白云揉成铜。他喜欢像一条黄鳝一样，在浊气和清气里自由自在地钻来钻去，阿尔做不了他的伴，无法陪着他玩耍。这使他很失望，于是他给阿尔起了个名：德布②。阿尔的名字，从此成了"德布阿尔"。后来更封德布阿尔为神匠，让他掌管浊气层。天地开辟出来后，德布阿尔便成为主宰人间的地神，被称为"米色③德布阿尔。"

---

① 译者注：蒲依三兄妹的名字，音节按次序排列，后者均比前者多一个音，似有以音节多少区别和确定胎次之意。

② 德布：意即又矮又胖的小人。

③ 米色：即地神，哀牢山一带又叫土主。

After dismissing the four immortals and fairies, Geng asked Puyi repeatedly for an equal partner. Puyi had no way but to pat her chest and ask Mazhimake in her heart, "Please cut off another half of your heart and that of mine to make a companion for Geng." Mazhimake replied, "The heart can not be sliced anymore. Let me try half of our livers." Puyi soon felt excruciatingly pain and dizzy. Later, a boy dropped out from her belly. Puyi named him A'er① and started to breastfeed him. Geng was happy to play with him and carried him on his back all day. But unfortunately, the little boy could only walk on the foul gas and could not go up to the clear gas. Also, as he could not grow tall, he was always only half of Geng's height. By then, Geng had already grown into a strong and handsome man, who was as tall as a great mountain with legs and arms like fir trees. The foul gas he grasped could be turned into iron, and the white cloud he rubbed could become copper. He was like an eel, getting into and out of the foul gas and the clear gas freely. But Aer could not be his companion to play with, which disappointed him. He gave Aer a name: Debu②. Therefore, Aer became Debuaer, which was later conferred by Geng as the immortal of craftsman, responsible for the foul gas area. After the separation of heaven and earth, Debuaer became God of Earth, also known as Mise③debuaer.

---

① Translator's note: the three brothers and sisters born by Puyi are named following a certain rule of number of syllables. It seems that when naming, the later born has one more syllable than the one born earlier.

② Debu: little man who is short and plump.

③ Mise: the God of Earth, also called earth master in areas around the Ailao Mountain.

更因为找不到伙伴，感到很孤独，一天到晚尽唱些叫人伤感的歌。蒲依一听见儿子的哀歌，心里就会一阵一阵地绞痛。她实在忍受不住了，便拍着胸脯，向心里的玛支玛珂神树说："玛支玛珂啊，我的心肝这么孤单悲苦，我们再想办法给他找个玩伴吧。"玛支玛珂为难地答道："我不知道给他找个什么样的玩伴才适合，你还是先问问你的心肝吧。"于是蒲依就问儿子说："我的更啊，你希望有一个什么样的伙伴呢？"更想了又想，告诉母亲说："一棵杉树里能跳出一男一女两个伙伴来，妈妈你不能也给我生一个像杉树仙女那样的人吗？"蒲依听了，说："等我问一问你父亲。"于是她拍拍心口，问玛支玛珂神树："你能不能再割一块心肝，做一个女孩出来给更做伴？"玛支玛珂神树说："心也不能割了，肝也不能割了，我割一块肺来试试吧。"

Geng felt lonely as he could not find anyone to play with. He sang sorrowful songs day and night, which saddened Puyi so much so that she could not bear it anymore. Again, she patted her chest and said to Mazhimake in her heart, "Mazhimake, my sweetheart is so bitterly lonely. Let us think of a way to find a partner for him." Mazhimake replied in an awkward tone, "I don't know what kind of partner suits him. Why don't you ask him in the first place?" So Puyi said to her son, "Dear Geng, what kind of partner do you want?" Geng thought for a while and told his mother, "Now that a fir tree can produce a boy and a girl, why not giving birth to a fairy like a fir tree?" Puyi replied, "Let me ask your father." Puyi patted her chest and asked Mazhimake, "Can you slice off a piece of liver again and turn it into a girl for Geng?" Mazhimake said, "Neither heart nor liver can be cut off again. Let me try your lung this time."

接着蒲依又一阵昏天黑地的剧痛，这次她翘了翘尾巴，果真从肚子里掉出来个女孩。这女孩名叫吾司木。因为她长大后喜欢穿红艳艳的衣裙，飘在天上，像一团黄灿灿、彩荧荧的云团，所以人们都叫她底诗底妮吾司木①。娇憨淘气的吾司木出生了，更有了最开心的玩伴；聪明美丽的吾司木长大了，更有了上天入地的好伙伴。蒲依既宠爱更又宠爱吾司木；而更却只宠爱吾司木一人。所以吾司木成了更的影子，只喜欢和更在一起，一步也不愿离开他。由于更太强壮了，更飞在空中时，吾司木便吊在他手上，骑在他脖子上玩耍，躺在他背上睡觉；更休息时，吾司木可以在他身上爬来爬去翻上滚下地玩耍。和更在一起，吾司木犹如有了依靠的藤子，可以长到天上去了。蒲依见自己的心肝常常忘记了她，又高兴又悲哀，于是住到德布阿尔家去了。吾司木和更隔一久去看她一次，其他时间都在浊气和清气里游玩。

① 底诗底妮吾司木：即红云黄云天仙女。

Afterwords, Puyi felt an excruciating pain. This time, she raised her tail all the way up, and a baby girl was born. She gave the girl a name, Wusimu. After growing up, as she preferred dresses of bright colors, which were like golden and colorful clouds when flowing in the sky, people called her Dishidiniwusimu①. Wusimu, ignorant and naughty, was born and became the best companion of Geng. When the smart and beautiful Wusimu grew up, she followed Geng everywhere. Puyi loved both Geng and Wusimu, but Geng only adored Wusimu. So Wusimu, like a shadow of Geng, only wanted to play with Geng, not willing to leave him at all. Being very strong, when he was flying in the sky, Wusimu would drag one of his arms, sitting on his neck for fun, and sleeping on his back; when he took a rest, Wusimu rolled on him to play. With Geng, Wusimu was like having a vine to depend on, which grew all the way to the sky. Puyi was happy yet depressed, as she found that his sweetheart had left her behind, so she moved to the place of Debuaer. Wusimu and Geng visited her once in a while. At other times, they played in the foul gas and the clear gas.

① Dishidiniwusimu: the fairy of red clouds and yellow clouds.

天宫的诞生

更和吾司木在清气和浊气里自由自在地游玩了很久，早先时还兴高采烈的，又新奇又陶醉。但慢慢地吾司木一天到晚嘟着嘴，更想逗她笑她却哭，问她要什么她又说不清，把更急得眼睛瞪成杯子大，好久不敢说话。正好这时德布阿尔要在浊气里盖一座华丽的宫殿，打算来请更去为他捏浊气造铁，捏清气造铜。德布阿尔这人，虽然没有上天入地的本事，而且身瘦力弱，但却非常聪明，是个很有发明创造本事的匠人。他已经掌握了铸铁锻铜的技术，而且叫蒲依抽浊气为树，为他生下个妻子，一下子儿孙满堂，日子过得很惬意。更和吾司木应邀去帮他捏铁捏铜。过了九九八十一天，阿尔的宫殿盖成了，黄闪闪的铜顶，黑亮亮的墙，又庄严又豪华。吾司木越看越喜爱，于是撅起小嘴对更说："我也要一座宫殿，得比二哥的堂皇，还要盖在清气顶上，进门要能做主人，出门要能观宇宙，还要把妈妈接来，做我们的伙伴。"

The Birth of the Heavenly Palace

Geng and Wusimu had lots of fun in the clear gas and the foul gas for a long time. They were exhilarating and curious about everything that they fell for. Gradually, Wusimu pouted all the time. However Geng tried to make her laugh, she only cried. Geng asked for the reason, but she could not tell, which upset Geng, who opened his eyes wide open as big as cups, not daring to speak. At that time, Debuaer intended to build a glamorous palace, so he asked Geng to make iron by moulding the foul gas and make copper by moulding the clear gas. Debuaer was smart, born with a talent in craftsmanship, though he was weak physically and could not move freely in between heaven and earth. He had already mastered the skill of casting iron and forging copper. Now, he led a very happy and content life, as he had a wife, produced by the tree drawn from the foul gas by Puyi, and numerous children born by his wife and grandchildren. Geng and Wusimu were invited to make iron and copper for him. After eighty one days, the palace was built, solemn and luxurious, with bright yellow cooper roof and bright black walls. The more Wusimu looked at it, the more she liked it. So, she pouted her mouth and said to Geng, "I also want a palace, a grander one than brother Aer's. I will build it on top of the clear gas, so that I can be the master inside and view the universe when I walk outside. I will also invite our mother to live with us."

更二话没说，便飞到清气顶上，选好了地盘，可是妹妹却不要用铜做顶、铁做墙的宫殿，这把更给难住了。他敲了三次自己的高额头，又学母亲拍着胸口打主意，但无论如何也想不出比铜和铁光灿的材料。于是他问躲在他的胳肢窝里数腋毛的吾司木：“你要的宫殿，到底像什么？”吾司木脸上笑眯眯，大眼亮闪闪，比手画脚地说：“我的宫殿吗？墙壁黄灿灿，房顶银汪汪，进门一个天，出门一个天。”更实在没有办法，只好去问蒲依：“妈妈呀妈妈，妹妹要一座墙壁黄灿灿，房顶银汪汪的宫殿，我该用什么材料做？”蒲依说：“等我问问你父亲。”接着她便拍着胸脯问玛支玛珂，玛支玛珂也说不清，蒲依只好对更说：“你去问问老二，看他有没有办法。”更依言去找阿尔，黑脸膛的矮个子阿尔，正在大汗淋淋地抽浊气造树。更问他：“二弟阿尔，你是个聪明的匠人，你知不知道，比铁还光亮的是什么？比铜还光灿的是哪样？它们该用什么来制造？”德布阿尔想了想，说：“比铁还亮的东西，应该是银了；比铜还光灿的东西，应该是金了。浊气只能捏出铁，清气只能捏出铜，你把清气和浊气掺在一起捏捏看，看能捏出什么来。”更觉得这办法应该试一试，于是先抓了三把浊气，合着一把清气捏，果然捏出了亮闪闪的银子，接着他又抓了三把清气，合着一把浊气捏，捏出了金灿灿的金子。金银捏成了，更便用银去盖房顶，用金去做墙

Without a doubt, Geng flew to the top of the clear gas and chose a location. But Wusimu did not like copper roof and iron walls, which stumped Geng. He knocked his forehead for three times and patted his chest like his mother did when she was in trouble, trying to think of materials shinier than copper and iron, but in vain. So he asked Wusimu, who was counting hairs in his armpit, "What kind of palace do you want?" Wusimu blinked her bright sparkling eyes with a smile and made lively gestures, "My palace? I want golden walls and silvery roofs. One sky in, one sky out." Geng had no idea, so he asked Puyi, "Mother, my sister wants a palace with bright yellow walls and silvery roof. What kind of materials do I need?" Puyi replied, "Let me ask your father." Then, she patted her chest and asked Mazhimake, who also could not tell. Then Puyi told Geng to ask her second child and see whether he had an idea. Geng went to Aer, a short man with dark skin, who was steeped with sweat while drawing the foul gas to make trees. Geng asked him, "My brother Aer, you are a smart craftsman, so do you know what material is brighter than iron and what material is shinier than copper? How to make these materials?" Debuaer thought for a while and said, "Silver is brighter than iron and gold is shinier than copper. The foul gas can only be made into iron, and the clear gas can only be made into copper. Why not mix the foul gas with the clear gas and see what will come out?" Geng thought that it worth trying. So, he grasped three streams of foul gas and mixed them with a stream of clear gas, which really produced sparkling silvers. Then he grasped three streams of clear gas and mixed them with a stream of foul gas, which turned into gold as expected. In this

壁，造出了一座大院套小院，高房套矮房，共有九千九百九十九个院子的宫殿。这宫殿都是金灿灿的墙，银汪汪的顶，辉煌的光芒洒出去，房左的云白了，房右的云红了，房前的云黄了，房后的云紫了。房上房下，清气化为千万道彩虹，群起群落地绕着宫殿飞舞。吾司木高兴极了，原先嘟成鸭子嘴的两唇，这会儿变成一朵娇艳的红花，白牙齿欢欢地往外跑，甜舌头嫩嫩地直探头。她嘻嘻呵呵地笑着，嘤嘤咛咛地唱着，像只花蝴蝶，骑在更的脖子上，要更驮着她满院子奔跑，还把这座宫殿取名叫“石姆岩哈”①。这样跑了九天，她的嘴又嘟起来了，眉头又皱起来了，话没有了，歌也听不见了。更一看妹妹的样子，心里真是难过极了。他问道：“妹妹，你还要什么？哥哥给你去找。”吾司木说：“宫殿这么大，只有我们兄妹，又清冷又孤独，这宫殿应该热闹一些才好。”更听了，心想：“找来些伙伴，宫殿虽然热闹了，妹妹不就把我忘了吗？”他想了又想，因为不敢违拗妹妹的心愿，便去抓浊气捏动物，捏出了牛羊猪马，捏出了飞禽走兽，然后朝它们吹一口气，这些动物都活了，欢蹦乱跳叫起来。动物们

① 石姆岩哈：意即至高无上的宫殿。

way, Geng built the roofs with silver and walls with gold. Finally, a palace with 9,999 courtyards, consisted of large and small courtyards and houses, was completed. The palace has shinny golden walls and bright silvery roofs, giving off brilliant lights, which made clouds on the left side of the palace white, on the right side red, in the front area yellow and at the back purple. Thousands of rainbows formed by the clear gas wrapped the palace like ribbons. Wusimu used to pout her mouth like a duck but was smiling as sweet as a red flower. Grinning with shinning teeth and tender tongue in and out, she sang joyous songs, as pleasant as a colourful butterfly, and rode on Geng's neck everywhere in the courtyard. They named the palace "Shimuyanha"①. After nine days of riding, Wusimu pouted and frowned again, not willing to say a single word or sing songs. Geng was very upset at the sight of it. He asked his sister, "What else do you want? I will find it for you." Wusimu replied, "The palace is big enough, but don't you think it is too chilly and lonely here with just two of us? I expect it to be a more lively palace." Geng thought to himself, "Will my sister forget me if I bring back some friends here?" Not daring to go against his sister's wishes, Geng came up with an idea. He grasped the foul gas to make animals, such as cattle, sheep, pigs, horses, all kinds of birds and other types of animals, which became alive, jumping and shouting everywhere, after a blow of breath from Geng. Having noses, eyes and long hairs all over their bodies, these animal could both speak and sing, but they could only walk

---

① Shimuyanha: the supreme palace.

虽然有鼻子有眼，也能说话唱歌，但必须四脚落地走，而且浑身长毛，没有人的灵性，只能凑热闹，不会成为人的知心朋友。更很满意，便把动物们全赶进天宫里去。天宫顿时热闹了起来，吾司木高兴极了，小嘴窝窝又开成了花，甜唇嫩舌地唱着笑着，一天到晚要更驮着她，赶起动物们进进出出地在天空游荡。后来有一天，吾司木看见了天宫四周的彩云，就对更说：“哥哥，我要穿彩裙，就像云霞一样美的彩裙。”更便把天宫四周的彩云撕下几幅，接成了一套鲜艳夺目的褶裙，给吾司木穿在身上。从此，吾司木飞到哪里，哪里便一片金黄，吾司木站在哪里，哪里就亮堂。

on their four feet. In this way, without the intelligence of human being, animals could only join the party, but not make real friends with human, which suited Geng's expectation very well. So he led all the animals into the palace which made the place lively instantly. Wusimu was so pleased that she grinned happily and sang pleasant songs again. She rode on Geng day and night, moving the animals in and out of the palace in the sky every day. One day, when Wusimu saw the colourful clouds around the palace, she said to Geng, "Brother, I want to wear a colourful dress, as beautiful as the clouds." So Geng tore several colourful clouds around the palace and put them together to make a brilliant pleated skirt for Wusimu. Since then, wherever Wusimu stood, the place would be filled with gold and light.

接着，兄妹俩把母亲蒲依接到石姆岩哈来，让她掌管兄妹的宫殿和野兽。蒲依接管了石姆岩哈后，便把动物分成两等，一等是蠢笨糊涂的动物，它们被命名为牛马猪羊鸡鸭鹅，专供更和吾司木宰食和骑用；另一等是精灵聪明的动物，它们被命名为虎兔龙蛇獐熊豹等，专门侍奉更和吾司木。以虎为领头的是不长角的肉食群，它们负责天宫的警卫和防务；以野猪为领头的是不长角的果根食群，它们负责耕种天宫的五谷杂粮；以老熊为领头的是其他草食动物，它们负责其他杂务；以凤凰为领头的是色彩最艳丽的鸟群，它们负责护理吾司木的起居饮食；以大雁为领头的是善于远飞的鸟群，它们是更的随从和护卫；以乌鸦为领头的是其他鸟类，在宫殿里听蒲依使唤。至高无上的天宫石姆岩哈，从此有规有矩，秩序井然，成为一个热闹繁华，但又异常庄严神圣的地方。更、吾司木和蒲依，出门一大群，进门一大帮，显得无比的高贵和气派。动物们把更叫更资，把吾司木叫木色嫫；把蒲依叫资洛果。更资开天辟地，缔造万物，主宰万物的时代，就从这时开始了。

流传地区：永仁县
讲述者：曲木阿石
搜集整理者：罗有能

Afterwards, the brother and sister invited their mother Puyi to live in Shimuyanha and asked her to be the master of their palace and beasts. After taking over the palace, Puyi divided animals into two types, one kind was clumsy ones, which were named cattle, horse, pig, sheep, chicken, duck and goose, and served as food or riding tools for Geng and Wusimu; the other kind was smart ones, which were called tiger, rabbit, dragon, snake, roe, bear, leopard, etc., servants to Geng and Wusimu. Carnivores without horn were led by tiger, taking responsibility for security and defense of the palace; animals that fed on fruits and roots without horn were led by wild boar, responsible for farming cereals and coarse grains for the palace; other herbivores were led by bear, dealing with all the chores; birds with bright colors were led by phoenix, taking care of diet and daily life of Wusimu; birds which could fly long distances were led by wild goose, following orders from Geng; other birds were led by raven, answering calls from Puyi. Since then, the supreme heavenly palace of Shimuyanha had rule and order, becoming a lively, prosperous, yet grand and solemn place. Geng, Wusimu and Puyi were accompanied by a crowd inside and outside of the palace, in noble and grand manners. Geng was called Gengzi, and Wusimu was Musemo and Puyi, Ziluoguo by animals. The era when Gengzi created the world and mastered heaven and earth began.

Spreading area: Yongren County

Narrator: Qumuashi

Collector and editor: Luo Youneng

人祖的由来

很古很古的时候，上没有天，下没有地，只有飘飘的清气和沉沉的浊气。慢慢地清气上升变成天，浊气下沉变为地。后来，从天边飞来一对银雀，这对银雀叫哎和哺①，哎与哺相配就有了人类。

那个时候，男人不知道娶媳妇，女人不知道出嫁，人们只知道母亲，不知道父亲，居住在森林中跟野兽相伴，饿了摘野果，渴了喝山泉。后来，哎和哺慢慢地兴起了嫁娶的规矩，有的娶来媳妇，有的嫁出女儿。

又过了许多年，他们生出的后代只有一只眼睛，叫独眼人。后来，独眼人生下了竖眼人，竖眼人生下了横眼人。

① 哎：乾，为阳。哺：坤，为阴。

The Origin of Human Ancestor

Long time ago, apart from the flowing clear gas and the heavy foul gas, there was neither sky above nor earth below. Gradually, clear gas went up and became the sky, while foul gas went down and became the earth. Later, a pair of silver sparrows, called Ai and Bu①, from heaven mated and produced human on earth.

At that time, neither men nor women knew anything about getting married. People only knew their mothers, without any knowledge of their fathers. They lived in the forest, in company with wild beasts, picking wild fruit for food and drinking spring water when they became thirsty. Afterwards, the custom of marriage started, so some began to take wives while others married their daughters.

After many years, their off-springs only had one eye, called one-eyed man. Later, one-eyed men bore vertical-eyed men, who afterwards produced horizontal-eyed men.

---

① Ai: Qian, means Yang. Bu: Kun, means Yin.

天上有个神仙叫兹阿玛①，他见人间一片混乱，决定要用干旱惩治人间。兹阿玛从天外请来九个太阳，八个月亮。白天，火辣辣的太阳晒得花草、树木都干枯了；夜里，月亮出来吸海水，把所有的海水都吸干了。飞禽走兽全晒死了，独眼人、竖眼人都死光了，只剩下他们的后代横眼人。

后来，九个太阳走了八个，八个月亮去了七个，于是，海里又有了水，花儿又开了，鸟儿又唱歌了，横眼人的日子好起来。天上派出策耿纪②来试试人间良心的好坏。他先到东方，东方有一家人很富裕，粮食堆成山，牛羊肥又壮，鸡群满山林。策耿纪骑着龙马走到这家门口，说："我是天神官，走的路太长，我的龙马甲已脱落，龙腰已折断，想要一点金银、绸缎、人血和人肉，好接龙腰，补龙甲，请你们各样给我一点吧！"这家人听过后，装穷叫苦地回答说："啊呀，仙官呀，我们穷得光打光。白天吃的荞粑粑，夜晚睡的木板床，哪有东西给你啊！"他们什么都不给策耿纪，他只好又往前走。但每到一处，遇到的富人都这么说，策耿纪一肚子气。

---

① 兹阿玛：天宫仙人。

② 策耿纪：掌管天地万物的天神，又叫"更资天神""恩梯古资"等。

There was a celestial in heaven called Ziama①. Having seen the chaos in the mortal world, he decided to use draught as a punishment. Ziama invited nine suns and eight moons from the outside to hang in the sky. During the daytime, grasses, flowers and trees were dried up and withered from the burning suns; at night, moons came out to suck up all the water in the sea. Fowls and beasts were all burned and died, so were the one-eyed men and vertical-eyed men. Only off-springs of the horizontal-eyed men survived.

Afterwards, eight suns and seven moons went away, leaving only one sun and one moon in the sky. Soon, the sea was again with water, flowers began to blossom and birds came to sing songs; the life of the horizontal-eyed men became better. Then, Cegengji② descended from heaven to test the conscience of people in the mortal world. First, he went to the east, where there was a wealthy household with piles of grain, fat and strong flocks and herds, and chickens running all over the mountain. Riding on his Ryoma (or dragon horse), Cegengji came to this family and said, "I am a god from heaven. I have travelled so far that the amour of my Ryoma has fallen out and its waist has broken. Would you give me some gold, silver, silks and satin, human flesh and blood to mend these?" Hearing this, the house owner began to poor-mouth, "Ah, dear god, we are the poor wretch. We can only eat buckwheat cakes during the day and sleep on plank bed at night. How can we offer you anything?" Cegengji had to leave without being offered anything. He was furious because he got the same answer wherever he went.

---

① Ziama: a celestial being in the heavenly palace.

② Cegengji: the God responsible for heaven and earth, also called "the God of Gengzi" "Entiguzi" etc.

一天，他遇到了一个贫穷的人。策耿纪上前问：“你是谁?”这人回答说：“我是居住在这里的笃慕①。”笃慕亲亲热热地问策耿纪：“请问客人从哪里来？如今要到哪里去?”策耿纪说：“我骑的龙马生了病，治马要用人血和人肉。”笃慕听了后，眼睛都没有眨一下，就叫策耿纪拿刀来，要割自己腿上的两块肉，放自己肘上的一股鲜血给策耿纪。策耿纪很感动，就把真情告诉了他：“好心的人啊，我来人间不是为了要什么东西，只是来试一下人们心肠的好坏，富人们都没有好心肠，唯独你这贫穷的人良心好。好心的笃慕啊，请你听清楚，等到一年零一百天的时候，我就要用洪水来整治人间，另外换一拨人!”策耿纪说着，拿出一颗葫芦种交给笃慕说：“你把这颗葫芦种种在门口，好好护理它，等它长大，你到山上去找三种蜂蜡来，以后好用。”笃慕按照策耿纪说的，等到春耕时，把葫芦种在家门口，勤浇水、勤培土，到了秋收时，又砍树搭架。

① 笃慕：人名，传说是彝族最早的祖先。

One day, Cegengji met a poor man and asked, "Who are you?" The poor man replied, "I live here and my name is Dumu.①" Dumu asked Cegengji with a warm heart, "Dear guest, where are you from and where are you going?" Cegengji answered, "My Ryoma is ill and I need human blood and flesh to cure it." After learning it, without hesitation, Dumu asked for a knife to cut off two fleshes from his thigh and bleed his elbow to offer blood to Cegengji. Cegengji was very moved and told him the truth, "Kind-hearted man, I am not here in the mortal world to ask for anything. I only want to test whether people have a good heart. The rich do not have one. Only you, a poor guy, have. Dear Dumu, listen carefully, when it is the one year and a hundred day from now, I will use flood to renovate the world and replace it with new groups of people!" Cegengji took out a gourd seed and gave it to Dumu, "Plant it by the front door of your house. Take a good care of it and watch it grow. Also, look for three kinds of beeswax from the mountain which will be useful in the future." Dumu did as he was told and planted the gourd seed by the front door in spring, watering and earthing up it frequently. When autumn was approaching, he cut down trees to make a support for the plant.

---

① Dumu: name. He is said to be the ancestor of the Yi nationality.

葫芦结出来了，又肥又大，长有一庹①，粗有半度。这时，策耿纪又来人间对大家说：“人们听好，老天要下大雨了，大雨要把大地淹没，你们各自备船逃命吧，有金的打金船，有银的打银船。”人们听后，有的说：“老天降雨灭干旱，正好犁田来栽秧。”有的说：“洪水来了也不怕，骑上牛背就无事。”有的说：“我家房后有棵又高又大的树，洪水来了我就爬树尖。”不过，他们还是半信半疑地造起了金船、银船。笃慕无金无银做不成金船银船，只是摘回了成熟的大葫芦当船。

一年零一百天到了，笃慕藏进葫芦里，用山上采来的三种蜂蜡封住了口。霎时间，天昏地暗，日月无光，天上只见黄龙抖身子，蓝龙舞巨爪，黑龙翻白眼，白龙翘尾巴，青龙张大口。五条巨龙一起翻腾跳跃，把大雨降到人间。大雨哗哗啦啦，整整下了七天七夜，万物都被淹没，大地变成一片汪洋，滔滔洪水一直翻滚到云间。石蚌、青蛙在天上叫，野鸭、大雁都上了天，金船和银船沉进了海底，只有葫芦顺水漂着，一直漂到洛尼山②。笃慕戳通蜂蜡，把头伸出葫芦口，

① 译者注：一庹=两臂向左右伸开的长度。

② 洛尼山：地名，在今云南省东川、会泽地区。

The fat and big gourd had grown, which was one tuo① in length and half tuo in width. Then, Cegengji came to the mortal world again and told people, "Listen, it is going to rain very heavily, which will flood the earth, so prepare a ship to run for your life. If you have gold, make a golden ship; If you have silver, make a silvery one." After learning it, one said, "The rain can remove the drought, so it will be about the time to plough the land and transplant the rice seedlings." One said, "There is no need to be afraid. When that come, we can ride on cows' back." Another one said, "I have a very tall and big tree in my backyard. I will climb to the top of it if flood comes." Still, they were dubious and started to build golden and silvery ships. Dumu neither had gold nor silver to make a ship, so he just picked the ripe gourd he had planted for preparation.

When it was the date of a year and a hundred day, Dumu hid into the gourd and sealed it with three types of beeswax collected from the mountain. In a moment, it became dark all around, without a slight light from the sun and the moon. In the sky, only five dragons could be seen. The yellow dragon shook its body, the blue dragon waved its huge claws, the black dragon rolled its eyes, the white dragon cocked the tail, and the green dragon had its mouth wide open. The five dragons rolled and leaped, bringing pouring rain to the earth, which lasted for seven days and nights, drowning everything and making the earth a vast ocean. The surging flood rolled up so high to the clouds that frogs croaked in the sky, and wild ducks and wild geese were thrown into the cloud, while all the golden ships and silvery ships submerged down into the bottom of the ocean. Only the gourd survived, flowing on the water all the way to the Luoni Mountain.② Dumu poked the beeswax open and stretched out his

---

① Translator's note: one tuo = two outstretched arms.

② Luoni Mountain: a place in Dongchuan, Huize Area, Yunnan Province today.

打算爬到山崖上去。他看见一蓬金竹，就抓住竹子往上爬，一直爬到洛尼山顶，在那里住了下来。

后来，大水落下去，地面露出来。可是，这里无人烟，冷了无火烤，饿了没饭吃，天亮鸡不叫，门前狗不咬，他的日子实在难过。策耿纪见他这样苦，就从天宫派下太白神来帮他。太白神变成一只大黑蜂，飞到一截木头上，用刺蜇木头，左转三转，右转三转，木头就冒烟起火，笃慕就跟黑蜂学会了钻木取火。

不久，策耿纪又来到人间，看见笃慕孤苦伶仃的，一个人独自淌着眼泪。策耿纪问：“好心的笃慕，你为什么两眼泪汪汪？”笃慕回答说：“十里路上不见人，百里路上无人家，孤孤单单一个人，没人来做伴。”策耿纪马上派三个仙女下凡，与笃慕结成夫妻。笃慕的三个老婆，大老婆叫蚩以武吐，生下慕雅考、慕雅切两个儿子；二老婆叫能以咪冬，生下慕雅热、慕雅卧两个儿子；三老婆叫尼以咪哺，生下慕克克、慕齐齐两个儿子。笃慕的六个儿子长大后，个个都很成器。他们就是彝族的六个祖先。

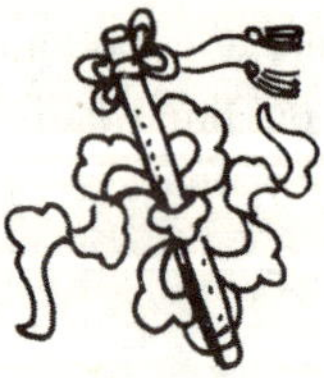

head from the mouth of the gourd, intending to climbed up to the cliff. Seeing a clump of golden bamboo, he quickly grabbed it and climbed all the way up to the tip of the Luoni Mountain, and settled there.

Later, the flood faded away and the earth emerged. However, the world was uninhabited and became lifeless. There was no fire to warm in coldness, no food to eat when getting hungry, no crow to remind a day at sunrise and even no barking dog to guard the door. Life was bitter for Dumu. Having observed his bitterness, Cegengji sent Taibai God from the heavenly palace to help him. Taibai God turned into a big black bee and flew to the top of a piece of wood. It stung the wood, rotating to the left for three times and then to the right for another three times, and thus the fire was made. In this way, Dumu learned to drill wood to make fire from the big black bee.

Before long, Cegengji came to the mortal world again. He found that Dumu was lonely and helpless, weeping silently by himself. Cegengji asked, "Kind-hearted Dumu, why are your eyes brimming with tears?" Dumu replied, "There is no one and no household in the nearby region. I am all alone without a companion." Cegengji immediately dispatched three fairy maidens from heaven and married them to Dumu so that he had three wives. The first wife was called Chiyiwutu, who bore two sons, called Muyakao and Muyaqie; the second wife was named Nengyimidong, who had two sons, Muyare and Muyawo; the third wife, Niyimibu, gave birth to another two sons, named Mukeke and Muqiqi. The six sons all grew up and became very capable, who were the six ancestors of the Yi people.

后来，这六个祖先子生孙，孙生子，子子孙孙多得如树干分枝。人越来越多，他们就分居到各个地方。武、乍二支的先祖是慕雅切、慕雅考，他们居住在楚吐①以南；糯、恒二支的先祖是慕雅热、慕雅卧，他们向洛博②以北开拓；布、默二支的先祖是慕克克、慕齐齐，他们在实液③中部地方发展。

讲述者：阿危·热默

搜集整理者：阿乍·莴芝

① 楚吐：地名，今云南东北一带。

② 洛博：地名，今四川一带。

③ 实液：地名，今贵州、广西一带。

Afterwards, these six ancestors gave birth to their children, and then had grandchildren. In this way, they had numerous off-springs, like a huge tree with countless branches. As population expanded, many left and settled to other places. The two branches of Wu and Zha, the off-springs of Muyaqie and Muyakao, settled in the south of Chutu①; the branches of Nuo and Heng, the off-springs of Muyare and Muyawo, came to the north of Luobo②; and the branches of Bu and Mo, the off-springs of Mukeke and Muqiqi, moved to the central region of Shiye③.

Narrator: Awei · Remo

Collector and editor: Azha · Wozhi

① Chutu: a place, in the northeast of Yunnan today.

② Luobo: a place, in Sichuan today.

③ Shiye: a place, in Guizhou, Guangxi today.

三兄弟

一

在很古的时候，滇南龙马山①上，彝家寨子星罗棋布。在这些众多的寨子里，有个名叫龙孔的小寨子。寨子前面开满了苦刺花，寨边长满了苦竹林，山坡上种满了苦荞。寨子里有三个穷兄弟，生活就像苦荞一样苦。老三刚生下地，阿妈就断了气，刚刚满周岁时，阿爹又死了。三个兄弟就像无娘的鸡，又哭又叫；就像无娘的牛，到处乱跑。他们的哭声传到上寨，寨里的乡亲们忙下来瞧；哭声传到下寨，寨里的乡亲们忙来关照。老大爷给他们送来油盐，阿哥们给他们送来柴草，老奶奶天天来帮他们做饭，阿姐们天天都给他们挑水。在乡亲们的热情关照下，三个穷兄弟一天天长大了，个个长得神威貌俊，伶俐聪明。乡亲们都夸奖三兄弟来日有出息。

① 龙马山位于云南省元江县东面。

The Three Brothers

I

Long time ago, the Longma Mountain①, now located in Southern Yunnan, was dotted with numerous stockaded villages of the Yi people. Among all those villages, there was a small one, called Longkong. Flowers bloomed in front of it; bamboos thrived around it; crops, more specifically buckwheat, were planted densely on the hill. But all of them tasted bitter. So, for the three penniless brothers in the village, they could not be more familiar with "bitterness" in their lives. Their mother passed away when the little one was born. When he turned one, their father left them as well. The orphans cried out too hard to catch their breath. Then they burst out of the door and charged everywhere. Their cries shook the upper village. People there went down to share their sorrow. And their cries was also heard, clearly, by people living in the lower village who came up to care for them. Old men gave them oil and salt; young pals brought them bundles of wood and grass; old women cooked for them every day; young girls fetched water to them. Having been taken well care of by their neighbors, the three brothers grew up gradually and became handsome and intelligent. In the eyes of neighbors, they were meant to achieve something one day.

① Longma Mountain lies in the east of Yuanjiang County, Yunnan Province.

三兄弟为了糊口，只得到他乡去帮工。他们帮了一村又一村，帮了一寨又一寨，但仍然缺吃少穿，日子很难熬。到后来，三兄弟只有分手各自逃生去了。为了来日好相互寻找，临别前，他们取了名字：老大叫夺艾，老二叫夺哩，老三叫夺勒。

二

三兄弟分手后，他们各自爬了很多山，过了很多河，穿过很多林，走过很多箐。夺艾找到了黑夺只①，跟他在林中学养鸟。夺哩找到了西夺只②，跟他在山中采草药。夺勒找到了亨夺方③，同她在一起学搓草索。

日子过得很快，一转眼飘过了三次冬雪，落过了三回春雨，三兄弟团聚了。久别相逢，多么高兴啊！他们各自讲了主人的恩德，讲了自己学到的手艺。

听说街子很热闹，他们想去看看。由于路途遥远，他们黄昏就睡觉了，半夜就起床赶路了。他们爬了九座山，过了九条河，来到了叫歌支的街场。这里的街场很热闹，人山人海，奇货样样有，各人在选购着自己需要的东西。只见阿姐们的背篓里装满了沉甸甸的好货，大妈们的背篓里装满了各种杂货，可他们三兄弟衣袋里无钱，什么也买不起。

① 黑夺只：即传说中的鸟神。
② 西夺只：即传说中的植物神。
③ 亨夺方：即传说中的山神。

To make a living, they had to work in other villages, but still struggled however hard they worked from one village to another. They still led a very poor life. Later, they had to part each other for a living. Before leaving, they named themselves in case they would meet one day. The oldest was called Duoai, the second Duoli and the littlest Duole.

II

After departing from each other, they each climbed over many mountains, crossed countless rivers and went through numerous forests. Duoai met Heiduozhi① and learned to breed birds in the forest. Duoli found Xiduozhi② and was trained to pick herds in the mountains. Duole went to Hengduofang③ and became an apprentice who could twist grass into ropes.

Time slipped by. After three fleeting years, the three brothers gathered together. Seeing each other again, they were eager to share virtues of their masters and skills they sharpened.

Having heard that the streets were bustling, they wanted to see for themselves. As it was a long journey, they slept at sunset and got up at midnight. Over nine mountains they climbed and ninc rivers they crossed, they finally reached a street market called Gezhi. The market was bustling with life where people flooded in and out with piles of exotic goods. Everyone was busy with purchasing. Young girls carried baskets filled with heavy good stuffs and senior women loaded themselves with sundry goods. But none were affordable to the three brothers.

---

① Heiduozhi: the deity of birds in legend.

② Xiduozhi: the deity of plants in legend.

③ Hengduofang: the deity of mountain in legend.

离开了歌支，三兄弟又继续朝前走。他们爬了九个坡，过了九条箐，来到了一个叫阿纳的街场。这个街场上卖的都是六畜：牛，马，猪，羊，鸡和狗。只见老大爷们笑眯眯地牵着买到的肥壮牛羊；阿哥们雄赳赳地骑在买到的骏马上。三兄弟两手空空，什么也买不起。大哥叹冷气，二哥皱眉头，三弟垂着头。他们无心再赶街，转身回家去了。走到一棵大树下，三兄弟已筋疲力尽，便坐在树下歇气。他们你一言，我一语，都说去向主人要三年的工钱，然后到街上买点自己喜爱的东西。

三兄弟歇了一阵后，又继续往前赶路了。他们穿过九片林，走过九道弯，来到一个叫洁莫山的地方。这时，太阳已经落山，林中百鸟叽叽喳喳鸣叫得十分快活。三兄弟被鸟叫声迷住了。他们拾起一些松枝，烧起一塘火，一边烤着火，一边静听百鸟唱歌。正当他们听得出神时，忽然呼呼地刮起一阵狂风，大地一时变得阴风惨惨，林中的百鸟惊飞出巢，凄惨哀鸣。

“深夜百鸟闹，遭难快来到。”夺艾三兄弟都说要提防灾难的到来，可因身子困倦，眼难张开，躺在草地上进入了梦乡。忽听轰隆一阵巨响，山摇地动，狂风呼啸，林涛怒号。三兄弟猛然惊醒，依偎着坐在一起，不敢行走，也不敢再入睡，盼着天快开亮。

After leaving Gezhi, they moved on. They climbed over another nine mountains and crossed nine trenches. A street market called Ana unfolded before them in which the six domestic animals, namely ox, horse, pig, goat, fowl and dog, were being sold. The three brothers saw smiling old men pulling their strong oxen and sheep, and young pals riding on their gallant horses. But to own one was like a dream for the three penniless brothers. The oldest brother sighed, the second one frowned and the little one drooped his head. In no mood for shopping, they turned around and went back. After a long walk, they were exhausted and sat down to relax under a big tree. They chatted and agreed to ask their masters to pay them for three years of work so that they could buy something to their delight in the streets.

After a short rest, they went on. They went through nine forests and took nine turns, arriving in a mountain called Jiemo. By then, the sun had gone done, but birds in the forests chirped joyfully. The three brothers were captivated by the chirps so they picked up some branches of pine tree to lit a fire and then sat around it, listening to those birds singing. While they were listening intently, a gust of wind roared past. All of a sudden, the earth was battered, scaring the birds away in shriek.

"Birds making a fuss at night does not augur well," The three brothers said. Although they wanted to prepare for the ominous, they were too sleepy and fell asleep on the grass. Suddenly, a deafening sound shook them up. Then, the earth shook with blowing wind and roaring forests. The three brothers sat close with each other. They dared neither to walk out nor to go back to sleep. They just prayed for the dawn.

三

一场狂风过后，东方渐渐发白了。此时，远处传来悲凄的哭声，撕肝裂肺，叫人心寒。三兄弟寻声快步赶去，惨景出现在眼前：四处墙倒梁塌，遍地血淋淋的尸首。一打听，才知道昨晚此地发生了地震。

三兄弟看着这惨景，你一言我一语议论开了。大哥夺艾说："昨晚雀鸟惊飞怪叫，说明地震要来临它们是知道的，人若能知鸟语，就不会遭此大难了。我要去求黑夺只教我鸟语，工钱我不要了。"二哥夺哩接着说："仙翁西夺只有九百九十种草药，我要去求他教我救人，工钱我不要了。"听了两位兄长的话，三弟夺勒点点头，接着道："我也要去求仙母亨夺方，她有九十九根索子，每根索子都是缩地筋，缩地筋一拉，山能聚拢到一起，救灾救难就快多了。我要去求她送我一根，工钱我也不要了。"三人商量妥当，一同向主人要宝去了。他们先找到了黑夺只，夺艾开口说道："仙翁黑夺只，我帮了三年工，求你送我一件东西。"仙翁道："我有金银山、谷米仓、好绸缎、壮牛羊，这些你要什么自己去挑选，你喜欢什么自己去搬。"夺艾道："我不要金银、绸缎，也不要谷米、牛羊，我要学会鸟语，去救受难的乡亲。"黑夺只看夺艾有这样的好良心，便叫乌鸦来教他鸟语。夺艾学会了鸟语，拜谢黑夺只走了。三兄弟一路上高高兴兴地走着。走了几天几夜，他们又来到了西夺只住的地方。夺哩忙开口道："仙翁西

III

After a gust of wind, the sky lightened. Then bitter cry wafted from the distance, making their hair stand on end. The three brothers ran towards the sound and saw nothing but a tragedy. Walls collapsed; beams fell down; and bloody dead bodies scattered everywhere. After making an enquiry, they learned that an earthquake happened last night.

Looking at this miserable scene, the three brothers talked to each other again. The oldest one said, "Last night, it was so weird to see the birds shrieking and flying in panic. They must have known that an earthquake was coming. If only human could understood chirps! I'm going to ask Heiduozhi to teach me that. I don't want money anymore." The second brother followed, "Lord Xiduo has nine hundred and ninety kinds of herbs. I'm going to ask him to teach me how to save people. That's what I need." Hearing what his two brothers said, the little one nodded and said, "I'm also going to Lady Hengduofang for one of her ninety-nine ropes. You know each one can pull mountains together. So these ropes can be used to stop disasters. I don't want my pay any more." After reaching an agreement, they set foot to their masters for what they needed. The three brothers went to Heiduozhi first. Duoai, the oldest brother, said, "Lord Heiduozhi, I have worked for you for three years. Now I'm asking you to give me something." Heiduozhi replied, "I have mountains of gold and silver, warehouses filled with crops, countless pieces of fine silk cloth, and herds of strong oxen and sheep. You can choose whatever

夺只，我帮了三年工，求你送我一件东西。”仙翁道：“我有各种各样的玉石、珍珠，这些东西你要什么就自己去拿吧。”夺哩道：“我不要玉石，我不要珍珠，我要不死药，拿去救受难的乡亲。”西夺只看夺哩有这样的好良心，便送了他一包不死药，耐心地教会他怎么使用。夺哩得到不死药，拜谢西夺只走了。他们一路笑语欢声，不知走了几天几夜，最后来到了亨夺方住的地方。夺勒忙开口道：“仙母亨夺方，我帮了三年工，求你送我一个东西。”仙母道：“你是不是想要我手中的宝？”夺勒恳求道：“求你送我一根缩地筋，让我拿去救遭难的乡亲。”仙母便拿出缩地筋送给夺勒，还教会他怎样使用。夺勒得到了缩地筋，拜谢亨夺方走了。

you like." Duoai said, "I don't want them. I just want to learn the language of birds so that I can save my fellow countrymen in their suffering." Heiduozhi knew Duoai was kindhearted and asked ravens to teach him the language. After mastering it, Duoai thanked Heiduozhi and left. The three brothers went on, happily, for several days and nights and arrived at the place where Xiduozhi lived. Duoli asked, "Lord Xiduozhi, could you give me a treasure since I have worked here for three years?" The lord replied, "I have various kinds of jades and pearls. You can take whatever you want." Duoli said, "I just want longevity pills so that I can help people afflicted by disaster." Xiduozhi saw benevolence in Duoli and gave him a bag of longevity pills and taught him how to use it. Duoli expressed his gratitude to Xiduozhi and left. The three brothers continued their journey with so much hope. After many days, they reached the dwelling of Hengduofang. Duole asked, "Lady Hengduofang, do you think I can ask you to give me something in return for my work here?" The lady answered, "Do you want something in my hand?" Duole begged, "Please give me one rope. I need to help those villagers in misery." The lady consented and taught him the way to use it. Duole said thanks to Hengduofang and went away.

四

三兄弟得了三宝，蹦蹦跳跳，一路走一路笑。他们爬过的山坡，数也数不清；他们攀过的悬崖，有九十九堵；他们走过的山箐，有九十九条；他们走过的岔路，有九十九道。走到了哈科风，又见雀鸟惊飞，又见雀鸟惊叫。三兄弟走近一瞧，原来是几只乌鸦在啼叫。几只乌鸦“哇哇哇”地叫了几声，便展翅飞走了。

两个弟弟望着哥哥问道：“夺艾大哥，乌鸦说什么，快告诉我们吧。”夺艾忧愁地说道：“乌鸦说，牛头斯大山出了三件事，有只大花虎，一时身抽搐，死在林中了；有只大黑狗，一时毛直竖，死在路边了；一只勾嘴鹰，扇断了翅膀，摔死在树脚了。”为救虎、狗、鹰，夺勒立即拿出缩地筋，这缩地筋，有九十九庹长，用时能伸长几十丈，不用时缩成一小团。夺勒把缩地筋使劲拉开，一头朝前边丢，一头朝后边甩，然后朝前拉三拉，朝后踩三踩，四周群山一齐聚拢来。夺艾三弟兄很快就走到了牛头斯山上，举目一看，乌鸦说的话句句都真实。夺哩立即拿出不死药，喂花虎一点，喂黑狗一点，喂老鹰一点，接着在虎头、狗头、鹰头上各拍了三拍。转眼一看，只见死老虎翻了一个身，站起来了；只见死黑狗鼻孔喘着气，汪汪汪叫了几声，站起来了；只见死老鹰翅膀上下扇了几下，突然飞起， 在天空转了一圈后又落在三

IV

The three brothers danced along the road with constant laughter. Countless mountains they climbed over; ninety-nine cliffs they scaled; ninety-nine trenches they crossed over; and ninety-nine crossroads they encountered. Finally, they walked to Hakefeng where birds flied in panic and shrieked constantly. Looking closer, the three brothers found that some ravens were clucking. At the sight of them, the ravens shrilled and flew away.

The two little brothers looked at their old brother and asked, "Duoai, what did ravens say? Tell us." Duoai replied with worry, "They said that three accidents happened in Niutousi Mountain. A huge dapple tiger got a cramp and died in the forest. A big black dog got his hair stand on end and died on the roadside. An eagle with crooked beak broke his wings when flapping them and fell to his death." To save those poor creatures, Duole took out his magic rope immediately, which extended to 99 chi long in use and shrank back to a small ball when it was not used. Having tried hard to pull the rope open, he threw its one end forward and the other backward. Then he went forward and pulled three times, and went backward and stepped

兄弟面前。花虎为谢恩人，要跟夺艾走；黑狗为谢恩人，要跟夺哩走；老鹰为谢恩人，要跟夺勒走。三兄弟带着虎、狗、鹰，又继续朝前走。他们来斗秃山，又见乌在飞，又听乌在惊叫。三兄弟走近一瞧，又是乌鸦在啼叫，它们“哇哇哇”地叫了几声又展翅飞走了。

两个弟弟又望着大哥问道：“夺艾大哥，乌鸦在说什么？快告诉我们吧。”夺艾满面愁容道：“斗秃山出现丧事了，有三个姐妹，大姐叫吾娌，二姐叫丢娌，三妹叫西娌。昨天，她们死去了阿爹，今天又死去了阿妈，三姐妹正哭得死去活来。”夺勒一听，立即拿出缩地筋，将山拉拢来。三兄弟走近一看，果真是三姐妹扑在爹妈的尸体上号啕大哭。夺哩拿出他的不死药，喂进爹妈的嘴里，拍拍爹妈的头，顿时，爹妈活起来了，两老笑眯眯地望着三个女儿。三姐妹见爹妈回生过来一时哭脸变成了笑脸。她们一齐跪在三兄弟面前，感谢他们的救命大恩。两老也忙从箱里拿出几两银子，送给三兄弟。三兄弟婉言谢绝了。他们正要转身出门，被三姐妹拉住了。吾娌拉着夺艾，丢娌拉着夺哩，西娌拉着夺勒，爹妈堵在门口。老阿爹笑呵呵地望着三兄弟，说：“三位大恩人，你们把我俩老从死里救活过来，总得留下个住地和姓名呀。”夺艾回答道：“大爹，我们三兄弟生在龙马山，家住龙孔地，

on it three times, which drew mountains around him closer. The three brothers ran to Niutousi Mountain so they could look closer. It turned out that everything ravens said was true. Duoli immediately took out the longevity pills to feed the tiger, the dog and the eagle. Then he patted their heads three times each. In a blink of an eye, the dead tiger turned over and stood up; the black dog puffed and barked; and the eagle flapped up, started to fly and then landed in front of the three brothers after a circle in the sky. The three grateful animals decided to follow their saviors. So the three brothers went on with three animals. Then, they reached the Doutu Mountain where birds were also flying in panic and shrieking unpleasantly. It turned out that they were ravens again who shrilled and flew away as the three brothers drew closer.

The two little brothers looked at their elder brother again and asked, "Duoai, what were they saying? Tell us quickly." Duoai replied worriedly, "Grieved things have happened in the Doutu Mountain. Three sisters there, Wuli, Diuli, and Xili, lost their dad yesterday and their mom today. They were sobbing heart out." After learning it, Duole took out his magic rope and pulled the mountain to him. As they looked closer, the three girls were really crying over the dead bodies of their parents. Duoli put his magic pills into the mouths of the three sisters' parents and patted their heads. Suddenly, the couple came back to life and smiled at their daughters. The three girls' sad face immediately turned into a bright smile. They knelt before the three brothers to show their gratitude. And their parents took out several silver coins from a box for the three brothers, who, however, refused politely.

从小死去父母，三兄弟相依为命，四处帮工度日。”老阿妈听了恩人的话，喜上眉梢，把心中的美愿倒了出来：“三位大恩人，若是不嫌我家的姑娘笨，不嫌我家的姑娘丑，我愿把她们许配给三位恩人，不知喜欢不喜欢？情愿不情愿？”夺艾三兄弟听了都点点头。三姐妹见恩人点头，就像喝了蜜水，满心甜透了。

五

夺艾三兄弟与吾娌三姐妹成婚后，日子过得很甜美。阿爹管着田地，五谷年年丰收；阿妈管着家务，年年吃穿不用愁。吾娌三姐妹在一起织布绣花，亲热和睦。夺艾三兄弟一同下山狩猎，时时形影不离。一家人在美满中欢度春秋。

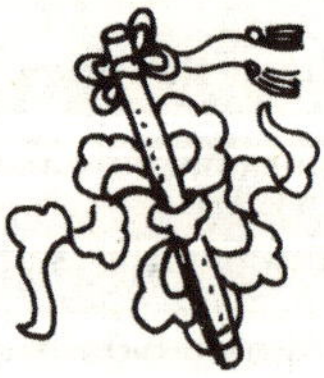

As they were about to leave, the three girls stopped them. Wuli grabbed Duoai; Diuli pulled the arm of Duoli; and Xili caught hold of Duole. At the same time, their parents blocked the door. The old man smiled at the three boys and said, "You are our saviors. At least let us know your name and address." Duoai replied, "We were born in Longkong Village in the Longma Mountain. Our parents died when we were little. Since then, we had relied on each other for survival and made a living by working everywhere." Having heard what he said, the old lady spoke out her wish happily, "If you think our girls are smart and pretty enough for you, I'd like you to marry them. Of course, if you want to." The three brothers nodded, which delighted the girls who felt as happy as a lark.

V

After the marriage, they lived a happy life. Their father took well care of fields which saw a bumper harvest every year, while their mother kept house for them so that they had no worry about food and clothing. The three sisters wove and embroidered together in harmony, and the three brothers went down for hunting, always staying close with each other. The whole family enjoyed a perfect time together.

“春风不常吹，好花不常开。”一天，三对小夫妻留下老两口守家，上了山。老两口闲得不自在，翻出不死药到门前来晒。太阳看见了，偷偷跑下大地，把不死药偷走了一半；月亮看见了，也偷偷跑下大地，把太阳偷剩的不死药全部偷走了。当老两口发现有人偷药时，偷药人已变成太阳和月亮向天空飘去。老两口急得大声哭喊着：“太阳，还我们的不死药！”“月亮，还我们的不死药！”可是，太阳和月亮已回到天空，任凭老两口怎样哭喊，它们都不理不睬。

傍晚，夺艾兄弟抬着猎物回来了，吾娌三姐妹背着柴禾回来了。老阿爹向三个女婿哭诉了失药的经过；老阿妈向三个女婿道歉。夺艾三弟兄听了，满腔怒火，决定打一把长楼梯搭到天上，把不死药夺回来。

做楼梯要用木材，砍木材要用砍刀，打砍刀要采铁矿，铁矿在遥远的格鲁北。夺勒用缩地筋把格鲁北拉了过来。三兄弟从格鲁北背回铁矿炼成了生铁。

打刀要请铁匠，铁匠在遥远的厄拉地。夺勒又用缩地筋把厄拉地拉了过来。三兄弟从厄拉地请回好铁匠，打了九十九天铁，打成了砍刀。

"Spring wind does not come often. Beautiful flowers do not always blossom." One day, the three couples went up to the mountain, leaving their parents at home. The two elders were so at loose ends that they took out longevity pills to have a sunshine in front of the door. At the sight of the pills, the sun crept down the earth and took half of them and the moon followed, stealing the rest. When the two old poor found out, it was too late. They had to watch the sun and the moon flying to the sky, crying out anxiously, "Give them back", but in vain. Hanging back in the sky, the sun and the moon simply ignored them.

At dusk, when the three brothers came back with preys with their wives loaded with bundles of wood, they were told about the stealing by their father-in-law with tears. The poor old mother-in-law apologized regretfully. The brothers were furious after learning the story. They decided to put a long ladder all the way to the sky and took their pills back.

They needed wood for ladder, machetes for cutting wood and iron ore for forging machetes. But iron ore was in the distant Gelubei. So Duole used his magic rope and pulled Gelubei to him. Then, the brothers carried the ore and smelted it into pig iron.

They also needed a blacksmith to forge machetes, but he lived in the far Eladi. So Duole hauled Eladi back with his rope. In this way, the brothers invited a talented blacksmith who successfully forged iron into a machete after working for ninety-nine days.

梯杆要用木头做，好木长在遥远的深山。夺勒还是用缩地筋把遥远的深山拉过来。三兄弟一起动手从山上砍回黑柚木，又从黑厄地请来了好木匠。木匠从春天做到了秋天，做成了九百九十九踩的楼梯。

栽梯要用石头，夺艾三兄弟从春天背到秋天，石头背够了。他们又请来了石匠，石匠凿石凿了九个月，凿出石头九百九十九块。石匠用石头砌梯脚，砌了九个月，梯脚砌得稳稳当当。

要把梯子扶起来搭到天上了，夺艾三兄弟请来众乡邻帮忙，把梯子搭到了天上。月亮见了心里十分着急，太阳见了心里十分恐慌。它们拿出不死药，一下子全部吞进肚里去了。

Also, they needed wood for making a ladder. But solid wood could only be found in the remote mountain. Again, Duole draw the distant mountain back with his rope. Then, the three brothers brought back some teak wood from the mountain and invited a skillful carpenter from Heiedi. The carpenter eventually made a ladder with ninety-nine rungs after working from spring to autumn.

To install a ladder, rocks were needed. In order to carry back enough rocks for the ladder, the three brothers worked from spring to autumn. Afterwards, they invited an excellent stonemason who chipped away at rocks for nine months and finally made nine hundred ninety-nine rocks. Then, he used the rocks to consolidate the bottom of the ladder after another nine months' hard work until it was as steady as Mount Tai.

The three brothers asked their neighbors to help lift the ladder all the way to the sky. The moon saw it and got very worried. So did the sun. Therefore, they took out the longevity pills and swallowed them all instantly.

夺艾叫来了花虎，花虎爬上了楼梯，爬了九天九夜，来到了太阳上；夺哩叫来了黑狗，黑狗爬上了楼梯，爬了九天九夜，来到了月亮上。虎、狗在天上爬了九天，人间已经过了九年，埋在地下的梯脚腐烂了。黑蚂蚁、白蚂蚁一起来啃，它们啃了九个月，朽木已被啃断，“哗啦”一声响，楼梯倒下来了。花虎和黑狗又急又气，向太阳和月亮狂吼怒叫。为报主人恩，花虎孤身和太阳相斗，每天大口大口地吃着太阳；黑狗孤身和月亮相斗，每天大口大口地啃着月亮。可是，吃进不死药的太阳和月亮，不怕花虎吃，不怕黑狗啃，吃掉长出来，啃缺又长圆。从此，月亮永远不会死，夜夜挂在天上，太阳永远不会死，日日挂在天上。地上的不死药断了根，世间的人，死后再也不会复生了。

流传地区：元江县龙马山

讲述者：白佑山

搜集整理者：宋自华

Duoai called on the tiger to climb up the ladder, who finally reached the sun after nine days and nine nights; Duoli summoned the black dog who arrived at the moon after climbing the ladder for nine days and nine nights. But time in the sky did not work as it did on earth. Though it took nine days for the tiger and the dog to reach the sky, actually nine years had passed on earth. During these long years, the bottom of the ladder was already decayed, as black ants and white ants had nipped at it for nine months. Finally, the ladder fell down. The tiger and the dog were anxious and furious, who howled at the sun and the moon wildly. To return favors of their masters, they chose to stay in the sky and fight. The tiger bit chunks off the sun every day, while the dog bit off the moon. However, the sun and the moon were not afraid at all because they had eaten longevity pills. Therefore, they grew back in full again no matter how hard the tiger and the dog bit. Ever since, the moon had hung up in the sky at night eternally, while the sun was high up during daytime. However, people on earth could not come back to life any more.

Spreading area: the Longma Mountain, Yuanjiang County
Narrator: Bai Yuoshan
Collector and editor: Song Zihua

史拉俄特“买”父亲

据说，彝族在史拉俄特以前是没有父亲的。家中事都由母亲和舅舅主张。这个故事讲的是史拉俄特“买”父亲、找父亲的事。

很久很久以前，诺苏①中有一个人叫史拉俄特。他从小聪明伶俐，爱动脑子，性格刚直倔犟，遇事非弄明白不可。他有一个心地善良的母亲，有一个漂亮能干的姐姐，没有哥哥弟弟。母亲和姐姐在家耕织，俄特上山打猎。由于从小喜欢骑马射箭，俄特练就了一手好箭法，每逢出猎都是满载而归。全家生活过得安静、幸福。

① 彝族的一个支系。

Shilae'te "Bought" Father

It is said that the Yi people did not have fathers before the endeavour of Shilae'te. All the family decisions were made by mothers and maternal uncles. This story tells how Shilae'te bought and looked for his father.

Long time ago, there was a man called Shilae'te in Nuosu①. He had been smart, inquiring, straightforward and somewhat obstinate since he was a child. He always insisted on getting to the bottom of the matter. He had a kind-hearted mother and a beautiful and capable sister, but no brother. His mother and sister stayed at home to do the farming and weaving, while E'te went hunting in the mountain. As he had a profound interests in riding and archery since childhood, he later developed into a master of archery and a fruitful hunter. The whole family lived a peaceful and happy life.

① A branch of the Yi ethnic group.

有一天，全家围坐在火塘边，吃着猎肉的时候，俄特向母亲和舅舅提出了思索已久的心事："鸟有母，兽有父，我家怎么没有父亲？"母亲被问住了，沉思了好久好久才答道："天上的彩云是父亲，地上的春风是父亲。"问舅舅，也不肯回答。他怎么想也想不出个道理来，就下了决心，要去"买"父亲，要去找父亲，不管到天涯海角也要找到父亲。

俄特带了九个随从，驮了九驮金子和九驮银子，白兔驮金子，狐狸驮银子，三月初三出发，踏上了寻找父亲的征途。

他们向着水的源头走，不知走了多少路。有一天来到一块平地，俄特看见一群群云雀在晨曦中飞舞，唱起了婉转的晨歌。听了云雀的歌声，俄特被吸引住了，呆呆地望着蹿上蹿下的云雀，不觉勾起了心思，自言自语地唱道：

欢快的云雀呀！
你有美丽的舞姿。
有嘹亮的歌喉。
你可告诉我，
我亲爱的父亲在哪里？

可是欢快的云雀哪能领会俄特的心思，它们仍旧飞舞歌唱。俄特静立了好久好久，长叹了一声，又赶路去了。

One day, when the family members were having the hunted meat by the fireplace, E'te asked his mother and maternal uncle a question, which had been hanging in his mind for a long time, "While birds have mothers and beasts have fathers, why isn't there a father in our family?" His mother was tongue-tied and answered after quite a while, "The colourful cloud in the sky is father and the spring wind on the ground is father." E'te then asked his maternal uncle, who kept silent. He could hardly figure out any reason in it, so he was determined to "buy" a father, however far he might travel.

E'te took nine attendants, nine loads of gold and nine loads of silver with him. The rabbits carried gold and wolves bore silver. They marched on the 3rd of March to look for his father.

Oriented to the source of water, they travelled days and nights, losing count of time. One day, they reached a plain where E'te saw skylarks dancing and singing in the morning light. He was deeply attracted to the beautiful voice. Staring at the skylarks jumping up and down, E'te could not help sighing with emotion, and sang to himself:

Lively skylarks!
You have beautiful dances,
Resonant voices.
Can you tell me
Where my dear father is?

But how could the lively skylarks understand E'te. They were still dancing and singing. Standing still for a long time, E'te sighed and continued his journey.

俄特艰难地走啊走，饿了用山泉水调把炒面充饥，困了就在山林中露宿。他来到了阿苏尼知山麓。茫茫的大森林，陡峭的山崖，他走了九天九夜，还没有走出阿苏尼知山林。林中蚊子像斑鸠一般大，大蟒像柱子一样粗，虎豹豺狼成群结队。他用金弓银箭射死了一只又一只虎豹豺狼，射死一条又一条毒蛇，不知多少次死里逃生。他终于翻越了阿苏尼知山，来到了阿俄脑依①边。

阿俄脑依水流湍急，波涛翻滚，漩涡一个挨一个。俄特乘牛皮船，越过了漩涡，战胜了恶浪，渡过了江，来到了华祖波尼②。

俄特从来没有见过这么大、这么平的地方，华祖波尼是九块很大的平地连成的，九块平地九村人家。村挨村，户连户，乌鸦飞过要被炊烟熏下来，斑鸠飞过也要歇九歇。他挨村访，挨户问，还是问不到父亲，还是“买”不到父亲，只好沮丧地离开华祖波尼。

① 阿俄脑依：意为黑水，指金沙江。

② 华祖波尼：地名，意为汉族居住的地方。

E'te went on his arduous travel. He mixed the spring water with the spiced noodles for food and slept out in the forest at night. He came to the Asunizhi Mountains, where he travelled in the deep forest and steep cliffs for nine days and nine nights and still could not get out. In the forest, mosquitoes were as big as turtledoves and pythons were as thick as pillars, with flocks of wild beasts. He could not count how many beasts and poisonous snakes he had shot with his golden bow and silver arrow before he barely escaped his life and managed to climbed over the Asunizhi Mountains and reached the area of Aenaoyi①.

The water in Aenaoyi was turbulent, with rolling waves and numerous whirlpools. Driving in a leather boat, E'te successfully crossed the turbulent river by surmounting the whirlpools and navigating the treacherous currents, and came to Huazunibo②.

E'te had never been to such a large and flat place before, as Huazunibo was stitched by nine big plains and settled with nine villages. Villages were close to one another and so were the households. Crows flying over could not survive the smoke from kitchen chimneys and turtledoves had to take a rest when flying past this area. He called upon every village and every household but still could not find or "buy" a father, so he had to leave Huazunibo in dismay.

---

① Aenaoyi: Heishui, the Jinsha River.

② Huazunibo: name of a Place where the Han Nationality lives.

梨花白了，桃花红了，时间又到了三月初三。他找了一年，“买”了一年，连个父亲的影子也没有见到。他历尽千辛万苦，翻越了千山万水，可是心愿未偿。他又来到了一个僻静处，夜幕已笼罩着山峦。鸟儿归巢了，兽儿归穴了，他只好在一棵大树下露宿。俄特过度劳累，心里想着心事，枕着树根，不知不觉睡着了。他梦见自己正在树林里艰难地行走，遇到一位白发苍苍的老毕摩①。他向老毕摩问起了心事：“我翻越千山万水，历尽千辛万苦，来‘买’父亲，来找父亲。尊敬的毕摩阿普②，请你告诉我，我的父亲在哪里？”毕摩叹道：“可怜的年轻人，你沿着山走，不远处有一片竹林，竹林中有一幢房子，有位姑娘会告诉你。”毕摩说完哈哈大笑。俄特想继续追问，却被黎明中鸟儿的叫声惊醒了。他匆忙上路，怀着侥幸的心情沿着山梁走去。没走多远就进入一片翠竹林，沿着林荫小道走去，见到了一幢房子。房子在翠竹的掩映下，灯火辉煌，传出阵阵优美的歌声。俄特走进房内，惊呆了：啊唷！金做的瓦，银做的柱，宫女来往如梭。

---

① 译者注：毕摩是整个彝族社会中的知识分子，是彝族文化的维护者和传播者。

② 阿普：彝语，意为爷爷。

Pear flowers turned white and peach blossoms grew red; it was the 3rd of March again. He had looked for and tried to "buy" a father for one year, but there was still no trace of him. He had gone through innumerable trials and hardships and travelled thousands of miles, but he could not get his wish. Again, he came to a quiet place where night had fallen over the mountains. Birds returned their nests and beasts came back to their caves. He had to spend the night over under a big tree. E'te was too exhausted, with a load on his mind, so he quickly fell into sleep on the tree root. In his dream, while taking an arduous journey in the forest, he met a grey-haired Bimo① and asked him, "I have gone through countless hardships and travelled numerous hills and streams to 'buy' and look for a father. Respectable Bimo Apu②, can you tell me where my father is?" Bimo sighed and said, "Poor young man, walk along this hill, and you will find a house in the not too distant bamboo forest, where a girl will tell you." Afterwards he laughed heartily. E'te wanted to question more closely, but he was waken by the sound of birds at dawn. He started off in haste and walked along the ridge of the hill to take chances. After a while, he entered into a bamboo forest, so he continued his walk in the avenue and saw a house. In the shadow of bamboos, the house brilliantly illuminated where melodic sound of singing was heard. Walking into the house, E'te was stunned: Oh! The house was made of golden tiles and silvery pillars where

① Translator's note: Bimo is the intellectual and man of wisdom in the Yi society, who guards and spreads the Yi culture.

② Apu: Yi language. It means grandfather.

一位少女坐在堂中织布。原来那歌是这少女唱的。她头上戴着珍珠玛瑙闪闪发光，衣服似鹦鹉的羽毛。俄特看花了眼，连连赞道："搓棚，搓棚①。"声音惊动了少女，她含羞默默地用袖口掩住脸问道："远来的客人，有什么事，要到什么地方去？"听了这话，俄特忽然想起梦中老毕摩的话，就连忙迎上前去答道："尊敬的姑娘，我越过千山万水，要去'买'父亲，要去找父亲，请你告诉我，我的父亲在哪里？"少女听了，先是感到惊奇，然后唱道：

蜜蜂不知晚，看见山崖就宿。
斑鸠不知晚，看见树林就宿。
云雀不知晚，看见平地就宿。
远来的客人，有心事也要宿。

俄特听了少女的话，想着问个究竟，又被少女那神奇姿态吸引，就解驮卸甲住下了。

这少女原是仙子子阿滴都家的幺女，名叫子尼史色。晚上，为了迎接这位凡界的客人，少女在宫前燃起了九塘篝火，摆出九坛芳香的美酒。在芦笙②声的伴奏下，客人和主人先后唱起了动听的彝家民歌。

---

① 搓棚：意即真了不起。

② 译者注：芦笙即古代簧管乐器。

maids were streaming in and out. In the middle of the hall, a maid sat and wove, from whom the sound of singing came. She wore sparkling pearls and agates on her head and dressed in parrot-like feathers. E'te was dazzled. He could not help paying compliments, "Cuoshan, Cuoshan①." The voice startled the maid. The shy girl covered her face with her cuff and asked, "Dear guest coming from afar, is there anything you want? where are you going?" This reminded Bimo's words in his dream, so E'te quickly came forward and answered, "Dear girl, I have travelled thousands of miles and endured numerous hardships to 'buy' and look for a father. Can you tell me where my father is?" The girl was amazed at first, but then she sang:

Bees do not know the night, and they rest at the sight of the cliff.

Turtledoves do not know the night, and they rest at the sight of the forest.

Skylarks do not know the night, and they rest at the sight of the plain.

Dear guest coming from afar, you also need to rest when you have worries in your mind.

E'te had thought of asking the reason, but fascinated by the maid's mysterious style, he unloaded the pack and settled.

The maid was called Zinishise, the youngest daughter of fairy Ziadidu. At night, the maid set on nine heaps of bonfire and laid out nine jars of good wine to welcome this guest from the mortal world. With the accompaniment of Lusheng②, the guest began to sang melodic folk songs of the Yi people with the host.

---

① Cuoshan: awesome and amazing.

② Translator's note: Lusheng refers to an ancient reed-pipe wind instrument.

俄特唱道：

百花丛中索玛花最美丽，
姑娘当中数史色最漂亮。
唱起歌来像云雀，
歌儿会唱千万箩。
心灵手巧赛金猴，
织出彩帛千万匹。

史色连忙答道：

百鸟当中布谷最可亲，
凡人当中俄特最忠厚。
姑娘的歌唱了千万箩，
只因宫中凄凉心里闷。
织出锦帛千万匹，
哪有人间粗布暖！

俄特又迫不及待地唱道：

为哪样白云朵朵绕山间？
为哪样蜜蜂嗡嗡闹花丛？
为哪样三月初三布谷声声叫？
为哪样俄特盼父盼不到？

史色没有马上回答，却向俄特提出：

什么东西像纱不能织？
什么东西像棉不能弹？
什么东西像盐不能食？
聪明客人你能猜得出，

E'te sang:

Azalea is the most gorgeous one among all the flowers,
Shise is the most beautiful one among all the girls.
Sing like a skylark,
and sing a thousand songs.
More skilful in hand than the golden monkey,
she can weave a thousand colourful silks.

Shise hurriedly replied:

Cuckoo is the dearest one among all the birds,
E'te is the sincerest one among all the mortal men.
The girl has sung a thousand songs,
because life in the palace is lonely and depressed.
The girl has woven a thousand colourful silks,
but how can they be comparable to the warmth of the coarse cloths woven in the mortal world!

E'te could not wait to reply:

Why do the white clouds surround mountains?
Why do the bees buzz around flowers?
Why do the cuckoos keep chirping on the 3rd of March?
Why can't I find my father?

Shise did not answer immediately, but asked E'te:

What can not be woven like yarn?
What can not be fluffed like cotton?
What can not be eaten like salt?
Dear guest, if you are smart enough to get the right answer,

我就把实心话告诉你。

俄特沉思了一会，便答道：

天上的云彩像纱不能织，
山间的云雾像棉不能弹，
溪间的冻冰像盐不能食，
我若猜得无差错，
快把实话告诉我。

史色见俄特聪明，心里便产生了爱慕之情，就唱道：

花香芬芳引蜂来，
山高峰峻绕白云，
三月初三春风暖，
娶媳养儿便成父。

俄特听了，顿时省悟过来，找父"买"父的心思散失了。仙子子阿滴都被俄特的行动感动了，就把幺女史色嫁给了他。俄特用九驮金子作聘礼，用九驮银子换来家当，娶了史色。夫妻和睦恩爱。后来史色生了三个儿子。从此养儿见到父，养女见到母，一代代男婚女嫁，繁衍后代。这就是史拉俄特"买"父、找父的故事，至今老幼皆知，每逢讨媳嫁女，讲的唱的就是这个故事。

流传地区：云南省永胜县

搜集整理者：莫新元

I will tell you the truth.

E'te thought for a while and answered:

Clouds in the sky can not be woven like yarn,
Mists in the mountain can not be fluffed like cotton,
Freeze in the stream can not be eaten like salt,
If I am right,
Please tell me the truth.

Shise had a feeling of affection at E'te's smart answer, so she sang:

Fragrance of flowers attracted bees,
Clouds only surround the high mountains and steep cliffs,
Spring wind is warm on the 3rd of March,
Take a wife and bear children, then you will be a father.

E'te learned the truth all of a sudden and decided to disregard his single-minded pursuit of "buying" a father. Fairy Ziadidu was moved by the action of E'te, so she married her youngest daughter Shise to him. E'te gave nine loads of gold as betrothal presents and exchanged the nine loads of silver for household belongings; then, he married Shise. The couple had a peaceful and happy life. Later, Shise gave birth to three sons. Since then, daughters and sons could meet their parents. For generations, men took wives and women married husbands to produce off-springs. This is the well-known story of E'te who tried to "buy" and find a father. Now when the Yi people get married, they will sing this story.

Spreading area: Yongsheng County, Yunnan Province
Collector and editor: Mo Xinyuan

搓日阿补征服女儿国

搓日阿补和他的母亲木古搓日

搓日阿补的妈妈木古搓日单家独户住在深山老林里。有一年，丈夫出门去打猎，一去就再也没有回来。

木古搓日去寻丈夫。一天，一座奇怪的大山挡在面前，抬头看去，只见山上红彤彤的，开满了各式各样的花。这种花大得出奇，颜色也怪，挂在麻线样细的小草尖上，大风吹过，不摇也不动。离得老远，那股香气就扑鼻吹来。木古搓日就像做梦一样，身不由已地爬上了高高的山顶。站在山顶上，可以看见很远很远的地方。山顶上的风也吹得怪，一会倒着吹，一会正着吹，吹一次要停好半天。风一来，刚出蒂的花蕾便突然开放了，小小的花朵也一眨眼变得大大的。木

Cuoriabu Conquered the Kingdom of Women

Cuoriabu and His Mother, Mugucuori

Mugucuori and her families lived in deep forests, alone. One year, her husband went out hunting but never returned.

Mugucuori went to find her husband. One day, she was blocked by a huge strange-looking mountain. Looking closer, she found that the mountain was coated in redness as kaleidoscopic flowers bloomed all over there, which were huge in size and odd in color. Attached to the grass as thin as strings, those brobdingnagian flowers never faltered a bit even if a gust of wind roared past. Besides, they were so aromatic that Mugucuori could smell them in a very long distance. Fascinated by this illusory scene, she couldn't resist climbing all the way to the top of the mountain. Standing on the peak, she could see things far in the distance. But wind there was also strange. It came sometimes head-on, sometimes from the back, at rather long intervals each time. When the wind came again, all the buds suddenly came into full blossom. The once small buds grew much bigger just in the blink of an eye. Mugucuori felt surprised, but

古搓日又惊奇，又高兴。心想，山高，声音就传得远，我在这里喊丈夫，他容易听见。她张了张嘴，可是声音还没喊出口，风就扑面吹来了。香呼呼的风，热热地吹进她的嘴里，使得她全身像着火一样发烫。她感到自己好像咽下了什么美味的东西，心里一阵发痒，便昏倒在草地上了。

从山上走下来，她便知道自己怀孕了，慌忙找个山洞住进去。过了九个月，生下个又白又胖的儿子，取名叫搓日阿补。

搓印阿补出世后，母亲摘了九十九种果子给他吃，使他比人世间所有的人都聪明；母亲找了九十九种兽肉给他吃，所以他比世上所有的动物都灵巧；母亲还挖了九十九种树根给他吃，因此他长得比大树还要标直。

搓日阿补三岁跟着母亲学织布，到了七岁，就能把火草织成漂亮的衣裳，还能用兽毛织出温暖耐用的披毡。妈妈见了，高兴地对儿子说："阿补呀，妈妈没有福气生姑娘，可你比姑娘还能干！不过男人是应该去寻找火草和兽毛的，织衣织布是女人的事哩。"于是，搓日阿补就上山找火草和兽毛去了。他一转眼就找了许多回来。七岁的时候，他又跟母亲

thrilled. She would like to call out her husband's name there, on the mountain peak, because she thought her voice could reach further at such a high altitude. When she was about to say the word, the wind came to her before she could make herself heard. The aromatic hot wind went into her mouth, which heated her all over. She felt like having taken in something very pleasant. Feeling itchy in heart, she fainted and fell down to the glass land.

When she went downhill, she found that she was pregnant, and therefore hasted to accommodate herself in a cave. Nine months later, a lovely chubby boy was born, called Cuoriabu.

After birth, his mother picked ninety nine kinds of fruits for him to eat so that he would be smarter than anyone else. Also, his mother hunted ninety nine kinds of animals as his food so that he would be the most agile among the living, and dug up roots of ninety nine kinds of trees for the same purpose, in the hope of making him grow even more upright than those trees.

At the age of three, Cuoriabu learned how to weave from his mother. When he was seven, he was able to weave gerbera into beautiful clothes, and animal fur into warm and durable wraps. Seeing all those achievements, his mother said pleasantly, "Abu, although I was not lucky enough to have a daughter, a son like you is even more crafty than a daughter. I'm happy. However, a man's duty is to forage gerbera and animal fur, not weave, for that is what women should do!" Therefore, Cuoriabu went up mountains to search for gerbera and animal furs. Soon he came back with a full basket. He learned farming from his mother at the age of seven, and became an expert at it when he was nine.

学种地。到了九岁，他又成了种地能手，一天能犁完一座山；十天犁的地，一夜就种完了。母亲见了，又夸奖说："阿补呀，妈妈没有福气生姑娘，可你比姑娘还顶用！不过男人应该去打猎，种地是女人的事，你去给妈妈找兽肉去吧！"于是，搓日阿补很快成了个英勇的猎手。

小人长成大人，大人变成英雄，母亲看着儿子大山一样的体格，石头一样的肌肉，树干一样的手脚，心里一天比一天高兴。不知不觉地，木古搓日老了，走不动路，做不成活了。搓日阿补放心不下，便天天背着母亲出门去打猎。母亲实在过意不去，便劝儿子说："阿补呀阿补，妈妈年老骨节松，一天到晚颠簸在儿背上，心好像要被抖落了，肝好像要被抖烂了。你把妈放在家里，别再把妈背在背上。如果再背的话，妈妈就不是儿的妈了。"搓日阿补听了摇着头说："妈妈呀，你不知道，房前边老熊在做窝了，房后边饿狼在下崽了，房梁上吃人的蚊子成堆了，床下边毒蛇在结队了，儿子怎能把妈妈放在家里！"不管母亲怎么说，儿子还是坚持背起母亲去打猎。木古搓日没办法，打了一个主意，要把儿子嫁出去。

He could till all land in the mountain in one day. And it took only one night for him to till the vast land while others needed ten days. His mother complimented again after seeing all his achievements, saying "Abu, although I was not lucky enough to have a daughter, a son like you can even till more land than a daughter. I'm happy. However, a man's duty is to hunt, not farm, for that is what women should do!" Therefore, Cuoriabu soon became a valiant hunter.

His mother was so proud to see that her child had grown up and became a hero, with stalwart figure, rock-hard muscle, and strong limbos like trees. As time passed by, Mugucuori grew feeble, and was no longer able to walk and work. Cuoriabu was worried so he carried her on his back every time he went out hunting. Being a burden, his mother felt awkward, so she said to her son, "Abu, my jolts are loosening. Please get me off. The shaking at your back will crumble my heart and liver. Let me stay at home, or you will not have a mother anymore." Cuoriabu shook his head and replied, "Mum, you need to know that bears are building their homes in front of our house, hungry wolves are breeding curbs in our backyard, cannibal mosquitoes are crowded over our beams, and poisonous snakes are gathering in groups under our beds. How can I leave you there, my mother!" No matter what his mother said, Cuoriabu insisted on carrying her on the back when he went out for hunting. His mother had to give in, but she came up with another idea, which was to find someone to marry him.

“阿补呀阿补，没有开过花的树不算树，没有成家的人不算人。妈妈有个主意，要找一家漂亮的姑娘，把你嫁出去。”

搓日阿补不同意：“妈妈呀妈妈，前半生你养我，后半生我养你，这才是正理。要我出门去嫁人，除非我从来没有你这个妈。妈妈呀妈妈，请你不要再往下说！”

木古搓日说：“阿补呀阿补，不愿离开妈也不难，你把妈妈吃在肚里去嫁人，这就是两全其美的好事了。不要为难呀阿补，妈的阿补就在妈的肚子里装过哩！”

搓日阿补还是不同意：“妈妈把我装在肚子里是给我生命，我把妈放在肚子里是害了妈的生命。我不能吃妈妈，我也不能离开妈妈去嫁人。”

两母子争执不下，闹了好几天。后来搓日阿补想出了个办法，决定去娶个媳妇来。可当时的规矩是男人出嫁，女人娶亲。母亲虽然不同意，但也无法阻挡他，只得让儿子把她藏在山洞里。这样，搓日阿补便出门说亲去了。

"Abu, a tree with no flower is not a real tree. A man with no wife is not a real man. I'm thinking about finding a beautiful girl to be your wife." his mother said.

Cuoriabu shook his head and said, "Mother, you spent half of your life raising me. Now it's my turn to look after you. That's what a son should do. How can I marry someone when I have a mother who needs to be taken cared of. Mum, please say no more!"

But his mother said, "Abu, there's a way that I can be with you. You can eat me. Then whoever you marry, I will still be with you. It's a good way. Abu, please don't feel sorry for me. You used to be in my body too!"

Cuoriabu still didn't agree and replied, "I used to be in your body because you were giving me a life. But if I put you in my body, it means that I will take your life. I can't do that. Neither can I marry someone nor leave you at home."

They argued for several days. Then, Cuoriabu proposed an idea which was to marry someone and bring her back to his home. But marital traditions at that time required men to live in his wife's house after their marriage. Although his mother did not agree, she had to compromise, and told her son to hide herself in a cave. Afterwards, Cuoriabu went out to find someone to marry.

搓日阿补和人世间的姑娘们

搓日阿补遵照妈妈的嘱咐一路上唱着歌，向花山的方向走去。刚翻过一座山梁，一只打扮得花花绿绿的金丝鸟绕着他飞，嘴里唱道："阿呷阿呷西哩色诺莫拉木曲达……"搓日阿补听了半天听不懂，不过还是高兴地想："好兆头哩，好兆头！"不久，又有一头野猪跟着他吵吵闹闹地叫喊："烘烘何何巴达拉乌则泥则……"搓日阿补听了半天听不懂，有点生气了，抽出长刀，把野猪给吓跑了。

又过了一会，碰到一群猴子拦住去路，比手画脚地说："哇啦伊哩加加莫莫阿鲁者曲……"搓日阿补听了半天听不懂，越发生气了，抓起一根木棒，把猴群追得满山遍野乱跑乱叫。

从此，动物们见了搓日阿补，都远远地躲开了。好不容易才遇着几只小松鼠，搓日阿补连忙问道："松鼠呵松鼠，过去是男人嫁女人，现在我想叫女人嫁男人，请你告诉我走哪个方向我才能说到媳妇？"松鼠听了他的话，用手指指前边，嘻嘻笑着说："往前走，媳妇有；说得着，说不着……"讲完就跑了。这使搓日阿补又高兴又担忧。

Cuoriabu and Girls in the Mortal World

Following his mother's advice, Cuoriabu walked towards the mountain with flowers and sang on his way. When he climbed over a ridge, a colorful canary flied around him humming, "agaagaxilisenuomolamuquda..." Cuoriabu listened but couldn't understand it. Still, he was happy because he thought it was a good sign to him. Later, a wild pig screamed to him, "hohohehebadalawuzenize..." He listened again, but still couldn't figure out what was said. This time, he was a little pissed off, and took out his long knife to scare away the pig.

Then, a group of monkeys stopped him, making gestures and saying, "Walayilijiajiamomoaluzhequ..." He listened, and again, he could understand nothing. He got angry, and chased the monkeys all over the mountain, scaring them into screaming.

Since then, animals would instantly ran away at the sight of him. He came a long way before he finally met several squirrels. He asked, "Squirrels, men used to live in his wife's house after their marriage. But now I want my wife to stay at mine. Please tell me where I should go if I want to find a wife like that." After hearing what he said, squirrels smiled and pointed the path forward, "Maybe there is a wife for you in that direction. Who knows. But that's all we can tell you." they said. Then the squirrels ran away. Those words made Cuoriabu both happy and worried.

几天以后，搓日阿补走到一个山坡上，遇到一位放猪姑娘。放猪姑娘一见搓日阿补，就亲亲热热地问道："过路的阿哥，你从哪里来？要到哪里去？你的母亲姓什么？你的名字叫哪样？看你满面春风，又走得这么急急忙忙，是不是想家人？"

搓日阿补连忙答道："像金丝鸟一样好的放猪小妹呵，我从花山后边来，要到花山前边去，我的妈妈姓搓日，我的名字叫阿补。我这样急急忙忙地走，不是想嫁人，是想娶个女人做媳妇。聪明的放猪姑娘，请你告诉我，世上有没有愿意出嫁的女人？"

放猪姑娘听了，好心地说："既然你这样想，那你就尽你的本事去做吧。不过我要告诉你，你想说个媳妇，比想生个娃娃还要难！"搓日阿补很感激她，就说道："好心的姑娘，愿你的猪关在圈里，比放到山上还胖。"从此，猪就不用再往外放牧了。

不久，搓日阿补又遇上了放羊姑娘。他俩互通了姓名，搓日阿补就问放羊姑娘："聪明的放羊阿妹，像野猪一样能干的放羊阿妹，我想改变女人娶男人的规矩，去说一个媳妇回家奉养母亲，你说我能不能实现自己的愿望？"

A few days later, Cuoriabu met a girl who was herding pigs when he walked on a hillside. The girl asked very graciously, "Young boy there, where do you come from and where are you going? What's your mother's name? What's your name? You must be missing your families since you shine with happiness yet walk so hastily."

Cuoriabu answered immediately, "Dear sister, you are as beautiful as a canary. I come from the back of the flower mountain and want to go to the front of it. My mother's family name is Cuori. And my name is Abu. The reason why I walk so hastily is to find a wife who can stay with me in my house instead of going to hers. Smart herding girl, please tell me whether I can find a girl like that."

The girl replied kindly, "Well, if that's what you wish for, just try your best. But I have to tell you that finding a wife like is even harder than giving birth to a baby." Cuoriabu was very grateful and said, "You are so kind-hearted. I hope your pigs can grow stronger and fatter in captivity than in the wild." Since then, people no longer needed to herd pigs.

Soon, Cuoriabu met a girl who herded sheep. After greeting each other, he asked the girl, "Smart sister as diligent as wild pigs, I want to change the rule that men can only live in their wives' home after their marriage. I want to find a wife who can stay in my house and serve my mother. Can you tell me if I can make my dream come true?"

放羊姑娘嘲笑道：“你有没有比我多的牛羊？如果有的话，我就嫁给你。看你光身一人，还想说什么媳妇，怕嫁出去也没人要哩！”

搓日阿补听了很生气，骂道：“从今往后，女人养不活羊子，养羊的福气归给男人才好！”从此，女人就真的放不好羊子了。

搓日阿补离开放羊姑娘走了半天，又遇着一大群妇女正在驾牛犁地。他们互通了姓名之后，搓日阿补又说：“猴子一样灵巧的姐妹们呵，我想来你们地方说个媳妇，有没有愿嫁给我的姑娘？”

犁地的妇女们都笑了起来：“你能像我们一样驾着牛犁地吗？如果不能呀，还是嫁给我们吧！”

搓日阿补生气地走，边走边说：“但愿从此牛不听妇女的话，除了男人谁也不能把牛制服才好！”从此，果然牛就再也不听妇女使唤了。

The girl laughed at him, "Do you have more cattle and sheep than me? If you have, I'll marry you. But it looks like that you have nothing but yourself. How can you find a wife? I doubt anyone will want you!"

Cuoriabu grew furious and cursed, "From now on, women can't raise sheep anymore. Only men will be blessed with this skill." Since then, women really turned out to be incapable of raising sheep.

Cuoriabu left the girl and walked for a while. Then he met a group of women who were riding cattle to plough the field. After exchanging their names, Cuoriabu said, "Hi, sisters as agile as monkeys. I'd like to find a girl to marry me and live at my home. Is there anyone?"

The women who were tilling the land all laughed, saying "Can you ride the cattle and till the land just like us? If not, you come with us!"

Cuoriabu got angry. He cursed again while turning away, "From this day on, I hope cattle will only obey men!" Since then, cattle really no longer followed instructions of women.

一天，搓日阿补走到一个寨子里，见场院里有很多小姑娘正在扬场。他走上去，还没等通报姓名，姑娘们早一窝蜂围住了他。他想："女人家要比男人懂得害羞才好；她们的婚姻不能让她们自己做主！三岁订婚、十三岁出嫁给男人，那就好得不得了啦！世上的女人，都不爱听从哥哥弟弟的话，要是把她们的女儿都嫁给哥哥弟弟的儿子，这样的规矩，那不知有多好啊！"果然，后来就实行姑舅表优先婚。变得和他想的一模一样了。

搓日阿补走呵走呵，走了很多路，一路上的遭遇使他很伤心，但他还是头也不回地照直走着，来到一个连男人的影子都见不着的地方。他路过一条山梁时，山头上站着个漂亮女子，笑眯眯地和他打招呼："走路的哥哥，你从哪里来？要到哪里去？你的母亲姓什么？你的名字叫哪样？看你一脸的哭相，是不是碰到了什么为难事？"

搓日阿补报了自己的姓名，然后说："松鼠样美丽的姑娘哟，我家里有年老的妈妈，我想说个媳妇去陪伴她。你能不能告诉我，这里有没有愿出嫁的姑娘？"

One day, as Cuoriabu entered a stockaded village, he saw many young girls winnowing on the farmyard. He went closer. Before he could introduce himself, a crowd of girls surrounded him. But he thought girls should not be so active and open. Therefore, he thought to himself, "Girls should be more shy than boys. Also, they should not make decisions on their marriage. They ought to be engaged at the age of three and marry away when they turn thirteen. That will be brilliant. Women in this world never listen to their brothers, but if there is a rule that requires their daughters to marry sons of their brothers, how awesome that can be!" Later, marriage was pervasive among cousins. Everything went exactly like what he had wanted.

Cuoriabu kept on walking for a long time. Though saddened by previous experiences, he still made up his mind to go forward, and arrived at a place where there was no sight of man. When he walked through the ridge of a mountain, he saw a beautiful girl standing on the top, waving at him in bright smile, saying, "Hi, brother, where do you come from? Where are you going? What's your mother's last name? Where's your name? You look so sad. Have you encountered anything that troubles you?"

Cuoriabu introduced himself and said, "Hi, sister, you are as beautiful as a squirrel. I have an aged mother back in my house, so I'd like to find a girl to be my wife and accompany my mother. Can you tell me whether there are girls here who would come home with me?"

姑娘听了，眉开眼笑地说：“知道呵，有愿出嫁的姑娘哩。不过你得先上山来，帮我找到了我要找的东西，我才告诉你！”原来，离这儿不远的地方，有个女儿国。女儿国的女人迎风站在山头上也能怀孕。生下的儿女，只留姑娘，不要儿子。女儿国的人到处抓男人过日子。天长日久，这一带的男人就被抓绝了。这里的女人娶不着男人，便走出门来，专候远来的男子，把他们骗回去成亲。这姑娘今天就是专门来等待男人的。

搓日阿补不知道这些，听了姑娘的话，就高兴地和她走在一起了。正好这时，天上飞过一群雁鹅，姑娘指着最后边那只说：“天上飞着的雁鹅，最后边那只没有伙伴，你如果把它射下来，你就有媳妇了。”

搓日阿补张弓搭箭，把那只雁鹅射落了下来。他看看雁鹅美丽的羽毛，很心疼，就拔了一把装在箭袋里。姑娘不住口地夸他。

过了一会，山头上爬下来一条大蛇。姑娘指着毒蛇说：“它也是来寻找伙伴的。你如果能拔下它的毒牙，我就是你的媳妇。”

The girl smiled broadly and replied, "I know there will be some here. But you need to go up the mountain and find what I want, then I will tell you!" It turned out that there was a kingdom of women not far from here. Women there could get pregnant when facing the wind at the top of the mountain. After giving birth, only daughters were left. Therefore, women from that kingdom tried to catch men everywhere to live with them. Over time, all the men nearby were caught and became their husbands. Those who couldn't find a man nearby had to go outside and waited for men coming from afar. This girl was waiting for her prey today.

Cuoriabu did not know that, so he followed the girl, happily. Just then, a flock of geese flew overhead. The girl pointed at the last goose in the flock and said, "Look at that one, so lonely without a companion. If you shoot it down, you will have a wife."

Pulling back the bow and shooting an arrow, Cuoriabu shot down the goose as told. He felt very sorry when he observed its beautiful features. So he pulled out some of the feathers and put them in his arrow bag. The girl kept complimenting him.

Later, a giant snake crawled down from the mountain top. The girl pointed at the snake and said, "He is looking for companions. If you pull out his fangs, I will be your wife."

阿补一纵步跳上蛇背，卡住蛇的脖子，硬是把蛇牙拔下来了。姑娘看他这样了不起，心里很高兴，拉起搓日阿补就走，一进家就对躺在床上的老母亲说："妈妈呀妈妈，你的福气可真好，女儿今天呀，给你娶来了个了不起的女婿，你睁大眼睛看他吧：他那石头一样硬的肌肉，可以砸断毒蛇的牙齿；他那大山一样的体格，可以一手提起地，一手托起天；他那大树一样的双手，可以把天和地捏成粉末。"她的妈妈见了搓日阿补，也很高兴，十分乐意让他俩成亲。

搓日阿补乐坏了，拉起姑娘就要走。姑娘的母亲火了："世间只有男人跟女人，哪有女人跟男人？你现在是我家女婿了，愿在也要在，不愿在也得在！"

姑娘也说："我跟你走是不合道理的，我母亲又年老了，我就更不能走了。你是心甘情愿嫁我的，所以你只能住下！"

搓日阿补一听，气得扭身就走。可还没有走出三座山，那姑娘又追了上来。她叫住搓日阿补说："我舍不得你，我还是要嫁给你。"搓日阿补问她："你妈准你走啦？"

"我把她带来了！"姑娘说。

搓日阿补问："哦，在哪里？"

Abu made a great stride and jumped on the snake's back. With one hand choking its neck, Abu mustered all the strength on the other hand and took out the fangs. The girl was very delighted to find this capable man, so she took him home, hand in hand. Upon arrivaling, she immediately talked to her old mother who was lying on bed, "Mum, how blessed you are. I have good news. I've found an outstanding son-in-law for you. Look at him. His muscle is as hard as rocks, enough to break snakes' fangs; his figure is as stalwart as a mountain, enough to support both sky and earth; his hands are as strong as trees, enough to crumble sky and earth." The girl's mother was indeed very satisfactory with Cuoriabu, and approved of their marriage.

Cuoriabu was so excited that he immediately took the girl's hands to ask her to go away with him, which angered her mother, "Men must stay with women after marriage. That's the rule, not the other way around. You are now my son-in-law, so you have to stay here, like it or lump it!"

The girl also said, "It is against the rules for me to go away with you. My mother is aged so I have to stay here to look after her. You marry me agreeably, so you have to stay here with us!"

Cuoriabu turned away and stormed outside in fury. Before he could walk through three mountains, the girl caught up with him. She called out to him and said, "I don't want you to leave. I still want to marry you." Cuoriabu asked her, "Does your mother approve of your going away with me?"

"I have brought her with us!" the girl answered.

Cuoriabu said, "Well, where is she now?"

姑娘说："在我肚子里！"

搓日阿补吓呆了："你把你妈吃啦？"

姑娘说："吃了不麻烦！"

搓日阿补惊骇得抖起来，连声叫道："不娶你，不娶你，活着不娶你，死也不娶你，你走你的路，不然我杀死你！"

姑娘眼看无法挽救了，一下子起了坏心，对搓日阿补说："那么你到前边另说一个吧，从这里照直走，翻三道红色的山梁，过三条黑色的河水，那里的姑娘，十个出来十个嫁，百个出来百个走。我罪该万死，就死在你面前吧。但愿你一定照我说的路走，不然你就再也说不着媳妇了。"说完，姑娘一头撞死在路边的大树上。她的灵魂变成红嘴白脸的美女雀，到现在还在山里伤心地叫着："不嫁你，不娶你，气死你，不娶你……"

搓日阿补和女儿国与猎神

搓日阿补没有料到姑娘会自杀，又后悔又难过。他架起火烧了姑娘的尸体，心想："她是一个好姑娘，我害了她了。"于是他就照姑娘留下的话朝着那个方向走去。

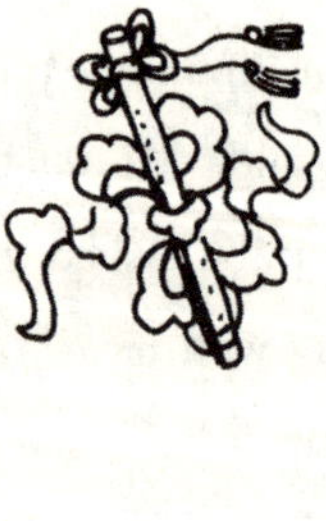

The girl replied, "In my stomach!"

Cuoriabu was startled, "You've eaten your mum?"

The girl said, "Yes, so she won't bother us anymore!"

Feeling frightened, Cuoriabu exclaimed in trembling, "You go. Please hurry. I will never marry you! You go now or I'll kill you!"

The girl wanted revenge after learning that there was no way to fix it, so she told Cuoriabu, "Then leave and find another one. Go straight forward. After climbing three red mountain ridges, crossing three black rivers, you will find girls who would be so willing to go with you. I've made horrible mistakes, so I am now paying the price with my life. I hope you will follow my advice or you will never find any girl to be your wife." Afterwards, the girl ran towards a tree along the path, hit it with her head, and died. Her soul turned into a beautiful sparrow with red mouth and white face. The sparrow's crying sound of "Mary you, no way!" could still be heard today.

Cuoriabu, the Kingdom of Women, and the Deity of Hunting

The suicide was out of Cuoriabu's expectation, which made him feel so regretted and disheartened. He lighted a fire and burned the body. He thought, "She is a good girl, but I killed her." So he continued his journey in the direction advised by the girl.

三道红色的山梁翻过去了，三条黑色的河水蹚过去了，搓日阿补来到了一个奇怪的地方。这地方天是红的，地是红的，空气是红的，连水也是红的。九十九层耀眼的金光中，出现了一个红色的寨子。在开着的寨门口，在寨外宽阔的坝子上，成千上万不穿衣裳裤子的年轻女人，背柴的背柴，挑水的挑水，放牧的放牧，做活的做活。所有的人都唱着一种迷人的歌，欢乐得不得了。原来这里就是女儿国。女儿国的人只会死，不会老，因此每个活着的人，都好像十七八岁的大姑娘。她们个个身材高大，力大无穷。搓日阿补很惊奇，不知道自己到了什么地方。他正想转身离去，忽见迎面来了几十个背着孩子的妇女，她们的乳房特别大，都把乳头从肩膀上甩过去让孩子吃，手里提着柴捆，嘴里哼着奇怪的歌。搓日阿补正在惊讶时，早被背孩子的妇女们看见了。她们不但不回避，反而笑眯眯地围上来，欢天喜地地把他上上下下看了个遍。其中一个叫了起来："嗬哟，老天赐给我们的福气来了，抓住他呀，别让他跑了！"这里话音刚落，那里几十个人便一起乱吼起来，接着，满山遍野的女人都放下手中的活计大喊大叫，刮风一样黑压压地扑了过来。搓日阿补一看势头不妙，连忙砍开一条血路，好不容易才逃出重围。可是，女儿国的人们也毫不放松，紧紧追上来了。

After climbing over three red mountain ridges and crossing three black rivers, Cuoriabu arrived at a very strange place where the sky was red, and so were the earth, air and water. A red stockaded village loomed over amid shinning golden lights. Its front gate was wide open. On the vast dam outside the village were tens of thousands of naked women, carrying wood, or fetching water, herding stock, or busy with other things. All of them were joyously singing melodic songs. It turned out that this was the Kingdom of Women where women who looked like in their seventeenth or eighteenth only died but never grew old. Besides, they were all very tall and strong. Cuoriabu was confused with his whereabouts. Just when he thought of getting out of there, he saw dozens of women with their kids on the back coming towards him. They had very big breasts, which were all flung up to their heads for their kids to suck. They sang odd songs, carrying bunches of wood on their hands. Those women had already seen Cuoriabu while he was still in dismay. Instead of feeling shy and trying to avoid, they all approached and crowed towards him for a closer observation. One of them shouted, "Oh, how blessed we are to have him here. Get him. Don't let him escape!" Suddenly, all of them shouted out loud. Before echoes tailed off, women all over the mountain dropped their work and joined in the shouting. They rushed to Cuoriabu like a roaring storm. Cuoriabu, keenly aware that he was in danger, fought his way out hurriedly and finally managed to get out. But those women were still chasing him without a thought of giving up.

搓日阿补眼看她们就要追上来了，急中生智，伸手去箭袋里取箭头。箭头没拿着，却取出一根雁鹅毛来。他看看来不及重换了，只得把它搭在箭上射了出去。只听一声轰响，一道红光闪过，大山断成两截，中间出现了一条又深又大的裂缝，把搓日阿补和追来的女人们隔开了。搓日阿补又用雁鹅毛射了一箭，裂缝里顿时洪水滔天。女人们再也过不来了。这条河就是今天的金沙江。

望着金沙江水，搓日阿补想到自己奔波了许久，依然一事无成，伤心地大哭了三声，又想到自己逃脱了灾难，高兴得大笑了三声。从此，金沙江水就一会儿笑，一会儿哭，一会儿洪水滔天，一会儿风平浪静。

出门时间已经很长了，搓日阿补决定回家去，可是他过不了江。他急得沿着江边不停地来回走动想办法。忽然，他觉得怀里有什么东西硬邦邦的，好像要往他的肚子里钻。他伸手一摸，原来就是那颗毒蛇的牙齿。他生气地把它丢进江里。奇怪的是，蛇牙一落到水里，马上变成了一条巨蟒，直直地搭在江两岸。搓日阿补踏着蟒背过了河，终于回到了江这边。

As they were coming closer, Cuoriabu had a quick wit. He tried to take out arrows from his bag, which he failed and took out a feather of the goose instead. In a haste, he had to put the feather anyway on his bow, and shot it out. Then a deafening voice came. A red light shined. The mountain was split into two halves, with a deep and wide valley lying in between, which separated Cuoriabu and those chasing women. He took out another feather and shot, which immediately flooded the valley, so that those women would never catch up with him again. The valley is where the Jinsha River lies today.

Looking at the river, Cuoriabu cried sadly for three times, for he thought that he had not accomplished anything despite of all those efforts. Afterwards, he laughed happily for three times, as his recent escape from dangers came to his mind. The Jinsha River down there responded to his emotions, sometimes roaring yet sometimes remaining calm.

It's been a long time since Cuoriabu had gone out, so he decided to return home. However, he could not cross the river lying in front of him, so he walked along the river bank back and forth in anxiety. All of a sudden, he felt something very hard moving towards his stomach, which turned out to be the fang he had retrieved from the giant snake. Cuoriabu tossed it angrily into the river, which unexpectedly turned into a big boa. The boa bridged the gap with its body, so that Cuoriabu could stepped on it and crossed to the other side of the river.

一天，搓日阿补走到一条清澈明亮的小河边，他口渴极了，蹲下去喝了一口，只觉得这水比蜜还甜。他抬头顺水流看去，只见离他不远的河边上，有一个身穿树叶衣的女人在洗手。这女人长得非常美丽，把搓日阿补给迷住了。他不知不觉地走过去，向女人问道："你是哪方的阿妹，你是哪家的姑娘，看你的双手就像竹笋，看你的脸庞就像月亮，只因为你在这条河里洗了手，整条河都香了。我顺着香味跑来，跑到了你的面前！"

洗手的姑娘笑眯眯地说："你是个了不起的英雄。你要做的事情我都知道。我在这里等你，是想知道你有没有要我帮忙的事情！"

搓日阿补喜出望外，连忙说出了自己的心愿。

姑娘不慌不忙地答道："大哥的心意我了解，大哥的来历我明白，我一百个心愿想嫁给你，但是有九万头畜生阻拦着我。那是父亲诗姆岩哈（天祖）的财产啊，我无法把它抛弃。就是我抛弃了畜生，我们中间也还隔着一层天呀，大哥！"

One day, Cuoriabu arrived at the side of a very clear stream. As he was very thirsty, he lowered his head and took a sip of water, which tasted sweeter than honey. Looking towards lower reach of the stream, he saw a woman dressed in leaves nearby washing her hands along the stream. The woman was so beautiful that Cuoriabu was enthralled. Unwittingly, he approached the girl and asked, "Dear sister, where do you come from? Where's your home? Your hands are straight and slim like bamboo, and your face is as bright and round as a moon. The whole stream becomes so fragrant just because you've washed your hands here. I have followed the aroma to you."

The girl smiled and said, "You are a great hero. I know what you are after. So I'm waiting for you here to see if I can be of any help!"

Cuoriabu felt so excited, and told her what was in his mind.

The girl answered slowly, "I know what you want and I've learned your stories. Although it is my utmost desire to marry you and live with you, I have to look after ninety thousands animals, which I can't abandon, as they are legacies from my father, Shimuyanha, the divine God. And even if I do, we are still no match because I live up there and you live down here!"

搓日阿补这才明白对方是猎神。这时，猎神安慰他说："大哥呀大哥，嫁不了你但我能帮你，你千万莫唉声叹气。你不在家的时候，我的马鹿和喜鹊，已经去你家照顾你的母亲；今后你碰到困难的时候，只要在大树脚下垫上青松毛，把刀弩摆在正上方，把我的名字念三声、喊三声，我就会派牛羊牲畜们来帮忙。"

搓日阿补听了，说了许多感激的话。猎神热情地把他送到家门口。他看见妈妈好好的，心里十分高兴。

从此两母子再也不想别的事，安安心心地住下来了。可是搓日阿补和猎神所说的话，顺着河水淌到女儿国去，被一个正在河边舀水的女人听见了。搓日阿补和妈妈安静地生活着的时候，那个姑娘也正在打主意。

搓日阿补和他的妻子海乃嫫

自从有了猎神的帮忙，搓日阿补出门打猎时，就再也不用背着母亲走了。猎神把马鹿和喜鹊仍留在他家，帮他照顾母亲。搓日阿补天天去找猎神玩，从此打猎也不用刀弩，伸手就可以把野物拉回来。

Then, Cuoriabu realized that in front of him stood the Deity of Hunting. To comfort him, the deity said, "Young boy, although I cannot marry you, I can still help you. Please don't feel upset. I've already sent a deer and a magpie to help your mother back home since you left. In the future, if you encounter any difficulties, you'll have my animals to help you, but remember to place pine needles on the foot of a tree, on which put your blade and bow, and then call and shout my names for three times respectively beforehand."

When Cuoriabu was told of this blessing, he expressed his gratitude for several times. Then, the deity kindly sent him home, where he felt very relieved to find that everything went well with his mother.

From then on, Cuoriabu and his mother thought of no other things than settling there. But what Cuoriabu and the deity said ran down the stream carried by water to the Kingdom of Women, and was heard by a woman fetching water by the stream. While Cuoriabu and his mother were enjoying a peaceful life, the woman was plotting.

Cuoriabu and His Wife, Hainaimo

With the help of the Deity of Hunting, Cuoriabu no longer needed to carry his mother on the back whenever he went out hunting, because the deity left her deer and the magpie to look after his mother at home. Cuoriabu went to play with the deity every day, so that he could hunt wild animals without using blade or bow.

冬天到来的时候，猎神要把老虎吆到遥远的黑格山躲雪，离开了这个地方。有一天，搓日阿补在打猎归来的路上，遇到一个遍体鳞伤的年轻姑娘，冷得缩成一团，倒在路边，眼看就要死了。搓日阿补很可怜她，就把她背回家里去养伤。姑娘好起来以后，十分感激他的救命之恩，苦苦求他娶她为妻。她说：“如果你娶了我，我就一天到晚把妈妈背在背上；到明年春天，还给你生下一个像你一样了不起的儿子。”搓日阿补被她说动了心，与这个来路不明、名叫海乃嫫的女人成了亲。

成家之初，海乃嫫的孝心是不能再好了。她果真一天到晚把木古搓日背在背上。第二年秋天，她又生下一个又白又胖的儿子来，把一家人都喜欢死了。搓日阿补把妻子和儿子当成眼珠子一样疼爱。慢慢地，儿子长大了，会喊爹妈了。木古搓日说：“我的孙儿和他爹小时一模一样。”

有一天，搓日阿补打猎回来，发现猎神留下来的灰喜鹊不见了，只有鹊毛飞得遍地都是。他奇怪地问海乃嫫，海乃嫫说：“你那宝贝儿子吵死哭活要吃喜鹊肉，我杀给他吃了。”搓日阿补很生气，觉得这样做太对不起猎神了。可喜鹊是被宝贝儿子吃掉的，他不好多说什么。

When winter was coming, the deity left because she needed to call out her tigers to a warmer place, the Heige Mountain far in the distance. One day, when he was on his way back from hunting, Cuoriabu met a young girl who was severely wounded. She looked as if she was going to die, lying on the road side and curling up to get warmth. Feeling sorry for her, Cuoriabu carried her on the back and went home to cure her. When she recovered, the girl thanked him for saving her life and coaxed him into marrying her. She said, "If you marry me, I'll carry your mother on my back everyday. By the next spring, I'll have given birth to an outstanding son just like you." Cuoriabu was persuaded and married the woman of questionable origin. Her name was Hainaimo.

At the beginning of their marriage, Hainaimo couldn't serve Cuoriabu's mother better. She carried Mugucuori on the back day and night. In the next autumn, she gave birth to a lovely chubby boy, which greatly pleased the whole family. Cuoriabu treasured his wife and his son like the apple of his eyes. Over time, his son grew up, and could speak. Mugucuori said, "My grandson looks just like his dad back then."

One day, when he returned home from hunting, Cuoriabu strangely found that apart from the scattering features, the gray magpie left by the deity was missing. He asked Hainaimo, who answered, "Your son yelled and wanted to eat the magpie desperately, so I killed and cooked it." Cuoriabu was furious as it disappointed the deity for her kindness. But it was his son who ate it, so he did not scold her.

又有一天，搓日阿补打猎回来，发现猎神留下的马鹿又不见了，只有鹿皮高高地挂在门上。他又奇怪地问海乃嫫，海乃嫫告诉他：“你那宝贝儿子寻死觅活要吃马鹿肉，我杀给他吃了。”搓日阿补一听，再也忍不住了，抓住妻子就要打。海乃嫫跪在他面前说：“如今妈妈和家都有我照顾，再也不用野兽帮忙了。反正猎神的东西你要什么就可以得到什么，我杀一只马鹿也不为过。”搓日阿补一想也对，就放了她。从此，人养着的牲畜就少了马鹿和喜鹊。后来天祖诗姆岩哈知道了这件事，认为人太贪心，改了天规，从此只能用刀枪才能获得猎物了。

一次，搓日阿补发觉妻子的乳房很大，喂奶时，常把它甩到背后去，就像那天他在女儿国看见的一样。他再仔细一看，发现妻子身材高大，双手有力，走路就像一阵风，不由得怀疑起来。他想试一试妻子，便对她说：“来，我们两口子摔一跤吧！”

聪明的海乃嫫马上猜出了丈夫的意思，三次都故意输给了丈夫。搓日阿补还是觉得妻子的力气很大，心里想：“世间的女人，都应该只有男人一只手的力量才好！”从此，世间的女人力气就变小了。

The other day, when Cuoriabu came back, he found that the deer left by the deity missing. This time, he could only see its fur hanging high on the door. He asked Hainaimo who told him, "Your son cried out for deer's meat, so I killed and cooked it." Cuoriabu couldn't curb his anger anymore. He grabbed his wife and was about to beat her. Hainaimo knelt down before him, asking for forgiveness. She said, "Now our mother doesn't need help from those beasts because I'm looking after her and the whole family. You can get whatever beast you want from the deity anyway. So please spare me for killing one dear." Cuoriabu was persuaded, and let her go. Since then, deer and magpies had been excluded from stock in human's captivity. After learning it, the divine God, Shimuyanha, regarded human as greedy creatures, so he changed the rule to the one that required human to use blades or bows to hunt their preys.

Once, Cuoriabu found his wife's breasts oddly big. When she breastfed her child, she flung them back. The scene reminded him of the Kingdom of Women. Looking closer, he began to notice that his wife was indeed very tall and strong. At the sight of her big hands and strength when she walked, he couldn't help doubting about her identity. So he decided to test her. He asked his wife, "Come on. Let's try wrestling."

The smart woman instantly knew what was going on, so she lost deliberately to her husband for three times. However, Cuoriabu still sensed great strength from his wife's hands. He thought to himself, "It's better for women to have strength equal to that of men's single hand." From then on, women became less strong.

由于海乃嫫三次都输了，搓日阿补不敢断定她就是女儿国的人，又生出一计说："来呀，我们两口子赛跑吧！"

聪明的海乃嫫又猜出丈夫的意思，跑的时候尽量把步子迈得零零碎碎的，迈步的时候脚朝两边甩，结果远远地落在了丈夫的后面。搓日阿补见了，心里想："世上的女人要是都这样跑就好了。"从此，世上的女人跑步时，都成了她这个模样。搓日阿补跑到前边，坐在山上，看着追上来的妻子想道："要是她的个儿没有这么高，我就没有理由怀疑她了！"从此女人的个头就变得矮小了。

晚上回到家来，海乃嫫呜呜大哭起来。搓日阿补问她哭什么，她说："我想起了我可怜的妈妈，分别三年多了，不知现在她怎么样了？阿补呀，我们背着儿子去看一看她吧！"

搓日阿补答应了，海乃嫫便吩咐道："明天天一亮，你就出门去打野物，我把家收拾一下，日出时半路来遇你，我们就带着野味给妈妈拜年去，这样好不好？"

搓日阿补答应了。他一觉睡醒过来，只见海乃嫫早就起来了。灶房的大甑子里，热烘烘香喷喷地蒸着什么。搓日阿补想和妈妈告别一下：往天这时妈妈早起来了，可是今天却看不见她的身影。他问海乃嫫，海乃嫫回答说："睡得香香的、甜甜的，别惊动她啦，你早该上山了。"

As his wife lost for three times, he couldn't be sure whether she was really from the Kingdom of Women. So he came up with another idea. He asked his wife, "Let's try racing."

The smart Hainaimo had already learned what was in her husband's mind. Therefore, she only took small steps and sometimes moved her legs sideways to slow her down, so that she lagged far behind in the race. Cuoriabu saw how his wife ran and thought, "If only all women would run like this." Since then, all women really ran like that. Having won the race, Cuoriabu found a place to sit in the mountain and watch his wife catching up. He thought, "If she were not that tall, I would have no reason to doubt her!" Since then, women became shorter.

After returning home at night, Hainaimo cried badly. Cuoriabu asked her what went wrong. She said, "I miss my poor mother. It's been three years since I have left. Abu, can we visit her with our son?"

Cuoriabu agreed. Hainaimo ordered, "Early in the morning tomorrow, you will go out hunting, and I'll stay at home and clear the house. We'll meet halfway when the sun rises. Then we'll go to visit my mother with preys. Is that okay?"

Cuoriabu agreed. The next day, when he woke up in the morning, he found that Hainaimo had already got up. Something in the cask was being cooked in the kitchen, smelling very delicious. He wanted to say goodbye to his mother because his mother should have got up by this time as usual. However, she was nowhere to be found today. So he asked Hainaimo who replied, "Your mother is still sleeping, sound and sweet. Let's not wake her up. By the way, it is high time you went up to the mountain."

“那么我背小儿子先去山上打猎，你背着礼物后边来！”搓日阿补说。

平时十分温顺的海乃嫫，突然变得粗野起来，朝他挥着洗锅帚破口大骂：“你是懒筋发了还是不想去见我娘，推三阻四没良心，再不动身我就死给你看！你上山不上山？”

搓日阿补只得上山打猎去了。他打了一头野猪和一只金鹿，便到半路上去等妻子。等了好半天，海乃嫫才背着娃娃，手提包袱，急急忙忙地走来。搓日阿补见她满嘴油渍，奇怪地问：“你吃了什么？吃得满嘴油水。”

海乃嫫说：“绵扯扯的腊肉，脆生生的肝。”

搓日阿补问：“哪来的腊肉哪来的肝？”

海乃嫫说：“房梁上挂的，柜子里装的，我藏着留给妈妈的。”

搓日阿补半信半疑地看了看海乃嫫，见她生气，便不再说话。海乃嫫踢野猪一脚，骂声：“臭猪！”踩金鹿一脚，骂声：“烂鹿！”再也不肯要野物。搓日阿补觉得很可惜，可还是丢下猎物跟妻子上路了。半路上，他想背儿子，可妻子却把手中的包袱塞给了他。他觉得包袱很重，偷偷地打开看时，只见里边装着大块大块的熟肉，肤色很像母亲木古搓日的。他惊奇地问：“这是什么肉？”

"I'm going to carry our son on my back and go hunting. You catch up with us later!" Cuoriabu said.

Hainaimo, a very gentle and obedient woman in the past, suddenly turned rough. She wove her broom at him and scolded loudly, "Are you getting lazy or just delaying visiting my mom? You have no heart to find those excuses. Go or I'll kill myself!"

So Cuoriabu had to go out hunting. After hunting a wild pig and a gold deer, he went back halfway to meet his wife. Having waited for a long time, he finally saw her coming in a hurry with the kid on her head and the bag on her hand. Then he saw something greasy on her mouth, and asked in confusion, "What did you eat? You got your mouth so greasy."

Hainaimo said, "Soft salted meat and crunchy liver."

He asked, "Where do you find salted meat and liver?"

She answered, "On the beam, in the cupboard. I stored them for mother."

Half convinced, Cuoriabu looked at Hainaimo. Seeing her getting angry, he said no more. Hainaimo kicked the pig, swearing, "Smelling pig!" And then stepped on the deer, shouting, "Rotten deer!" She did not want those preys. Pity as he felt for the loss, Cuoriabu had to leave the preys and go with his wife. In the middle of their travel, he wanted to carry his son on the back, but his wife gave him the bag, which was very heavy. He opened it secretly before his wife could notice. Inside were many chunks of cooked meat looking like those from his mother because of the same color. He asked in shock, "What's this?"

"人肉!"海乃嫫怪声恶气地叫道。

搓日阿补被海乃嫫激怒了，便不再理她。

走了三天后，搓日阿补发现儿子在海乃嫫的背上一直不哭也不动，静悄悄的。他心里十分疑惑，便对海乃嫫说："把孩子放下来喂喂奶呀!"

海乃嫫答："我的奶头在背上呢!"

走了一会儿，搓日阿补又问："儿子为什么睡得这样死呀？他平常可是一觉醒十次的呢。"

"小孩子在娘背上，睡三年都是平常事!"

"把他头上盖着的布拉开呀，要闷死人呢!"

"揭盖布着了凉才死人呢!"

搓日阿补说不过海乃嫫，可是他边走边想，越想越觉得不对头。这时，一只花花绿绿的金丝鸟飞来，绕着他唱道："阿呷阿呷西哩色诺莫拉莫曲达……"那鸟唱完，飞落到他肩上。海乃嫫见了，便一巴掌将它打死了。搓日阿补很惋惜，把它拾起来装进口袋里。

不久，路边又有一头野猪对着他大声叫喊："烘烘何何巴达拉乌则泥则……"还没听懂它说了些什么，海乃嫫便抽出丈夫腰间的长刀把它砍死了。搓日阿补惋惜地把老野猪五寸长的獠牙掰下来装在口袋里。

"Human flesh!" Hainaimo snapped.

Pissed off by Hainaimo, he decided to ignore her.

Having walked for three days with his wife, Cuoriabu noticed that his son remained always still on her back, not crying or moving a bit. In confusion, he said to his wife, "Put the kid down. You need to feed him!"

She said, "My nipples are up there!"

After a while, Cuoriabu asked again, "Why is our son having a dead sleep? Normally, he would wake up ten times for a sleep."

"On the back of their moms, children could sleep for three years!" she answered.

"Open the cloth covered on his head, or he will be stifled!"

"If I open the cloth, he will catch a cold and die!"

Cuoriabu could not win the argument, but he felt something wrong more strongly as he continued his journey. Just then, a colorful canary flied around him, humming "agaagaxilisenu-omolamoquda..." Then the bird landed on his shoulder. Hainaimo saw it, and killed it with a slap. Cuoriabu felt very sorry and put it in his pockets.

Soon after, a wild pig along the road shouted to him, "honghonghehebadalawuzenize..." Before he could understand what it said, Hainaimo took out the long knife on his waist and killed it. He felt regretful and collected its five-inch bucktooth in his pockets.

再过了一会儿，又有一群猴子拦住他们的去路，朝他比手画脚地说：“哇啦伊哩加加莫莫阿鲁者曲……”还没听清它们说些什么，海乃嫫便拿起丈夫的弩箭，把领头的小猴射倒了。搓日阿补很惋惜地把猴皮剥掉，装在羊皮口袋中。走不多远，搓日阿补又看见许多松鼠坐在路边的树上，一会儿“哇哇”大哭，一会儿又“嘻嘻”乱笑。

搓日阿补觉得今天兆头不好，心里七上八下的。他想起了猎神，不由得轻声叹道：“猎神呵猎神，我怕是要遭难了！”

他刚说完，四面八方的山上，忽然出现了成千上万的野兽，悄悄地尾随着两人朝前走。搓日阿补看见这一切，心神就安定了。

他们来到一个岔路口，有两个大个子姑娘正坐在那里玩。她们一见来了人，有一个扭头就走开了，有一个欢欢喜喜迎上来，亲亲热热地和海乃嫫打招呼。

“这是我的亲妹妹！”海乃嫫对丈夫说。

正说着，只见四五十个年纪一样大的女人，跟着刚才走掉的那个，一窝蜂跑来，围住了他们。没等搓日阿补反应过来是怎么一回事情，便被扑上来的几十个女人夺了刀弩，按翻在地，又被手腕粗的篾绳捆起来，一点也动弹不得。这时，海乃嫫便和女人们又唱又跳，然后抬着气昏过去的搓日阿补，翻过三道红色的山梁，趟过三条黑色的河流，来到红彤彤的女儿国。

Later, a group of moneys stopped them, making gestures and shouting, "Walayilijiajiamomoaluzhequ..." Again, before Cuoriabu could figure out what it was talking about, Hainaimo grabbed the bow from his shoulder, and shot down the leading little monkey. He peeled the monkey in sadness, and put the monkey in his sheepskin bag. Then he kept on walking. Before long, Cuoriabu saw many squirrels sitting on trees along the path, sometimes crying and sometimes laughing.

Cuoriabu thought it ominous today, and grew very anxious. Then he thought of the Deity of Hunting and sighed, "My deity, I'm going to have troubles!"

Suddenly, tens of thousands of beasts showed up on mountains in every direction, and followed him and his wife quietly, which greatly relieved him.

Cuoriabu and his wife came to a crossroad where two tall girls sat by the road side and had fun. Upon seeing him and Hannaimo, one of them ran away and the other came forward and greeted.

"This is my younger sister!" Hainaimo said to him.

Suddenly, forty to fifty women of the same age followed the girl who just ran way, and surrounded him and Hainaimo. Before he could realize it, those women jumped to him, took his knife and bow, and pushed him to the ground. Soon after, He was unable to move, bound by ropes as thick as human wrists. Hainaimo and those women sang and danced happily around him. Then, they carried Cuoriabu, having fainted due to agony, all the way to the red Kingdom of Women, after climbing over three red mountain ridges and crossing three black rivers.

原来，海乃嫫就是那个偷听了搓日阿补和猎神对话的女人。

搓日阿补征服女儿国

搓日阿补被五花大绑着送到国王的面前。国王见他体格强壮，精神饱满，高兴地重赏了海乃嫫。然后，就叫人把搓日阿补脱得赤条条的，送到密不透风的铜造的公房里去，安排女人们轮流和他同房。搓日阿补一心想着复仇，哪有心思搭理姑娘们，于是就拿出野猪牙齿来对付女儿国的人。

第二天早上，国王刚起来，头晚去和搓日阿补同房的三个姑娘，便跌跌撞撞地跑进来，惊慌失措地说："妈妈呀妈妈，怪事呵怪事，昨晚上我们一进公房，刚睡下就什么都不知道了。今早起来后，我们的奶子忽然变得只有碗大。"

国王感到很奇怪，亲自去试了一下，果然和三个姑娘说的一样。国王看着自己比桶还大的奶子忽然变成了一小砣，吃惊得目瞪口呆，伤心地哭了。她的哭声一响开，全国所有的人，大奶同时变小奶，再也大不起来了。接着，国王又显出了老相，全国所有的女人也跟着变，一下子变得像人间一样有老有少，个头也矮小了。

It turned out that Hainaimo was the woman who overheard the conversation between Cuoriabu and the Deity of Hunting.

Cuoriabu Conquered the Kingdom of Women

Cuoriabu was sent to the queen with his hands and feet tied. Seeing that "the prey" had a stalwart body and a good mental condition, the queen felt happy and rewarded Hainaimo handsomely. Then she asked one of the servants to take off his clothes, and sent him to an impregnable public house where women were told to lie with him one after another. Cuoriabu wanted nothing else but revenge, so he took out the wild pig's fang in his bag to fight those women.

The next morning, when the queen just woke up, three girls she arranged for to sleep with Cuoriabu entered in stumbling steps, shouting in panic, "Mother, so weird. Yesterday when we went into the house, we fell asleep immediately. And when we woke up this morning, our breasts became as small as bowls."

The queen felt confused, so she decided to find out by herself. She had the same experience as the previous three girls, as she found that her breasts also turned small overnight. The queen felt shocked and cried sadly. Once her cry spread out to the whole country, everyone's big breasts turned small and could not grow again. Soon afterwards, the queen aged all of a sudden and so did other women in the kingdom. Some people looked very old, others young, and they all became shorter, just like ordinary people.

女儿国的人很气愤，要把搓日阿补杀了吃掉。国王同意了，便把搓日阿补抓过来，对他说：“我们要杀你吃，你有没有话说?”

搓日阿补答道：“我手指一点，就能点小你们的大奶，显出你们的年龄，你们还敢来杀我?”

国王心虚了。大臣们商量了一会，才对他说：“我们要考考你，如果你赢了，我们就不杀你，还让你做国王，如果你输了，我们还是要把你杀掉。”

搓日阿补说：“那就随你考吧!”

第一考是犁地。在女儿国的门口，有一块一百五十架牛才犁得过来的地。国王不给他牛，也不给他犁架，却叫他一天就要全部犁出来。搓日阿补跑到山上，砍来十架犁，套上一百头野猪，连拱带犁，不出半天就把地犁完了。犁完之后，搓日阿补问国王：“女人强还是男人强?”国王早被吓得伸长舌头，连声说：“男人强男人强!”

第二考是种地。国王要搓日阿补把犁好的地种好。搓日阿补叫来成千上万的松鼠，一眨眼的工夫便把地种好了。

All women in the kingdom were so furious that they wanted to kill Cuoriabu and eat him. The queen approved and sent a servant to bring him to her. She said to him, "We are going to eat you. Any last words?"

Cuoriabu said, "With a flip of my fingers, your breasts became small, and your oldness showed. You dare to kill me?"

The queen felt afraid. The lords discussed for a while, and said to him, "We are going to test you. If you win, you will live and become king. But if you lose, we will still have you killed."

Cuoriabu said, "Bring it on!"

The first test was tilling the land. In front of the gate of the kingdom lied a vast land which could only be tilled with efforts of one hundred and fifty cattle. But the queen gave him neither cattle nor plow, and asked him to till the whole of it within one day. Cuoriabu ran up the mountain, and chopped wood to make ten plows. He also called out one hundred wild pigs. It turned out that he tilled all of the land in less than half a day. After completing the challenge, Cuoriabu asked the queen, "Are men stronger than women?" Still in shock, the queen said voluntarily, "Yes, indeed!"

The second test was farming. The queen asked Cuoriabu to farm all the tilled land. Cuoriabu called out tens of thousands of squirrels, and finished it in a blink of eyes.

第三考是收包谷。国王要搓日阿补在一天之内把整片坝子里的包谷收回来。搓日阿补又叫来了比松鼠还多的猴子，半天时间就把包谷全部收起来了。

“男人强还是女人强?”搓日阿补问。

国王冷笑道：“那还说不定，我还没考完呢！再说，请野兽帮忙，不算你的本领!”

“那就再考!”搓日阿补说。

“限你在一个月之内，用山草织出够全国人穿的布来，用羊毛织成十件衣裳来。”国王说。

搓日阿补这次什么动物都没有请，割来山草，找来羊毛，他把山草和羊毛一堆一堆的放好，然后掏出口袋里的金丝雀来，对着山草点一点，山草成布了；对着羊毛点一点，羊毛成衣了。不出半个月，他便织出了够全国人穿的布，每人还有十件温暖耐用的羊毛披毡。此外，还用金丝鸟的红花羽毛，织成五光十色的花围腰，让女儿国的女人围在胸前。因围腰十分漂亮，人们都争着来要去围在胸前。

The third test was reaping corns. The queen asked Cuoriabu to harvest all the corns nearby in one day. Cuoriabu called out monkeys, more numerous than squirrel to help him finish the task in just half a day.

"Are men stronger than women?" Cuoriabu asked again.

The queen sniffed, "Don't get cocky now. It is not finished! Besides, asking help from beasts makes no real hero!"

"Then let's do it again!" Cuoriabu said.

"You need to weave grasses on the nearby mountains into a cloth large enough for the whole kingdom, and make wool from those sheep into ten garments in just one month, one month!"

This time, Cuoriabu did not turn to beasts for help, but reaped grasses and had sheep shearing all by himself. Then he piled them up, took out the dead canary from his pocket, and pointed it at them. Suddenly reaped grasses turned into a cloth, and wool became a garment. He did the same thing to the rest, and finished the task in less than half a month. Besides, he wove colorful feathers of the canary into glamorous clothes for women to wear on their breasts. They were so beautiful that all women scrambled to put them on.

国王见这么多难题都考不住他，也想不出别的办法来了，很着急。正好到了三月间，国王便推说女儿们要去山上“打野”，等“打野”回来，要再考一次。原来，每年一到三月，女儿国的人都要跑到花山顶上去，迎着风站几天，回来就会怀孕，生孩子。她们把这叫做“打野”。据说花山上的风，每到三月，就会从天下各地把男人的阳气刮来，所以当今世上男人一到三月，总是精神不振的。

不久，“打野”的人都回来了，国王的办法也想出来了。她对搓日阿补说：“如果你能像我们的人一样，生下个孩子来的话，我就服你了！”搓日阿补哈哈笑道：“我这两天正感到肚子里有东西呢，我现在就生一个给你瞧。”说着，他从肋下把那天被海乃媖打死的猴子扯了出来。人们见那人模人样的血淋淋的肉团，都惊叫一声，全部跪下。国王也不敢怠慢，跟着跪了下去。

搓日阿补说：“你们从花山回来都好一会了，也把孩子生出来呀！”

“天神公公饶命啊，我们实在生不出来了。今年花山上的风失灵，我们都没有怀孕啊！”人们悲声哀求着。原来，系上搓日阿补的花围腰，女儿国的人从此再不能迎风怀孕了。

Having failed so many times with her tests, the queen thought of no other ways, and got very anxious. It happened to be about in March. The queen found an excuse, saying that all the women needed to go up mountains to "Daye" and the tests would go on until they came back. According to their traditions, all the women in the kingdom would go to the top of that Flower Mountain, and stand there embracing the wind for several days from January to March. When they came back, they would get pregnant and give birth to children. That was called "Daye". It was said that the wind on that mountain carried energy from all the men across the land. That's why nowadays men still feel so dispirited from January to March.

Soon, all the women who went out to "Daye" returned. And the queen had thought of another test by then. She said to Cuoriabu, "If you could give birth to a baby like us, then you will win!" Cuoriabu laughed, and said, "I am feeling something right in my belly these days. Now watch, I'll give birth to a baby now." He took out the dead monkey which Hainaimo killed that day. At the sight of the bloody meat like human flesh, everyone screamed and knelt. The queen knelt too.

Cuoriabu said, "It's been a while since you have come back from the Flower Mountain. You need to hurry up to give birth to a baby!"

"Have mercy, our king. We really can't. This year, the wind has no effect. All of us are not pregnant!" They begged in despair. It turned out that women wearing the cloth made by Cuoriabu on their breasts would never get pregnant just by embracing the wind.

“你们都给我做媳妇吧!”搓日阿补坐到王位上去，对女儿国所有的人说。

“是!”大家连忙答应。于是大家都成了他的媳妇。

过了好久，搓日阿补发现很多女人都在暗暗地哭。他奇怪地问：

“好吃好睡的，你们哭些什么呀?”

女人们答道：“大王呀，我们虽是你的媳妇，可一年都见不着你一面。加上如今我们力气小了，人也弱了，不能吃苦，不够干活，无儿又无女，越想越伤心。”

搓日阿补说：“那么你们都去嫁人吧。”从此，女人们都嫁人去了。

猎神从黑格山回来。搓日阿补离开女儿国，跟猎神做伴，去给天家放牧牲畜。后来，他和猎神做了夫妻，一个管有角的野兽，一个放无角的野兽。直到现在，我们打猎的时候，还要把猎物的心脏献给他吃呢。

讲述者：苏绍相，李玉兴，何正芳

搜集整理者：基默热阔

Cuoriabu sat on the throne and said, "All of you be my wives!"

"Yes, my lord!" Everyone hurriedly nodded and became his wives.

After some time, Cuoriabu found many women crying behind his back, so he asked in confusion, "Now you don't have to worry about food and sleep. Why are you crying?"

The women answered, "My lord, although we are your wives, we can hardly see you even for once in a year. Besides, we are weak with little strength now. We can not do hard work and easily get tired. With no son or daughter, the more we think about these, the sadder we feel."

Cuoriabu said, "Well, you can all leave here to find husbands." Since then, it was women who left home to marry men.

When the Deity of Hunting returned from the Heige Mountain, Cuoriabu left the Kingdom of Women to play with her and help herd stocks for deities. Later, he and the Deity of Hunting got married, one in charge of beasts with horns and the other beasts with no horn. Up to now, when we go out hunting, we still offer hearts of our preys to him.

Narrator: Su Shaoxiang, Li Yuxing, He Zhengfang

Collector and editor: Jimorekuo

阿什色色和布阿诗嘎娓

据说很古的时候，男人不娶，姑娘不嫁，一家骨肉围着妈妈的火塘，团团圆圆地生活在一起。后来的娶妻嫁女是一个叫阿什色色的人兴起来的，他是婚嫁的始祖。

阿什色色是阿司色匹地方的人，他是妈妈最娇贵最宠爱的独儿子，也是彝山上最顽强最勇敢的男子汉。他长大成人之初，一天到晚站在门口，盯着房屋发呆。他的妈妈奇怪了，就问他：“阿什色色，你为什么总是这样看房屋？”

阿什色色反问道：“哦，妈妈！一棵树是不是有花才好看？”

“是啊，开花的树最好看！”母亲说。

阿什色色又问：“如果没有水，山是不是会好看？”

“如果没有水，山就没看头了。”母亲答道。

阿什色色说：“我看我们家的房子又矮又黑，就像没有水的山，没有花的树，总是不好看。”

The Story of Ashisese and Buashigawei

It is said that in the very ancient time, neither men nor women would marry. Kindred family lived together around the mother's fireplace. The marriage was later thrived from its ancestor, Ashisese.

Ashisese, born in Asisepi, was the only blue-eyed son dearly loved by his mother as well as the most tenacious and bravest man of the Yi mountain. After growing up, he stood at the door all day long, staring at the house in a daze. His mother asked him with puzzle, "Why do you always look at the house like this?"

Ashisese asked back, "Mom, is a tree beautiful only because it has flowers?"

"Indeed. Trees with blossoms are the most gorgeous!" His mother replied.

"Will mountain be more picturesque without water?" He asked again.

"Definitely not. Without water, what's the point of viewing the mountain anyway?" His mother answered.

"But our house, low and black, is not nice-looking, just like a mountain without water, or a tree without flowers." Ashisese said.

母亲说："这事有点不好办，你打算怎么来弄呢？"

阿什色色毫不犹豫地答道："雌雄箐鸡住在一起，一花一绿配着才好看；英雄的男人居住的房屋，要有美丽的姑娘相伴才会光彩夺目。我要去找父亲，让父亲来与母亲同出同入；我要去说个媳妇，让媳妇来做我的伙伴。"

母亲阻止说："太阳和月亮不能见面，男人和女人不能做伴。这事最好莫提！"

可是母亲说服不了儿子，阿什色色还是上路找父亲说媳妇去了。他穿着浦莫列衣织的布衣，背着哈依德谷用过的弩箭，带着色色坡尔酿制的美酒，拿着阿尔得坡制作的竹笛，披着特子洛俄编织的蓑衣，戴着热可阿吉编织的篾帽，发编勒则比克的冲天英雄结，口唱穆尔都惹创作的歌曲，骑着达里阿宗马，一路问着找着去了。

阿什色色走啊走，来到日诺吉觉地方，看见一群放羊的姑娘，正在玩用树枝和草搭房盖屋的游戏。阿什色色走过去，和她们互通了姓名，然后问她们说："你们知不知道我的父亲是谁？我要找他给我说个媳妇，请你们告诉我知不知道我的父亲，他在哪里？"

姑娘们非常喜欢阿什色色，想留他在身边，于是争着对他说："你的父亲是谁，在哪里，我们都知道，但是你得留下和来我们一起玩，我们才告诉你。"

"It's a tricky issue. What do you suggest?" His mother said.

Without hesitation, Ashisese answered, "Like the male and female pheasants, which are good looking because red ones are matched with green ones, so the house where a heroic man lived would be splendid only with a beautiful lady as a company inside. I'm going to look for my father to make a companion with you, and as well, a wife to be my partner."

His mother hurriedly stopped him, "The sun and the moon could never meet, and men and women could never be partners under the same roof. Do not say that again!"

However, she failed in persuading him, who, nevertheless, headed on his way to find his father and his own wife. Wearing the clothes made by Pumolieyi, the coir raincoat by Teziluoe, the bamboo cap by Rekeaji, and taking the arrow used by Hayidegu, the wine brewed by Sesepoer and the bamboo flute made by Aerdepo, Ashisese sang songs produced by Muerdure and rode the Daliazong horse with his hair knotted like Lezebike, forward on his way.

Ashisese went to the place of Rinuojijue, where he saw a group of sheep-herding girls playing games of building houses with branches and grasses. Ashisese moved forward, exchanged names with them, and then asked, "Do you know who my father is? I want him to help me marry a wife. Please tell me where he is."

The girls adored Ashisese very much and would like him to stay, so they told him eagerly, "We know who and where your father is, but we won't tell you unless you stay and play with us."

阿什色色依言留了下来。他和姑娘们一起玩盖房子，盖出了一间木房子。姑娘们不敢把他带回家去，晚上就让他一个人住在木房子里，白天才来找他玩，给他带各自认为最好吃的东西。

这样的日子过了很久，姑娘们总不告诉他父亲的下落，这使他感到无聊起来。后来他忍不住了，就问放羊姑娘："请你告诉我，我的父亲到底在哪里？"放羊姑娘说："你没有父亲，所以你不用去找了，你和我们在一起多快乐！"他不相信，又去问放牛姑娘，放牛姑娘回答说："你的父亲有没有我不知道，但我知道你是我怀中孩子的父亲！"放猪姑娘也说："你要找父亲，还是去问你的妈妈吧，她知道你的父亲在哪里。"

阿什色色很感激放猪和放牛的姑娘，给了她们良好的祝愿，猪从此不用放牧了，牛从此听话不跑了，但放羊姑娘受到了诅咒，她的羊一天要跑九架山。

阿什色色按放猪姑娘的吩咐，回来问母亲。母亲告诉他说："你面向东方，迎着太阳走，第一个碰见的人，就是你的父亲。"阿什色色依照母亲的指点朝东方走去，走到帕布里之山，在山洞里，遇见了一个白胡子长齐脚尖、已病得奄奄一息的老人。这老人一见阿什色色，便面露笑容，用很兴奋的声音问："你是不是阿什色色？你是不是我的儿子？如果你是阿什色色，请你治父亲的病，请你救父亲的命。"

Ashisese agreed. He played with the girls and built a wooden house. Not daring to take him home, the girls left him alone in the wooden house at night and only came to play with him during the daytime. But they all brought him the most delicious food to their taste.

Long time had passed, the girls never mentioned his father, which bored Ashisese. Later, as he could on longer stand, he asked them, "Please tell me where my father is." The sheep-herding girl responded, "It's a wild goose chase! You have no father at all. Why not stay with us happily?" He did not believe, and then asked the cattle-herding girl who answered, "I know nothing except your being the father of the child in my arms." The pig-herding girl also said, "You'd better ask your mother. She must know it."

Ashisese was grateful to the cattle-herding and the pig-herding girls and blessed them with good wishes, so that pigs and cows became domesticated ever since. But the sheep-herding girl was cursed with heavy work on herding.

Ashisese returned home to ask his mother, as suggested by the pig-herding girl. His mother told him, "Go to the east where the sun rises and the first man you meet is your father." Ashisese did as his mother instructed and arrived at the Mount Pabuli. In the cave, he met an old dying man with white beards reaching the tip of his toes. The old man turned into smile the moment he saw Ashisese, and asked excitedly, "Are you Ashisese, my son,? If so, please cure your father's disease and save your father's life."

阿什色色高兴地说："我是你的儿子，我是阿什色色，我来治你的病，我来救你的命。"

父亲告诉儿子说："在你母亲的枕头下边，压着我的命；在你母亲的针线袋里，装着我的魂；在你母亲的贴身包里，装着我的火草、火石。你把这一切给我偷来，我的病才会好。你用火石火草，打出火来烧掉我的胡子，我就会变得年轻。"

阿什色色依言把父亲要的东西偷来了，父亲的病好了，人变得又年轻又健壮。可是母亲病倒了，而且转眼变成了一个风烛残年的老太婆。阿什色色很着急，便来问父亲，该怎么医治母亲。父亲告诉他说："你母亲的命在我口袋里，你母亲的魂在我手心上。要治好她的病，只有叫我去和她做一家。"

父亲的话正合儿子的心愿，回到家里后，他便对母亲说："妈妈呀妈妈！如果爸爸是树你是花，如今花不在树上，你哪能不枯萎；如果父亲是水你是山，如今水不在山上，山怎么会不荒废。我还是把父亲找来，和你做一家。"母亲觉得儿子的话很好，于是同意了。阿什色色把父亲接来跟母亲做了一家，母亲的病就好了，人也变得又年轻又漂亮。父亲和母亲，出门是一双，进门是一对，有说不完的话，乐不够的事。母亲生弟弟妹妹，父亲来抚养，日子过得越来越热闹。阿什色色见了这一切，去说媳妇的信心更坚定，于是他又穿着浦莫列衣织的布衣，背着哈依德谷用过的弩箭，带着色色坡尔酿制的美酒，拿着阿尔得坡制作的竹笛，披着特子洛俄编织的蓑衣，戴着热可阿吉编织的篾帽，发编勒则比克的冲天英雄结，口唱穆尔都惹创作的歌曲，骑着达里阿宗马，一路找着问着唱着去了。

Ashisese answered happily, "Yes, I am! I'm here to cure and save you."

The old father told his son, "My life hinges on the stuff under your mother's pillow; my soul is stored in your mother's sewing bag; my fire weed and flint is hidden in your mother's personal bag. Steal them for me, and then I'll get recovered. Burn my beards with fire sparked by the fire weed and flint, and I'll be young again."

Ashisese did as told. His father was cured and became young and strong, while his mother tuned into an old woman cursed with illness. He was anxious and asked his father how to save her. His father told him, "In my pocket holds her life, and on my palm lies her soul. She can only be cured if she accepts me as family."

His father's words were exactly what he wished. After returning home, he said to his mother, "Supposing father is a tree while you are a flower, and flower without tree is bound to wither; supposing he is water while you are a mountain, and mountain without water is to be deserted. It's better to be with him." She was persuaded and agreed. Therefore, Ashisese took his father home and had them married. Since then, his mother got well and became young and beautiful again. They were always in pair with endless talks, happily. Later, his mother gave birth to younger brothers and sisters, and his father brought them up. Life of this family was getting more joyful and lively. Having seen it, Ashisese was more determined to find a wife. For this reason, Ashisese set foot on his journey again, wearing the cloth made by Pumolieyi, the coir raincoat by Teziluoe, the bamboo cap by Rekeaji, and taking the arrow used by Hayidegu, the wine brewed by Sesepoer, the bamboo flute made by Aerdepo, he sang songs produced by Muerdure and rode the Daliazong horse with his hair knotted like Lezebike.

阿什色色朝东走了又走，不知穿过了多少密林和村寨，不知跨过了多少悬崖和江河，在寒风像乱马、白雪铺地的图尔山脚下，他遇上了一个遍身长脓疮、满头生烂肉的人，正疼得呼天叫地地在树林里打滚。他一遍又一遍地哀求阿什色色说："年轻人，救救命吧！"阿什色色很同情这个病人，决心帮助他。于是问道："我该怎么救你的命呢？我该用什么治你的病呀？"病人告诉阿什色色说："如果你真心帮助我，如果你是个勇敢的人，那你必须背着我穿过图尔山口的三十三道乱刀风，爬上图尔山冰雪坡上的九十九层岩，我的病才会好！"阿什色色毫不犹豫地答应了。病人告诫他说："三十三道乱刀风是魔鬼的世界，魔鬼会把你撕成碎片；九十九层岩是狼虫虎豹的乐园，它们将使你死无葬身之地。如果你中途后悔，不变石头就变成冰块。这一切你不怕吗？"阿什色色说："人是要脸的，嘴是要人尊重的，说过的话不反悔！"病人说："那好，只要你对什么都不理睬，什么都不能伤害你；只要你不回头，你就会成功。"

Ashisese went eastward. After crossing countless forests, villages, cliffs and rivers, he arrived at the foot of the snow-covered Tuer Mountain where the wild cold wind blew. He met a man with abscesses over his body and gangrened flesh on his head, rolling and ululating painfully. He piteously entreated Ashisese, "Please save me, young man!" Ashisese was sympathetic to him and decided to offer his help, so he asked, "What can I do to cure your disease and save your life?" He told Ashisese, "If you are sincere and brave enough, carry me across thirty-three gusts of wild winds at the mountain pass and climb up the cliff with ninety-nine levels on the snow-covered slope. Only then will I be cured." Ashisese agreed without hesitation. The man warned, "The thirty-three gusts of wild winds is the world of devils which will tear you up; and the cliff with ninety-nine levels is the territory of wild beasts where your tomb lies. If you regret halfway, you will turn into stone or ice. Aren't you afraid?" Ashisese said, "People value faith in promise. I'll never eat my words!" The patient said, "Alright. Nothing will hurt you as long as you turn a blind eye. Only faith will lead to success."

阿什色色背着病人，闯过了三十三道魔鬼乱刀风，爬上了九十九层虎狼岩，魔鬼扑来他不理，毒蛇猛兽挡道他不睬，也不回头望，只管大步朝前走，很快就安全到达了图尔山顶上。病人一到山头上，马上变成一个红光满面、健壮魁伟的男人。他对阿什色色说："我不是什么病人，我就是天地万物之主恩梯古资。因为北方日浦觉觉地方，人们完全违背了祖传的规矩，各家族不是友好相处，而是互相侵吞，杀得尸横遍野，血流成河；他们不敬奉共同的族魂，不祭祀万物之灵，不遵守天神的安排，荒芜了土地去吃草木，放弃了六畜去抢人，我想用天神的力量来惩罚他们，又怕拖累其他安分守己的人。所以我只好寻找一个勇敢的凡人，带着兵去征讨他们。现在你就代我办这件事，办成了会有你的好处。"

恩梯古资说完，给了他一把蚕豆、一把豌豆。阿什色色把这两把豌豆蚕豆撒出去，满山遍野都是兵和将。阿什色色带着黑压压的豆兵豆将，很快把日浦觉觉地方平定下来了。他把动乱者全集中起来，问起动乱的根源，很快就把事情的来龙去脉搞清了。

Ashisese went ahead directly with the ill man on his back. He successfully went through the thirty-three gusts of wild winds and climbed up the cliff with ninety-nine levels, in disregard of devils or wild beasts. He just strode forward without a turning back, until they reached the top of the Tuer Mountain. Upon arrival, the patient immediately turned into an energetic and strong man glowing with health. He told Ashisese, "I'm not ill at all. I'm Entiguzi, the master of heaven and earth. People in the northern place of Ripujuejue have utterly broken the ancestral rules, replacing friendly co-existence with invasion and slaughter. They do not worship the shared spirit, make sacrifice to lords of the universe and obey the arrangement of gods. They desert land and exhaust grasses and trees afterwards; they abandon farming livestock and plunder people everywhere. I want to punish them with the power of god, but I'm also worried about hurting the obedient ones. So, I decide to find a brave mortal, which is you, to go on a punitive expedition against them. You'll be rewarded for that."

Then Entiguzi gave a handful of broad beans and another handful of peas to Ashisese. He spread them, which miraculously turned into a huge army all over the mountain. Ashisese led this army and settled the chaos in Ripujuejue very soon. He gathered the rioters and interrogated the origin of chaos, making clear of the ins and outs of the event in a very short time.

原来，在日浦觉觉地方，出了一个惊世绝俗的美女，名叫布阿诗嘎娓。布阿诗嘎娓到底美成什么样，没法把她的美貌描述下来。但据说她坐在房子里，房子就会变得又高又大又明亮，就像安着一个太阳；她走在山路上，树木就会开满了鲜花；她唱起歌来，万物都会围着她舞蹈；她喝过的水比蜜还甜，她织在布上的飞禽走兽都会飞会跑；她在阴天出走，天空便会云开日出；她在热天出走，彩云就要飘来护卫。

布阿诗嘎娓是嫉妒产生的根源，嫉妒是从她身上开始的。

布阿诗嘎娓和哥哥，是坐在妈妈的两条大腿上生长的，一个坐在一边；兄妹是吊着妈妈的两只奶长大的，一个吊在一边。哥哥拉着妹妹的手，兄妹俩是拉着手长大的。哥哥是妹妹的魂，妹妹是哥哥的心，魂离不开心，心离不开魂。哥哥生怕别人看见了布阿诗嘎娓把她抱走，就盖了一间九层楼的木房把妹妹关起来，自己坐在门口把守。妹妹很感激，给他唱最好听的歌，讲最动人的故事。兄妹俩就这样快快乐乐地过了一天又一天。但为时不久，她美妙的歌声被放牧的儿童听去了，放牧的儿童就到处去传，结果九十九个部落的小伙子闻讯跑来瞧。看见了布阿诗嘎娓的美貌，谁也离不开一步了，都争着去求爱。布阿诗嘎娓见一个答应一个，九十九个小伙子都得到了她的爱情，但他们都不能走近布阿诗嘎娓，更不能和她同枕共乐，把爱献给她。原因是嘎娓的哥哥从中作梗，不肯把妹妹让给外人。九十九个小伙子嫉妒起来，最后发了疯，他们把九层楼的木房用火烧了，把嘎娓的哥哥捆起来送进石洞，把布阿诗嘎娓抢跑了。

It turned out that there was an amazingly beautiful lady named Buashigawei in Ripujuejue. The record describing her beauty did not survive. But it was said that houses would be tall, huge and bright like sun light inside once she entered; trees would blossom once she walked by; all creatures would dance around her once she sang; water would be sweeter than honey after she drank it; animals could run and fly as long as she embroidered them on the cloth; cloudy days would turn into sunny ones once she went out; and colourful clouds would come out to shield her in hot days.

Buashigawei was the origin of envy. Envy spread from her.

Buashigawei and her brother grew up on their mother's legs, sitting on each leg side by side; they grew up through hanging on their mother's breasts, hanging on each side. She grew up with her brother, interdependent like soul and heart. As her brother worried that Buashigawei might be found and taken away, he built a nine-floor wooden cabin to shelter her. Out of great gratitude, Buashigawei sang the most melodious songs and told the most touching stories to him. They had lived happily for a long time. However, a shepherd boy once accidentally heard the beautiful voice and spread away. Young men from ninety-nine tribes went there out of curiosity. Captivated by her beauty, everyone stayed and struggled for her love. But her brother was reluctant and managed to exclude her from others. Consequently, though no one was refused, no one could get close and shared love with her. The ninety-nine young men grew envious and crazy, they burned the wooden cabin, left Buashigawei's brother bound in the cave, and snatched her away.

布阿诗嘎娓落入九十九个部落手中后，九十九个部落内仇杀和嫉妒就开始了。布阿诗嘎娓落入这个部落，其他部落就来抢；落入那个部落，其他部落又去夺。人们忘记了敬奉祖先，祭祀万物之灵，忘记了种田和放牧，无休无止的暴乱就是这样开始的。

阿什色色问明了这一切情况后，把布阿诗嘎娓叫来，又从岩洞里放出她的哥哥，让兄妹俩回去耕种放牧。可是布阿诗嘎娓的哥哥说：“大英雄阿什色色呀，你如果不把九十九个部落全部杀尽，抢夺我妹妹的战争就无法平息。这块地方永远不会安宁。”阿什色色听了，去问被他降服的人们。九十九个部落的人异口同声地说：“大英雄阿什色色，最好的办法是你把布阿诗嘎娓杀死，否则我们不能保证，在你走后能不能平静下来。”

阿什色色觉得这事他无法做主，于是回到图尔山上去找恩梯古资，把事情的本末对他说了一遍。恩梯古资说：“在告诉你怎么处理这事之前，我想问问你，你为我做了这么大一件好事，你有什么愿望要我帮助实现？”

阿什色色说：“我的愿望就是娶一个妻子，让她时时刻刻和我生活在一起，共同管理土地财产，共同祭祖生育儿女。”

Since the seizure of Buashigawei by the ninety-nine tribes, envy and slaughter began. Tribes fought with each other back and forth for her. As a result, people left behind worshiping the ancestors, sacrificing to lords of the universe, farming and grazing. Endless chaos started.

After learning the situation, Ashisese called for Buashigawe and freed her brother from the cave. He instructed this pair of brother and sister to return home and take care of farming and grazing. But the brother said, "Great hero, if you do not extirpate the ninety-nine tribes, the war to grab my sister would never end and peace would never be treasured on this land." After learning the brother's idea, Ashisese went to the captives who all spoke with one voice, "Great hero, the best solution is to kill Buashigawei. Otherwise, we can't guarantee the peace after your leave."

Ashisese felt hard to make a decision, so he returned to the Tuer Mountain for Entiguzi, telling him the whole story. Entiguzi said, "Before I tell you my decision, I want to know what reward you wish for as you have done me such a big favor."

Ashisese replied, "I wish to have a wife, who stays with me all the time, and manage our land, worship ancestors and procreate children together."

恩梯古资说："两件事可作一回办，你就把布阿诗嘎娓娶来做媳妇，这样就能平息九十九部的争斗。但你不能让她回到她生长的地方，见到她的父母兄弟和亲友。如果这事你能做到，那就请你去召集日浦觉觉的人，我要从云上给他们传话。"

阿什色色奉命把日浦觉觉的人召集在一起，恩梯古资就从天上传下话来说："日浦觉觉的美女布阿诗嘎娓，要嫁到遥远的阿司色匹地方去，给阿什色色做妻子。这事如果有人阻拦，那日浦觉觉就要陷入无穷的灾难，六畜要死光，人烟要绝种。如果布阿诗嘎娓出嫁后往回逃，那么天下的女人从此都要嫁人，谁不嫁人谁就浑身腐臭，谁不嫁人谁就灾难重重，九死一生。"

天神的话是不能违抗的，人们虽然舍不得嘎娓，但不敢不让阿什色色把她娶去。嘎娓出嫁的那天，她的哥哥抱着她哭，哭诉了三天三夜，把兄妹从小到大的情谊说了一遍又一遍。接着她的母亲又来哭诉，把母女的深情哭诉了三天三夜。然后亲邻的姐妹女友都来哭，把大家的深情讲了三天三夜。这样哭着唱着，唱着诉着，一直哭了九天九夜，才让姑娘启程上路，到阿司色匹去了。

Entiguzi told him, "Well, the two things, the solution and your wish, can be done at the same time. Go and marry Buashigawei, so the fight can be ended. But you should keep her from returning home and meeting her family. If you can do that, then just gather the people of Ripujuejue, and I will send words to them from heaven."

Ashisese followed the instruction. After gathering people of Ripujuejue, Entiguzi told them from heaven, "Buashigawei, the beauty in Ripujuejue, is going to marry Ashisese as his wife, to the remote place of Asisepi. If anyone dares to resist, Ripujuejue will then be trapped in infinite disasters. All your livestock and people will go extinct. If Buashigawei flees back after the marriage, all women on earth will get married; otherwise they will get rancid and suffer from everlasting disasters and tortures."

Though with reluctance, no one dared to disobey the god and go against the marriage. On the wedding day, Buashigawei's brother hugged her, recalling their experiences since childhood tearfully over and over again for three days and nights. They talked about their sentiments towards one another over and over again. Then her mother came to her and wept out her sorrow with profound sentiments for three days and nights. Afterwards, her sisters and friends all went to her and cried, recalling their love and friendship for three days and nights. Therefore, it was not until nine days later that Buashigawei finally set foot to Asisepi for marriage.

布阿诗嘎娓嫁到遥远的阿司色匹地方后，日里想哥哥，眼泪下饭吃；晚上想父母，眼泪作床铺。她把出嫁时哥哥唱的话唱了一遍又一遍，又把父母唱的话唱了一遍又一遍，最后把姐妹唱的话唱了一遍又一遍。因为天神恩梯古资有话在先，头年她想回家不敢回，二年她想回拜哥哥父母不敢回。到了第三年，她实在不能忍受了，在收麦的时候，她去拣麦穗；割荞的时候，她去拣荞粒，总共拣得三斗三升①麦粒和三斗三升荞料。她用麦粒和荞粒煮出了六坛酒，先拿两坛去拜见公公和婆母。她问公公和婆母说："公公和婆母啊，你家有没有嫁出去的姑娘？如果有出嫁的姑娘，她们能不能来拜望你们？如果她们能来拜望你们，那我也该回去拜望父母兄弟了，请你们答应我这个小小的愿望。"公公和婆母回答说："我家没有嫁出去的姑娘，如果有，你也不能回去拜望父母兄弟。"布阿诗嘎娓的第一层心绝望了。她又拿了两坛酒去求小姑子："姑娘啊，姑娘，你想没想过有一天你要出嫁？你出嫁后还回不回来见父母？如果你会回来的话，请你允许我回去见父母。姑娘回答说："我是不会出嫁的，如果我真会出嫁，也不允许你回家。"布阿诗嘎娓的第二层心也绝望了。她最后拿了两坛酒，去拜见自己的丈夫阿什色色："尊敬的阿什色色，你是不是有妹妹？如果你的妹妹会出嫁，你让不让她回来拜望你？如果你允许她回来的话，请你允许我去见一次哥哥。"阿什色色因为牢记着天神的话，不允许她回去："泼出的水不能舀回瓢，出嫁的姑娘不能回娘家，我不允许你去。"布阿诗嘎娓的最后一层心，就这样彻底绝望了。

---

① 译者注：古代一斗是 40 斤，一升是 4 斤，一斤是 500 克。

After marrying into the remote Asisepi, she missed her brother and parents very much, weeping day and night. She repeatedly sang what her brother, parents and sisters sang on that wedding day. For fare of what Entiguzi had said, she didn't dare to return home in the first and second year of marriage, however desperate she wanted to visit her brother and parents. But she could no longer stand in the third year. So, she collected ear of wheat and buckwheat at the time of their harvest, and gained three dou and three sheng① for each, from which, she brewed six jars of wine. Buashigawei first visited her parents-in-law with two jars and asked them, "Are there any married girls in your family? Could they return home and visit you after their marriage? If so, then I want to visit my parents and brothers as well. Please grant me this little wish." They answered, "Whether there is a married one or not, you are not allowed to go back anyway." She got frustrated for the first time. Then she turned to her sister-in-law with two jars, "Have you ever thought of getting married one day? Will you come back to see your parents? If you will, please permit me to go back and visit my parents." She replied, "Whether I marry or not, you will never be permitted to go back." She grew desperate for the second time. At last, she took the rest two jars to her husband, "You have a sister, right? If she gets married, will you allow her to return and see you? If you will, please allow me, too." Bearing the God's words in mind, Ashisese refused, "You can not put the spilled water back into the bowel. Likewise, married women can not return home. What's done is done. I will not allow you to go back." Having lost the last hope, she was in utter despair.

---

① Translator's note: in ancient time, one dou equals 40 jin, and one sheng equals 4 jin. One jin is 500 grams.

山头上杜鹃叫，山腰里阳雀催，山箐里石蚌喊，蓝天上大雁唱。布阿诗嘎娓一天也不能停留了。在一个月黑风高之夜，她逃出了阿司色匹地方，跨过九条河，翻过九座山，穿过九片林。当她来到蕨草梁子时，跳出雌雄仔三只老虎来。雄虎分去了她的头，雌虎分去了她的肢，仔虎分去了她的腰，蚂蚁分去了她的心肺肠肚，苍蝇分去了她的血。美女布阿诗嘎娓，再也走不出蕨草梁了，再也见不到父母哥哥了。因为布阿诗嘎娓违反了恩梯古资的话，天下的姑娘从此都要嫁人。人间的婚嫁就是这样开始的。

布阿诗嘎娓的哥哥，因为太思念妹妹，就在妹妹逃离阿司色匹时，也正好赶来探望妹妹。结果在蕨草山梁上，他看见妹妹变成了老虎的食物，从此痛不欲生，成为一个无所依附的流浪汉。他做成了口弦，制作了芦笙，把妹妹的苦难和自己的思念编成了《哭嫁歌》，专门在婚礼场上唱。彝族婚礼中的《哭嫁歌》，就这样流传下来了。

流传地区：永仁县
讲述者：曲木阿石
收集整理者：罗有芬

To Buashigawei, chirps of cuckoos on the mountain top and mountainside, white blotched snappers in the mountain valley and gooses in the sky all urged her to go back. She could not stay here for one more day. So she fled from Asisepi in a dark and windy night. After crossing nine rivers, nine mountains and nine forests, she arrived at the ridge of the Juecao Mountain where three tigers, a male, a female and a little one, jumped out in front of her all of a sudden. The male tiger dragged off her head; the female one torn up her body; and the little one took her waist. Afterwards, ants ate up her viscera, and flies sucked up her blood. The beauty Buashigawei finally died there and could no longer meet her brother and parents. Since then, girls on the earth had to marry because of Buashigawei's disobedience to Entiguzi's order, which marked the start of marriage in the mortal world.

As Buashigawei's brother missed her badly, he set out to meet her when it was about the time she escaped from Asisepi. But when he arrived at the ridge of the Juecao Mountain, what he saw was the remains of his sister torn apart by tigers. He was overwhelmed with sorrow and became a vagrant with nothing to rely. Then, he composed the wedding laments of his sister's sufferings and his missing with the buccal reed and reed-pipe wind instrument he made. Wherever there was a wedding, he would sing this lament. In this way, the wedding lament of the Yi ethnic group passed down.

Spreading area: Yongren County
Narrator: Qumuashi
Collector and editor: Luo Youfen

阿鲁举热

阿鲁举热出世

迭朴索洛有一个美丽聪明的姑娘，名叫朴莫乃日。她是滇池龙王的孙女，是彝家第一个会织布、第一个会做罗锅帽、第一个会缝裙子衣裳的人。

朴莫乃日十六岁那年，有一天，她手拄牙巴骨，坐在织布架上想心事。忽然天上飞来一只神龙鹰，影子罩在她身上，飞了三转，影子罩了她三次。一次滴一滴血下来，三次滴了三滴血下来。一滴落在罗锅帽上，一滴落在披毡上，一滴落在裙子上。又有一天她放猪到三道箐，坐在箐边想心事。忽然天上飞来一朵云，滴下三滴水，一滴落在罗锅帽上，一滴落在披毡上，一滴落在裙子上。从此以后朴莫乃日的肚子一天天大起来。怀孕九个月零九天，她生了一个儿子。这个儿子是个怪人，生下地以后只是哭，不吃人的乳，不

Alujure

The Birth of Alujure

In Diepusuoluo, there was a beautiful and intelligent girl named Pumonairi, who was the granddaughter of Dianchi Dragon King. She was the first person who could weave, made the Luoguo hat, and sewed skirt clothes in the Yi ethnic group.

One day, Pumonairi, at the age of sixteen, held her tooth bone and sat on the weaving rack, pondering. Suddenly, a dragon hawk flew in the sky, with its shadow covering her. It flew around for three times, and she was covered for three times. Afterwards, blood dripped down, one drop each time, and altogether there were three drops of blood, with one drop on the Luoguo hat, one on the felt, and the third one on the skirt. Another day, she herded pigs to Sandaojing, sitting on the sidelines and pondering. Suddenly, a cloud appeared in the sky and three drops of water dropped down afterwards, with one drop on the Luoguo hat, one drop on the felt, and the third one on the skirt. Since then, Pumonairi became pregnant. After nine months and nine days, she gave birth to a son who was a weirdo. Apart from crying, he refused to take any breast milk and wear

穿人的衣。朴莫乃日想，怕是大树的儿子，便把他抱到大树脚。可儿子不吃树的果，不穿树的皮。她又想怕是石头的儿子，便把他放到岩石脚。可儿子不吃石头的乳，不穿石头的皮。她想怕是斑鸠的儿子，便把他抱到斑鸠窝旁边。可儿子不吃斑鸠的食，不穿斑鸠的衣。朴莫乃日拿儿子没有办法，她想起神龙鹰的影子，就把儿子抱到神龙鹰那里去，儿子才止住哭。神龙鹰的食他吃了，神龙鹰的衣他也穿了。朴莫乃日把儿子交给神龙鹰走了。神龙鹰精心地把她儿子抚养长大。后来人们叫他阿鲁举热。

阿鲁举热找阿妈

神龙鹰把阿鲁举热养到十六岁，阿鲁举热已经长大成人。他想起生身的母亲，要去找阿妈。神龙鹰也想让儿子自己去闯闯世面，练练本事，就让他走了。阿鲁举热找阿妈，找到东方没找着，找到西方没找着，找到南方和北方也没找着。最后走到一个平展展的大地方，还是没有找着母亲，却找到大头领日毋家。

human clothes. Pumonairi thought maybe he was the son of a tree, so she placed him beside a tree root, but the boy refused to eat its fruit and wear the skin of the tree. Pumonairi thought maybe he was the son of a stone, so she put him by the foot of a stone, but the boy did not eat from the stone or wear the skin of the stone. Then she thought maybe he was the son of a turtledove, so she put him next to the nest of a turtledove, but the boy still rejected food eaten and clothes worn by the turtledove. Pumonairi ran out of ideas. Suddenly, she thought of the shadow of the dragon hawk, so she immediately took her son to the dragon hawk, and the boy stopped crying. He began to eat hawk's food and accepted clothes worn by hawks. Pumonairi gave her son to the dragon hawk who took precious good care of him and raised him up. Later, people called this boy Alujure.

Alujure Looking for His Mother

The dragon hawk raised Alujure up to the age of sixteen. When Alujure grew up, he thought of his mother and decided to look for her. As the dragon hawk also wanted his son to see the world and practice his skills, it let him go. Alujure set out on his journey, but his mother was nowhere to be found, not in the east, west, north or south. Finally, without any trace of his mother, he arrived at a flat place, where he found the house of the chieftain—Riwu.

日毋叫他去放猪，交给他七头老母猪。过了一久，他放的七头母猪都下了崽，主人很喜欢。可是有一天，七头母猪领着七窝小猪，跑呀跑，全都跑散了。阿鲁举热找到山头找不着，找到山脚找不着，找不着猪又不敢回日毋家。他走呀走，走到天黑才看见一个住家户。他走进去要求借住一晚，这家人答应了，还把他当贵客接待。主人说：“尊敬的贵客，我家没有东西接待你，家里还有三只鹅，杀一只来接待你。”听说要杀鹅，公鹅、母鹅和小鹅商量开了。公鹅说：“把我杀了接待客人，你们母子俩好好活着。”母鹅说：“把我杀了接待客人，你们父子俩好好活着。”小鹅说：“把我杀了接待客人，你们二老好好活着。”阿鲁举热听到鹅的议论，就对主人说：“你家不要杀鹅了，我是长翅膀的儿子，不吃长翅膀的肉。”主人家听了也就不杀鹅了。

Riwu asked him to herd pigs and gave him seven old sows. Before long, the seven sows all gave birth to piggies which pleased the chieftain greatly. But one day, seven litters of piggies led by seven sows ran away. Alujure could not find them anywhere at the top or the foot of the mountain. Not daring to return to Riwu, he walked for a long time and finally saw a household at night. He was allowed to a stay overnight and even treated as an honored guest by the owner, who said, "Respected guest, there is nothing in my family to treat you but three geese. We will kill one of them in your honor." After hearing the conversation, the three geese began to discuss. The male goose said, "Kill me for the guest, and my son, you can stay alive with your mother." The female goose said, "Kill me for the guest, and my son, you can stay alive with your father." The gosling said, "No, take me, and my dear father and mother, you two stay alive." Alujure heard their discussion and said, "Do not kill any goose. I'm a son of a hawk which has wings, so I do not eat anything that has wings." Therefore, the three geese survived.

第二天早上天刚亮，阿鲁举热就起身走了。刚走到河边，只见三只鹅早已在那里等着。老鹅们感谢阿鲁举热说："因为你不吃长翅膀的肉，所以，我们都活着。你这样匆匆忙忙地走，究竟有什么事？"阿鲁举热说："我把日毋家的七窝猪放丢了，找不着猪不敢回家去。"公鹅说："你是个好人，你有难处我们应该帮助你，你只要找着两件宝物，就可以制服日毋。"阿鲁举热问："哪两件宝物？到哪里去找？请你们告诉我。"公鹅说："你莫急，等我们抖抖身子看。"公鹅抖三抖，没有抖下来；母鹅抖三抖，抖下一根毛。母鹅告诉阿鲁举热说："这不是一根普通的毛，是一支神箭。你拿着这根毛到对门大石板上绕三转，石板自己会开门。里面丢出小针你莫接，丢出大针你莫接，丢出一顶罗锅帽，你就赶快接着，因为罗锅帽里装着九十九庹长的头发，那就是神线。你拿着神箭和神线，指山山会垮，指海海会干，指人人会死。你有这两件宝物，再也不用怕日毋。"

阿鲁举热照着母鹅说的去做，果然找到了九十九庹长的头发。他拿着这两件宝物往回走去，回到了日毋家。日毋责问他："你不好好去放猪，拿着鹅毛和头发玩，你要干什么？"

The next morning, as the day just broke, Alujure went up and left. As he walked to the side of the river, three geese had already waited there. The old geese thanked Alujure and said, "We owe our lives to you because you don't eat meat of animals with wings. Why are you in a hurry? What happened?" Alujure replied, "I lost Riwu's seven litters of piggies, so I do not dare to go back unless I find them." The male goose said, "You are a kind-hearted man. If you have any difficulty, we are happy to help you. As long as you find the two treasures, then you can subdue Riwu." Alujure asked, "What are the two treasures? Where to find them? Please tell me." "Don't worry," said the male goose, "Let's shake ourselves up." It shook for three times, but nothing was shaken off. Then the female goose quivered for three times and shook off a feather. "This is not an ordinary feather," said the goose, "it is a magic arrow. Take the feather and walk around the large slate in opposite to the door for three times; the door will open. If a small needle is thrown out, do not pick it. If it's a big needle, also leave it alone. But if a Luoguo hat comes out, pick it up at once because there is a long hair, 99 duo in length, inside, which is actually a magic thread. You take the arrow and the thread, then the mountain will collapse if you point at it; the sea will dry up if you point at it; and the person will die if you point at him. With these two treasures, you have no need to fear Riwu anymore."

Alujure did as told and found the hair. So, he took these two treasures and went back. Riwu scolded him, "You, stupid guy! Why do you hold the stupid hair and feather instead of herding pigs? What's wrong with you?" Alujure said, "I am holding the magic arrow and the magic thread. The mountain will

阿鲁举热说："我拿的是神箭和神线，指山山会垮，指海海会干，指人人会死。"日毋不相信，说："那你就指给我看看。"阿鲁举热用神箭和神线向对面岩子斜着指一下，岩子垮一半；直着指一下，岩子全垮了。然后对门前的水塘斜着指一下，水干了一半；直着指一下，水全干了。日毋心里惊慌，但嘴还硬。他说："你有本事再指指我的坐骑试试。"阿鲁举热拿起神箭和神线对着日毋的马斜着指一下，马站不稳；直着指一下，马倒地死了。日毋的心"怦怦"跳，但仍不服气。他想狗会避邪，就对阿鲁举热说："你再指我的白狗试试。"阿鲁举热指一下，白狗倒地死了。这下日毋害怕了，不跑，生怕神箭指着自己；要跑，又怕丢失脸面。他定神想想：我是主子，他是奴隶，哪有主子怕奴隶的道理。于是他壮着胆子对阿鲁举热说："你指死的那些都是些命小鬼，你有本事来指我试试。"阿鲁举热说："你是主子，我是奴隶，我咋个指你。"日毋认为自己真的命大，阿鲁举热不敢指他，就大声说："我叫你指，你就指。"阿鲁举热只好抬起神线对着日毋指一下，日毋就站立不稳；对心窝指一下，日毋倒地死了。从此以后，日毋的家产变成了阿鲁举热的财产，日毋的两个老婆，都归阿鲁举热所有，阿鲁举热在这块地盘上当起了主子。

collapse if I point at it; the sea will dry up if I point at it; the person will die if I point at him." Riwu did not believe, so he questioned in doubt, "Then show me." Alujure pointed to the rock obliquely with his two treasures, and half of the rock immediately collapsed; then, he pointed straight to it, the whole rock fell apart. Afterwards, he pointed obliquely at the pond in front of the house, and half of it dried up; then he pointed straight to it, and the whole water was gone. Riwu grew in panic, but he still pretended not to show it. "Point at my horse again if you dare," Riwu said. Alujure took the arrow and the thread and pointed at the horse obliquely, and then the horse hobbled; then he pointed straight to it, the horse fell down and died. Riwu, whose heart pounded hardly in fear, was still unwilling to submit. Riwu thought that dogs could ward off the evil, so he said to Alujure, "Try to point at my white dog again." Alujure did as told and the white dog fell down and died. Now, Riwu was convinced, feeling threatened. If he stayed, he was afraid of being pointed at; if he ran, he was afraid of losing face. After a while, on a second thought, he told himself that he was the master and Alujure was the slave, so there was no reason why the master should be afraid of the slave. Therefore, he emboldened himself and challenged Alujure, "What you pointed at were low-class lives. Try to point at me if you dare." Alujure replied, "You are the master and I am your slave. How can I point at you?" Riwu did think that he had nine lives and Alujure was afraid of pointing at him, so he said loudly, "Just do it as I told." Alujure had to follow his order with his arrow and thread, and soon Riwu could not stand steadily; afterwards, Alujure pointed at Riwu's heart, and Riwu died. From then on, Riwu's property, together with his two wives, belonged to Alujure, who became the master of this land.

阿鲁举热射日、月

日毋的两个老婆都很喜欢阿鲁举热这位英俊的大神人，都愿意做他的妻子。但两个妻子给他出了个难题说："你手里有两个宝物，指山山会垮，指海海会干，指人人会死，你能用它制成箭射月亮和太阳吗？现在天上有七个太阳，晒得万物不能生存；天上有六个月亮，弄得白天和夜晚分不清。"阿鲁举热回答说："让我试试看。"阿鲁举热砍来岩桑做弓，用鹅毛做箭，九十九庹长的头发做弓弦。他带上弓箭去射太阳、月亮。他先站在蕨枝上射，蕨枝倒在地上。阿鲁举热封赠蕨枝说："蕨枝呀蕨枝，你不成器，以后人们把你的头掐来当菜吃。"从此以后，蕨一发嫩芽，人们就把它掐来当菜吃。阿鲁举热站在青松树上射，松树的枝丫又踩断了。阿鲁举热封赠松树说："青松树呀青松树，你骨头是硬的，树叶也是青的，想不到这么脆弱，以后世人把你砍来做火把，砍了不会发。"从此松树砍掉以后就再也长不起来，只有借风的力量把松子吹到别处去生长。阿鲁举热爬到羊耳朵树①上去射太阳、月亮。可是羊耳朵树叶子团在一起张不开，不好站

① 译者注：羊耳朵树即杨翠木。

Alujure Shooting down Suns and Moons

Riwu's wives all adored Alujure, the great handsome hero, and were willing to be with him. But the two wives gave him a difficult question, "You have two treasures, which can make mountains collapse, oceans dry up, and people die. Can you make these two things into arrows to shoot down moons and suns? You see, there are seven suns in the sky which burn all lives on earth to death; also, there are six moons in the sky, confusing day and night." Alujure replied, "Let me have a try." Then, he cut down rock mulberries to make a bow, and used goose feathers to make arrows and the long magic hair to make bowstrings, with which, he prepared to shoot down the suns and moons. First, he stood on the fern branch, but it fell to the ground. He said to the fern branch, "You are good for nothing. In the future, people will take your head off and eat it as a dish." Since then, when ferns sprouted, people would pick the fresh leaves as food. Then, he stood on a pine tree which immediately broke. He said to the pine tree, "You have hard bones and green leaves, but you are so fragile. In the future, people will cut you down to make torches, and you won't be able to sprout any more." From then on, pine trees could no longer grow up once they were cut off. Their nuts could only be blown everywhere and grew at the mercy of winds. Afterwards, he climbed on a sheep ear tree①,

① Translator's note: sheep ear tree refers to Pittosporum Kerrii Craib.

上去。阿鲁举热封赠羊耳朵树说："羊耳朵树呀羊耳朵树，你叶子团在一起张不开，以后你不会长成材。"从此羊耳朵树就长不成材。阿鲁举热站在马缨花树上射，马缨花树撑住了。七个太阳射下来六个，六个月亮射下来五个，太阳和月亮各剩下一个。阿鲁举热封赠马缨花树说："马缨花树呀马缨花树，你是好样的，以后你不要长成材，人们就不来砍你了，只是用你做饭勺、用你做酒杯，人们吃饭喝酒都不会忘记你。你的花是金花银花①，到处都可以见到你。"从此以后，彝家人最崇拜马缨花。阿鲁举热把多余的太阳和月亮射掉了，白天，夜晚分得清了，万物能生长了，他的两个妻子更敬佩他了，所有的彝家人，也都感谢这位能干的主子。

朴莫乃日想儿子

朴莫乃日把儿子抱到神龙鹰那里后，鹰的食他吃了，鹰的衣他穿了，哭也不哭了。她放心地转回来，可是半路遇到老妖婆吹了一阵妖风，把朴莫乃日吹进妖洞去了。老妖婆想

① 金花银花：指红马缨花和白马缨花。

whose leaves, however, remained closed, which made it difficult to stand on it. He said to the sheep ear tree, "Your leaves can not open, so you won't grow into useful timber." Since then, sheep ear trees could never grow to full size. Finally, he stood on a silk tree which held it, where he shot down six suns and five moons, leaving only one moon and one sun in the sky. He said to the silk tree, "You are a good one. If you don't grow into timber, people won't cut you down. You will be used to make cooking spoons and wine glasses. People will not forget you when they eat and drink. Your flowers will become golden flowers and silver flowers① on spoons and glasses, so that you can be seen everywhere." After that, the Yi people began to adore silk trees as their favorite. As Alujure shot down the needless suns and moons, people could differentiate between day and night, which enabled everything on earth to grow and flourish. Because of it, his two wives admired him more. All members of the Yi family were grateful to this capable master.

Pumonairi Missing Hcr Son

After Pumonairi took her son to the dragon hawk, where the boy ate hawks' food, wore hawks' clothes and didn't cry any more, she felt relieved and left. However, halfway back, an old witch blew a demon wind which carried Pumonairi into a devil's hole. The old witch wanted to eat Pumonairi, but she could

① golden flowers and silver flowers: means red flowers and white flowers of the silk tree.

吃朴莫乃日，但是吃不了。因为朴莫乃日是龙的后裔，她身上又有神龙鹰的三滴血、天龙的三滴水。老妖婆几次想吃她，可一触她的身子，老妖婆就会全身麻木。老妖婆不敢吃朴莫乃日，但也不放她，让她在妖洞里受折磨。

朴莫乃日扳着指头数数，她在妖洞里整整十六年了。她自言自语地说："儿子呀儿子，神龙鹰把你养大成人了吧？妈妈想看看你。"说也奇怪，母亲自言自语地一说，阿鲁举热的心就"怦怦怦"地跳起来。他拥有了日毋的地盘，过上了主子的日子，又射下了太阳、月亮，名声也大了，人们都很敬仰地。可是心一跳，他就想起寻找生身母亲的事。阿鲁举热背上弓箭，向两个妻子和家人告别，继续寻找母亲去了。

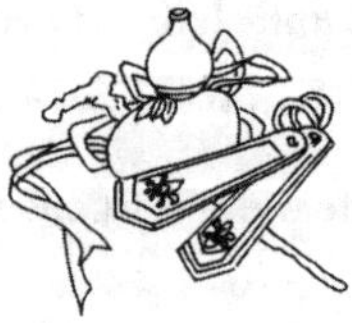

not do it, because Pumonairi was a descendant of dragon and had received three drops of blood from the dragon hawk and three drops of water from the dragon. The old witch tried several times, but once she touched Pumonairi's body, she would be numb. Therefore, the old witch did not dare to have another try. However, Pumonairi was kept in captivity in the hole and tortured.

Counting with fingers, Pumonairi found that she had been in the devil's hole for sixteen years. She murmured, "My son, you must have been brought up by the dragon hawk. Your mother wants to see you." Strangely, when Pumonairi murmured, Alujure's heart jumped hardly, which reminded him of his mother. Though he had already become reputable and admirable as the master in Riwu's land and a hero who had shot down suns and moons, he decided to embark on the journey to look for his mother. So, he took his bow and arrows and bid farewell to his two wives and families.

阿鲁举热东、南、西、北到处寻找母亲。他走到西边的一个山寨里，看见一群姑娘躲在屋里不敢出门。阿鲁举热去找她们，见那些姑娘个个愁眉苦脸，问她们有什么苦楚，谁也不敢说话。阿鲁举热对她们说："我是阿鲁举热，有什么难处你们可以告诉我。""哦！你就是大神人阿鲁举热。"这下姑娘们一拥而出，有的拉住他的手，有的抱住他的脚，苦苦哀求救救她们。原来在西边的木克哈尼山岩洞里住着一个老妖婆，善于耳听八方，谁说她的背后话，她都知道，并且马上就来害你，所以谁也不敢议论她。这个村的姑娘只要长到十五六岁，就要被老妖婆抓去吃。老妖婆专门吃十五六岁的大姑娘。阿鲁举热心中暗想："难道我母亲也被这个老妖婆抓去了吗？"阿鲁举热抬起脚就要去找那妖婆，姑娘们不让他走，哀求说："大神人呀！愿你永远和我们在一起，不然我们难得活命。"阿鲁举热说："我先去把那妖婆除掉，才能保住你们的性命，你们还是让我走吧！"姑娘们依依不舍地送了他一程，指给他妖婆居住的山。

He looked for his mother everywhere in the east, south, west, and north. One day, he arrived at a stockaded village in the west where he found that girls hid in their houses, not daring to come out. He went to them and saw the worried faces of the girls. He asked for the reason, but no one dare to speak. He comforted them, "I am Alujure. If you have any difficulty, let me know. I can help you." "Oh goodness, you are the great hero Alujure." Exclaimed the girls, who all came out all of a sudden, some holding his hand and some holding his feet, all pleading for help to rescue them. It turned out that there was an old witch living in the cave of the Mukehani Mountain in the west, who was quick-eared. Whoever said bad words about her behind her back, she could know it and immediately come to do the harm. Therefore, no one dared to talk about her. Girls in the village would be caught and eaten by the old witch once they fifteen or sixteen years old. He said to himself, "Is my mother also caught by this old witch?" So, Alujure decided to go for the witch, but the girls refused to let him go. They pleaded, "Mighty hero! Please be with us, otherwise we will die." He said, "I need to kill the witch first. Only in this way can I save your lives! So, let me go." Having no way to persuade him to stay, the girls had to bid farewell to him and pointed to the mountain where the witch lived.

阿鲁举热按姑娘们指的方向走去。路过一块草坪，忽然遇到一匹神马。这匹神马长着九层翅膀，经常在草坪上横行，无人敢接近它。阿鲁举热看到神马反而心里高兴，暗想把它拉来当坐骑该多好。那神马看到有人走进草坪，就气势汹汹地扑过来，阿鲁举热趁机一跃骑上马背，把神马压倒在地，使它动弹不得。神马说："从来没有人把我压倒过，大神人阿鲁举热，请你饶我一条命吧！我愿当你的坐骑听候你的使唤。"这样阿鲁举热收得了一匹会飞的神马当坐骑。

当他骑着神马来到一片松林的时候，忽然跑出一头野牛精，头上长着三只角。那野牛撞倒一棵树，然后大吼一声，表示它的力气大。神马告诉野牛精说："这是大神人阿鲁举热，你不要和他较量。"野牛精说："他本事再大，力气也不会有我的大，哪有被力气比我小的人降服的道理。"野牛精一头撞向阿鲁举热，阿鲁举热顺手把野牛精的角拔掉一只。那野牛精血流满面，只好跪在阿鲁举热面前求饶说："大神人，饶我一命吧！以后我不再作恶，老老实实为人们拉犁。"从此牛为人犁地，现在的牛也只有两只角了，因为有一只角被阿鲁举热拔掉了。

He walked in the direction instructed by the girls. Suddenly a magic horse came out as he passed by a lawn. This horse had nine wings and often ran wildly on the lawn, so no one dared to come close to it. But Alujure was happy at the sight of the magic horse, because he thought it would be a good mount. As soon as the horse saw someone walking into the lawn, it rushed to him with great force. At that moment, Alujure caught the opportunity to ride on it and pushed it to the ground so that it could not move. The magic horse said, "No one has ever overthrown me. Alujure, the mighty hero, please spare me! I am willing to be your mount and obey you." In this way, Alujure obtained a horse which could fly.

When he rode on the horse to a pine forest, a demon buffalo with three horns on his head suddenly ran out. The buffalo knocked down a tree and screamed, indicating that it was strong. The horse told the buffalo, "This is the great hero Alujure. Don't challenge him." The buffalo said, "However strong he is, he is no match for me. How can I surrender to a person who is weaker than me?" The buffalo crashed into Alujure, but he pulled out a horn of the buffalo just the moment. Bleeding, the Buffalo had to kneel in front of Alujure and ask for mercy, "All mighty hero, please spare me! I promise that I will never do any harm again. In the future, I will faithfully help people pull the plough." Since then, buffalo became the tamed cattle and plowed the ground, which had only two horns left, as one horn had been pulled out by Alujure.

阿鲁举热骑着神马继续往前走，要到妖洞里去寻找阿妈。神马告诉他，妖婆特比阿莫非常厉害，她嘴里喷出的水，能把人喷倒；她念咒语，能把人咒死；她的爪像刀子，能一把抓出人的心。阿鲁举热准备了三把倒钩，来到妖洞前。妖婆闻到生人味就走出山洞来。妖婆刚张开嘴，还没来得及喷水，阿鲁举热用一把倒钩一下钩住了妖婆的舌头，妖婆有咒语也念不成了。另两把倒钓一把钩住妖婆的一个手掌心。然后阿鲁举热用铁链把三把倒钩连起来，牵妖婆带他到洞里去找阿妈。在妖洞里关了十六年的朴莫乃日瘦得像一根草，阿鲁举热很伤心地朝着母亲哭了起来，妖婆便趁机逃跑了。可是不管她跑到哪里，倒钓都取不出来。妖婆从此再也不能抓人、咒人了。阿鲁举热背着母亲，骑着神马，回到了原来的住处扎扎结列①。

① 扎扎结列：地名，在迭朴索洛北面。

Alujure continued his journey forward on his horse, in the hope of finding his mother in the devil's cave. The horse told him that the witch, called Tebiamo, had great power who could spray water from mouth to push people down, read spells to kill people and grabbed out a person's heart with her fingers as sharp as knives. So, Alujure prepared three barbs before he came to the cave. When the witch sensed the smell of a living person, she walked out of the cave. As she was about to open her mouth, Alujure hooked the witch's tongue with a barb at once, leaving her no time to spray water or read spells. He took the other two barbs to hook the palms of the witch's hands, and then connected the three barbs with an iron chain. Afterwards, Alujure guarded the witch to the cave for his mother. Pumonairi became as thin as grass after spending sixteen years in captivity in the cave. At the sight of it, Alujure grieved and cried. The witch took this opportunity to flee away, who, however, could never catch or curse people anymore as there was no way to remove the barbs. Alujure carried his mother on his back and rode his horse back home to his former residence—Zhazhajielie①.

① Zhazhajielie: name of a place, north of Diepusuoluo.

朴莫乃日试儿子

回到扎扎结列以后，朴莫乃日才知道她儿子就是射太阳、月亮的大神人。她高兴地说：“我儿不愧是神鹰的后代。”但是她还要试试儿子的为人和孝心。她对儿子说：“妖婆折磨我十六年，我天天夜里出冷汗，听说獐子血可以补虚，你能找到吗？”阿妈的话音刚落，阿鲁举热就出门了。不到一锅烟的时间，他提回来两只獐子交给阿妈。朴莫乃日又说：“妖婆恐吓了我十六年，我日日夜夜心跳，听说鹿心可以医治。”转眼儿子又打回了三只马鹿。母亲又说：“我在妖洞十六年，听不到外边的声音，现在一听到声响，我就胆怯，听说熊胆可以医这个病。”一会工夫，儿子就从外面打回三只黑熊。朴莫乃日喝了獐血，吃了鹿心、熊胆，身体很快恢复了，又像十六年前那样好看。

Pumonairi Testing Her Son

After going back to Zhazhajielie, Pumonairi knew that her son was the hero who had shot down suns and moons. She said to herself proudly, "My son is a worthy descendant of the dragon hawk." But she still wanted to test her son's manner and filial piety. She said to her son, "The witch had tortured me for sixteen years; as a result, I feel cold every night. I hear that the blood of the river deer can boost health. Can you find it?" Alujure immediately went out to find the river deer. Within a few minutes, he brought back two river deer to his mother. Pumonairi said again, "The witch has threatened me for sixteen years, so my heart shuddered frequently. I learn that the heart of deer can cure it." Her son came back with three deer at once. She said again, "Since I have been in the devil's cave for sixteen years, I could not hear any sound from the outside. Now, any sound outside will frighten me. To my knowledge, the bear's bile can cure it." After a while, the son came back with three black bears. After having bloods of river deer, hearts of deer and the bile of bears, Pumonairi recovered and looked as beautiful as she was sixteen years ago.

朴莫乃日知道儿子既能干又有孝心，很高兴。但是她还要试儿子的胆量。她对儿子说："我发烧，头晕眼花，你到大雪山危杰尔曲去取三块冰凌回来给我吃。"阿鲁举热去找神马商量说："危杰尔曲大雪山我听说过，但不知在何方，这事请你帮帮忙。"神马点点头表示可以帮忙。神马是有九层翅膀的飞马，经常在半空中飞行，没有它不知道的山，不认识的水。阿鲁举热骑着神马去到危杰尔曲大雪山取回了三块冰凌给阿妈做药。母亲这下也感到自己对儿子太苛刻了，今后再不能叫儿子去做危险的事情，所以她再也不给儿子出什么难题了。过了几天安稳的日子，阿鲁举热又想南方的家。他告诉母亲，在南方迭朴索洛地方，他已拥有日毋的地盘和妻室。朴莫乃日知道自己的母亲也是从迭朴索洛嫁到扎扎结列的，那里是祖宗在的地方。她对阿鲁举热说："儿呀，迭朴索洛是个好地方，既然那里有你的地盘，有你的妻室，我们应该搬到那里去住。"于是阿鲁举热又背着阿妈，骑着神马，回到迭朴索洛居住。

Pumonairi felt very happy after making sure that her son was both capable and filial. However, she still had to test whether her son was a brave man. She said to her son, "I have a fever and often feel dizzy. Please go to the snowy mountain of Weijieerqu and bring back three icicles for me." Alujure went to discuss with the magic horse, "I have heard of this mountain before, but I have no idea where it is. So, please help me." The horse nodded and agreed to help. With nine layers of wings, it often flied here and there, and therefore knew everywhere. Then, Alujure rode on the horse, setting out to the snowy mountain and finally brought back three icicles to his mother to make medicine. At this time, his mother felt that she was too harsh on her son and she would no longer ask him to do any dangerous things in the future, which meant that she would not cause trouble to her son anymore. After living a few peaceful days, Alujure missed his families in the south. So he told his mother that he had Riwu's land and two wives in Diepusuoluo in the south. Pumonairi knew that this was his land of ancestor, because her mother was also married from Diepusuoluo to Zhazhajielie. She said to Alujure, "My son, Diepusuoluo is a good place. Since your land and wives are there, we should move there to live." So he mounted on his horse, carrying his mother on his back, and went back to Diepusuoluo.

龙鹰大战

朴莫乃日想，儿子终日奔波，斩妖除害，射掉了多余的太阳、月亮，为人间做了很多好事，应该让他平平安安过几天日子。她对儿子说："阿鲁举热啊，你从生下地就一直在奔忙，我这当妈的看着实在不忍心，部落的事由阿妈来料理，你去找你的两个妻子，好好过几天日子吧！"阿鲁举热想，母亲是部落里最受尊重的人，有母亲料理部落的事情，自己一百个放心，于是就骑着神马去找他的两个妻子去了。

大老婆住在迭朴索洛的西面，小老婆住在迭朴索洛的东面。阿鲁举热骑着神马，飞越迭朴索洛大海，东边住几天，西边住几天，两个老婆对他都很好。可是这种甜蜜的日子不长久，过了一段时间，小老婆心里嫉妒了，她要阿鲁举热长期住在她那里，不让他去看大老婆。一天夜里，她用剪刀把神马的翅膀偷偷剪掉了三层。天还没有亮，神马就"咴咴"叫起来。阿鲁举热以为神马催他回西边去，又骑上神马飞越迭朴索洛大海。飞到海中央，神马飞不动了，渐渐向海里落去。阿鲁举热伸手摸摸神马的翅膀，发现九层翅膀被剪掉了三层，这才知道是小老婆下了毒手。水淹到齐脖子的时候，他朝天喊道："我的父亲神龙鹰呀！我中了女人的诡计。"话音刚落，涌来一股海浪，阿鲁举热和神马便一齐淹没在大海之中了。

Fighting between the Dragon and the Hawk

Pumonairi thought that as her son had not taken a rest for so many good deeds such as killing the witch, shooting off the extra suns and moons, it was time for him to be blessed with a stable and happy life. So, she said to her son, "My son, you have been busy since you were born. As a mother, I can not bear to see you deal with endless work all the time. I will help you with the tribe's affairs, so that you can have several happy days with your wives." Alujure was convinced that his mother, as a respected person in the tribe, could do the job perfectly. So, he rode on his horse and went to see his two wives.

His first wife lived in the west of Diepusuoluo, and the second lived in the east. Alujure flied over the sea back and forth on his horse so that he could stay in the east for a few days with his first wife, and went to the west for a few days with the second one. Both of them were very kind to him. However, this happy moment did not last long. After a period of time, the second wife was jealous, because she wanted Alujure to live with her all the time, instead of going to his first wife every few days. So, one night, she used scissors to cut off three layers of the horse's wings. Before daybreak, the horse cried out. Alujure thought that the horse was urging him to go back to the west, so he rode on it to fly across the sea. But midway above the sea, the horse ran out of strength and could not fly further; then, it gradually fell down to the sea. After checking the wings, Alujure found that the nine-layered wings were cut off by three layers. Only then did he know that it was the second wife who laid this murderous hands. As the water was flooding to his neck, he shouted to the sky, "Father! I was tricked by a woman." Then, a wave came, drowning Alujure and the horse.

神龙鹰听到儿子的呼喊，成群结队地飞到迭朴索洛上空，向海龙王要儿子。龙王说："阿鲁举热是龙的后代。"鹰说："阿鲁举热是鹰的儿子。"两家都不肯让，因此发生了龙鹰大战。龙鹰大战惊动了整个迭朴索洛，朴莫乃日和阿鲁举热的两个妻子都知道了阿鲁举热落入大海的事。她们跑到海边哭喊"还我儿子"、"还我男人"。朴莫乃日坐在大海的北边哭，阿鲁举热的大老婆坐在迭朴索洛的西边哭，小老婆坐在迭朴索洛的东边哭。哭呀，哭呀，后来，朴莫乃日在大海北面变成了一座大山，阿鲁举热的大老婆也在海的西面变成一座大山。小老婆良心不好，在海的东面变成一块大石板，天天被人踩。

流传地区：金沙江沿岸

讲述者：肖开亮，黑朝亮，李守芳

搜集整理者：李世忠，祁树森

After hearing the call from his son, the dragon hawk flew above Diepusuoluo with a flock of hawks, and asked the dragon king to return his son, who argued, "Alujure is a descendant of the dragon." The hawk refuted, "He is the son of the hawk." As the two sides refused to make any concession, a war between dragons and hawks took place, which stunned the entire Diepusuoluo. Pumonairi and Alujure's two wives knew about the event and ran to the seaside, crying and yelling, "return my son" and "return my man". Pumonairi sat in the north of the sea and cried; Alujure's first wife cried on the west side of the Diepusuoluo; his second wife cried on its east side. Later, Pumonairi turned into a mountain in the north of the sea, and the first wife also became a mountain in the west of the sea. But the second wife became a big slate, stepped on by people every day because of her wickedness.

Spreading area: Banks along the Jinsha River

Narrator: Xiao Kailiang, Hei Chaoliang, Li Shoufang

Collector and editor: Li Shizhong, Qi Shusen

南诏始祖细奴逻

唐初，在云南洱海地区有六个大部落，就是人们常说的六诏。六诏中，南诏部落经济繁荣，诏主细奴逻是个很有才干的人。到了他的曾孙皮逻阁的时候，就统一了洱海地区，建立了有名的南诏国。南诏国前后有二百五十三年历史，诏王十三代。民间流传着许多南诏王的传说，下面就说说始姐细奴逻的故事。

一

细奴逻出生在哀牢山区。妈妈叫摩利羌，是个眉清目秀、聪明能干的彝家姑娘。摩利羌十八岁的时候，有一天，她到离家不远的龙潭边洗衣服，看见水面上有一块滑溜溜的木板。木板慢慢漂到她脚边，她就把它捞起来，蹲在上面搓衣服。过了几天，摩利羌再去龙潭洗衣服时，这块木板还在老地方，她又蹲到木板上去洗。这样经过两次，摩利羌就怀了孕。十个月后，她生下了九个儿子。

Xinuluo, The Ancestor of Nanzhao Kingdom

In the early Tang dynasty, there were six tribes located in the Erhai Region of Yunnan Province, also commonly known as the Six Zhaos. Among the Six Zhaos, the Nanzhao tribe was prosperous and thriving, for its chief, Xinuluo, was a very talented leader. During the rule of his grandson, Piluoge, the Erhai Region was successfully unified, and the famous Nanzhao Kingdom was therefore established. The Nanzhao Kingdom has two hundred and fifty three years of history with thirteen generation of kings. There are many folk tales about the Nanzhao kings. Here is the story of its first king—Xinuluo.

I

Xinuluo was born in the Ailao Mountain area. His mother, Moliqiang, was a beautiful and clever Yi girl with bright eyes. At the age of eighteen, one day, when she washed clothes at the dragon pond, not far from home, she saw a piece of slippery plank floating on the water. The plank slowly drifted to her feet, so she picked it up, squatted down above it and rubbed the clothes. Days went by, she went to wash clothes again, only to find that the plank was still there. So she squatted on it to wash her clothes for a second time. After that, Moliqiang was pregnant and gave birth to nine sons ten months later.

在九个儿子出生的那天晚上，有条龙飞进了摩利羌的屋子，变成一个年轻俊俏的小伙。他对摩利羌说："这九个儿子是我的，今夜我领走八个，留下最小的一个给你，他的名字就叫宠龙，你把他好好养大，让他服侍你。"说完就不见了，八个儿子也不见了，只有最小的儿子还在。从这天起，小儿子身上闪着一圈红光。摩利羌小心地把宠龙裹在包头布里，给他喂奶，养他长大。宠龙一天比一天长大，他身子周围的红光也显得更明亮了。

在皇帝住的京城里，有一个道士，天天在观测天象。有一天，他发现西南边天上出现奇异的红光，就去禀报皇帝。皇帝问他是怎么回事，他说："南天出红光，必有圣人降。"皇帝害怕有圣人降世，将来会和自己争皇位，就派大臣到西南方来察访，一定要把有红光的人抓到。

皇帝派了一个名叫弥芮忽的酋长查办这件事。弥芮忽带着兵马来到哀牢山区，挨家挨户进行查找。这时，哀牢山一个头人的儿子因为想娶摩利羌遭到拒绝，对摩利羌有怨恨，就向弥芮忽禀报说："摩利羌养着一个私生子名叫宠龙，从小就有一团红光罩在身上。"弥芮忽一听非常高兴，便化装成阿毕(即毕摩①)模样，穿上羊皮褂，戴上挽发帽，拿上小铃铛，"叮叮当当"摇着来到了摩利羌家。

① 译者注：毕摩即祭师，"毕"意为"念经"，"摩"意为"有知识的长者"。

The night when the nine sons were born, a dragon flew into Moliqiang's house and turned into a young handsome man. He said to her, "These nine boys are my sons, and tonight, I will take away eight of them and leave the youngest one to you. His name will be called Chonglong. Raise him properly, and he will serve you when he grows up." Then he disappeared, along with the eight sons with him, except for the youngest one. From this day on, the little son was surrounded by a circle of red lights. Moliqiang carefully wrapped him in the cloth, nursing him and raising him. Days went by, as Chonglong grew older, the red lights became brighter.

In the capital city, where the emperor lived, there was a Taoist master, who observed the natural phenomena every day. One day, he found that there was a ball of red light flashing in the southwest sky. So he immediately reported it to the emperor, claiming it to be a symbol for the arrival of a king. The emperor, fearing that the arriving king would overthrow him in the future, sent a minister to the southwest region, and wanted him to be captured.

The emperor sent a chieftain named Miruihu to look into this matter. The chieftain arrived at the Ailao Mountain region with a group of troop, and searched the village door to door. Just then, the son of the village chief, holding the grudge for Moliqiang as having been turned down by her before, reported to Miruihu, "Moliqiang has been keeping a bastard son named Chonglong, who had been surrounded by red light since he was born." Miruihu was thrilled at the news, so he disguised himself as a Bimo① and came to Moliqiang's house, wearing a sheepskin vest and cap, and with a bell in his hand rattling.

---

① Translator's note: Bimo refers to priest. "Bi" means reciting scriptures; "Mo" means knowledgeable seniors.

弥芮忽一进摩利羌家，就看见眼前有一闭红光在闪耀。他高兴极了，心想如能拿得这个有红光护身的圣人归朝，皇帝一定有重金赏赐。他迫不及待地向摩利羌走去，边走边大声嚷嚷："听说你喜得一子，快抱出来让我为他祈祷，请祖宗神灵保佑他!"摩利羌正在院子里缝衣服，见这个陌生的阿毕一进门就看孩子，觉得有些蹊跷，不知怎么办才好。这时她哥哥波洗匆匆忙忙地从门外进来，几大步走进屋子，抱出一个孩子递给弥芮忽说："好啰好啰，这就是我家妹的孩子，请阿毕祈福。"弥芮忽接过孩子，马上变了嘴脸，甩掉挽发帽，砸掉手中的铃铛，恶狠狠地说："这小孩是妖儿，我奉朝廷之命，前来降服。"说完，抱起孩子大步走出门去。

事情这样突然，等摩利羌明白过来，弥芮忽已经抱着孩子走远了。摩利羌悲痛欲绝，放声大哭。这时波洗放低声音说："妹妹，不要难过了，宠龙还在里间睡着呢，刚才被带走的是乌呷。"原来他在外面听到朝廷派人来捉拿宠龙，就急忙回家给妹妹报信，但来的时候已经晚了，刚进家门就看见化装成阿毕的人要看宠龙。他急中生智，跑进自己屋中，把自己的儿子乌呷抱出来，交给了弥芮忽。宠龙和乌呷是同一天出生的，所以弥芮忽也没看出来。

The moment he stepped into the house, he saw a beam of red light glowing in front of him. He was extremely delighted at the thought of the emperor's abundant reward if he could return with this sage with red light. Then, he hurried to Moliqiang and shouted, "I learn that you are blessed with a boy. Quickly bring him to my side, so that I can pray for him, and pray for blessings from our ancestors." Moliqiang was sewing her clothes when she saw this strange Bimo coming into the house who asked for her son. She felt confused. It was at this time when her brother Boxi hurried into the house, walked quickly into his room and came out with a baby. He handed the baby to Miruihu and said, "Here, here, this is the child of my sister, please pray for him." Miruihu took the baby and turned into a nasty face. He threw away his cap, smashed the bell and said ferociously, "This child is a demon, and under the order of the imperial court, I am hereby to surrender this demon." After that, he strode out of the house with the baby in his arms.

It all happened out of a sudden. By the time Moliqiang finally realized what was happening, Miruihu had long gone with the boy. Moliqiang abandoned herself to great despair and burst into tears. However, Boxi whispered to her, "Don't feel sad, sister. Chonglong is still asleep inside. It is Wuxia that he took away." It turned out that Boxi overheard the news in the street that a commissioner had been sent by the emperor to come after the child with red light, so he hurried home in the hope of delivering the message to his sister. But it was too late. The moment he stepped into the house, he heard the disguised man asking for Chonglong. At that time, an idea flashed through him, which was to replace Chonglong with his own child, Wuxia. So he ran to his room and handed his son to Miruihu. As the two boys were born on the same day, so Miruihu wasn't able to tell the difference.

乌呷虽然被抱走了，但是波洗和摩利羌都知道，乌呷身上没有红光，只能哄过一时，朝廷派来的人发觉后，必定还要来搜家。为了保护宠龙，他们想出一个办法；把家中的大母狗杀了，掏空肚子，把宠龙裹好放进狗肚子，用狗皮遮住宠龙身上的红光。放好后，他们把狗放进狗圈，再引小狗来吃奶。果然，弥芮忽发觉了抱去的小孩身上没有红光，波洗和摩利羌刚刚安置好，他就带着人，来摩利羌家搜查。但是他们翻遍了屋里屋外，都找不到一个小孩。从狗圈旁边走过无数次，他们也没有发现什么可疑的地方，只见母狗闭着眼睛好好地睡在地上，小狗在吃奶。折腾了半天，他们一无所获，也没有发现家中还有红光，只好垂头丧气地走了。

弥芮忽带着人马一走，波洗忙从狗肚子里抱出宠龙交给摩利羌。摩利羌背着宠龙连夜逃出了哀牢山。

Though Wuxia was taken, Boxi and Moliqiang knew that Wuxia was not surrounded by the red light, so Miruihu eventually would realize the truth and return for Chonglong. In order to protect him, they came up with an idea. They butchered their big mother dog, emptied its belly and stuffed Chonglong inside, so that the dog's skin would cover the red light. After settling him inside the belly, they put the dog in the dog yard and lured the puppies to suck its breasts. As expected, Miruihu found the boy he carried had no red light surrounding him, so he returned to the house immediately and arrived right after the moment Chonglong was settled. They searched the house from top to bottom but failed to find any trace of a child. Though they had passed the dog yard countless times, they failed to notice anything suspicious, only to find that the mother dog lying down peacefully with puppies surrounding it. And after all that trouble, they got nothing, not even the red light, so they left with disappointment.

Right after Miruihu and his troop left, Boxi took Chonglong out from the dog's belly and handed him to Moliqiang. She carried her little son and escaped from the Ailao Mountain overnight.

二

摩利羌背着宠龙一直朝着西南方走去，一路跋山涉水，走了十来天，来到巍宝山。巍宝山山势雄伟，气候温和，土地肥沃，这里的人生活习惯、风俗礼节和摩利羌的家乡一样。母子俩就落脚在巍宝山下，开荒种地，放牧牛羊。为了躲避朝廷的追赶，摩利羌改名为“羌壶”，宠龙也改名为“细奴逻”。

羌壶带着细奴逻在巍宝山住了十多年，细奴逻长成了力大非凡的小伙子，能够帮母亲上山干活了。这一年，他在山坡开了一大片荒地，种上了庄稼。但是山上没有水，庄稼长不起来，他便想挖一口井浇地。他发现在一块巨石耸立的地方，有叮叮咚咚的流水声，就决定搬掉石头，把水引出来。但是这块石头大得很，和他在一起种地的乡亲们见了都摇头。细奴逻独自砸开石头，把井挖出来。泉水从山肚子的白沙中渗出来，清甜凉爽，他就给这口井取了一个好听的名字，叫“白沙井”。从此他们栽田种地就不愁没有水了。

Ⅱ

Moliqiang carried Chonglong and headed southwestwards. They scaled mountains and forded streams for days, and finally arrived at the Weibao Mountain, a place with magnificent peaks, mild climate and rich soil where the locals' habits and traditions were just like that in their homeland of Moliqiang. So they settled down, cultivating and grazing. Moliqiang renamed herself Qianghu, and the boy's name was changed into Xinuluo, in case the court would chase after them again.

Over a decade, they lived in the Weibao Mountain region where Xinuluo grew into a young lad with incredible strength who could help his mother with all the farm work. One year, he cleared a field of wasteland to grow corps. But the corps could not grow as there was no water in the mountain to irrigate. So he decided to dig a well to water the land. He found a spot where a huge rock standing on top of it, with tinkling sound of water flow coming from below. He wanted to move the rock and drew the water out. However, the rock was so heavy that the villagers all thought it impossible to move it. But Xinuluo was able to crack the rock and dig out the well all by himself with ease. As a result, the sweet and cool spring water seeped from the white sand of the mountain soil, which he delightfully named, the Well of White Sand. From that day on, villagers never had to worry about watering their corps.

这时候羌壶得了皮肤病，细奴逻到处为她寻医找药。有一天，他见山脚下有一个地方白气腾空，好像云烟密布一样，下去一看，原来是一潭热气腾腾的温泉，就跳进去洗了个澡。洗过后，他感到特别舒服，就把母亲搀到这里来洗澡。洗过后，羌壶的皮肤病居然就好了。从此以后，人们知道了温泉可以治病，大家都来这里洗澡治病，还给温泉取了个美名，叫“蒙诏汤池”。这个温泉今天还在巍宝山下。

三

巍宝山属蒙舍诏，诏主常和邻居蒙嶲诏争夺领地，你攻我打。有一年，蒙舍诏诏主张乐进求决心挑选精兵，征服蒙嶲诏。他听说细奴逻力气大，有胆量，很受人尊敬，就亲自来到巍宝山，招收细奴逻入营当兵。

细奴逻这时已是一个魁梧的壮汉，不仅会耕地放牧，还会张弓射弩。张乐进求把细奴逻招进兵营，叫他当兵丁头目。

Later, Qianghu suffered from a skin disease, so Xinuluo searched for cure and doctors everywhere. One day, at the foot of the mountain, he found a place shrouded with white fog, looking like gathering clouds from a distance. Taking a closer look, it turned out to a hot spring. He jumped into it and took a shower, feeling very comfortable. So he carried his mother here for a bath. Afterwards, her skin disease was miraculously healed. Since then, people learned that this spring could cure diseases, and they all came down here to bath and seek for heal. Afterwards, this spring was named Mengzhao Spring, which can still be found at the foot of the Weibao Mountain today.

III

The Weibao Mountain was ruled by the Mengshezhao tribe. Its chieftain occasionally waged war for land against the neighboring Mengxizhao tribe. One year, the chieftain of the Mengshezhao tribe, Zhanglejinqiu, decided to recruit for the finest soldiers to conquer the Mengxizhao tribe. He heard that Xinuluo was a man of remarkable strength and courage, respected widely by people, so he came to the Weibao Mountain to recruit him in person.

At that time, Xinuluo had already grown into a strong man with exceptional martial skills. Not only could he farm and graze, but also was he good at bow and arrows. So Zhanglejinqiu drew him into his camp and appointed him as the general of his troop.

细奴逻英勇善战，屡建战功，深得全诏兵士的爱戴。经过一年多的战争，细奴逻辅佐张乐进求打败了蒙嶲诏，统一了蒙舍川。

战争结束了，细奴逻凯旋回乡，巍宝山的乡亲父老们特地开辟了一块“打歌场”，为他聚会打歌，庆贺胜利。

这个时候一个名叫蒙织的姑娘爱上了细奴逻，细奴逻也喜欢美丽、勤劳、善良的蒙织。他们在打歌场上建立了感情，第二年就办了喜事，第三年生下了一个儿子，祖母羌壶为他取名叫“逻晟”。

逻晟一天天长大，到七八岁时，细奴逻常常带他去劳动。

有一天，父子俩在山上犁地，蒙织去送午饭，路上看见一个老道人闭着眼睛，盘腿坐在一块石头上。当她走近时，老道人忽然睁开眼睛说：“阿嫂，我三天没有吃饭了，把你的饭给我一点吧！”她见老道人可怜，就把午饭送给了他；自己又回家重做。当她重新做好上山时，老道人又说了：“好心的阿嫂，你给我的饭不够吃，再给我一点吧！”她想，

Xinuluo led many heroic battles and fought courageously against the enemy, and thus was deeply respected and loved by all the soldiers of the tribe. After more than a year of war, Xinuluo assisted Zhanglejinqiu in defeating the Mengxizhao tribe and unifying the Mengshe region.

After the war was over, Xinuluo went home with triumphant return. The fellow countrymen opened a field called the Song-Beating Field, so that people could gather here, holding parties and singing songs for him to celebrate for his heroic victory.

It was at this time when a girl named Mengzhi fell in love with him, and Xinuluo was also fond of this beautiful, diligent and kind girl. They became lovers after their acquaintance at the Song-Beating Field, and married soon in the next year. In the third year, they gave birth to a son, whom his grandmother Qianghu named Luocheng.

When Luocheng grew up to around eight years old, Xinuluo often took him to do labour work.

One day, when the father and son were plowing the land up in the mountain, Mengzhi went to send lunch for them. Alongside the path, she found an old Taoist priest sitting on a rock with his legs crossing and eyes closing. When she approached, he suddenly opened his eyes and said, "Dear ma'am, I haven't eaten for three days. Please spare me some food!" Feeling pitiful, she gave the lunch to him and returned

救人要救到底，于是又把午饭送给了他，自己再回家做。她第三次上山时，老道人还没有走。蒙织说：“你老人家是不是还没有吃饱？”道人点点头。蒙织叹口气，又把午饭给了他，自己又回家再做。等她第四次做好饭，送到山上时，太阳已经落山了。细奴逻父子肚子饿，已经解了犁耙，坐在树下歇气。见她才来，问起原因，她就把路上的经过一五一十地说了出来。

细奴逻父子感到很奇怪，就跟她去看，果然看到路旁的一块石头上，一位老道人盘腿而坐。更怪的是，他前面有一条青牛、一只白象，头上盖着五彩云气。

老道人见他们过来就笑着问：“你们需要什么？”

细奴逻忙回答：“我们小户人家，只求神仙保佑我们五谷丰登、六畜兴旺。”

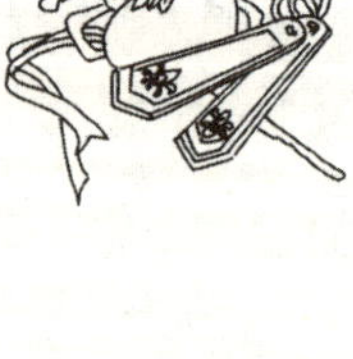

home to cook for more food. Afterwards, as she climbed up the mountain again, she found that the priest was still there who said, "Oh dear, the food was not enough for me. Could you please kindly spare me some more?" She thought that she ought to give whatever help she could offer if needed, so she gave the lunch to him and returned home to prepare again. When the third time she came up the mountain, the priest was still there. She asked him, "Are you still hungry?" The old priest nodded. Mongzhi signed and gave the lunch to him again. By the fourth time she sent lunch to Xinuluo and Luocheng, it was already sunset. As they were so hungry that they had already taken off the plough and rested under a tree. At the sight of her, they asked her the reasons and she told them the story.

Xinuluo and Luocheng felt strange at it, so they followed her to look for the old Taoist priest. Indeed, there was an old priest sitting cross-legged. What was even more mysterious was that a black ox and a white elephant stood in front of him and a ring of colorful halo covered over his head.

As they walked closer, the old priest smiled at them and asked, "What do you need?"

Xinuluo replied hurriedly and humbly, "We are only ordinary family. We wish nothing but good harvest and thriving livestock."

老道人听了，笑着说："你们是好心的人家，会有好报的。"边说边用手中的扇柄在细奴逻的犁把上敲了十三下，然后驾着五彩云飞走了。细奴逻一家再看时，只见大石头上还留着道人的衣痕和牛、象的足迹。这个时候他只感到奇怪，不知道老道人敲的十三下，竟是指明以后南诏国王的代数。

又有一次，蒙舍诏举行祭柱大典。祭柱就是祭祀诸葛亮①立下的白崖铁柱。那天，全蒙舍川的男女老少都赶来参加，细奴逻一家也来了。祭柱活动刚开始，铸在柱顶上的金丝鸟突然飞了起来，"扑哧""扑哧"拍着翅膀，在空中盘旋了三圈，然后落在细奴逻的左臂上。细奴逻十分惊奇，也不去惊动它。这只金丝鸟在他臂上整整停了一天才飞走了。这件事引得整个蒙舍川的人都议论纷纷，说："细奴逻要当王了！"酋长张乐进求知道细奴逻是个能干的人，就想让位给他，但细奴逻硬是不肯，这件事就放下来了。

---

① 译者注：诸葛亮为三国时期蜀汉丞相，是一位足智多谋的政治家、军事家、文学家、书法家、发明家。

"You are kind-hearted people, and you will be repaid with kindness." said the old priest, smiling, after hearing his request. He knocked Xinuluo's plough for 13 times with the handle of his fan while he was talking. Afterwards, he drove on the colorful halo and flew away. When Xinuluo's family looked at this place again, traces of the priest's clothes and footprints of the ox and elephant were still there. They felt odd at that time, without knowing that the 13 knocks meant thirteen generations of kings in the Nanzhao kingdom.

Another time, when the Mengshe tribe held the Column Rituals, which was to sacrifice for the White Cliff Column set by Zhuge Liang①. On that day, everyone of the Mengshe region gathered together to attend this event, including Xinuluo and his family. When the ceremony just started, the golden canary at the top of the column suddenly came alive. It first flew up in the sky, waving its wings, and then landed on the left arm of Xinuluo after circling three times above the air. Xinuluo felt amazed and chose not to disturb it. The canary stood on his arm for an entire day before flying away. Later, there were many discussions in the tribe about this sign, and people all believed that Xinuluo would become a king in the future. After learning Xinuluo's fine characteristics, the chieftain, Zhanglejinqiu decided to abdicate in favor of him. But Xinuluo declined resolutely, so the king had to put it aside.

---

① Translator's note: Zhuge Liang was a prime minister of Shu Han, in the period of Three Kingdoms, who was a statesman, militarist, litterateur, calligrapher and creator with resourcefulness and wisdom.

过了不久，一天中午，细奴逻正在吃饭，忽然有一条青蛇哗哗地梭到他的脚上盘着。过了好一会，青蛇才慢慢地梭走。走的时候，蛇身在地上拖出几条线，组成了“守境术”三个字。后人说，这是神蛇教给他的治国法术。

酋长张乐进求知道这件事以后，更是要让位给细奴逻了，但细奴逻还是不肯。两人相持不下，细奴逻指着一块巨大的石头说：“我们不必争，如果我一剑砍得进这块石头，我就当首领，砍不进，还是你当。”他举起剑砍去，砍进石头三寸①深。细奴逻不好再推辞，就当了蒙舍诏的首领。

流传地区：巍山县
讲述者：郝青龙等
搜集整理者：王丽珠

① 译者注：1 寸=3.3 厘米。

Not long after, Xinuluo was having lunch one day, and all of a sudden, a green snake appeared out of nowhere and coiled around his feet. After a while, the snake slowly glided away, drawing several lines with its body, forming the letters of Shoujingshu, meaning the Art of Governance. Later, the story goes that it was this divine snake that taught him the skill of governing the nation.

After learning it, Zhanglejinqiu was ever more determined to give him the throne. However, Xinuluo still refused to do so. Under such a deadlocked situation, Xinuluo had a proposition, saying, "Let's stop arguing about this. If I can hack the stone with one wave of my sword, I will accept your offer; otherwise, you will still be our chieftain." So he hacked the stone, holding his sword high, and the sword cut three cun① into the stone. Therefore, Xinuluo could not declined anymore and became the leader of Mengshe tribe.

Spreading area: Weishan County

Narrator: Hao Qinglong, etc.

Collector and editor: Wang Lizhu

① Translator's note: 1 cun = 3.33 cm.

阿乍利

阿乍利捉龙卖

现在楚雄州府所在地“鹿城”的彝名叫做“峨碌”，峨是大的意思，碌是龙的意思，即有大龙的地方。据传说，远古的时候，鹿城附近都是汪洋大海。后来出了个了不起的人物，这个人的名字叫董麻乍利，人们尊称他为阿乍利。因为他懂降龙伏虎法，能把水多地方的龙捉去卖给缺水的地方。① 所以凡是有水患的地方都请他去捉龙，凡是干旱无水的地方就请他去卖龙，他就以卖龙为营生，走遍了天南地北。因为龙被他捉得太多了，所以楚雄坝子的水逐渐少了，大海变成了陆地，只剩得一条青龙河。青龙河两岸现出了一些平展展的小坝子，就是现在的楚雄坝子。有一次他捉了很多龙，放在背箩里，边走边卖。走到一个山坡上，他想找点水喝，忽然看见一家小茶店，他就走进去，叫茶店老板烧水泡茶。茶店老板说：“这里干旱无水，水要到半里②以外去挑，现在挑来的水已用完了，无法接待你；如果要酒，酒还可以倒一碗给你喝。”阿乍利喝完酒以后，心想：“没有水怎

① 译者注：在中国神话中，龙掌管雨水。

② 译者注：1 里 = 500 米。

Azhali

Azhali Selling the Catched Dragons

Nowadays, "Lucheng", an important city in Chuxiong Autonomous Prefecture, is called "Elu" in the language of the Yi nationality. To break it down, E means big, and Lu means dragon, so all together it represents a place with huge dragons. According to a legend, there was a vast sea near Lucheng in ancient times. Later, a great man, Dongmazhali, became well-known and was called Azhali by the locals. Being able to subdue dragons and tigers, he sold dragons caught in places with too much water to places that suffered from water shortage.① Therefore, he was invited to catch dragons wherever there was a flood, and to sell dragons wherever there was drought. In the long run, he came to make a living through the sales of dragons and had travelled to a lot of places. Gradually, the sea was reduced into land with the shrinkage of water area near Chuxiong plain because the dragon was over-caught by him. Only the Qinglong River survived the shrinkage, but flat patches emerged

① Translator's note: as Chinese mythology goes, dragon is in charge of rainfall.

么能开茶店!”他叫茶店老板拿个钵来。茶店老板不知道阿乍利要干什么，便顺手把瓦钵拿给他。只见阿乍利提起装龙的背箩一倒，倒出九条小泥鳅(就是九条小龙)，用瓦钵罩好，然后嘱咐茶店老板说：“你需要水的时候，用筷子轻轻敲一下瓦钵，一股筷子粗的水就会从瓦钵下面淌出来。”嘱咐完以后，阿乍利就走了。茶店老板半信半疑，看着阿乍利走远了，才拿一支筷子轻轻敲了一下瓦钵，果然流出筷子粗的清丝丝的一股泉水来。茶店老板高兴极了赶快向阿乍利走的方向顶礼膜拜：“谢谢仙人恩赐，谢谢仙人恩赐!”有了水，这个小茶店便兴旺了起来。可是，过了段时间，贪心的茶店老板认为水只有筷子粗，不满足，就用锄把去敲，不小心就把瓦钵敲烂了，淌成一条大河。小茶店变成了九龙店(一说是水淌铺)。

on either bank of it, which is the Chuxiong plain now. Once, he caught many dragons, so he put them in the basket on his back and peddled along the way. Walking to a hillside, he felt like drinking some water when a small tea shop came into his view. He entered the shop, asking the owner to make tea for him. The owner replied, "You know, it's dry without any rain here, and we have to fetch water from places half a li① away, and worse still, we have used up all the water available. So, we can't make tea for you. But we can give you a bowl of wine, if you like." After drinking the wine, Azhali thought, "How can he run a tea shop without water!" He asked the tea shop owner to bring a pottery bowl. The owner, not knowing what Azhali was going to do, gave him a bowl. Then Azhali lifted up the basket and nine small loaches (i. e., nine small dragons) came out of it. Having covered them with the bowl, he told the shopkeeper, "When you need water, tap the bowl with chopsticks, and then a stream of water as thick as chopstick will flow out." Then Azhali left, but the tea shop owner was dubious about the magic, so he tried himself after Azhali went far away. It turned out that a thin stream of spring water really came out. He was so excited that he hurriedly bowed in worship in the direction where Azhali left, adding "Thank you for this gracious and magic gift! Thank you for this gracious and magic gift!" Without worries of water supply, the business of this small tea shop boomed. However, after some time, the greedy tea shop owner wanted something more than the chopstick-thick water flow, so he tapped the bowl with a hoe, only to leave the bowl broken. As a result, the original water flow evolved into a wide river and the small tea shop became a nine-dragon shop or water-flowing shop.

---

① Translator's note: 1 li = 500 m.

阿乍利一路卖龙，到了苍山脚下，他又叫喊着："卖龙啰，缺水的地方来买龙啰!"人们走过来一看，都说："小小泥鳅，算什么龙!"他叫了几天几夜，不但没有人，反而听到人家说，他把泥鳅当龙卖，骗人。阿乍利一气之下，把背箩里的龙全部倒在苍山脚下，这些龙都爬上了苍山。于是苍山上冒出了九十九股水，从苍山上流下的水汇成了现在的洱海。从这以后，阿乍利再也不干卖龙的营生了。

阿乍利为什么会降龙？这个本事是哪里学来的？话得从头说起。

原来阿乍利有一个姐姐，在阿乍利年幼时就被嫁到很远的地方。他长大成年后，很想念姐姐，就背上许多干粮，按老人们指点的方向去找姐姐。他走呀走，不知翻过了多少山，渡过了多少河，干粮吃完了吃野果，渴了喝山泉水，终于找到了姐姐。可是，到了这时他才知道，他姐姐嫁给了狗头国里的人。这里的人长得奇怪，狗头，人身，还长着狗尾巴。狗头国里最大的禁忌是外来人不能耻笑他们，若耻笑他们，就会被咬死。阿乍利刚到姐姐家时，他姐姐就告诉他这些禁忌，并特别叮嘱他说："吃完饭你姐夫就用尾巴来扫桌子，你看了千万不能笑。"开始几天，阿乍利也比较注意，没有什么事情。住的日子长了，他就习以为常了。突然有一天吃完饭，姐姐收了碗以后，狗头姐夫又用尾巴来扫桌子，左扫右扫，扫来扫去，非常认真。阿乍利忍不住扑哧一声笑了出来，狗头姐夫不高兴地走出去了。姐姐知道大祸要临头，拿了一些干粮给弟弟，叫他赶快逃跑。姐姐又给他一万支筷子，一罐香油，告诉他："如狗兵狗将来追你，你就用筷子蘸香油丢在路上，那些狗兵狗将忙着去舔香油，你就赶快跑；筷子丢完了还跑不脱，你就爬上大树，抓把米含在嘴里。"阿乍利按姐姐的嘱咐出门就跑。没跑多远，果然狗头

Azhali peddled dragons all the way to the foot of the Cang Mountain, still shouting, "Dragons on sale. No water? Come and buy some dragons!" People came over and said, "Look, they are just little loaches! These can be called dragons?" After several days and nights, still nobody came to buy and people even thought that he was a cheater selling loaches as dragons. Azhali was so irritated that he released all the dragons in his basket on the foot of the Cang Mountain, which all climbed up the mountain. Later, ninety-nine streams of water flew down, becoming the current Erhai Lake. From then on, Azhali no longer sold dragons as a living.

But why can Azhali control dragons? Where did he learn this skill? Well, here is how the story goes.

Azhali had a sister who was married far away when Azhali was young. When he grew up, he missed his sister very much. He prepared food and set out to find her in the direction given by the old people. He walked on and on, not knowing how many mountains and rivers he had crossed. He ate wild fruits after his prepared food ran out and drank spring water when he got thirsty. Finally, he met his sister. However, he found that his sister married a man in Dog-head Kingdom, where locals looked strange with dog heads, human bodies and long dog tails. The biggest taboo here was that outsiders who laughed at them would be bitten to death. Azhali's sister told him this taboos upon his arrival, and specifically exhorted him, "Do not laugh at your brother-in-law if he uses his tail to sweep the table after a meal." In the first several days, he was prudent, so nothing happened. Gradually, he even became used to living there. Suddenly one day after dinner, while his sister was putting away dishes, the dog-head brother-in-law was sweeping the table again with his tail carefully from left to right, which amused Azhali, so he couldn't help laughing. Then, his brother-in-law went out, unhappy.

姐夫领着狗兵狗将来追他。阿乍利用筷子蘸香油丢在路上，让狗将去舔。狗舔完了筷子又继续追来。筷子丢完了，阿乍利把油罐敲烂丢在路上，仍无济于事，狗兵狗将舔舔油罐上的香油又继续追。阿乍利想起姐姐的话，只得迅速爬上树，狗兵狗将们就在树下围守。时值中午，太阳当空，阿乍利在树上急，狗兵狗将们在树下晒，晒得他们舌头长伸。阿乍利想起姐姐的嘱咐，张开嘴，仰起头，抓米含在嘴里。狗头姐夫看见阿乍利张着嘴，里面又有蛆一样的东西，以为阿乍利死了，就对他的狗兵狗将们说："你们看阿乍利已经死了，嘴里都生蛆了，我们回去吧！"于是狗兵们一声吆喝，前呼后拥地回去了。阿乍利解了围，慢慢梭下树，准备上路。正在这时，忽然看见狗头姐夫的道袍丢失在路边。阿乍利穿起这件道袍，很快便回到了青龙河边。到家后，他无意中发现道袍里有一本天书，就打开读了起来，越读越有兴趣，因为里面写的是降龙伏虎法。阿乍利捉龙卖的本领就是这样学到的。

Knowing that his brother was about to be in trouble, his sister prepared him some food and told him to flee. She also gave him 10,000 chopsticks and a bottle of sesame oil, telling him, "If the dog soldiers chase you in the future, you can drop chopsticks dipped with sesame oil along the way. Those dog soldiers will be busy licking the sesame oil and you can run away; If you can't escape, you should climb up trees and put a handful of rice in your mouth." Azhali fled as her sister told him. Soon, his brother-in-law did lead the dog army to chase after him. Azhali tossed chopsticks with sesame oil on the road, so that the dogs would lick it. After licking all the chopsticks, the army continued to chase. Now Azhali had to break up the oil bottle into pieces before throwing them on the road, but all in vain. So he had to climb up a tree quickly as told by his sister. The dog soldiers circled under the tree in guard, until it was noon, when the sun was burning. Azhali was anxious on the tree, while the dog soldiers were stretching out their tongues for cooling in the parching sun. Suddenly, his sister's instructions kicked in. Raising his head, he opened the mouth and grabbed rice to stuff in it. Seeing that there were something like maggots in Azhali's opened mouth, the dog-head brother-in-law thought that he was dead and said to his soldiers, "Can't you see? Azhali is dead. There are maggots in his mouth. Hey, let's go back!" Finally, they went back in a chorus of yelling. Azhali, now out of trouble, slowly came down from the tree. He was about to continue his journey when he suddenly saw his brother-in-law's robe left by the road. Azhali put it on, and soon reached the Qinglong River. When he got home, he accidentally found a heavenly book in the robe and started to read it. The more he read it, the more arresting he found it became, because the book was about how to tame dragons and tigers. This is the end of the whole story of how Azhali learned this skill.

阿乍利使鬼

阿乍利因为得到他姐夫道袍里的天书，不仅会降龙，并且还会使鬼。后来，阿乍利来到荷花村落脚。这村子缺水，人们商量去挑一个坝塘，积点水到栽秧时候用。但是坝塘附近有很多鬼，人们白天去挑坝，晚上鬼们又把土填回去。村里的人没有办法，只有请阿乍利去解决。阿乍利知道是鬼在捣乱，他就告诉人们说："你们不要挑了，我一个晚上就帮你们挑好。"那天晚上，阿乍利就召集众鬼夜间去挑坝，挑到下半夜，阿乍利想，应该煮点饭去给鬼们吃。他就叫他老伴煮饭挑去，并嘱咐挑去摆着就行了，不要说话。阿乍利的老伴真的煮了饭挑去了，她把饭挑去摆在那里，等了好久也没有人来吃。她等得不耐烦了，就说了一句："鬼都不见一个，哪个来吃！"就把饭挑回来了。这时坝塘中还有一个山包没有挑完，鬼们听见阿乍利的老伴骂，于是提起脚来都走了。老伴回来时，阿乍利问道："怎么就挑回来了？"老伴说："鬼都不见一个，挑给哪个吃！"阿乍利说："叫你莫说话，你怎么要多嘴多舌，今晚这个坝挑不好了。"第二天早上，阿乍利到坝上去一看，还剩一个鸭嘴形的山包没挑完。所以荷花村的那个坝塘一直到现在还留下了一个鸭嘴形的小山包，大家

Azhali in Command of Ghosts

Thanks to the book in his brother-in-law's robe, Azhali could not only subdue dragons, but also control ghosts. Later, Azhali came to the Lotus Village as a stopover where villagers planned to dig a pond to hold some water in advance for planting rice due to water scarcity in the local area. But there were many ghosts nearby, who would refill the pond dug by the villagers during the day with soil at night. They had no choice but to ask Azhali to solve it. He knew that the ghosts were making trouble, so he told the villagers, "You can stop digging and I'll fix it for you in one night." That night, Azhali called on all the ghosts to dig. In the second half of the night, Azhali thought, he should cook some food for these laborers. He asked his wife to prepare some food, but instructed her not to say anything when she sent it. She did as told, but didn't see anyone come to eat after a long time. Impatiently, she complained, "There is not even a ghost here, not to mention any trace of human. Who on earth will eat it!" She took the meal back home. At the time, there was still a hillock that had not been leveled and dug. On hearing her complaint, the ghosts all walked away. When she came back, Azhali asked, "Why do you bring it back?" She said, "There was not even a ghost there, not to mention any trace of human. Who on earth would eat it!" Azhali said, "I've told you not to say anything! Why not keep silent? Probably the work won't be finished tonight." The next morning, Azhali went to have a look, finding that there was a duck-billed hillock left. Therefore,

都称它为玉鸭嘴。下雨以后，这个坝塘满满地积了一塘水，阿乍利站在坝埂上，自言自语地说：“坝塘有了水，可惜没有田，这坝塘下面有几片田就好了。”那些鬼听了阿乍利的话，以为只有坝塘不好玩，既有坝塘又有田才好玩，便用一个晚上的时间开垦出好多田。阿乍利知道那些鬼们又去给他开田去了，便叫他老伴煮些饭送给鬼们吃。可是老伴不肯，说：“要送你自己去送，我才不耐烦呢。”阿乍利想，如果他自己去送饭，那些鬼怕他，都要吓跑掉，干脆就不送了。第二天，阿乍利到坝塘下边一看，已开出了好几片平平整整的田。他去找黄牛坝的两条小黄牛(是两条黄龙变的)，请小黄牛为他犁田耙田。晚上，他想连夜去放田水，可是走过去一看，田里都是些碎石块和碎瓦片。他知道那些鬼又在捣乱。原来那些鬼认为他们为阿乍利挑了坝、开了田，而一顿饭都不得享受，连闻闻都办不到，所以故意搬些石头在田里让他种不成。阿乍利若无其事地站在田头自言自语说：“一个石头三两油，一泡狗屎烂田头。”说完哈哈大笑而去。他的话又

the pond in Lotus Village had a small hillock in the shape of duck bill, which everyone called it the Jade Duck Bill. After rain, this dam pond would be filled with water. Azhali stood on the ridge of the pond, talking to himself, "There is water in the pond, but no field around. It would be better if there is." On hearing this, those ghosts thought it's not fun to just have the pond; instead, having both pond and field would be more amusing. So they cultivated many lands in one night. Azhali knew what the ghosts were going to do and asked his wife to cook some rice for them to eat. But his wife refused and said, "Go there yourself! I'm fed up with it." Azhali calculated that if he himself brought the meal there, those ghosts would be scared away. So he simply didn't go. The next day, Azhali went to the pond and found that several flat fields had been developed. Then he brought two little dragon-turned oxen from the Huangniuba village to plow the fields for him. At night, he wanted to draw water to the fields, but as he walked closer, he found that the fields were covered with gravels and broken tiles. He knew that it must have been the ghosts that played the tricks. They thought that they had built a pond and opened a field for Azhali, but they had not been rewarded with any food, not even the smell. So they intentionally carried some stones into the field so that Azhali could not grow anything in the field. Azhali stood casually in front of the land and said to himself, "A stone produces three-liang-oil and a pile of dog shit gets many fields rotten away." Then he left, laughing. His words were heard again by the ghosts who discussed, "If a stone produces three liang of oils, those many stones we put in the field can produce a huge sum. That means

被那些鬼听见了。鬼们商量说："一个石头三两油，我们丢了这么多石头在田里，不知有多少油，白把他的田弄肥了。一泡狗屎烂田头，我们把石头搬掉，换成狗屎把他的田咬烂掉，他就种不成谷子了。"那些鬼又把石头搬掉，拾来很多狗屎放在田里。后来阿乍利的田比其他家的田都肥。那些鬼看到为阿乍利耕田的两条黄牛是两条龙，就再也不敢来捣乱了。

阿乍利之死

由于楚雄的龙被阿乍利捉得多了，水少了，露出大块的土地可供人们开田种地，所以阿乍利也以盘田为生，不再捉龙卖了。可是黄牛坝那两条小黄牛经常出来挑架，力气再大的壮汉也劝不开，而阿乍利穿着道袍去中间一隔就劝开了。因为两条黄牛是两条黄龙变的，只有阿乍利才降得住，所以只要发现小黄牛挑架，人们都请阿乍利去劝架。年长日久，他那件道袍又脏又烂，他的老伴好心把他的道袍拿去用热水

his field will become fertile for free! But if a pile of dog shit can rot many fields, we can replace the stones with dog crap to destroy his field so that he can't grow the millet." Therefore, the ghosts removed the stones and put a lot of shit in the field. But later, his field, instead of getting rotten, was more fertile than that of other families; that is because two dragon-turned oxen had been plowing for Azhali. Knowing this, those spirits no long dared to mess things up here.

The Death of Azhali

As dragons in Chuxiong was caught heavily by Azhali, water became scarce. Instead, there were more patches of land for cultivation and planting. Therefore, Azhali now made a living by cultivating land rather than selling dragons. The two small oxen often fought with each other and even a strong man was unable to stop their fighting. But the oxen would stop fighting when Azhali stood near them in a robe. That is because the two oxen were originally two yellow dragons, which would only be controlled by Azhali. So whenever the two oxen started to fight, people would send for Azhali for help. Day in and day out, his robe turned dirty and worn-out. His kind wife took his robe for a washing in hot water, and as a result, the heavenly book in the robe was also soaked. Once, he was asked to stop the two little oxen from fighting. He hurriedly put on the robe and went there to do his

泡洗，结果把天书也洗烂了。有一次，黄牛坝的两条小黄牛又在挑架，乡亲们又来喊他去劝架。他急忙穿上道袍去劝架，可是这一次不灵了，因为他道袍里的天书已经洗烂，所以不仅没有劝开牛，反而被牛挤死了。这位捉龙卖的好汉，就这样结束了他的一生。

流传地区：楚雄市
讲述者：王德茂
收集整理者：李世忠

job as usual. But this time, it didn't work at all, as the book in his robe had been ruined through washing. Consequently, Azhali was gored to death by the two oxen, so he was unable to stop the fight. The man who caught and sold dragons ended up his life in this way.

Spreading area: Chuxiong City
Narrator: Wang Demao
Collector and editor: Li Shizhong

我们的大地

Our Land

火把节的传说

阿细①人的火把节

农历六月二十四日，是阿细人民的传统节日——火把节。每年到了这一天，远远近近的青年，到摔跤场上比武，姑娘们来摔跤场上跳月②，老人和小孩也纷纷到跤场上看摔跤。人声、炮声、三弦声……闹得整个西山③天覆地翻。二十五日晚上，青年小伙子高举着明亮的火把，从村东头游了

---

① 阿细：彝族的一个支系，主要居住在云南省弥勒市西山区。
② 跳月：一种热情豪放的舞蹈，又叫“阿细跳月”。
③ 西山：指弥勒市西山区，是阿细人民的聚居区。

Legends of the Torch Festival

The Torch Festival of the Axi[①] People

June 24th of the lunar calendar is the Axi people's traditional Torch Festival. Every year on this day, young people from far and near come to the wrestling field to compete in martial arts; girls come here to dance Tiaoyue[②]; the elderly and children also come to watch the match. At that time, voices of people, sound of firework and music played by sanxian instruments intertwine with each other lively and can be heard in the entire Xishan[③] region. On the night of June 25th, young men, holding their flaming torches high, walk in line from the east side of the village, and girls, holding their flaming torches as well, walk in

---

① Axi: a branch of the Yi Ethnic Group, who mainly lives in the Xishan Region of Mile County in Yunnan Province.

② Tiaoyue: an enthusiastic and vigorous dance, also called Axi Tiaoyue.

③ Xishan: the Xishan Reigon in the Mile County, where most Axi people live.

过来；姑娘们也举起火炬由村南头游过去，当两条火龙游到公房①门前的时候，广场上火龙飞舞，时而成对，时而两对并列，你出我进，好像火龙在翻腾。老年人也点燃火把，在屋内绕来绕去，驱魔除灾，熊熊火炬，户户通明，一派奇观。

这个传统节日，究竟怎么来的呢？

相传，在那召②那个时代，我们的祖先还住在拖登来若③。这里天气暖和，古木参天，一年四季都有香花开放，都有鸟儿歌唱，森林里有鹿、麂子和箐鸡，江河中有鱼、虾和蛙。住在这里的人，不愁吃，不愁穿，老人能活九十九岁，小孩一生下来就有十来斤。

---

① 公房：在中华人民共和国成立前青年男女娱乐游戏的地方，每个村子都有一两个这样的房子。

② 那召：阿细语音译，是一个年号，是否南诏有待考证。

③ 拖登来若：传说中的地名，阿细语音译，据传在金沙江畔。

line from the west side. When the two dragon-like lines meet in front of Gongfang①, it's like two fire dragons dancing in the square, sometimes in pairs, sometimes in parallel, going forward and backward in turn. The elderly also ignite torches and walk around indoor, in the hope of exorcising evil spirits and disaster. It's a wonder to see the flaming torches and luminous houses during the Torch Festival.

Do you know how this traditional festival began?

It is said that this festival began in the era of Nazhao②, when our ancestors lived in Tuodenglairuo③. They lived in a place with warm weather and towering trees, where there were blooming flowers every season and singing birds every day, running deer, muntjacs and wild chicken in forests and swimming fish, shrimp and frogs in rivers. At that time, our ancestors lived comfortably without worries of food or clothing. The elderly could live to be ninety-nine years old and infants were born with healthy and strong bodies.

---

① Gongfang: a house for young men and women to have entertainment before the founding of the People's Republic of China. There were one or two such houses in every village.

② Nazhao: the transliteration of the Axi Language, a reign title. Whether it is Nanzhao remains to be verified.

③ Tuodenglairuo: the name of place in legend, the transliteration of the Axi Language. It's said to be by the side of the Jinsha River.

离这儿很远很远的地方，有个名叫那迢迢的首领，他们家有钱有势，从外地来做官的人都要先求他。他们家的奴隶，比天上的星星还要多；他们家的牛羊，像地上的草，数都数不清；他们家的田地，骑上马跑上十天半月也没法子跑到边。可是他还不满足，想把奴隶一个接一个地排列起来，一直排到京都和皇帝比个高低。有一天，他叫家人拿来登记奴隶的簿子，按上面的数字，一个挨一个地排了一下，只排到湖面地界就没有了，要排到京都还差好大一截。他很失望，后来听说四川成都人很多，他的口水就淌下一尺来长，想把那里的人抢来当奴隶。于是他把心腹们都找来，商量到成都去抢奴隶的办法。有的说，从贵州去，由沙衣①回来，沿路老老小小裹在一起抢来。有的讲，从沙衣去，由贵州回来，只抓壮实的，不要老太婆和小孩。人多话多，争论不下。那迢迢想：我要的是个数，只要人头在，脚跛眼瞎，老人，小孩都要。这样，他叫管家带领一队人马从贵州去成都，把男的、女的、老的、小的，只要是活人，都统统抢来当奴隶。管家不敢怠慢，敲锣打鼓，打起黑旗，带上人马，浩浩荡荡地出发了。

① 沙衣：阿细语音译，传说中的江河名称，据传指金沙江。现在阿细语中无“金沙江”这个词。

In a place far away from Tuodenglairuo, a chief called Natiaotiao was affluent and powerful. Whoever came to seek employment must beg him for recommendation firstly. His slaves were more numerous than stars; his cattle and sheep were as countless as grasses; his farmland was so large that horses could not run away in half a month. But he was too greedy to be satisfied. He hoped that if his slaves stood in lines, the line would extend from his house to the capital, so that he could compete his wealth with the emperor's. One day, he asked slaves to stand in line and listed them one by one, but the line only stopped by a lake nearby, far away from the capital. The chief was extremely disappointed. Later, he learned that there were many people living in Chengdu City of Sichuan Province. Mouth-watering, the greedy chief decided to grab people there as his slaves. So he summoned his subordinates to discuss ways of grabbing slaves. Some proposed grabbing young and old all the way from Guizhou to Shayi①; while others suggested grabbing only the strong, leaving the old and little ones behind, from Shayi to Guizhou. Many mouths were talking but no decision was made. The chief Natiaotiao thought quietly, "I only care about the number. With enough slaves to list, who cares whether they are lame or blind." Then he settled his mind. He asked his housekeeper to lead a group of subordinates from Guizhou to Chengdu, grabbing whoever was alive to be his slaves. The housekeeper led a team and set off right away, holding black flags and beating drums and gongs.

---

① Shayi: the transliteration of the Axi Language. The name of a river in legend. It is said to be the Jinsha River. There is no word of "Jinsha River" in the Axi Language today.

五月端阳那天，沙衣附近各村各寨的人都来沙衣边玩。男的跳进江里摸鱼，女的在江边洗衣服，娃娃们沿着江边跑着玩，老头子坐在树荫下聊天，熙熙攘攘，把沙衣边闹得个底朝天。正玩得起劲的时候，有个小伙子急急忙忙跑来说："那边来了好多人，前面黑旗飘飘，后面锣声阵阵，中间的人一个拉一个，两边的人举着长杆子。"有经验的老人听了着急地说："不好！这一定是抢人的人来了，快跑！"刹那间，江边上的热闹景象不见了，妇女们跑回家去，拿木杆顶住门悄悄地躲在里面，连气都不敢喘。小伙子没进村，都躲在村外了。

长长的队伍越来越近，看得越来越清楚了。原来两边是拿着长矛的兵丁，中间是用绳子拴着的奴隶，男的拴在左手，女的拴在右手，两人一对拴在一起。队伍来到村边，少数兵丁留下看守奴隶，大部分窜进村里，乒乒乓乓，闹得鸡犬不宁，把村子里的男人、女人、老人和小孩一个不剩地抓走了。躲在村外的小伙子实在忍不住了，就跑出来跟他们讲。可是，人家有刀枪，有长矛，人多势众，鸡蛋碰石头，只有自己倒霉，小伙子们也全部被抓。兵丁拿绳子把这些新抓来的奴隶的手拴起来和原来抓的奴隶一起带走了。据说，现在阿细人每到五月端阳这天就要用黑线或花线拴在手上，男的拴左手，女的拴右手，据说就是这样来的，是为了怀念当初被抓来当奴隶的祖先。

On the day of Duanyang in May, villagers around Shayi all gathered there. Men jumped into river to catch fish; women washed clothes by the riverside; children ran along river happily; elderly men chatted under trees. The entire Shayi was lively with crowded people and sound of loud laughter. As everyone was enjoying the time, a young lad ran over in a hurry and said, "I saw many people coming, with black flags and beating drums. People on each side hold poles, and people who walked between are tied up." Some experienced elders said anxiously, "They must come here to grab people as slaves! Everyone just run away!" All of a sudden, the lively scene by the the riverside disappeared. Women ran back home, placing poles and sticks against doors, hiding indoor breathlessly and young men all ran out and hid outside the village.

As the long group walked closer, people could observe them more clearly. They saw soldiers with lances walking on each side, with the caught slaves tied in between. Left wrists of male slaves were tied to the right wrists of female slaves, two in pairs. As soon as they arrived, the majority of soldiers broke into the village, leaving a small number to guard the slaves. They turned the village upside down, catching everyone in sight. Young men hidden outside couldn't stand it anymore, so they jumped out to negotiate with soldiers and were caught right away with no weapon. Newly caught slaves were tied up with former ones. So it's said that on the day of Duanyang in May today, Axi people all fasten black and colorful strings on their wrists, men on the left hand and women on the right, to memorize their ancestors who were caught as slaves in this event.

抢来的奴隶最后都被赶到了冷衣①边。那迢迢见抓来了这么多的奴隶，喜欢得三天三夜合不上嘴，睡不着觉，满以为这么多的人可以排到京都去了，殊不知没排出湖南又没人了。这时，有个心腹向那迢迢说：“大老爷，你这样做没有用啊！你把奴隶排到京都，皇上也不会赏你钱，不如把奴隶卖了，凑上些钱，建一个塔，把你的名字刻在上面，让后代人知道你那迢迢有多少庄子，多少奴隶，多少牛羊。”那迢迢一听，心里像放进一块冰糖，便想在冷衣边建一座很高很高的塔。于是，他叫人把老头子、小孩、妇女统统拉到昆明城里去卖掉，用卖来的钱买砖、买瓦、买石头，留下的青壮年，被赶到工地上去干活。

① 冷衣：阿细语音译，据传指洱海。

Those slaves were taken to Lengyi①. Seeing so many slaves, Natiaotiao was too happy to sleep. He thought that this time his slaves could line up all the way to the capital, but it turned out that the line ended by the time it reached Hunan. Then, a henchman said to the chief, "My lord, I think it's useless to care about how long the line can be, for the emperor won't give you any prize for that. How about selling them to make some money, with which you can build a tower and engrave your name on it, so that people in later generations will know how many villages, slaves, cows and sheep you have." Natiaotiao felt sweet inside at this brilliant idea, like eating a spoon of honey. So he made up his mind to build a tall tower in Lengyi. The old, weak and female slaves in Kunming were sold to buy bricks, tiles and stones, while the strong young slaves were left to do the labour work of building the tower.

---

① Lengyi: the transliteration of the Axi Language. It is said to be Erhai.

塔要修几十丈高，用的砖瓦千千万，一块石头好几百吨重，都要用两只手来搬，奴隶们累死累活，也不知道死了多少。可那迢迢一点也不在乎，死了一个，添上两人，不干活就打，谁歇下就揍，逼得奴隶们实在活不下去。不知哪个人说了一声："那迢迢是人，我们也是人，为什么要逼我们这样干？我们不干了，伙计们，跑啊！"大家早就不愿意干了，听了这句话，工地上立刻像炸了锅一样，奴隶们四处奔逃，一会儿就跑了许多人。监工眼睁睁看着没有办法，只好禀报那迢迢。那迢迢听说奴隶暴动，就派兵来镇压。一夜之间抓回来两三千奴隶。第二天，那迢迢站在一个高高的台子上，大声地对着奴隶们说："你们是我的奴隶，活着是我的人，死了也是我的鬼。我要你们今天死，你们就不能活到明天。我要吃你们的心，你们也得高高兴兴地给我送来。现在我要你们修塔，你们得老老实实给我干活。今天抓来的先杀五百，剩下的关在牢里，等建好塔再杀了祭神。谁想死就逃，谁要活就乖乖地干活。"那迢迢的话没有吓住奴隶，却在奴隶们心中种下了更深的仇恨，大家在下面悄悄地议论要跟那迢迢大干一场。有的说："跑也是死，不跑也是死，得有个法子呀！"有的讲："干脆跟那迢迢拼了！"大家你一言我一语，想不出合适的办法，于是一齐去找阿真。

The tower was extremely high, which used thousands of tiles and bricks. A single stone weighted several hundred tons, which were all carried by slaves with their bare hands, leading to numerous deaths. But Natiaotiao did not care about it. When he saw one died, he would sent two more to continue the work. Also, anyone who dared to take a rest would be whipped. Finally, slaves could not stand it anymore. One of them said, "We are all living people like Natiaotiao. How can he force us in this way? We won't work for him anymore. Guys! Let's escape!" All the slaves who had long been unwilling to work answered the call right away and escaped. Suddenly the place was out of control like boiled water jumping out of a kettle. Natiaotiao's subordinates had no way but reported to him. Upon hearing it, Natiaotiao sent his army to suppress the slaves immediately; thousands of them were caught overnight. The next day, he spoke to slaves loudly from a high stage, "You are all my slaves whether you are alive or dead. If I want you to die today, you will not live to tomorrow. If I want to eat your heart, you have to send it to me with a smile. Now I require you to build a tower, so just do it as I told. For slaves I've caught back today, five hundred of them will be killed, and the rest will be imprisoned at first. When the tower is built, they will be killed to sacrifice to deities. If you want to die, just try to run away again; if you want to live, honestly do your work." However, instead of frightening the slaves, these words planted seeds of greater hatred. They discussed secretly to prepare a fight against Natiaotiao. One of them said, "We are dead if we escape or stay. What's the difference? We need to come up with an idea to survive!" Another one proposed, "Just rise up to kill Natiaotiao!" Everyone spoke but no idea won, so they went to ask Azhen.

阿真心肠好、办法多，他说的话，没有一个不听，他做的事，没有一个不佩服。这天奴隶们都来求他想办法，要他领大伙去跟那迢迢斗。阿真说："鸟要合群，人要齐心，只要大家心齐，那就好办了。斗一定要斗，关在牢里的人，也一定要救出来，不过我们也得准备准备，不能眼睁睁地去送死。大家先准备，哪天动手，到时候告诉大家。"听了阿真的话，奴隶们暗暗地做着准备。

时间一天天地过去，等准备停当的时候，已经到六月二十三日了。早上，阿真告诉大家："现在就去打那迢迢，把关着的弟兄救出来。"阿真一发话，奴隶们像河堤崩了似的，拿棍棒，捡石块，提镰刀，扛锄头，成群结队往那迢迢家冲去。那迢迢看了，心惊胆战，急忙派兵镇守，同时叫羊倌把羊群从圈里赶上山去，免得被奴隶们抢走。

Azhen was a kind and clever man. Whatever words he said, everyone followed; whatever he did, everyone praised it. When slaves came to ask Azhen to lead them to fight against Natiaotiao, Azhen said, "Birds should be in groups, and people should be united. Only in this way, can we ensure success. Of course, we will fight and rescue those in prison, but we need to prepare well. Otherwise, we are going to die for nothing. So start preparation from today, and I will inform you when to take action." Therefore, slaves all went back and prepared for fights secretly.

Time flied. Everyone finally got well-prepared on the date of 23rd June. In this morning, Azhen informed them, "It's time to fight against Natiaotiao and rescue our friends!" As soon as the call was given, all the slaves with sticks, rocks, sickles or hoes as weapons ran in groups towards Natiaotiao's house. Natiaotiao was scared when he saw it, so he immediately dispatched soldiers for defence, and ordered shepherd to herd goats to the mountain, in case they would be grabbed by slaves.

兵丁有刀枪，奴隶赤手空拳，攻了一天也没有攻进那迢迢的家。聪明的阿真，看见那迢迢把羊群赶到山上去了，赶快派人到山上把羊群圈进石窝里，让它们饿着。二十四日傍晚，阿真让人在每只羊的角上捆上一束火把。等天黑尽了，他叫大家点燃羊角上的火把，让羊走在前面，奴隶们捧着火炬跟在羊群后头。这群羊本来就饿慌了，再加上角上点着火，便一个挨着一个拼命地向那迢迢家跑去。兵丁见那么多的火光，分不清羊和人，乱砍乱射。不一会，羊倒了一地。那迢迢见了心疼起来，叫兵丁们不要砍，不要射，先让羊群进去。阿真乘机带着奴隶跟着羊群冲进那迢迢家，用火烧死了那迢迢，救出了被抓的奴隶。那迢迢的家也被熊熊的大火吞没了。

天亮了，太阳出来了，阿真和奴隶们聚集在冷衣边上。这时冷衣边上蝴蝶飞舞，冷衣里鱼儿在跳跃，奴隶们弹起三弦，吹起笛子，尽情地唱歌跳舞，跳得太阳落西坡，唱得月儿从东来。

With full preparation, slaves still could not break into Natiaotiao's house after a day's fight, as soldiers had swords and spears, but they only had bare hands. At that moment, the clever Azhen saw that goats were herded to the mountain, so he asked some slaves to starve goats in a cave. On the night of 24th June, Azhen told people to tie torches on the horn of goats. When the sky was in deep darkness, he ignited those torches and herded goats to Natiaotiao's house, followed by slaves holding torches. Those starving goats were frightened by fire, so they dashed to Natiaotiao's house. When soldiers saw so many torches, they just shot and killed randomly without being able to distinguish slaves and goats. After a while, many goats fell down. Natiaotiao was disheartened to see it, so he ordered soldiers to cease shooting and allowed goats to come into the house first. Taking this chance, Azhen led slaves broke into his house together with goats and burned him to death. Afterwards, they rescued all the slaves in prison and left Natiaotiao's house swallowed by fire.

When the day broke and the sun rose, Azhen and other slaves gathered together by the side of Lengyi, where butterflies danced in sky, fish jumped in water and slaves played sanxian instruments. They danced and sang to their hearts' content until sunset, until the moon came out.

从那以后，每年农历六月二十四日，各村各寨杀猪宰牛纪念这个日子。二十五日晚上捧着火把游行，并且把端阳那天拴上的黑线或花线剪断丢进火里烧掉。阿细人把六月二十四这天叫做“火把节”。

搜集整理者：昭乌初扎

撒尼[①]人的火把节

在彝族撒尼人居住的圭山二十四寨里，流传着这样一个传说：

相传，很古很古的时候，大地上的人过着穿树叶、吃野果的生活。天上有位阿番神，看到人们生活太凄惨，于是背着大王，偷偷地推开大门，把天上的五谷籽种撒到地上。

人们得到了五谷籽种，但不会耕耘、栽种。人们没办法，就去请勤劳的蜜蜂教人们怎样耕耘，怎样栽种，怎样收打粮食，怎样绩麻做衣服。由于籽种来自天上，得到神力的帮助，长出的庄稼茎秆粗，籽粒饱满。每到扬花季节，远远看去，就像成群的绵羊，白花花的，铺满了山坡，盖满了平坝。花谢结籽出穗，一吊吊的谷穗，就像松毛扭成节。到了收打时节，打场上，一对对连枷舞双蝶，一堆堆粮食装进仓。

① 撒尼：彝族的一个支系。

Since then, on 24th June every year, villagers slaughter pigs and cattle for celebration. On the night of 25th June, people parade with torches, and cut off and burn the tied black and colorful strings. Therefore, 24th June is called the Torch Festival by the Axi people.

Collector and editor: Zhaowuchuzha

The Torch Festival of the Sani① People

There was a story told the by the Sani people in twenty-four stockaded villages of the Gui Mountain.

It was said that long time ago, people wore leaves and ate wild fruits for survival. A deity called Apan sympathized with the miserable life that people lived, so he threw seeds of five grains to earth secretly behind the Emperor of Heaven.

However, people had no idea how to plow fields and plant seeds. So they went to ask the hardworking bees, which taught them how to plow fields, plant seeds, harvest grains and used hempen threads to weave clothes. As their seeds came from the heaven with deities' power, grains they grew were all bountiful and strong. When it came to the season of flowering, fields were all white through, like groups of sheep crowding the entire slope and dam. When flowers faded and bore seeds, their ears were like twisted pine leaves. When it came to the season of harvest, people's flails were moved as butterflies, and tons of grains were loaded into granaries.

---

① Sani: a branch of the Yi Ethnic Group.

从此以后，人们过上了丰衣足食的生活。

这事，后来被天王知道了，眼看人间的生活就要超过天上。他一怒之下，招来大力士神，命他到人间，把人们种的庄稼全毁掉，让人们重新回到穿树叶、吃野果的时代。

这个大力士神，趁月黑星回的时候，降落到人间。他来到地里，手拔脚踏地破坏刚扬过花的庄稼。

大力士神正卖力地执行着大王的命令，人们从四面八方围拢来，纷纷质问大力士神："凭什么要破坏我们人间的幸福生活?"大力士神依仗着浑身的力气，蛮横地说："我是天上大力士神，浑身都是力气，在天上用不完，来到地上出气。你们这些可怜的人呀！谁敢来和我比摔跤？要是你们摔倒了我，我就转回天上，再也不管人间事。要是不敢出来比，就趁早快些闪开，我今天要拔光所有从地上长出来的东西。"

大力士神为显一显浑身的力气，看见山边正牧着牛，便走过去，首先选了一条腰圆、肩高的黄牯牛，双手一托，将牛丢到山脚下。随后，他又找到一条排角的大水牛，双手抓住牛角，用力一扭，就一把把水牛扭翻在地上。正因为有过这桩事，所以，以后过节时，首先要斗牛。可是，人们谁也不愿充当那凶恶的大力士神，就只好让牛与牛斗了。

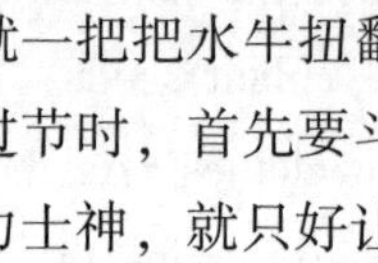

Since then, people lived a rich life with ample food and clothing.

However, the Emperor of Heaven knew it later, who felt very upset as people's life was about to surpass his. So he summoned the Deity of Strength to ruin every crop, forcing people to go back to the time when they could only eat wild fruits and wore leaves as clothes.

Then, the Deity of Strength descended to the mortal world in the middle of night, pulling out and treading on crops.

While he was busy following the Emperor's order to destroy the crops, people gathered around him and questioned, "How dare you destroy our grains and life?" The deity replied overbearingly, "I am the strongest deity in heaven, and my endless strength need to be released in your fields. You poor guys, who dares to compete wrestling with me? If you defeat me, I will go back to heaven and never return. But if you dare not, just go away! I will pluck every plant here."

To show his strength, the deity walked to the mountain and picked a strong yellow bull, which was raised up and thrown away immediately by him. Later, he found a strong buffalo, which was pushed down to the ground by the deity again, who held its horns, twisted them and managed to overthrow it with bare hands. Because of it, bull fighting became a custom still celebrated today. As no one wanted to play the role of the fierce deity, they just let bulls fight with each other.

大力士神摔翻牛以后，更是洋洋得意。他向着围观的人群，双手叉着腰，迈着步子走圆圈，边走边说：“谁敢出来比一比？我好再出出气。要不敢就快些让开，我好……”

“慢着！别逞凶！”这时，从人群里走出英雄朵阿惹恣来。只见他裸露着身子，浑身上下黑油油的，腰上紧紧地用一条黑布扎着，“要摔跤，我们找块宽敞的地方去斗一斗，别在这里踏坏了庄稼。”

说完话，惹恣头也不回地走向深深的老圭山。接着，大力士神和人们都也跟着来到圭山头上。

大力士神与朵阿惹恣在荒山上，你抓着我，我扯着你，展开了一场恶斗。他们整整扭摔了三天三夜，分不出胜负。这时，山头上，小伙子们拨响了三弦，吹响了短笛，姑娘们拍红了手，跺痛了脚，都在为惹恣助威。突然，朵阿惹恣一下失了手，膝盖落了地。大力士神拼命压下来，想把惹恣压翻在地。惹恣单脚跪在地下，直压得地上出了个深窝窝，后来积满了水，天长日久，就变成了今天的圆湖啦！

After beating the bull and the buffalo, the Deity of Strength became more arrogant. With hands on hips, he looked at the surrounding people, "Who dares to go out and compete with me? If you can't, just go away."

"Hold on! Don't boast yourself!" A hero Duoarezi stepped out from the crowd. Shirtless, he was strong with shiny black skin, tied with one black cloth on the waist, "Let's go and find a spacious filed to wrest. Don't trample crops here."

As soon as Duoarezi proposed the challenge, he went to the Gui Mountain without hesitation, followed by the deity and the villagers.

On the bare mountain, the deity and Duoarezi caught each other and had a fight. They fought for three days and nights, but it was still a draw. At that time, in order to encourage the hero, young men started to play sanxian instruments and flutes, and girls clapped hands and stamped their feet ceaselessly until their hands were red and feet were sore. All of a sudden, Duoarezi missed one step and knelt down. The deity seized the opportunity to push him hardly in order to overthrow him. Duoarezi had to kneel on one knee, which was pressed so hardly that a deep hole was made. After many years, the hole was filled with water from rain and became the Yuan Lake today!

眼看大力士神就要取胜了，只见惹恣一收腰，吸口气，双手卡住大力士神的腰腿，猛一用力，站了起来，乘势将大力士神甩出去，直落到十几里外的独石山边，掼在地上，把平平的地上压出一条长长的深沟来。大力士神的头，撞通了跃宝山，山中的水淌到长长的深沟里，便成了今天的长湖。

这一下，大力士神再也不敢抖威风了。他悄悄地回到了天上。从此，每到这一天，人们都要用摔跤来欢庆胜利。

人们看到朵阿惹恣斗败了天神，小伙子更起劲地拨响了大三弦，短笛也吹得四周回响，而姑娘们随着乐曲，不停地拍手跺脚。这就是今天跳三弦的来由。

再说天王听到人们斗败了大力士神，看见人们欢歌起舞，气得眼冒火、嘴生烟。他亲自抓起案前的香灰炉，顺手撒向人间。这些香灰面，在空中飘飘荡荡，后来就变成了各种害虫，渐渐飞落在大地上，爬到地里，嚼食着刚刚灌浆的庄稼。眼看庄稼就要被毁坏了，聪明的人们很快找来了松树枝，点燃了一束束熊熊的火把，抓起松香面，撒向火把，喷出一股股火龙来，直烧得天王撒出来的害虫焦头烂翅，再也难逞凶了。

As the deity was about to win, Duoarezi inhaled a deep breath, gripped the deity's wrist tightly and made a strong move to stand up. Afterwards, he threw the deity away within one breath, all the way to the side of the Dushi Mountain dozens of miles away. It was such a heavy blow that a long and deep ditch in the plain ground was made. The deity's head knocked on the Yuebao Mountain, creating a huge hole, which began to be filled with water from the mountain in later years and finally became the Chang Lake today.

Therefore, the Deity of Strength dared not to show off his strength anymore, so he went back to heaven in shame. Since then, people held wrestling games to celebrate this event on that day every year.

After Duoarezi defeated the Deity, young men played sanxian instruments and blew flutes more enthusiastically, while girls clapped hands and stamped feet together with music more energetically. That's how the custom of dancing with sanxian comes.

When the Emperor of Heaven learned it, he was too angry to watch people sing and dance with happiness. So he took a censer and threw it to earth. Ashes in the censer spread and flew across the sky, turning into all kinds of pests. As they landed on the ground and spread to the fields, they ate crops which had just been filled. While the crops were about to be ruined in a moment, clever people lit branches of pine trees as torches and then added resin into flames, which turned into raging fires, burning all the pests spread by the Emperor to death. In this way, damage by pests was brought under control.

自此以后，每年到了月黑星回的六月间，朵阿惹恣斗败大力士神的二十四日这一天，人们都要穿上节日的盛装，打牛、宰羊来庆祝。节日里都要举行斗牛、摔跤、打火把活动，以此纪念人们斗败天王，迎来新的丰收年。

搜集整理者：罗希吾戈

撒梅[1]人的火把节

撒梅人把六月二十四日的火把节称为“过小年”。这一天，男女老幼，喜气洋洋。晚上老人要祭牛王、念《牛王经》。还要把吃剩的鸡骨头拿去烧了，点燃麻秆火，边烧边祈祷，念些“风调雨顺，六畜兴旺，人畜平安”之类的吉利语。老妈妈要把姑娘们在五月端阳节扎在手腕上的五色彩线剪下来用麻秆火烧了，祈祷神灵和撒梅王保佑孩子们快快长大，保佑一家老小健康长寿。青年小伙子则点上松明火把到田里转悠，到村子四周游戏玩耍，遇上小伙伴，撒上一把松香，火焰升起五六丈高。老人们还点上火把到灶房、卧室、牛圈、猪圈照亮一通。据说今天撒梅人点燃火把是为寻找撒梅人的祖先——撒梅王的精灵哩。

① 撒梅：彝族的一个支系。

Since then, on 24th June every year, the day when Duoarezi defeated the Deity of Strength, people would wear festival costumes and slaughter cattle and sheep for celebration. Also, activities like bull-fighting, wrestling and torch holding were held to memorize the day and welcome a new harvest year.

Collector and editor: Luoxiwuge

The Torch Festival of the Samei① People

Samei People call the Torch Festival "the Little New Year" on 24th June, when people of all ages are radiant with joy to celebrate it. At night, elders offer sacrifices to worship the King of Ox and recite its scriptures. Also, they burn leftover chicken bones and recite and pray for "favorable weather and good harvest, and a peaceful year for families and livestock" while igniting stems of hemp. Old women cut and burn colorful strings tied on girls' wrists, and pray for deities and King of Samei to bless children and families to live long and healthy. Young men light up torches made by pine wood and stroll in the fields and around villages. When they meet friends halfway, they sprinkle rosin to raise fires together. Elders also light up torches to check kitchens, bedrooms and pigpens. It's said that the reason why Samei people light torches today is to look for the spirit of the King of Samei, their ancestor.

① Samei: a branch of the Yi Ethnic Group.

撒梅人中，流传着这样一个古老的故事：

相传在很古很古的时候，滇池周围，土地肥沃，气候温和，水草丰美。这块宝地上，居住着撒梅人。勤劳、勇敢、忠厚、淳朴的撒梅人，热爱自己的领袖——撒梅王。

这撒梅王出身就不平凡。他的母亲是个十分勤劳的撒梅妇女，临产前还天天上山干活，撒梅王就生在山谷里。由于从小热爱劳动，饱尝风霜，青年的撒梅王本事就十分出众，很自然地被撒梅群众拥戴为领袖。他被选为撒梅王之后，更是处处关心百姓，事事为大伙着想。他为人宽厚，办事公道，得到天神暗中指点，本事也就更加超群出众。

有一年秋天，一个部族的首领带领部下侵入滇池地区，他发誓要把撒梅人撵走，把滇池畔肥美的水草地据为己有。撒梅王眼看情势危急，立即把撒梅人组织起来，对付这个入侵的恶魔。这个部落的头领派了两员大将带兵进攻撒梅村寨，被撒梅王杀得一败涂地，丢下尸体逃回去了。

An old story goes among the Samei people:

Long Long time ago, the Samei people lived around Dianchi, a place with fertile earth, mild weather, plenty of water and lush grasses. The hardworking and brave Samei people all admired their leaders, the King of Samei.

The King of Samei was born in a decent family. His mother was a hardworking woman, who even went to work in the mountain days before giving birth, so the King of Samei was born in a valley. As he enjoyed working and had accumulated experience from many difficulties he had gone through since childhood, the young lad was outstanding and admired by people, so he was naturally chosen the King of Samei. Afterwards, he cared more about people and considered their interests in all affairs. This justice and benevolent king, also guided by the deities, became more outstanding.

In one autumn, a tribe attacked Dianchi region, aiming to kick the Samei people away and conquer this lush grassland. In quick response, the king united the Samei people to defend against this invading enemy. As a result, the enemy troop was utterly defeated, with its two generals fleeing, leaving dead bodies of their soldiers behind.

这个部落的首领不甘心自己的失败，不久又派来更多的人马、更多的猛将来与撒梅王决一死战。终因寡不敌众，撒梅王被杀害了。撒梅群众十分伤心，一路哀号着将他的尸体抬回寨子。谁知到夜里星星出齐的时候，撒梅王的颈项上又长出一个人头来，与被砍掉的头一模一样，而且还瞪大眼睛，责怪哭他的人说："哭哪样！准备好刀枪，再与他们干吧！"撒梅王的父老兄弟，一看撒梅王复活了，个个转悲为喜，一夜磨刀擦枪，准备与侵略者再战。他们心更齐了，意志更坚了。

第二天，那个部落的首领正在欢庆他们的胜利，撒梅王又来挑战了。那个头领大惊失色，心里想道："奇怪，昨天才杀掉的头领，今天怎么又回来了？"忙命手下的几员大将迎战。撒梅王冲进敌人的队伍，杀了敌人几员大将，胜利返回村寨。撒梅人在寨内杀猪宰羊庆贺胜利。

The chief of that tribe could not reconcile his failure, so he summoned more soldiers to join the fight. Because they outnumbered the Samei people, the king was killed. The Samei people took back his corpse in grief, but the neck of the king grew a new head when the night fell and stars went out. The king opened his eyes on this new head and scolded them, "Do not cry! Prepare your weapons! Let's fight with them again!" At the sight of this miraculous restoration to life, everyone turned from sorrow into joy. They sharpened weapons overnight and prepared for another fights with even stronger determination.

The second day, the king went to challenge the chief again while the tribe was celebrating, which almost scared the chief to death. He thought to himself, "What an odd thing! How can the head cut off yesterday grow back today?" He sent several experienced generals to fight, but they were defeated by the king. The king went back with victory. The Samei people all slaughtered pigs and sheep for celebration.

第三天，吃了败仗的部落头领，又重整旗鼓，亲自率领大队人马和无数猛将来决战。他一定要抓住这个撒梅王，看看这个怪人。虽然撒梅人带着部落的人拼命死战，终因人少武器少而失败了，撒梅王的头又被砍掉了。半夜，撒梅王又长出头来，第四天又去敌营挑战。那个部落头领大怒，他大声吼道："我今日非把你捉住不可，一定要亲手砍掉你的脑袋，看你还长不长出一个头来!"撒梅王放声大笑道："莫生气，你们永远也杀不掉我的!"两人在草地上大战，杀得天昏地暗，日色无光，撒梅王又被他们捉住了。那个部落头领亲自砍掉撒梅王的头。只见撒梅王的脖子上闪出一道红光，慢慢地又长出一个头。撒梅王笑道："我说你们永远杀不死我，你们偏不信。我的头不又长出来了吗!"兵士们吓得面如土色，刽子手们一个个被吓得脚瘫手软。连头领也被眼前这奇异的景象吓慌了。到星星出齐的时候，撒梅王的头长得和原来一模一样。一连几天，都是这样。奸猾、歹毒的部族首领心生一计，装着一副笑脸说："放了他！让我们两家和好吧!"憨厚、勤劳的撒梅王信以为真，就回到自己的土地上，领着撒梅人种庄稼过日子了。

The third day, the defeated chief went back with a huge army led by himself for a final battle. He was determined to catch the odd king and figure out what was happening. Although the Samei people fought bravely and desperately, they still lost the battle because they had too few soldiers and were poorly equipped. So the head of the King of Samei was cut off again. At midnight, the king grew a new head for a second time, and he went to challenge the chief the next day. Seeing him, the chief was furious. He yelled, "I must catch you today and will personally chop your head! Let me see whether you can grow a new one again!" But the king laughed loudly, "Don't be angry. You will never kill me!" Then two leaders fought on the grassland fiercely from day to night. After the fight, the king was unfortunately caught again. The chief cut off his head, but the neck grew a new one after a slash of red light. The new head laughed loudly, "I told you I will never be killed. See! I have grown one again!" Those soldiers were frightened with pale face, and executioners were scared to death, and even the chief was in great panic. When stars came out at night, the king's head had grown completely, which happened many times for several days. So the cunning chief came up with a plan. He smiled deceptively and said, "Let him go, we shall reconcile!" The honest and hard-working king believed him and went back to his land.

这个部族的头领想："撒梅有这样的异人，看来硬打不行，只能用软办法，俗话说：'一物降一物，癞蛤蟆降怪物。'必须设法把他除掉，不除掉是个后患啊。"于是，他暗中派出不少侦探，到撒梅人中去打听撒梅王杀不死的奥秘。不久，一个狡猾的暗探，终于弄清楚了事情的奥秘。这秘密是从撒梅王的妻子口中泄露出来的：

撒梅王的妻子十分羡慕撒梅王"杀不死"这项特异的功能，她对撒梅王说："你不会死，也不会老，能永远活在人世。我嫁给你这样一个丈夫实在有福气，就是老了，死了，也高兴。"撒梅王对妻子讲了实话："孩子的妈呀！我也会死的。别人砍了我的头，只要拿尖刀草扎成扫帚在我的脖子上扫三下，我的头就再也不能长出来了。"撒梅王的妻子是个没有心计的女人，她把撒梅王告知她的秘密全部泄露出去了。结果被那个狡猾的奸细打听到了，他立刻禀告给自己部落的头领。

这个部落头领得知后，立即领着浩浩荡荡的人马来攻打撒梅寨。他们把撒梅王团团围住，因人多势众，撒梅王又被捉住了。部落头领命人砍掉他的头，用尖刀草扎成的扫帚在他脖颈上扫了三下。撒梅王的脖子上不再出现红光了，撒梅王的头不再长出来了。撒梅王真的死了。撒梅人失去了自己的领袖，只有各自奔走，逃往四乡。所以撒梅人又被称为"散民"。尖刀草的叶子，也因为染上撒梅王头上的血而变红了。

After he left, the chief thought to himself, "We can't fight directly if their king has deity's power, so we need to adopt a soft approach if force is not available. After all, there is saying that everything has its conqueror. Anyway, the king must be killed; otherwise we won't have good days to live." So he sent many detectives to tap the secret of the immortal king. Soon after, a crafty one figured it out, which was released by the king's wife.

The king's wife admired his husband's immortal power and said, "You will not die or grow old. How lucky I am to marry the man who can live forever! I am so happy even though I will get old and die eventually." The king told the truth to his wife, "Oh my dear! Of course I will die. If anyone who cuts off my head sweeps my neck for three times with a broom made of hedyotis diffusa at once, I will never grow a head again." Later, this secret was told by this simple-minded woman and heard by a spy.

After learning the secret, the chief immediately led his army to attack Samei village. Because the enemy was outnumbered, the king was caught, and his head was cut off again. But this time the chief swept his chopped neck with a broom made of hedyotis diffusa for three times. As a result, there was no red light and no head grew again. The King of Samei died. Samei people lost their leader. They had to run and escape to other villages, who were later called the "dispersed villagers". Since then, leaves of hedyotis diffusa became red because the blood of the King of Samei spilled on it.

撒梅人尽管离散了，他们永远怀念自己的领袖——撒梅王。为了纪念他，每年六月二十四日——撒梅王被害的日子，大家都点上火把，四处寻找撒梅王的精灵，纪念撒梅人自己的祖先。

讲述者：张福德，李灿，李元
搜集整理者：浪涛，燕华，思勤

纳苏[1]人的火把节

很早以前，在东方的蒲乌觉觉地方，我们彝家出了很了不起的人。这个人名叫支朵阿吾[2]。支朵阿吾这个人，论性格，山也没有他清纯；论机敏，飞鹰也没有他灵活；论才智，大海也没有他深广。他小的时候，父母一边让他拜天下最有才智的毕摩为师，一边送他去坝区学汉人的知识。到了十五岁，天下就已经没有能教他的人了。

北方的皇帝听说这件事后，有点不相信，就派了两个人来考他，结果反被支朵阿吾考倒了。皇帝很高兴，便封他做了俄吾司木的俄么后。彝家有了自己的天下，一下子繁荣富强起来，子孙遍布黑水以南的千山万水；凡是彝族人的地方，就有满山的牛羊，满地的庄稼，日子越来越好过。

---

① 纳苏：彝族的一个支系。
② 支朵阿吾：即孟获。

Although the Samei people were separated, they still missed their king. Therefore, on 24th June every year, the day when the king was killed, people would light on torches and go around to look for the king's spirit, in memory of him and their ancestors.

Narrator: Zhang Fude, Li Can, Li Yuan
Collecter and editor: Lang Tao, Yan Hua, Si Qin

The Torch Festival of Nasu① People

Long time ago, there was a remarkable person born in Puwujuejue, called Zhiduoawu②, whose character was even purer than mountains, response quicker than eagles and minds deeper than oceans. When he was a child, his parents sent him to be the apprentice of Bimo, the wisest men in the world. They also sent him to Ba region to learn the Han people's knowledge. When he was fifteen years old, no one had enough knowledge to teach him anymore.

An emperor in the north heard about him but didn't believe it, so he sent two people to test Zhiduoawu, but they were asked speechlessly by him in turn. The emperor was delighted to learn it and granted him the king of the region. Since then, the Yi people had their own land and became prosperous, whose generations lived across regions to the south of the Heishui River. As long as there were the Yi people, there would be countless cattle and sheep, as well as fruitful crops and grains, so their lives thrived day by day.

① Nasu: a branch of the Yi Ethnic Group.

② Zhiduoawu: Menghuo.

当时，在俄吾司木国的北方，隔着黑水有一个刹哈国①，那个国的俄木听说俄吾司木地方富饶广大，打算征服它。于是就派了一个名叫诸葛亮(彝语称者名勤)的人，带兵前来征伐。诸葛亮的人马刚到碟帕克米城，就被支朵阿吾带着彝家人团团围住。支朵阿吾的坐骑是只猛虎，可吓人啦，诸葛亮的人马突围时，只要一见支朵阿吾骑着猛虎冲来，便大叫“猛虎来了！猛虎来了！”立时乱成一团，退缩回去。彝家人不懂汉语，以为猛虎就是英雄或俄木的意思，一打起仗来，也高声喊着“猛虎来了！猛虎来了！”诸葛亮的兵又把音听走了，听成是“孟获来了”，以为支朵阿吾就叫孟获，所以后来汉人都管支朵阿吾叫孟获。

围了一段时间，诸葛亮的人马粮草殆尽，支朵阿吾的彝家人疲惫不堪。

① 刹哈国：意为汉人国。

There was a kingdom of Chaha① in the north of their land across Heishui River. The greedy king of Chaha heard about their prosperous land and decided to conquer it, so he sent a man called Zhuge Liang (Zhemingqin in the Yi's Language) to lead the army. However, upon arrival at Diepakemi, the army was instantly surrounded by the Yi people under the leadership of Zhiduoawu, who rode on a ferocious tiger. Whenever Zhuge Liang's troop attempted to break out of the encirclement, at the sight of Zhiduoawu dashing to them on a tiger, they would yelled in panic, "Tiger is coming! Tiger is coming!" and fell back. The Yi people didn't understand their language and thought tiger (Menghu in transliteration) means hero. So when fights began, they also yelled "Menghu is coming! Menghu is coming!" Zhuge Liang's army misunderstood it as the name of Zhiduoawu, so Han people called Zhiduoawu "Menghu" after that.

The encirclement lasted for quite some time until Zhuge Liang's army ran out of food and the Yi people were exhausted as well.

---

① Kingdom of Chaha: it means the Kingdom of the Han people.

支朵阿吾是个最爱属民的人，是个最聪明的人，什么都想到了，什么办法他都有。为了使彝家人得到休整，同时又让诸葛亮走不了，他叫人砍来很多很多的松明子；后来松明子砍光了，他又让大家去找来干蒿枝杆、干树枝，捆成一把一把的火把，围着碟帕克米城插了九圈，燃起九道火墙。他又叫一些人举着火把，在九圈火墙里穿插走动。这样一来，诸葛亮的兵就不敢往外冲了。彝家人高兴得举起火把边唱边跳起来。再说诸葛亮从城里往城外看，只见到处都是火把，忙对他的兵说："彝人多得很，看来这次很难突围，还是去和彝人认亲戚和解吧！"于是，他就派使者去对支朵阿吾说："龙生九子，九子分九方，汉彝是一族，汉彝是弟兄，兄在弟跟随，弟在兄保护，我现在后悔来打你们了，我们还是和好吧！"支朵阿吾说："汉人重父母，彝人重弟兄，如果真是弟兄，我就和你们和解，我就放你们一条生路，不过怎么让我相信呢？"后来诸葛亮听了使者回话，就亲自到彝家营地对支朵阿吾说："彝家是哥哥，汉人是兄弟，请你来考验我们，看我们是不是同宗弟弟吧！"支朵阿吾说："好，彝家最会唱古事，彝家的古事只有彝兄弟会听，现在我们就来对歌吧！如果我问的你都能答，我就认你们是兄弟！"

Zhiduoawu loved his people, and he was also the cleverest man who had thorough thought and numerous ways to solve problems. To ensure a rest for the Yi people and continued encirclement of Zhuge Liang's troop, he asked people to cut many dry branches and tied them up into torches, with which, they encircled nine layers of walls outside the city and lit them up, making nine layers of fiery walls burning with flames outside. The Yi people were asked to hold torches patrolling between walls, which frightened those soldiers who wanted to escape, so the Yi people were so happy that they sang and danced with torches outside. When Zhuge Liang looked outside, he saw countless torches and said, "the Yi people outnumber us. Our attempt to break through could hardly succeed, so let's reconcile with them!" Then he sent an envoy who delivered his message, "Long time ago, the dragon gave birth to nine sons who went to nine directions, and the Han people and the Yi people belonged to the same family. So, we are brothers. The younger brother followed the old and the older brother protected the young. We regret coming to attack you, and we want reconciliation!" Zhiduoawu replied, "We know Han people value parents, and we Yi people value brothers. If you are our real brothers, I shall reconcile with you, and I shall let you go. But you need to convince me at first." Then, Zhuge Liang came to the Yi people's base and said, "Yi people are our older brothers, and we Han people are younger brothers. You can have a test!" Zhiduoawu replied, "Very well. We are best at singing historical stories known by the Yi people, so let's have antiphonal singing. If you can answer all my questions in the songs, I will admit you to be our brothers!"

于是，支朵阿吾和诸葛亮就在城外平坝上摆开了歌场，两边的人马都来围观。两人一直对唱了三天三夜，从开天辟地一直到洪水朝天，支朵阿吾所问的，诸葛亮都答上了。支朵阿吾说："我看你三份中，有一份很像我们的同宗了。彝家最喜欢摔跤，彝家兄弟也会摔跤，现在我们来摔跤，如果我的人赢了，我就认你做兄弟，如果你的人输了，这三份中就没有一份了。"角力的结果，双方的人不输不赢。支朵阿吾说，这事难说准，还得看天意。双方又拉牛羊来斗，结果斗牛斗羊，依然是不输不赢，支朵阿吾说："现在三份中，有两份说明我们是同宗了，最后一份，我还得考一下：你得做出一种玩物来，要能飞到天上去，又能落回地上来，而且双方的人都同时可以玩。"诸葛亮想了想，就在坝子中间支了一架磨担秋，果然一边一个人，双方都能同时玩，不但能上天，还能落回地，在天与地之间飞转。支朵阿吾一看这事没难住诸葛亮，于是便遵守诺言，认诸葛亮做兄弟，与汉兵和解了。

Therefore, Zhiduoawu and Zhuge Liang built a stage for singing in Pingba outside the city where both the Han people and the Yi people came to watch. They sang for three days and nights, and the contents ran from the creation of the world to the flooding up to the sky. All questions asked by Zhiduoawu were answered by Zhuge Liang in singing. Zhiduoawu said, "I think one third of you look like our brothers. The Yi people also like wrestling, so the Yi people's brothers should be good at it as well. Now let us have a wrestling competition. If the Han people win, I will admit you to be our brothers." The result of the competition turned out to be a draw. Zhiwuaduo said, "It's hard to say. It still depends on the will of God." So they brought cattle and goats to fight again, but they ended in a draw as well. So Zhiwuaduo said, "I think two thirds of you look like our brothers, but there is one last test: you need to make a toy which can fly to the sky and come back to the ground, and people from the two sides can play at the same time." After a brief thought, Zhuge Liang made a special swing in the center of Pingba, which indeed could be played by two people each time, flying up to sky and then falling down to earth in turns. So Zhiduoawu kept his words, admitted them to be brothers, and reconciled with the Han people.

汉兵退走后，支朵阿吾的人马欢天喜地，又燃起火把，在碟帕克米城整整狂欢了三天。当时的日子，正是六月二十四到二十六，后来每年到了这个日子，支朵阿吾便大宴部属，让人们学着当时的样子尽情玩乐，以示纪念。这习惯一代一代地传下来，就成了“火把节”。

流传地区：武定县，禄劝县
讲述者：杨自荣
记录者：罗有能

腊罗[①]人的火把节

古时候，人间没有火，人类只能吞生肉，吃生饭，猛兽来了没有火拦，寒气来了没有火烤，生活很不方便。而且因为人类吃不到熟肉熟饭，病灾很多，寿命也很短，活到三十岁的人，就算是很了不起了。人们很希望这种状况能够改变，但又没有办法。那时的火只天宫里有，天宫凡人是很难去的，而且把守很严，即使去了，也不一定能把火种带出来。这事怎么办？谁能去天宫里盗火呢？

① 腊罗：彝族的一个支系。

After the Han army left, the Yi people were so happy that they lit up torches again and enjoyed a three-day revelry from June 24th to 26th June. Every year since then, Zhiduoawu treated his subordinates with great feasts to memorize that event and enjoy revelries. After several generations, this custom becomes the Torch Festival.

Spreading area: Wuding County, Luquan County
Narrator: Yang Zirong
Recorder: Luo Youneng

The Torch Festival of Laluo① People

Long time ago when there was no fire, people had to eat raw meat and uncooked rice. Without fire, life was not convenient, for people could not scare away beasts and shield from cold wind to get warmth. Also, as people could not cook their food, they easily caught illness with very short life expectancy. Those who lived to thirty years old were very rarely seen. People desperately wanted to change this situation, but there was no way. As fire was only possessed by deities at that time, and the heavenly palace banned mortal people from entering. What should people do? Who could go to the heavenly palace and steal the fire out?

① Laluo: a branch of the Yi nationality.

世上的人们商量着要找火，商量去商量来，吃了三斗商量饭，杀了三头商量牛，商量了三年三月又三天，还是没有办法。这时候，东方的主宰尼克木俄木(皇帝)着急了，就向天下发布命令说："世间万物，不管是不是人，只要为人类找采火种，我就把三个公主嫁给他做媳妇。"俄木家的三个公主是三朵鲜花，个个长得像仙女一样。西方、北方、南方的俄木都曾三番五次来求亲，但是东方的俄木一直拿不定主意，三个公主的婚事就给拖下来了。俄木的命令一下，三个公主也很高兴，传出话来说，只要谁找来了火种，她们都愿意嫁给他。

尼克木俄木的命令一传出，天下的人都在想办法、打主意，没有一个人不想去找火种，没有一个人不想当皇帝的姑爷，但是没有一个人能够有这样的本事。

后来，在我们地方，出了个名叫者洛的小伙子，这人不但懂鸟语，还会听兽话，从小以打猎为业，翻山越岭，风餐露宿，练出一身本事和力气，上山可以擒虎，下海能够捉龙。有一次，者洛打猎来到哀牢山最高最深的密林里，看见所有的飞禽走兽正在一起选王，他就走过去说："你们这王还是不要选了，如果一定要选，那谁的本事都没有我大，该我当你们的王呢!"凤凰听了首先说："我能飞到天上去，你能吗?"者洛说："你飞飞我看。"凤凰刚飞起来，者洛一箭就把它射落了。蛇说："这凤凰真没本事，看见人就不会飞了，

People all talked about it. Having had three meals and killed three cattle and talked for three years, three months and three days, still no one could come up with a good idea. Then the king, Nikemuemu, in the east got anxious, so he told the world, "To everything in this world, whether you are a human or not, as long as you can bring back the fire, I shall marry my three daughters to you." People around the world had long learned that his three princesses were live fairies, as beautiful as the most delicate flowers, even kings of the west, north and south had asked for marriage alliance many times but failed. Once the order was published, three princesses were very delighted and would like to marry whoever succeeded.

With this order, everyone began to think about stealing fire and marrying the princess, but on one was able to do it.

There was a young man in our place named Zheluo who understood languages of birds and beasts. He made his living by hunting. As he hunted on mountains and valleys every day since childhood, he grew up to be the most experienced and skillful hunter, who could catch tigers on mountains and catch dragons underwater. One time when he hunted in the highest and deepest forest in the Ailao Mountain, he saw animals gathering to select their king. He went there directly and said, "Don't bother to select a king! If you want a king, I should be your king, because I am the best among you!" A phoenix heard it and said, "I can fly to the sky, can you do that?" Zheluo replied, "Show me how you fly." Zheluo shot the phoenix down as soon as the phoenix just spread its wings. Then a serpent said, "This clumsy phoenix doesn't know how to fly now. Let me show you how good I am underwater."

还是我亮亮水中的本事给你看。”蛇刚钻到溪水里，者洛把有毒的箭头放进水中搅了搅，蛇便昏死过去，沉到水底不动了。老虎一看，哈哈大笑起来：“蛇老弟，蛇老弟，你不是说你能上天入地吗，这下一见人，怎么不会爬了？这下该我亮亮本事给人瞧啦！”说完，老虎就爬到山头上，张开嘴大吼一声，震得地动山摇，然后闪电一样从山头朝者洛猛冲过来，吓得所有的飞禽走兽都“轰”一下全逃走了。老虎好不得意。但快到者洛面前时，却见者洛仍一动不动地站着，老虎心理顿时疑惑起来，连忙刹住脚步，说道：“你再不逃跑，我可要吃掉你啦。”者洛说：“我吃老虎时，是从不打招呼的，你要吃我，你就来吃一吃看看！”老虎心虚了，问：“你敢吃我？”者洛说：“别说老虎，连野猪我也不知吃了几千几万只。”老虎是最怕野猪的，他不相信地说：“你别唬我了，我不相信！”者洛说：“不信，你跟我去看看，我吃一只给你瞧。”

者洛就把老虎带到青玉米地边守着。晚上，有三只野猪来吃青玉米包，吓得老虎藏在人背后，动也不敢动。者洛问老虎：“你要吃公的还是吃母的？”老虎说：“公的母的我都不敢吃，我吃小的吧。”者洛说：“小的留着做种，母的留着下儿，我们俩吃公的算了。”说着，一箭射在公野猪的头上。公野猪惨叫道：“人来了，快跑！”说完就死了，母野猪和小野猪一听人来了，一溜烟逃开了。者洛就用刀子把公野猪砍成两半，和老虎分吃。老虎很佩服者洛，便和他做了朋友。后来，蛇和扎布里鸟也来找者洛，和他做朋友。从此，虎、蛇、扎布里鸟和者洛，便天天在一起玩耍、打猎。

When the serpent just swam in river, it fainted right away when Zheluo put a poisoned arrow in water. A tiger saw it and laughed loudly, "You poor serpent, did you just brag yourself? Do you even know how to crawl? Now let me show my skill!" After saying it, the tiger jumped on a mountain and howled, making mountains tremble and quaked, then it rushed to Zheluo like a flash of lightning, scaring other animals away in a moment. The arrogant tiger walked towards Zheluo, who stood still, so the curious tiger stopped and said, "I will eat you if you don't run away." Zheluo replied, "I never ask tigers before eating them. Don't you dare to eat me?" The tiger were frightened and asked, "You dare to eat me?" Zheluo said, "I have eaten thousands of boars already, let alone tigers." The tiger feared boars most, but it was still not convinced, "Don't bluff me. I won't believe it." Zheluo said, "Then you can follow me, and let me show you how I eat a boar."

Zheluo took the tiger and asked it to wait for him beside a corn field. When three boars showed up at night to steal unripe corns, the tiger was so frightened that it hid behind Zheluo breathlessly. Zheluo asked it, "Do you want to eat the male one or female one?" The tiger replied, "I only dare to eat the little one." Zheluo said, "Keep the little one to grow up, and keep the female one for reproduction. Let's have the male one." Then he shot an arrow on the male boar's head, which was down and yelling, "Run! It's human beings to catch us!" Afterwards, the boar died. Upon hearing it, two other boars ran away quickly. Zheluo tore the boar apart, and ate it with the tiger together. The tiger admired him a lot and made friends with him. Later, the serpent and a bird went to find Zheluo to be friends. And they four friends played and hunted together since then.

当时，天下的人都在议论要找火，者洛也想去找火，他和三个朋友商量说：“我想去天宫里把火偷到人间来，你们愿不愿跟我去?”三个朋友听了，都爽快地答应去帮者洛试一试。者洛很高兴，便对三个朋友说：“如果你们帮我找来了火种，我就叫东方的尼克木俄木，把他的三个公主嫁给你们。”老虎听了很高兴，说：“那好呀，如果你把公主嫁给我，我就拼死去找火种。”蛇也说：“那二公主归我了，我的本事是上天入地，我驮你们到天上去吧!”扎布里鸟却说：“我不想要媳妇，三公主就给者洛吧。如果我偷来了火，我只想和人住在一起。”者洛说：“可以。”于是蛇便把者洛、虎和扎布里鸟驮到天上去了。

临走的时候，者洛对四方八面九山十箐的人说：“我者洛要找火种去了，请你们在最高的天生营山头上等着，等我找来了火种，好把它分给你们带回去。”人们听了很高兴，远远近近的人，都到天生营山上去等火种。后来连东西南四个天下的俄木，也都带着自己的属民来了。尼克木俄木还带来了自己的三个公主，等着者洛盗来火种后，履行自己的诺言。

When everyone in the world was talking about stealing fire, Zheluo also wanted to have a try. So he asked his three friends, "I want to steal fire from the heaven, will you come with me?" His friends agreed. Zheluo was delighted and said, "If you help me find fire, I will ask the king, Nikemuemu, in the east to marry his three daughters to you." The tiger was delighted, "Great! If I can marry a princess, I would like to risk my life stealing fire!" The serpent said, "The second princess is mine. I can fly and swim, so let me take you to the heavenly palace!" And the bird said, "I don't want princess. I just want to live with human beings forever if I have fire." After Zheluo agreed, the serpent prepared to fly them to the heavenly palace.

Before leaving, Zheluo told people around the world, "I am going to bring back fire. Please wait for me on the highest ground of the Tianshengying Mountain. After bringing it back, I can share it with you there." People were very delighted at it and all went to the mountain to wait for the fire. Even kings of four directions came with their subordinates. The king in the east brought his three daughters along and was ready to fulfill his promise.

者洛、老虎和扎布里鸟骑着蛇到了天上后，者洛对几个朋友说："凡人很难进天宫，你们几个先轮流去偷，如果偷不出来，我再想办法。"蛇说："我先去试试!"蛇偷偷摸进玉皇大帝的住房里去，看见灶房里烧着很大的火，它正想拿一根烧着的木头回来，结果一下子被烫伤了，脱了一层皮。蛇从火堆里逃出来，惊惊慌慌地回来说："哦哟，火会咬人，我怕得很，不敢偷了。"从此以后，蛇身上每年都要起一次火泡，大疼一次。每次起火泡，都把蛇疼得钻沙堆、滚刺丛、缠糙树、进石缝，直到把身上的皮脱掉一层才会好。这就是它每年都要蜕一次皮的原因了。

老虎听了后，有点心惊胆战。它说："什么火那么厉害，我去看看!"者洛对老虎说："只要你不去钻火堆，火就不会咬你了。你去时看见了火堆，最好把一头有火一头没有火的火柴头咬回来。"老虎说："可以!"然后就窜进天宫里去了。这时玉皇大帝家的灶火快要熄了，烧火丫头就睡在灶门口，老虎因为心慌，跑进灶房里时没看清楚那是个人，把她当作了"一头有火一头没有火的火柴头"，用嘴叼住就要跑。烧火的丫头很生气，顺手抓起火钳，朝虎身上乱打。因为丫头刚用火钳头熄火，火钳还是红的，打一下，就把虎毛烙掉一块，烙出点点道道的斑痕。老虎强忍着，把烧火的丫头叼到大门口，实在被打得耐不住了，只得放开姑娘一溜烟逃了回来，连声叫苦说："哦哟哟，火会咬人，火柴头会打人，我偷不回来。还是扎布里鸟去吧!"扎布里鸟说："我去我去!"者洛担心地说："连老虎和蛇都偷不来，你这么小……"扎布里鸟说："有憨力使憨力，有巧计使巧计，我去了，一定能偷来火种。"蛇和虎都不相信，但者洛说："扎布里鸟说得对，就让他去偷火种吧!"

They rode on the serpent and arrived at the heavenly palace. Zheluo told his three friends, "Human beings could not enter the palace, so you guys go to steal fire in order. If you all fail, I will come up with other plans." Then the serpent said, "I want to try at first!" After sneaking into the palace, it saw burning fire in the kitchen. When it was about to take one burning branch, it was burned with injury, which shed its skin suddenly. After running from the burning fire, the serpent was in panic and said, "Dear god! The fire bit me! I am too scared to get closer again!" Since then, serpents got blisters of burning and suffered from its pain every year. Every time the blisters came out, they had to crawl in sand and bush to shed their skin. That's why they shed skin every year.

After learning the serpent's story, the tiger was feared of fire and said, "How can fire hurt you like this. Let me have a look!" Zheluo told it, "Fire won't bite you if you don't touch it. If you see a pile of fire, just take one branch back and make sure that only one side of the branch is lit." The tiger agreed and ran to the palace. The fire in kitchen was about to extinguish, and there was a servant girl in charge who slept beside. The panic tiger didn't see clear where the fire was, so it just seized the servant and ran. The angry servant took fire tongs to hit and poke it heavily. The hot fire tongs hit and burned tiger's fur, whose skin were then covered with dotted scares. The tiger could not bear it and let the servant go. On its way back, it yelled constantly, "Ouch! The fire bit me. The fire wood hit me. I failed to steal it. Just let the bird try." Then bird said, "Let me try! Let me try!" But Zheluo was worried and asked, "Can you this small guy steal it? Both the tiger and serpent failed!" The bird replied, "They have their ways, and I have my own tricks. Trust me. I will steal fire back!" Although the tiger and serpent didn't believe it, Zheluo agreed to let it try.

扎布里鸟飞到天宫里，钻进灶房看了看火，也不去偷火，就飞到玉皇大帝夫妇的床头去了。玉皇大帝和王母正在谈论老虎叼烧丫头的事，玉皇大帝说：“下方大地上的人，正在议论火种，东方的尼克木俄木已经诏告了天下，说是谁能来天上偷回火种，他就把三个姑娘嫁给他，看来今天跑到灶房来的蛇和虎，都是为此事而来的。”王母说：“凡间的人真笨，在东方尼克木的土地上，到处都有铁；在南方的哀牢山上，到处长满了火草；在北方的大河边，到处有马牙石。只要拿一把火草贴在马牙石上，用铁块去擦石头，火草就会燃起来，那就是火了呢。”扎布里鸟听到这里，高兴得失声大叫起来：“我知道了。”玉皇大帝见扎布里鸟偷听他们夫妇俩的话，便伸手去抓，可只抓住尾巴。扎布里鸟一挣，挣掉又长又美的尾巴，从烟囱里钻出去逃走了。从此，扎布里鸟的尾毛再也没有长出来，让烟囱弄黑了的全身仍是黑漆漆的。

When the bird flew into the palace, instead of stealing it right away, it checked fire in kitchen at first. Then, it flew to the bedroom where the Emperor of Heaven lived, who was talking with his Queen about the servant who was almost caught by a tiger. The Emperor said, "Human beings are discussing about fire. The king in the east has told people that whoever brings back fire can marry his three daughters. The serpent and tiger which come to the kitchen today must have come here to steal fire." Then the Heavenly Queen said, "They are all stupid idiots. There is iron everywhere in the land of east, igniting grasses on the Ailao Mountain in the south and Maya rocks in the riverside of north. Just put a bunch of grass on the rock and clash iron on it, then the grass will burn and fire will show up." The bird was so happy to learn it and yelled, "I get it!" The Heaven Emperor went to catch the bird immediately, but he only caught its tail. In struggle, the bird cut off its beautiful and long tail quickly and escaped the palace throw a chimney. Since then, birds of this type could never grow a long tail and was all black because of dirt in the chimney.

扎布里鸟从烟囱里钻出来，逃离天宫，一见到几个朋友，便大喊大叫："我找到火种啦!"老虎讥笑道："我看你全身糊臭，连尾巴也被烧掉了，是吓疯了说疯话吧?"蛇也说："你不用你的身子把火引来?"者洛问："火种在哪里呢?"扎布里鸟把自己从玉帝的床头听来的话复述了一遍，虎和蛇都不相信，者洛说："可能是真的呢，我们去看看吧!"于是蛇又驮着几个伙伴，先飞到北方的大河边，找来了马牙石，又飞到东方找来铁块，然后回到哀牢山，从山坡上找到了火草。把三样东西拿到一起一试，果然火燃起来了。几个朋友高兴得不得了，就到天生营山顶上去，把火种分给了所有的人。从此，人间有火了，可以吃到熟饭熟菜，可以烧地、御寒了。因为有了火，人们的寿命越来越长，可以活到七八十岁了。东方的尼克木俄木，为表彰者洛他们几个盗火的功劳，把大公主嫁给老虎，老虎和大公主住到山上去，变成了彝族；把二公主嫁给蛇，蛇带着她住到了水边，变成了傣族；把三公主嫁给者洛，者洛住在坝区里，变成了白族。对扎布里鸟呢?按照它的要求，尼克木封赠说："从皇宫到民宅，只要有房屋，你都可以去住。"扎布里鸟很高兴，从此就一直跟着人烟走，人住到哪里，它也到哪里。

After running away from the chimney and escaping from the palace, the bird said to its friends loudly, "I have found fire!" But the tiger mocked it, "You are burned and sticky without tail. You are probably shocked and saying crazy words." The serpent also agreed, "Were you trying to burn yourself to bring fire back?" And Zheluo asked, "So where is it?" The bird repeated what it heard in the room, but the tiger and serpent didn't believe it. Zheluo said, "It can be true! Let's check it." So the serpent carried its friends and flew back to a riverside in the north. After gathering Maya rocks, they flew to the east to take iron blocks and to the Ailao Mountain to pick igniting grass in slope. Then they put three things together and clashed them. Fire really came out right away. They were so happy that they went to the mountain at once and shared fire to everyone. Since then, people could use fire to cook food and get warmth. Their life expectancy became longer, to seventy and eighty years old. The king of east decided to praise them, so he asked his first daughter to marry the tiger. They settled on a mountain later, and their descendants are the Yi people. He asked his second daughter to marry the serpent, who went to live beside a river later, and their off-springs are Dai people. Then he asked his third daughter to marry Zheluo who moved to Ba region later, and became ancestor of the Bai people. What about the bird? The king granted his wish and made a promise, "You can live wherever you like in people's houses," The bird was contented. So it always followed people wherever they went.

因为找到火种那天是六月二十四日，后来每到这一天，人们都要高举火把，唱歌跳舞，并学公主与盗火者婚配的样子，谈情说爱，寻找意中人，举行各种纪念活动。这习惯一代一代传下来，就成了“火把节”。

讲述者：李开鑫，罗正旺
记录者：罗有俊
整理者：罗有能

Because they found fire on 24th June, every year on this day, people would raise torches to sing and dance. They would also hold many commemorative activities, like seeking Mr. and Mrs. Right as princesses and fire-stealers in stories. These customs passed on generations after generations, which becomes the Torch Festival today.

Narrator: Li Kaixin, Luo Zhengwang
Recorder: Luo Youjun
Editor: Luo Youneng

赛衣节的传说

大姚赛衣节

很久很久以前，在美丽的白草岭山麓，有一个叫作“洪水潭”的水潭，这个水潭深不见底，清凉甘甜，山上放牧的人们常到这里饮水乘凉。

每天最早来到潭边的，总是那个叫阿米尼的聪明美丽的牧羊姑娘。她到了潭边，对着平静的潭水梳头洗脸，唱起悠扬的曼么若调①，然后，赶着羊群到白草岭去放牧。每天最晚一个回到潭边的，也总是阿米尼姑娘，她到潭边喝饱清醇甘甜的潭水，又唱起优美的曼么若调，赶着吃得饱饱的羊群回家去。

阿米尼做梦也没有想到，在洪水潭对面的密林中，有个人每天都在偷看她梳头洗脸，偷听她动人的歌声。这个人就是白草岭上著名的年轻猎人阿达西。阿达西深深爱着阿米尼，但他无家无业一直不敢向阿米尼倾吐埋在心底的爱情。

---

① 曼么若调：大姚县三台区一带的彝族牧歌。

The Legend of the Saiyi Festival

Saiyi Festival in Dayao County

Long time ago, a beautiful pond called "Hongshui" lay in the foot of the Baicao Mountain. The depth of the pond could never be predicted but the sweet and cool water always attracted lots of herds to rest around the pond.

A clever and beautiful shepherdess named Amini was always the first person to appear by the pond in the morning. She combed her hair and cleaned her face in the mirror of the pond, singing a melody of Manmero①. And then she herded sheep in the Baicao Mountain. In the evening, however, Amini was the last one to return to the pond, fully enjoying the clean and sweet water and singing Manmero again. Having rested well, she would drive the satiated sheep back home.

Amini did not realize that she was being watched and heard by a person in the woods in opposite to the pond. That person was a lad called Adaxi, a famous hunter in the Baicao Mountain. He was in deep love with Amini but never dared to express himself due as he was homeless and unemployed.

---

① Manmero: the Yi people's pastoral song in Santai District, Dayao County.

有一天，阿米尼坐在潭边唱歌，阿达西再也抑制不住炽烈的感情，就在密林中跟阿米尼对起歌来。阿米尼听到是一个男人跟她对歌，羞得满脸通红，急忙赶着羊群，头也不敢回地回家去了。从此阿米尼不再到潭边梳妆和唱歌了。阿达西心里非常难受。

过了几天，阿达西听人说：龙头大人①正召集九山十八寨的未婚青年在白草岭撒马坪进行骑射比赛，夺第一名的，将被封为带兵打仗的将领，而且还可以在九山十八寨中挑选一个漂亮的姑娘做妻子，婚礼费用也全由龙头大人出。阿达西高兴极了，他决心去夺取第一名，然后，请龙头大人把阿米尼送给他做妻子。

阿达西背起像金子一样发亮的岩桑宝弓，骑上像乌云一样的乌骡，向撒马坪奔去。当他到达撒马坪时，比赛快要结束了。参加比赛的小伙子个个骑技娴熟，箭法精良，众人正为推举第一名相持不下。阿达西来到赛场，人们的议论停止了，双双眼睛都转向这个年轻猎手。

① 古代，三台地区以河段划分地界，河的源头称“龙”，彝族群众把这一地区的头人称为“龙头大人”。

Until one day, when Amini was singing again by the pond, Adaxi could not hold his love anymore, thus he gave response to Amini in a song. Hearing the responsive song from a man, Amini blushed and drove the sheep back home without watching back. From that day on, she had not appeared by the pond any more, saddening Adaxi greatly.

Several days later, Adaxi heard that the Governor of Dragon Head① was calling for single men from eighteen stockaded villages across nine hills to participate in a riding and shooting match held in horse-riding lawn on the Baicao Mountain. The winner would be endowed with a position of general, leading an army to fight in wars, and a chance to select a beautiful lady as wife. Besides, all the cost of wedding would be born by the governor. Adaxi was extremely happy to learn that, so he made up his mind to win the first prize so that he could ask the governor to marry Amini to him.

Adaxi carried his Yansang bow, shining like gold, and rode his mule, as dark as black clouds, rushing to the horse-riding lawn. When he arrived, the match had almost ended. All the participants were skillful in equitation and archery. Just as people were arguing about the final winner, Adaxi showed up. Everyone stopped discussion to watch this young hunter.

---

① In ancient times, Santai Area was divided by river reach, and the source of the river was called dragon. The Yi people regarded the leader of area the "Governor of Dragon Head".

阿达西的表演非常出色，他在场上拣了十个酒碗，用左手托着，飞身上马，两腿一夹，那马就在撒马坪草场上飞奔起来。马跑得像闪电一样，人们看不清阿达西的身影，一股呼呼的风声紧紧追随着阿达西。突然，阿达西把身子往下一俯，将手中的十个酒碗均匀而神速地摆到草地上，然后催马绕场一周。回来时，只见他身子又一俯，十个酒碗早已回到手中。赛场上爆发出打雷一样的欢呼声。在欢呼声中，阿达西马不停蹄，把手往上一扬，十个酒碗被抛到空中形成一条弧线，紧接着他向空中一连射出十箭，十个酒碗被射得粉碎。

九山十八寨的人都推阿达西为第一名，龙头大人也喜欢这个本领非凡的年轻猎人，他一连赏了阿达西三大碗酒，然后对阿达西说："我将提拔你为高贵的将领，还将招你为我的女婿。"阿达西惊呆了，他急忙告诉龙头大人，自己已爱上了牧羊姑娘阿米尼，请求龙头大人让他娶阿米尼做妻子。阿达西的话使龙头大人十分为难。原来，三台地区常常受到外来人的抢劫，人们的生命财产受到极大的威胁。龙头大人已上了年纪，很想找一个英勇善战的人替自己带兵打仗，阿达西是最好的人选，但必须把他招为女婿，才能把兵权交给他。龙头大人没有料到阿达西会拒绝做自己的女婿。这事不能强求，龙头大人沉思半晌，提出一个条件：一百天之后，召集九山十八寨的姑娘来比赛新衣，如果阿米尼的新衣最漂亮，就嫁阿达西。否则谁的新衣最漂亮，谁就做阿达西的妻子。

Excellent performance was presented. Adaxi held ten bowls with his left hand and jumped onto the horse. With a skillful push, the horse thundered across the lawn, like a flash. People could barely follow him. All of a sudden, Adaxi bent over to arrange the bowls in line on the lawn rapidly but steadily. Then he rode around the lawn. When he came back, he bent down again and quickly retrieve the ten bowls. Thunderous applause burst in the court. But Adaxi did not stop. He lifted his arm and threw the ten bowls in the air like a curve and then shot ten arrows towards the bowls without intervals. Each bowel got shot and fell into pieces.

All the participants agreed that Adaxi should be the winner, so did the governor who also appreciated this excellent young hunter. Therefore he awarded him three large bowls of wine and said, "I will appoint you to be the general and marry my daughter to you." Adaxi was shocked. He hastily replied to the governor that he had fallen in love with a shepherdess named Amini. Also he asked for governor's permission to their marriage, which embarrassed the governor. In fact, the Santai District had often been invaded by outsiders, threatening residents' life and property. As the governor grew old, he desperately needed a brave and talented young man to be the army-leader, but under one condition that he had to be his son-in-law first. Adaxi was the best choice, but he didn't expect the young man's refusal. After all, marriage was the sort of thing that could not be forced. Thinking twice, the governor made a requirement which was to hold a competition of dressmaking for all girls from nine hills to participate. If Amini's new dress was the most beautiful, then she could marry Adaxi; otherwise, the winner would be his wife.

阿米尼也在场，她听到这个消息，真是又喜又悲，喜的是比赛场上的英雄阿达西竟然看中了自己，悲的是自己连穿麻布都困难，到哪里找布料来做漂亮的衣服。

阿米尼仍然到白草岭上去放羊。她的羊子几天来一连丢失了好几只，于是，她被龙头大人送进了白草岭上的木垛房里。

夜晚，白草岭上的山风送来了阵阵狼嗥，阿米尼害怕极了。这时，阿达西很关心她，就来到她的身旁，整夜地守卫在木垛房外，使阿米尼能安心入睡。白天，龙头大人只派人送来些残汤剩饭，但阿达西每天都给阿米尼送来两只美味的锦鸡。

日子一天天过去了，离新衣比赛的日子越来越近了，阿米尼姑娘也越来越伤心了。她心里想：达西阿哥是最好的人，如果我能做他的妻子，我一定好好地报答他，但是我到哪里找漂亮的衣服去参加比赛呢？

在泪水中，阿米尼熬过了九十九天。这一天，她抱着阿达西刚送来的锦鸡迷迷糊糊地睡着了。朦胧中，她梦见目已变成一只美丽的锦鸡，飞出了木垛房，飞过了白草岭，飞到一片幽静的树林中，在那里她找到了心爱的阿达西。百鸟都飞来向他们祝福，唱着歌儿赞美她那身美丽的羽毛。阿米尼高兴极了，她跟着阿达西飞呀飞，飞过高山，飞过丛林……突然，她惊醒了，她看着怀中的锦鸡，越看越觉得好看，五光十色的羽毛是那样的美丽，纵横交错的花纹排列得多么巧妙。她心想：“啊呀，我怎么不用锦鸡的羽毛纺织一套衣服呢？”

Amini was present, but she had mixed feelings when she heard the news. On the one hand, she was joyous because the hero Adaxi was in love with her; on the other hand, she felt sorrowful as she could hardly find any linen to wear, how on earth could she find the expensive materials to make the most beautiful dress.

After that, Amini still herded the sheep in the Baicao Mountain. But she lost several sheep for successive days, and thus was sent to a pigsty by the governor.

At night, Amini was frightened at the sound of the blowing wind from Baicao Mountain mingling with wolves' howls. Just then, Adaxi came, out of concern, to protect her in the outside of the pigsty until she fell asleep. During the daytime, the governor sent Amini scraps, but Adaxi would bring her two delicious golden pheasants.

Time flew day by day. The closer it was getting to the competing date, the sadder Amini was getting. She thought to herself, "Adaxi is the best man. If I can be his wife, I will certainly reward him. But where can I get the beautiful clothes?"

Amini spent 99 days in tears. One day she fell asleep with the pheasant sent by Adaxi. In unconsciousness, she dreamed to be a beautiful pheasant, flying over the pigsty, over the mountain, into a peaceful woods. Over there she found her beloved Adaxi. And all the birds gave their blessings to them, singing songs to praise her beautiful feather. Amini was extremely happy and she flew with Adaxi over mountains and woods. Suddenly she woke up. Staring at the pheasant in her hug, she found that the colorful feather was more beautiful and attractive with delicate patterns. She thought to herself, "why not knit a cloth out of feathers?"

时间只剩下最后一天了，但阿米尼并不害怕，她是彝家最能干的姑娘，她的手巧得出奇。她看着挂在木垛房中的许许多多的锦鸡皮，相信自己能纺织出一套她梦中穿过的那种衣裳。

新衣比赛的日子到了。九山十八寨的彝家姑娘都穿着自己精心制作的衣服来参加比赛。龙头大人的姑娘也来了，她穿的衣服，是从外地请来的九十九个裁缝、七十七个银匠，做了九九八十一天才做出来的。九山十八寨的姑娘灰心了，她们的衣服没有谁比得上龙头大人家的姑娘。

就在龙头大人得意洋洋的时候，阿米尼穿着锦羽衣来了。锦羽衣在太阳下闪闪发光，每一道花纹、每一个图案都是人们从来没有见到过的。所有的彝家姑娘都簇拥着阿米尼，请阿米尼传授刺绣技术，连龙头大人请来的裁缝和银匠也不得不认输。

大家都推举锦羽衣是最漂亮的衣服，阿米尼是彝家最聪明最能干的姑娘。龙头大人家的姑娘受到众人的冷眼，心中非常气愤，她要父亲把阿米尼赶出彝家山寨，但龙头大人却高举酒杯对阿米尼表示祝贺，并答应阿达西的请求，让阿米尼做他的妻子。

Even with one day left, Amini was not afraid because she was the most talented and skillful girl among the Yi people. Looking at plenty of skins of pheasants on the walls, she believed that she could weave a dreamlike cloth.

The competing date finally came. All girls in nine hills participated in the match, including the Governor's daughter. Her clothes was carefully knitted by 99 tailors, 77 silversmiths through 81 days. Staring at her clothes, other girls were disappointed at themselves, holding no confidence to win over her.

When the governor was treading on air, Amini turned up with her feather clothes shining in the sun and every piece of the pattern was completely new for other people. All the girls from the Yi families gathered around Amini, asking her to teach them her embroidery technique. Even the tailors and silversmiths invited by the Governor had to admit that their work was inferior to hers.

Everyone agreed that the feather cloth was the most beautiful one and Amini was the most brilliant and talented girl, while the Governor's daughter was coldly treated. In fury, she required her father to chase Amini out of the village. But the Governor made a toast to Amini, promising to marry her to Adaxi.

办喜事这一天，龙头大人亲自赏了阿达西三大碗酒。阿达西做梦也没有想到，龙头大人在酒里下了麻醉药，他喝了三碗酒，迷迷糊糊地在龙头大人家睡了三天三夜。等他酒醒之后，才知道跟他结婚的不是阿米尼，而是龙头大人的三姑娘。三姑娘告诉他：阿米尼并不喜欢他，她已经远走高飞了。阿达西怎么也不相信，他立刻离开了三姑娘，去寻找阿米尼。但他寻遍了白草岭的山山水水，哪里也见不到阿米尼的踪影。

一天，阿达西正在悲伤，山风突然从洪水潭方向送来一阵歌声。阿达西立刻向洪水潭奔去。远远地，阿达西看见阿米尼穿着美丽的锦羽衣，正在洪水潭边梳妆。阿达西喊着阿米尼的名字，飞快地跑到潭边，却不见阿米尼，只惊起一只美丽的锦鸡，向丛林飞去。阿达西毫不犹豫地跨入丛林，朝锦鸡飞去的方向紧紧追去……

从此，人们再也没有看到过阿达西的踪影。据说，阿米尼变成锦鸡飞走了，阿达西也变成锦鸡飞走了。

阿米尼虽然变成锦鸡飞走了，但她教给彝家姑娘的刺绣技术却代代相传，直到今天。彝家人为了纪念这个聪明美丽的姑娘，每年三月二十八都到三台街上聚集，比赛新衣，唱歌打跳。慢慢地，就形成了彝族传统的“赛衣节”。

流传地区：大姚县三台区
搜集整理者：黄自权

When the wedding day came, the Governor awarded Adaxi three bowls of wine. Adaxi would have never expected that the Governor had dropped anesthetic in his wine. After drinking it, he slept in the Governor's house for three days. However, when he woke up, he realized that he didn't marry Amini, but the daughter of the Governor who told him that Amini didn't love him and she had gone far away. But Adaxi didn't believe her. He left the Governor's daughter right away to look for Amini. But he couldn't find any trace of her even though he had searched in every corner of the Baicao Mountain.

One day when Adaxi was in grief, he heard a song from Hongshui Pond. He rushed to that direction right away. From a distance, he saw Amini in beautiful feather clothes combing by the pond. He rushed to the pond calling her name, but she was nowhere to be found instead of a beautiful pheasant flying up into the woods. Without hesitation, Adaxi rushed into the woods and chased after the pheasant...

Since then, people never saw Adaxi again. It was said that Amini flew away in the shape of a pheasant, and so did Adaxi.

Though Amini flew away, her embroidery techniques remained and were passed on to the girls of Yi till today. In honor of this beautiful and clever girl, the Yi people would gather together on 28th March of the Chinese lunar year to compete with each other on making new clothes, singing and dancing. That was the origin of Saiyi Festival.

Spreading area: Santai District, Dayao County

Collector and editor: Huang Ziquan

永仁赛衣节

很久很久以前，直苴①地方是一片茫茫的原始森林，森林中野兽成群，没有人烟。森林外边的寨子里，住着两个勤劳勇敢的彝家兄弟，哥哥叫朝里若，弟弟叫朝拉若，兄弟俩终年以打猎为生。

有一年的正月十五，朝里若和朝拉若带着弩箭，到茫茫的原始森林里去打猎。已经很多天了，兄弟俩还没有打到一头野兽，而他们却已经筋疲力尽。他们来到直苴的尼泥博，看到一个野猪打滚的烂泥潭，潭中水草丰茂，泥土油黑肥沃。哥哥朝里若说："这里土地这样肥沃，泉水这样清甜，一定是一个米粮之地，如果能在这个地方种上粮食，那该多好呵！"说也凑巧，在弟弟朝拉若蹲下喝泉水的时候，从他背着的箭筒里骨碌碌滚出三粒金黄饱满的谷子。兄弟俩高兴极了，立即把三粒谷子播进了泥潭中，并虔诚地祝愿说："这里若是米粮之地，适合人居住，等到秋天收获时，这三粒谷子一定会长成金黄饱满的谷穗。"

① 直苴：地名，在永仁县。

Saiyi Festival in Yongren County

Long time ago, Zhiju① Village was a vast area of primeval forests with groups of beasts and barely any trace of human. In the stockaded village outside the forests, there were two brave and diligent brothers of the Yi. The older one was named Zhaoliruo and the younger one was Zhaolaruo. They made a living by hunting all the year round.

On 15th January of the lunar year, the two brothers took the bows with them to go hunting in the primeval forests. They had hunted for several days but got nothing and became exhausted. Then, they came to Ninibo in Zhiju where there was a rotten mud with abundant grass and fertile soil, and a wild boar rolling in. The older brother said, "fertile soil and sweet spring promise a land of rice. How wonderful it will be if we can farm here!" By coincidence, when the younger brother squatted to drink the spring, three golden plump seeds rolled out from his arrow barrels. They were so happy and planted the seeds into the muddy pond right away, praying sincerely, "If it is truly the land of rice which is suitable for living, then these seeds will grow into full ears when autumn comes."

---

① Zhiju: name of a place, in Yongren County.

兄弟俩回到寨子里，把这段经过告诉了寨中的长老。长老听后对兄弟俩说：“要收获丰硕成果，不能只靠祝愿等待它的到来，而要付出辛勤的劳动。”朝里若和朝拉若听了以后，当即收拾好毡毯，背上吃米，带上打猎的弩箭，来到了直苴的尼泽博，在泥潭边搭起了窝棚，日夜守护着三粒谷子，从萌芽、生长，直到扬花、结果都不离开。兄弟俩射死了来威胁他们的豺狼、来泥潭里打滚的野猪、来伤害禾苗的老鼠，以及来啄食谷粒的山雀。到了金色的秋天，三粒谷子发成了三大窝谷丛，长长的谷穗像马尾巴一样垂下，饱满的谷粒黄爽爽、金灿灿。寨子里的长老和乡亲们热情地祝贺他们。

第二年春天，山林中的布谷鸟叫时，寨里的长老和朝里若、朝拉若带着愿意迁居的男女老少，来到直苴，起房盖屋，开垦土地，又从深深的山涧中引来了清甜的泉水，在田里播下谷子，在地里种上荞麦、绿豆和大麻。兄弟俩带领着大伙，披星戴月，薅锄耕耘，防兽防雀，保护庄稼，到了秋天，又获得了丰收。

When they went back, they told the experience to the elder in the stockade village, who taught them, "If you want a harvest, praying is not enough. You need to work hard." After learning it, they made full preparations to Nizebo in Zhiju with food and arrows for hunting. They built a shack by the muddy pond, and sheltered the three seeds from its sprouting, blossoming to yielding fruits. Meanwhile, they shot wolves, wild boars, mice and titmice which tried to threaten either the seeds or themselves. Finally, when the golden autumn came, the seeds grew into three large clumps of grains. The long ear of grains was in shape of the ponytail with the plump grains shining like gold. The elder and other villagers all expressed their congratulations to the brothers warmly.

In the second spring when cuckoo sang in the valley, the elder and the two brothers led the villagers who were willing to move to Zhiju to start a new life. They built houses from the ground, cultivated the land, brought into clear and sweet spring from the afar mountain, planted seeds in the cropland and grew buckwheat, mung bean etc. Under the leadership of the brothers, the villagers worked hard day and night, cultivating the land little by little and protecting the village from the invading beasts. Finally, there was a bountiful harvest in autumn again.

寨中的长老因为朝里若、朝拉若对开发直苴有功，要为他们缔结美满的姻缘。寨里的姑娘们听到这个消息，都争着要嫁给勤劳勇敢的朝里若和朝拉若。长老问他们最喜欢哪一家的姑娘，朝里若说："我最喜欢心灵手巧的姑娘。"朝拉若说："我最喜欢直苴的山水、树木、花草，哪个姑娘能把这些美丽的花草山水搬在衣裳上，我就娶她做媳妇。"长老向全寨宣布了朝里若、朝拉若兄弟俩选择媳妇的条件，决定在春耕大忙前的正月十五，全寨姑娘集中比赛服装，让兄弟俩挑选媳妇。心灵手巧的姑娘们为了能被选上，日夜织麻纺线，织出精美细白的麻布；又从山上采来了最鲜艳的花朵、最嫩绿的春草，从花丛中选来最美的花瓣，把细白的麻布染成赤、橙、黄、绿、青、蓝、紫各种颜色；在衣裳上、鞋帽上、围腰上绣上了高高的山、清清的泉水、美丽的奇花异卉图案。到了正月十五这天，姑娘们穿着艳丽的服装，打扮得漂漂亮亮的进行比赛。朝里若和朝拉若终于在众多的赛装姑娘中选择了自己的意中人。后来，每年春耕大忙前的正月十五日，为了纪念朝里若和朝拉若兄弟俩开发直苴的功劳，也为了动员春耕生产，彝族姑娘就要穿着盛装互相比赛。年复一年，祖祖辈辈，这个习惯流传了下来，变成了传统的民族节日——赛衣节。

流传地区：永仁县
搜集者：杨云忠
整理者：杨志光

To reward Zhaoliruo and Zhaolaruo for their contribution to develop Zhiju, the elder planned to help them find a satisfactory marriage. Girls in the village all desired to marry them when they were informed of the news. Therefore, the elder asked the brothers about their preferences. Zhaoliruo said, "I prefer ingenious girls." Zhaolaruo said, "I love the nature of Zhiju the most, so any girl who can reflect the beautiful grass and flowers, mountain and river onto the clothes shall be my wife." Then, the elder announced the standards to all villagers and set 15th January of the lunar calendar—a date before spring plough for girls to compete with their prepared garment. In order to win the competition, all the ingenious girls wove and spun day and night to make delicate and exquisite white flax. And then they selected the most colorful flowers and freshest grass to extract pigments to dye the white flax into red, orange, yellow, green, cyan, blue, and purple. High mountains, clear spring, and beautiful flowers were embroidered onto the clothing, shoes and hats. When the day came, beautiful girls in colorful clothes made by themselves competed with each other. And finally, the brothers, Zhaoliruo and Zhaolaruo, found their ideal wives. Since then, on 15th January of the lunar calender every year, girls of the Yi ethnic group would compete with each other in splendid attire to honor the contribution made by Zhaoliruo and Zhaolaruo to Zhiju and also mobilize spring plough. Finally, this custom has been passed on generation after generation and become a traditional festival—Saiyi Festival.

Spreading area: Yongren County
Collector: Yang Yunzhong
Editor: Yang Zhiguang

牟定三月会的传说

河边杨柳排对排，年年有个三月街，三月街子两头赶，阿哥阿妹跳脚①来。牟定三月会，又名三月街，是当地彝族人民的歌舞盛会。

传说，很早以前，牟定城外有一个龙潭，潭里有一条恶龙，每年一到栽插之际总要兴风作浪，发大水，冲田地，毁房屋，使人民生活困苦不堪。虽然年年祭奠，但是并无一点效果。

① 跳脚：一种彝族舞蹈。

The Legend of the Third Month Fair in Mouding

Row in row, stands the riverine willow; year after year, presents the Third Mouth Fair. When that day comes, people from all directions gather on the street with boys and girls dancing Tiaojiao① along the way. The Third Mouth Fair, also called Third Month Street Fair, is a festival for local members of the Yi ethnic group in Mouding to sing and dance.

According to the legend, there was an evil dragon living in a pond outside the Mouding County long time ago. The dragon would make trouble in yearly planting season, causing floods to ruin the farmland and houses, which caused misery to people's life. Though sacrifices were made year after year, nothing changed.

① Tiaojiao: a kind of Yi dance.

有一年，牟定新来了一个知县，他刚刚上任就遇上恶龙作怪，城里城外乱成一片。人们赶着牲畜，拖儿带女向四山避难。县衙门也只得搬上翠屏山顶。转眼间城内外汪洋一片，房屋没了，家具什物到处漂流，田里刚插上的秧苗全被冲走。人畜死伤无数，好不凄惨。知县见此情景，只有含泪安慰黎民百姓。洪水一过，他便把东西两屏山国库粮仓打开救济灾民。人们对他是交口称赞，但是他整天眉头紧锁，心想："这样下去，连年饥荒，民不聊生，皇粮收不上，还得救济，身为一县的父母官，于心何忍！"于是他喊来文书官商量，决定除掉恶龙。文书官说："知县大人，这恶龙作怪，年年如此。前任县令就因无法制服它，只好离任而去，我们何苦与这恶龙作对呢？再说，要制服恶龙，谈何容易，要是有个三长两短，大人你……"知县说："恶龙不除，定远①这坝子难得治理，百姓难得安居乐业，你我也难得安定啊！"他要文书官去请来彝家众头人共谋除恶大计。

① 定远：今牟定。

One day, a new county magistrate took office. Upon his arrival, the dragon started its evil plan, messing the whole county up. Residents had to flee to the Si Mountain with their families and livestock. The magistrate also had no choice but to remove his inquisition chamber to the top of Cuiping Mountain. All of a sudden, floods devastated the whole county where houses were submerged, furniture floated on the water and newly-planted rice seedlings were rushed away, which led to countless casualties of human and livestock. At the sight of it, the county magistrate wept and comforted residents. As soon as the flood was over, he opened the government granaries in the East Ping Mountain and the West Ping Mountain to help the refugees. Though people all spoke highly of the magistrate, he frowned all day long. He thought to himself, "If we don't do anything to change the current situation, people will starve from the endless flooding. Not only the government granaries can not be filled, hungry mouths are to be fed. As the magistrate, how can I stand by?" Therefore, he was determined to get rid of the evil dragon after a discussion with the clerical officer, who said, "My lord, it is nothing new that the dragon makes trouble year by year. And the preceding magistrate left the job just because he failed to defeat it. Why should we try again? Besides, it is definitely not an easy job to do. What if anything bad happen to you?" However, the magistrate answered, "It's impossible to properly govern Dingyuan① without killing the vicious dragon. If residents here can not live a peaceful life, how on earth can you and I work and live in peace?" Afterwards, the magistrate asked the officer to gather all the leaders of Yi together to work out a plan to kill the dragon.

---

① Dingyuan: Mouding today.

一番商议，大计定下，知县便通告全县百姓知晓，并要大家第二年三月二十八日那天，每户送几斤栗炭，到城外龙潭旁去烧。

很快，三月二十八日到了。人们都纷纷来到龙潭旁燃起了炭火，炭火烧红了天空。知县一声令下，将所有烧得红彤彤的栗炭都倒进了龙潭里。霎时，龙潭水滚沸起来，恶龙被烫得浑身是伤，动弹不得。后来人们又抬来石头，挖来泥土，把龙潭填了。为了使恶龙永世不得翻身，大家便在填好的新土上欢乐地跳起舞来，借以踩实泥土。从此以后，恶龙再也没有出来作怪，人民安居乐业了。

为了纪念这个胜利，大家便把每年三月二十八定为赶会跳歌的日子。知县还规定：每年三月街，人们不但可以在街上跳，还可以到县衙门①二堂跳，官民同乐。

流传地区：牟定县
讲述者：普启兴
记录整理者：罗桂森，李世忠

① 译者注：衙门是旧时的官署。

A final plan was decided after the discussion, and the magistrate informed all the people in the county, requiring every household to bring some chestnut charcoals and burned them by the Dragon Pond outside of the county on 28th March of the lunar calendar.

Soon after, when the day came, all the people went to the Dragon Pond to build a fire with the charcoals, lightening the sky. Once the magistrate gave the order, all of the burning charcoals were poured into the pond. The water in the pond was boiling instantly, which burned the dragon so heavily that it could hardly move. Afterwards, people filled the pond with stones and soil and they danced happily on the new ground to make it more solid so that the dragon could never come out again. Since then, people in the Mouding County had never been disturbed by the dragon again.

In honor of this triumph, 28th March of the lunar calendar was set as a day for gathering, singing and dancing. In addition, the magistrate issued a special regulation that residents could not only dance on streets, but also in the second chamber of the magistrate's yamen① so that officials and citizens could share the happiness together.

Spreading area: Mouding County

Narrator: Pu Qixing

Recorder and editor: Luo Guisen, Li Shizhong

---

① Translator's note: yamen refers to the government office in feudal China.

摔跤的来历

古时候，有个汉族小伙子离乡背井，流落在撒尼地区谋生。有个撒尼小伙与他一见如故，结为了兄弟。汉族小伙年长为哥，撒尼小伙年幼为弟。

有一天，弟兄俩上山放牛，忽然发现有一头牛得了草结食，老是定定站着，一动不动，不吃草，也不饮水，肚子胀得鼓鼓的。弟兄俩一看，都很着急。后来，撒尼弟弟对汉族哥哥说："哥哥，我俩得想想办法，不能眼巴巴看着牛胀死。我俩快给牛找点草药吃吃吧！"哥哥说："找点什么药呢？我不知道该吃什么药呀！"弟弟说："山上有一种药能治牛马结食病，这种药我知道，只要能找到，牛吃了肚子就会消下去。"两人便在山上找起药来，并终于找到了这种草药。他俩把药放在石板上，用木棒砸成糊状，扳开牛嘴，把药给牛喂了下去。不一会，牛拉了一摊稀屎，甩甩尾巴，就吃起草来了。

The Origin of Wrestling

In ancient times, a man of Han nationality left his hometown and came to Sani, where the Yi people lived, to make a living. A man of Sani people felt much acquainted with this man of Han nationality and therefore became sworn brother with him, the Han being older brother and the Yi younger.

One day, when they herded cows in mountains, they found that a cow had grass concretion in its stomach. So it stood still with a swollen stomach, without having any food or water, which worried the two brothers so much that the younger one of Sani people said to the older one of Han nationality, "Brother, we have to come up with a solution to rescue the cow; otherwise, it will die of swollen stomach. Certain herbs maybe useful!" The older brother replied, "But I have no idea what kind of herbs can be of a cure." "I know a herb which can cure grass concretion of cows and horses. As long as we can find it, the cows can be saved." The younger brother answered. Therefore, they began to search for the herb and finally found it. They put the herb on a flagstone, smashed it into paste, and fed it to the cow. Within a second, after having loose bowels, the cow came back with energy, starting to eat grass normally.

他俩见牛病好了，心里万分高兴，便一个搂着一个的脖子，在草地上乐得直打滚。这时对面来了个放羊老人，老人误认为他们在打架，忙来劝解。他俩就把发生的事说了一遍。老人说：“牛是庄稼人的命根。牛的病好了，是值得好好庆贺一番的，你们就比比谁的力气大吧。”他俩说：“得说咋个分输赢，不然，一天摔到晚也不知道谁的力气大哩。”老人说：“好，就以脊背落地为输，三跤两胜为赢。”两个小伙子都同意。两人便互相搂着脖子，抱着大腿，比赛起力气来了。比了一次又一次，两弟兄和老人都乐得合不拢嘴。

过了些时，汉族哥哥思乡心切，要辞别撒尼弟弟回家去。离别那天，两人依依不舍。汉族哥哥对撒尼弟弟说：“弟弟，千山万水隔不断我弟兄的感情，我俩分手不分心，将来有时间，望弟弟到我的家乡去玩一玩。”撒尼弟弟说：“将来一定去转一转。”便依依不舍地分别了。

Having cured the cow, the brothers were so happy that they embraced with each other and rolled on the ground. At that time, an old shepherd saw the scene and thought they were fighting mistakenly. Thus he hurried to get them reconciled. After the brothers explained the story, the old shepherd said, "Cows play a key role in farming. It indeed deserves a celebration for its recovery. Then how about you two competing strength with each other to celebrate?" The brothers asked, "What is the scoring rule? Without it, the winner can not be judged even if we compete for a whole day." The old man replied, "Well, anyone whose back touches the ground will lose. The best of three rule will be adopted." The two young man agreed and began competing. They held the thigh of each other, trying to put the other one down to the ground. One round after another, the brothers and the old man enjoyed themselves greatly.

A few days passed, the older brother of Han nationality felt seriously homesick, so he left the younger brother of Sani people and went back home. At the farewell day, they parted with reluctance. The older brother said, "My brother, the distance can not separate our friendship. We are physically separated but mentally connected. Some day, I expect you to visit my hometown." "I will. I promise." Answered the younger. Then, the older brother left.

几年过去后，撒尼弟弟已经变成嘴上长胡子的人，他讨了妻子，而且有了孩子。家里放牛的事，已经交给娃娃们去做了。他交了放鞭，却又理起了养蜂桶。他一人养起了很多蜜蜂，每年秋天都收得大桶大桶的蜂蜜。有年收蜜以后，他又想念起了那个汉族哥哥，很想到汉族哥哥那里去，约他尝尝香甜的蜂蜜。

一天，他告别了妻子和儿子，来到汉族哥哥的家。汉族哥哥和他一样也有了妻室儿子。两人相见，分外亲热，高兴得无法言语，又互相搂着脖子抱着腰，亲亲热热地摔起跤来，越摔越欢乐。前来为他们兄弟俩久别重逢庆贺的人们见了，越看越有趣。后来，人们认为最能表现喜庆气氛的莫过于摔跤，于是凡是喜庆的日子都要举行摔跤。

讲述者：云金

搜集整理者：毕有光

Time flied by. The younger one entered into adulthood, got married and fathered the children. He passed his cowherd job to his children and set out his apiculture. His business was so large that he could collect vats of honey every autumn. One day, after finishing collecting the honey, he missed the brother of the Han people again, longing to visit him and bring him some sweet honey to have a taste.

Later on, the younger brother left his family to meet the brother of Han nationality in his home. Same as the younger, the older brother was married as well as parented. The two intimate brothers were so excited to meet again that they held the neck and the waist of each other to begin wrestling happily. Their joy was beyond words. People who came to congratulate on their reunion were much attracted by their wrestling. After that, wrestling became the best way to express happiness. Since then, wrestling has never been absent in any festive activities.

Narrator: Yun Jin

Collector and editor: Bi Youguang

尼施传彝文

传说，哀牢山的彝家原先没有文字，记事靠刻木绳。可那时候，人们每天要做很多活，要记很多事，木块草绳也就装满了屋子，积成了山。母资莫①看见了，为人们焦愁不安。他叫来了一个管文字的仙女，对她说道：“刻木结绳记事，累坏彝家人了，你下凡去给他们传播文字吧。”于是仙女带了一颗金种和一颗银种下凡了。

仙女来到凡间，在哀牢山最高最陡的悬崖上栽下了银种和金种。她天天用雨给它们浇水，用风给它们培土，用云给它们施肥，用雾给它们松土。一个月后，金芽银芽冒出来了，金枝银枝长出来了，金叶银叶发出来了，金花银花开出来了。花香飘千里，引来采蜜的蜜蜂，引来了看稀奇的人群。仙女对人们唱道：“金花开了三千朵，银花开了三千朵，哪个小哥有心采，拿着礼物来娶我。”金花、银花使人迷醉，仙女的美貌更使人爱恋。人人都想做采花人，个个都争着来攀亲。

① 母资莫：天神。

Nishi Spread the Yi Language

It was said that formerly the Yi people in the Ailao Mountain kept record by curving on wood and tying knots with ropes as they had no written language. But at that time, people had a lot of work to do and many things happened every day, so their houses were piled up with wood blocks and grass ropes, which worried Muzimo① greatly. He asked for a fairy responsible for writing and told her, "the Yi people are worn out by curving and tying. Go to the mortal world and teach writing to them." So the fairy descended to the world with a golden seed and a silvery seed.

The fairy came to the mortal world and planted the golden seed and the silvery seed in the highest and steepest cliff of the Ailao Mountain. She watered the seeds with rain, earthed up the plants with wind, applied fertilizers with cloud and loosened the soil with frog every day. A month later, golden sprout and silvery sprout came out, followed by golden leaves and silvery leaves, and later golden flowers and silvery flowers. The heavy fragrance of the flowers travelled far, which attracted honey bees and curious people. The fairy sang, "Three thousand golden flowers blossom and three thousand silvery flowers blossom. If any lad has a mind to pick them, bring gifts and marry me." People were fascinated by the golden and silvery flowers and deeply attracted to the beauty of the fairy. Everyone wanted to be the one to pick these flowers. So they competed to seek a match with the fairy.

① Muzimo: a deity.

官家鸡叫头遍就起床，天刚发白就赶路，挑着一大箱金银来了。他一见仙女就得意地唱道："天上星星千万颗，官家金银如星多。姑娘若是嫁给我，穿金戴银一生乐。"仙女听罢，冷笑一声，摇摇头拒绝了。官家只好眨着一双馋眼，贪婪地看着仙女，垂头丧气地走了。

官家刚走，财主又挑着绸缎来了。他一见仙女便得意地唱道："天上白云千万团，财主绸缎满家园。姑娘若是嫁给我，好绸好缎穿不完。"仙女听后，又冷笑一声，摆手拒绝了。财主只得舔着流出的涎水，醉眼细眯地看着仙女，扫兴地离开了。

有权有势的人都碰了壁，穷人谁还敢去高攀？可人们却迷恋着闪闪发光的金花银花，迷恋着如花似玉的姑娘。

一天，有个挎弓佩剑的英俊猎人，左手拿着一把箐鸡毛，右手拿着一团红土，笑眯眯地来到仙女面前，开口唱道："我没有金银送给你，送你一坨红泥巴，这是我勤猎的见证。"仙女听罢，喜笑颜开，收下了猎人送来的礼物，同猎人结为夫妻。

An official got up when the rooster crowed for the first time and hurried on with his journey as the dawn was just breaking, along with a large box of gold and silver. At the sight of the fairy, he sang proudly, "Like the sky with countless stars, an official's house also has countless gold and silver; should you marry me, you will enjoy a lifelong luxury of gold and silver." The fairy sneered and shook her hand, declining the offer. Looking at the fairy greedily, the official had to leave, in downcast spirit.

As soon as the official left, a rich man came with silk fabrics. When he saw the fairy, he sang with great pride, "Like the sky with numerous clouds, a rich man's house is also piled with numerous silks and satin; should you marry me, you will have endless premium silk fabrics to wear." The fairy sneered again and shook her hands, refusing the rich man. The rich man had to leave in great disappointment, though with mouth watering and intoxicated eyes still squinting on the fairy.

As both man with influence and man with money ran up against stone wall, how could a poor gay dare to have a try? But people were infatuated with shinny golden and silvery flowers and the fair lady as pretty as a flower.

One day, a handsome hunter carrying a bow and a sword came with a bunch of pheasant feather in his left hand and a pile of red soil in his right hand to the fairy. He sang with smile, "I have no gold or silver for you, but here is red soil, as a witness to my hunting." Smiling broadly, the fairy accepted the hunter's gift and married him.

小两口恩恩爱爱，日子过得如糖似蜜。不久，仙女生下了个胖儿子，夫妻俩爱儿子如掌上明珠，取名叫尼施。

尼施聪明伶俐，生来就爱画画。他看见太阳，就在地上画太阳；看见月亮，就在地上画月亮。反正是见山画山，见水画水，见花画花，见草画草，见鸟画鸟，见兽画兽，见什么都画。说来也怪，尼施画什么像什么，可就是画不像仙女种出来的金花银花，尼施为此很难过。有一天，他哀求爹妈："阿爹、阿妈，金花银花我怎么画也画不像，怎么画也画不好，教我画画吧。"阿爹听了干着急，阿妈听了笑眯眯："好儿子，金花银花六千朵，是六千个字呵。你要把它们一朵一朵地摘下来照着写，才写得像，写得好啊。"尼施听后高兴极了，他拿阿爹送阿妈的箐鸡毛当笔，拿阿爹送阿妈的红土用水和了当汁，用阿妈织好的布当纸。尼施从金树上把花一朵一朵地摘下来照着描，描出的字像金花一样美丽；尼施又从银树上把花一朵一朵地摘下来照着描，描出的字也像银花一样美丽。一天又一天，一月又一月，尼施一共写了一百天。金树上的三千字写完了，银树上的三千字也写完了。

They were affectionate couple and had a life as sweet as honey. Before long, the fairy gave birth to a plump little boy, who was treasured like pearls and named Nishi.

Nishi was very smart and born with an interest in drawing. If he saw the sun, he would draw it on the ground; if he saw the moon, he would draw it as well. He drew whatever he saw, whether it was mountain, water, flower, grass, bird or beast. It was also strange that he could draw very realistically and accurately whatever it was. However, he could not draw the golden flowers and silvery flowers planted by the fairy well, which disappointed him deeply. One day, Nishi begged his parents, "Dad, mum, however I try, why can't I draw the golden flowers and silvery flowers well? Please teach me how to do it." His father was worried, but his mother smiled and said, "Good boy, the six thousand flowers are six thousand characters. You have to pick them one by one and draw accordingly like you write. Then you can write accurately as well." Nishi was very happy. He took the pheasant feature given to his mother by his father as pen, mixed the red soil, another gift from his father, with water to make ink, and used cloth woven by his mother as paper. Then, he picked the flowers from the golden tree one by one, and copied the shape, which displayed characters as beautiful as the golden flowers; he also picked the flowers from the silvery tree, and drew accordingly, which were as beautiful as the silvery flowers. Day by day, month by month, Nishi wrote for a hundred days. All the three thousand words from the golden tree had been Written, and so had been the three thousand words from the silvery tree. By that time, the fairy said to Nishi in a

这时，仙女意味深长地对尼施说："好儿子，从今以后，彝家千千万万的事，你都用这些字去记吧。"接着又对丈夫道："我要回去看我的阿妈，你带着尼施去给彝家传文授字吧。"

仙女离开后，没有再回到人间，尼施父子俩遵照她的嘱咐，把彝文传遍了彝家山寨。

流传地区者：元江县洼垤

讲述者：黄文宝

搜集整理者：宋自华

significant way, “Good son, from today on, keep record of all the things that happened in the Yi families with written words.” Then, she turned to her husband and said, “I need to go home to visit my mother. Take Nishi with you to spread these characters to the Yi people.”

The fairy left and never returned to the mortal world. According to her request, Nishi and his father spread the Yi language to all the stockades of the Yi people.

Spreading area: Wazhi, Yuanjiang County

Narrator: Huang Wenbao

Collector and editor: Song Zihua

三弦的来历

从前，有一个帮土司家放羊的小伙子，家里很穷，只有个老母亲，二十五六岁了，还讨不起媳妇。一天傍晚，他吆着羊群回家，突然发现路旁有一匹小马驹。他想：小马驹这么小，如果没有母马保护，野兽会来咬的。他把羊群赶回去关好，又转来替小马驹找妈妈，可怎么也找不到。

他只好把马驹抱回家去。妈妈见儿子抱着小马驹回来，非常喜欢，因为他家养不起什么牲畜，现在却有了自己的小马驹。从此，母子俩便精心地喂养这匹小马驹。

The Origin of Sanxian

Long time ago, there was a poor lad who herded sheep for a chieftain. Though he was already 25 years old, he still lived with his mother, because he was too poor to wed. One day, when it was at dusk, as he herded the sheep home, he found a pony by the road. He thought to himself, "what a small pony; it would be bitten by beasts without its mother's protection." So after shutting the sheep, he came back to the pony and helped it to find its mother. But he could find the mare nowhere.

He had to take the pony home. When his mother saw this little creature brought back by her son, she liked it very much. As his family was so poor that they could not afford raising any animal, but now, they had their own pony. Since then, the mother and son took great care of the pony.

每天清早，小伙子赶着羊群，牵着小马驹，到山上放牧。小马驹在山上，活蹦乱跳地跑来跑去，吃一会儿草，又跑到小伙子身边，望望他，舔舔他的手，绕着他转转走走。小伙子非常喜爱小马驹。阿妈呢，每天都要割好一篮青青的草，给小马驹做夜草。小马驹长到一岁了，白天小伙子骑着它赶着羊群上山放牧；晚上，小伙子把它和羊群关在一起。有一天晚上，一只狼钻到羊圈里来，小马冲着狼又踢又蹬又叫。小伙子惊醒了，点着明子火到羊圈里去看，只见小马一身湿漉漉的，直喘粗气。狼被小马撵跑了。

这样一来，小伙子更加热爱小马，更精心地喂养小马。

小马长到三岁，小伙子遛马的本事也练出来了，成了寨中出色的骑手。

土司家有个姑娘，长得十分漂亮，要招个骑马的能手做姑爷。为此土司出了告示：某月某日，在土司家城外广场上，举行赛马会，哪个赛赢了，就招哪个做女婿。

很多财主的阔少爷，都想当土司家的女婿，不惜钱财备办高头大马，金鞍银镫。

Every morning, the young man led the pony and grazed the flock of sheep in the mountain. The joyous pony would run here and there. It grazed for a moment and then came back to the lad looking at him, licking his hand and circling around. The young man adored the pony, and his mother also prepared a basket of grasses for it to eat at night every day. When the pony reached one-year old, the lad rode on it and herded the sheep during daytime; at night, he shut the pony together with the sheep. One night, a wolf sneaked into the sheepfold. The pony rushed to the wolf, kicking, driving and yelling at the wolf, which woke up the young man. He immediately lit a light and came to the sheepfold, where he saw the pony was all wet through and breathing heavily. The wolf was driven away.

In this way, the lad loved the pony even more and took a greater care of it.

Two years later, the lad could walk the three-year old pony very well and became the best horseman in the stockade.

There was a very beautiful girl in the chieftain family, who sought for a match with a skillful horseman. Therefore, the chieftain posted a notice that a horse racing event would be held in the plaza outside the town of the chieftain's family on a designated day and the winner of the race would marry the girl.

Many rich young men wanted to be the son-in-law of the chieftain, so they spent a large fortune on preparing for a large horse with golden saddle and silvery stirrup.

一位好心的老大爷，对小伙子说：“小伙子，二十多岁了，还讨不起媳妇，这次土司家要赛马招女婿，你也去试试吧！”

小伙子心想：我是土司家放牧的帮工，赛赢了也做不了土司家的女婿。但他转念一想，和那些公子少爷赛赛也好，赛赢了，可以杀杀他们的威风。因此他也准备去参加赛马会。

赛马会的日子到了，土司家的广场里，人山人海，广场中央，搭起了台子，土司家的贵客，坐在台上观看。

来参赛的少爷公子们，个个穿绸穿缎，跨着高头大马。小伙子穿的却是补丁衣裳，骑的马虽然也很壮实，但不那么高大，样子一点也不出众。“轰轰轰”三铁炮响了，赛马会开始了。说来也奇怪，少爷公子们的高头大马四蹄翻飞，再快也赶不上小伙子的小马驹。那小马驹行走如飞，奔跑似箭。比赛结束，小伙子轻轻松松拿到了第一。可少爷公子们不服气，要求再赛。结果又赛两场，还是小伙子夺得第一。少爷公子们只得认输，个个垂头丧气，像泄气的猪尿泡。

再说，土司一看得胜的竟是他家放牧的帮工，皱了皱眉头，对小伙子说：“今天赛马，你赛赢了，奖你三两银子。你这匹骏马，只配我土司爷骑，把马留下来吧。”

A kind-hearted old man said to the poor young man, "Lad, you are over twenty years old, but you still cannot get a wife. Now the chieftain is looking for a son-in-law. Why not go and have a try?"

The lad thought that only as a helper with the farm work in the chieftain's family, he could not be accepted as the son-in-law even he won the game. But on a second thought, he would like to compete with those rich gays so as to deflate their lordly pride if he won. Therefore, he decided to take part in the race.

On the racing day, the plaza of the chieftain was crowded with people, in the center of which, a stage was set up. Honored guests of the chieftain were invited to watch the race on the stage.

The rich young men were dressed in silk fabrics and rode on high horses. But the poor lad, dressed in shabby clothes, was leading a strong yet not tall horse, looking very ordinarily. "Hong, hong, hong", the cone drum was fired and the race began. It was strange that though tall and strong, the rich gays' horses could not catch up with the pony, which walked as if on wings and ran as if on arrows. When the race was over, the poor young lad got the first place easily. But the rich gays were not convinced and demanded another round. After two more failed tries, the rich men had to admit their failure. Downcast in spirit, they were like the deflated pig's bladder.

As to the chieftain, when he learned that the winner was just the helper in his family, he frowned and said to the lad, "Today you win the race and will be rewarded 150 grams of silver. But leave the horse, as only me deserves to ride on it."

小伙子听了，十分气愤，对土司说："我是来赛马的，不是来卖马的。"

土司一听，这还得了？便叫兵丁拿来鞭子，把小伙子抽打了一顿，关了起来。小马驹也被土司扣压下来。

土司夺得了小伙子的小马驹，非常高兴。一天，他请了些山官到家里来，吃过饭，他要骑这小马驹给山官们看看，以此显显威风。土司刚跨上马鞍，小马驹就双脚乱踢，一下子把土司摔了下来，并拼命地挣扎，把两股缰绳挣断溜跑了。

土司跌跌撞撞地站起来，狂叫着，命兵丁们把小马驹射死。几十个兵丁，端起弓弩向小马驹射击，小马驹身上虽中了很多支箭，但它没有倒下，直往家里跑去。土司看看满身带箭的小马驹，得意地说："反正这马活不了啦。"

小伙子的伤，经医生治后，慢慢好了起来。这天夜里，他想起了土司夺马的事，悲愤万分，久久不能合眼。半夜里，阿妈听到棚子门响，便对儿子说："你去看看，是不是我们的马回来了？"小伙子听了，一骨碌翻爬起来，点了明子火去看，果真是小马驹回来了。马身上插着密密麻麻的箭，小伙子看了十分心痛，他一边哭着拔去马身上的箭，一边给它擦上药。但是由于受伤过重，过了没几天，小马驹还是死了。母子俩日夜坐在小马驹身边哭泣，舍不得把它埋掉，整整哭了三天三夜。

The lad was furious. He said to the chieftain, "I am here to race my horse, not to sell it."

The chieftain could not believe that this lad dared to defy his master. He called for a soldier to bring the whip and stroke him heavily. The lad was shut away and his pony was also withheld by the chieftain.

The chieftain was overjoyed to have the pony. One day, he treated local officials at his house. After meal, he wanted to ride on the pony and impress his guests. As soon as the chieftain mounted the pony, he fell down as it kicked wildly and struggled desperately. Then the pony ran away by breaking the rein.

The chieftain went up, staggering. Then, he yelled and called for soldiers to shoot the pony to death. dozens of soldiers took up bow and crossbow, and shot the pony with many arrows. Instead of falling down, the pony ran straight home. Looking at the heavily injured pony, the chieftain was very proud and said, "Anyhow, this horse will surely die."

The lad's injury was cured by a herb doctor. At night, when he thought how the chieftain took away his pony, his grief and indignation rose in the mind, so he was unable to fall asleep. In the midnight, his mother heard a noise from the shed, and she said to her son, "Go and have a look. Is our pony back?" Bouncing up, the lad immediately lit a light to check and found that it was really the pony. But he was disheartened to see that the pony was stuck with arrows. He cried, pulling out arrows and applied medicine on his beloved pony, but the pony was too badly hurt that it still died several days later. The lad and his mother cried by the side of the pony for three days and night, feeling too grieved to bury it.

一天晚上，小马驹托梦给小伙子，说："主人啊，你别再为我悲伤了。我是你养大的，我也舍不得离开你。你用我的皮箍个弦筒，用我的脚杆做弦杆，用我的尾毛做弦线，让我们一起来咒土司骂土司。闲时我俩还可以一起欢快呢。"

小伙子醒来，按小马驹的话做了个精精巧巧的弦琴，用手一弹叮咚叮咚地响，这声音有时欢乐，有时哀伤，有时愤怒。这就是三弦。

从此，彝族人民就把这弦子一代一代地传下来。每逢节日，青年们就弹起大三弦，欢快地跳！老人们，在火炉旁，边弹小三弦，边讲着古老的故事……

流传地区：楚雄三街一带

讲述者：者从政

搜集整理者：者厚培

One night, the pony appeared in the lad's dream and said to him, "Dear master, don't feel sorrow for me. I was raised by you and I also did not want to leave you. Use my skins as the string tube, my legs as the string pole and my tail hairs as the string line. Let us curse and scold the chieftain. In leisure time, we can still play together joyfully."

The lad woke up and made an exquisite string plucked musical instrument. When he played it, it would produce the sound of Dingdong Dingdong, which sometimes sounded happy, sometimes sorrow, and sometimes furious. This is Sanxian.

From then on, the Yi people handed down this instrument in generations. During festivals, young people would play big Sanxian and dance happily; the elderly would play small Sanxian by the stove and tell ancient stories...

Spreading area: San Street, Chu Xiong County

Narrator: Zhe Congzheng

Collector and editor: Zhe Houpei

白车勒的故事

在南盘江与路南巴江交汇的地方，有两座山肩并肩地坐落在巴江两岸。它们像一对亲兄弟，紧紧相依，共同迎来朝阳，送走晚霞，又陪伴那里星星点点的渔火。这就是象征着彝汉两族人民兄弟情谊的老竹山和左列山。

相传好几百年以前，这老竹山上有一片宽阔的山场，住着彝家老爹阿靥①一家。每日里阿靥老爹带着儿孙们种地打猎，撒麻织衣。虽说是粗茶淡饭，但日子也还过得平平静静。阿靥老爹给这山寨取名叫“白车勒”。

一天，阿靥老爹打猎归来，突然发现山路上躺着一位不省人事的汉族老人。阿靥老爹赶忙上前扶起老人，从腰中解下葫芦，给老人喂上几口山泉水，然后把老人背回家中，煎汤煨药，终于把老人抢救了过来。

① 靥：云南方言，音 man，胖的意思。

The Story of Baichele

In an area where the Nanpan River meets the Lunanba River, there were two mountains side by side, along the two banks of the Ba River. They were like brothers, close to each other, embracing the sunlight, bidding farewell to the sunset glow and accompanying the sporadic lights on fishing boats. These are the Laozhu Mountain and the Zuolie Mountain, symbols of friendship between the Yi and Han people.

It was said that several hundred years ago, an old man called Aman① of the Yi ethnic group and his family lived in a broad tree farm in the Laozhu Mountain. Everyday, Aman led his children and grandchildren to till the farm, go hunting, spread linen to make clothes. Though living on weak tea and scanty meals, they were content with ordinary and peaceful life. Aman name the stockade Baichele.

One day, when Aman went back from hunting, he found that an old man from the Han nationality lied on the mountain road, losing conscience. Aman immediately came to assist the old man to stand up, opening his gourd to give some water to him. Then, Aman carried the old man on his back and took him home. After taking some soup and medicine, the old man finally came back to life.

① Man: Yunan dialect, which means fat.

原来，这位汉族老人姓施，是澄江府出名的老石匠，因为受不了官家的敲诈勒索，便来到这高寒山岭，要为村里人寻找一块官家管不到的清静山场居住，不想却饿昏在半山坡上。

阿靥老爹收留了施家阿公，用大碗水酒、大块鲜肉招待了几天，又打发施家阿公下山去把施家儿郎们接上山来同住。

就这样，彝家子孙和施家儿女们在这片土地上男耕女织，和睦地过着不愁温饱的日子。

阿靥老爹过世前，招拢儿孙们，一遍又一遍地嘱咐："谁要和汉族施家大哥的儿郎们闹别扭，谁就算不得彝家的好儿郎。"

施家阿公临终前也流着泪要儿孙们发誓，记住那宝葫芦的恩情，世世代代和彝家同胞和睦相处，然后才闭上了眼睛。

彝、汉两家的后代遵循先辈的遗言，互助互爱，和和睦睦地过了好多年月。但传到阿鲁老爹这一辈，就出了烦恼的事。

Later, it was found that this old man from the Han nationality had a family name of Shi, who was a famous stonemason in Dengjiang Prefecture. As he could not bear blackmail and extortion from the local officials, he came all the way to this high and cold mountain in order to find a peaceful tree farm where the local officials could not reach, but unexpectedly he fainted from hunger halfway up the mountain.

Aman accepted the old man and treated him with large bowls of water and wine, and large chunks of fresh meat for several days. He also invited the Shi family to move to the mountain.

In this way, off-springs of the Yi people and the Shi family lived harmoniously on this land. Men did farm work and women engaged in spinning and weaving, without worrying about food or clothing.

In his deathbed, Aman gathered his children and grandchildren and required repeatedly that everyone should stay peacefully with brothers in the Shi family; otherwise, they could not be regarded as good off-springs of the Yi ethnic group.

Before death, in tears, Shi also asked his children and grandchildren to make a promise that they should remember the kindness of Aman, and lived harmoniously with the Yi people forever. Then, he closed his eyes in relieve.

Descendants of the Yi and Han people followed the teachings of their ancestors. They helped and loved each other, leading a life in harmony for many years. But troubles came in the generation of Alu.

原来官家道台①老爷知道了白车勒这个地方是块一挤便出油的肥肉，馋得直淌口水。他用一张张传票把施家的族长施三公公传到衙门②，封官许愿，软硬兼施，硬要施家子孙赶走彝家兄弟，好给官家上税纳捐。施三公公义正词严地拒绝了道台的无理驱逐，怒气冲冲地回到山场。从此以后，他再也不下山和官家打照面了。

那时，路南州的彝家土司也派人来笼络阿鲁老爹："黄牛角，水牛角，各干各！快撵走那些汉人！"阿鲁老爹一吹胡子发了脾气，收起了待客的酒肉，打发土司派来的客人上路，然后闷闷不乐地一个劲抽起了旱烟。

官家和土司怀恨在心，又派人在彝、汉两家的子孙中间挑拨离间。后来，由于山场上的人口和牲畜不断地增多，宽阔的山场就越来越挤了，两姓儿孙们之间也难免渐渐引起了纠纷。

为避免不愉快的事情发生，阿鲁老爹和施三公公想出了一个权宜之计：在彝家耕种的土地埂边，一律用埂草打结为记。在施家经管的田地边，垒石为界。两家儿孙尽可能脱离接触，避免冲突。

① 译者注：道台是清代的官名。
② 译者注：衙门是旧时的官署。

A Daotai① in the government learned Baichele and found with mouth watering that it was a place like fat meat, where he could fringe benefits like squeezing oil from fat. He issued a number of summons, asking Shi San, leader of the Shi family to yamen②, to drive away the Yi people with promises of official post in both gentle and soft ways, so that the government could receive taxes from this place. Shi San sternly refused the unreasonable request and went back to the tree farm angrily. From then on, he declined any contact with the officials.

At that time, the chieftain of the Yi ethnic group in Lunan Prefecture also dispatched people to draw over Alu, "Cattle's horn and baffle's horn went desperate ways! Drive away those Han people!" Alu lost his temper and immediately pack up the meat and wine treated to the guest from the chieftain and sent him back on road. Then, Alu smoked a pipe for a long time, depressed in spirit.

Both the official and the chieftain harbored resentment in heart and sent people to alienate the Yi people from the Han people. Later, as people and animals all rose in number, the broad tree farm became increasingly crowded, which inevitably gave rise to dispute among the descendants of the two families.

In order to avoid unhappy conflict, Alu and Shi San came up with an expedient, which was to mark the land of the Yi people by tying grass knots in the surrounding area and mark the land of the Han people by piling up rocks around. In this way, off-springs from these two families could hardly meet each other and therefore reduce the likelihood of conflict.

---

① Translator's note: Daotai is an official title in the Qing dynasty.

② Translator's note: Yamen refers to the government office in feudal China.

可是，阴险毒辣的官家派人暗中移动了石桩，又放火把所有的草结标记烧得精光。这样一来，迎合了施家一些晚辈的私心。

彝家土司也乘机在阿鲁的部落里煽风点火，彝家的儿女们也忍不住嚷嚷起来了。

施三公公严厉地追查自家的不肖子孙，可没有人敢承认干过这种缺德事。老人家叹着气，带上那只当年救活老石匠施阿公的葫芦，领着儿孙们到阿鲁老爹的茅屋去赔情。

阿鲁老爹客气地接待了施三公公，并讲出了使施姓全族人震惊的一席话："没有不散的酒席，没有不缺的月亮，树长高了要发杈，弟兄大了要分家。施家老哥哟，阿靥家的孙孙们早该挪动个地方啰，明天我们就往左列山上搬家。白车勒是个好地方，老哥一定安排好它啊!""阿鲁兄弟，千万走不得哪！要这样搬，施老三跳下巴江也洗不掉这罪孽哟!"施三公公泪水纵横，伸出颤抖的手，紧紧抓住阿鲁老爹不放，再三恳求着。

"彝家人打定的主意，九十九条牛也拖不转啊!"阿鲁老爹平静地笑着，给施三公公送上一碗水酒。

"阿鲁兄弟，我……我一定把干这缺德事的坏种查出来，交给兄弟处置。再不然，我们施家离开这山场，说啥也不能让阿鲁家的人往外搬啊!"施三公公激动地说。

However, the sinister and ruthless official sent people to move the stone mark in secret and set fire to burn up all the grass knots, which catered to selfish motives of some younger generation of the Shi family.

The chieftain of the Yi nationality also took opportunity to stir up trouble among people from the Alu family, so children of the Yi people could not help complaining.

Shi San severely investigated the unworthy descendants of the family and no one dared to admit this wicked thing. The old man signed and led all his families with the gourd which had saved the life of Ashi to the bothy of Alu to apologize.

Alu received Shi San courteously and shockingly said, "No feast never ends, and no moon never breaks; tall trees will have branches and grown-up brothers will break up the family and live apart. My brother Shi, it is long time that we moved to somewhere else. We will go to the Zuolie Mountain tomorrow. Baichele is a good place, so please make a good use of it." "My brother Alu, don't go. If so, my sin can never be washed away!" Shi San was all in tears. Reaching out his shaking hands, he grasped Alu firmly and pleaded him repeatedly.

"Once the Yi people make up their mind, ninety-nine buffalo can not turn us back!" Alu smiled at Shi San calmly and offered him a bowl of wine.

"My brother Alu, I... I will definitely find out who has done this wicked thing and give him to you for your disposal. Or I will lead the Shi family to leave the tree farm. There is no reason why your family should move out!" Shi San said emotionally.

“啊，哈哈哈，看老哥说到哪里去了!”阿鲁老爹望着施三公公，一阵憨厚爽朗的大笑，又连连声明：“用不着，用不着，哪能这样！我看这事也未必是施家后生干得出来的。这火一烧，我倒有了主意，老哥住的石板屋，可不能随意挪动；阿鲁家住的是茅草屋，走到哪山还缺草呢？阿鲁不趁这年纪给儿孙寻个好山场，怎么对得起彝家的老祖宗！来，老哥，这碗离别酒您一定得喝下去。”

施三公公始终无法留住阿鲁一家。第二天，阿鲁老爹率领着彝家儿孙们过了巴江，在与老竹山相邻的左列山上安下了家。

多少代过去了，直到如今，老竹山上住着的施家子孙后代们，始终珍视白车勒这一彝家村名，怀念着勤劳、善良、无私的彝家兄弟。

巴江两岸，人们争相传颂着彝、汉先辈们创业的故事，传颂着那象征彝、汉兄弟情谊的老竹山与左列山的传说。

搜集整理者：刘植

讲述者：李多才

"Ah, hahaha, what nonsense are you saying? My brother!" Looking at Shi San, Alu laughed in a simple and honest way. He said immediately, "There is no need, definitely no need. How can you do that! I don't think it's done by one of the descendants from your family. Because of this fire, I figure out that it is easier for us to move since you live in the slabstone house which can hardly be moveable, while we live in the thatch house and grasses can be found everywhere. If I do not take the opportunity to find a good place for the children and grandchildren of my family while I am young, I will feel guilty for our ancestors. Come, my brother. Please drink this parting wine."

Shi San had no way to persuade the Alu family to stay. On the second day, descendants of the Yi family crossed the Ba River led by Alu and settled in the Zuolie Mountain, next to the Laozhu Mountain.

After many generations, until today, descendants of the Shi family who live in the Laozhu Mountain still treasure the Yi name of Baichele and cherish the memory of their hardworking, kind-hearted and selfless Yi brothers.

On the two banks of the Ba River, the enterprising stories of the Yi and Han ancestors and the legends of the Laozhu Mountain and Zuolie Mountain, symbols of their brotherly friendship, are still eulogized.

Collector and editor: Liu Zhi

Narrator: Li Duocai

灵魂与人生

Spirit and Life

流浪孤女蛇娘

从前，有一个姑娘名叫蛇娘。她是一个水灵灵的美女，站在哪里，哪里亮堂堂，坐在哪里，哪里光闪闪。她从小失去了父母，也没有家支，找不到安身处，只好漂流四方，到处流浪。她把自己的遭遇编成一首歌，一路走一路唱。凡是她走过的地方，老人们都在把她赞美，小伙子们都在把她看了又看。

蛇娘的境遇并没有因此改变。她依然找不到安身立足的地方，依然必须不停地流浪乞讨。因为人们赞美的只是她的外表，人们怀疑她出身低贱，谁也不愿收留她，更不可能娶她做媳妇①。蛇娘明白这一点，所以尽管她不停地用歌声倾诉自己本来出身的高贵和血缘的纯洁，心里并不抱什么希望。

---

① 彝族旧时的婚姻，等级观念极严，实行严格的姑舅表婚制，对不同等级的通婚现象，有一套专门的惩处酷刑。

Homeless Orphan Sheniang

At one time, there was a girl called Sheniang. She was so pretty that she was always the most shining star wherever she went. Her parents died in her childhood, leaving her no family at all. Being homeless, Sheniang started her vagabond life since then. She wrote her stories into a song and sang it along the way of wandering. Wherever she went, Sheniang always earned much praise from the elderly and affectionate glances from young lads.

However, her situation was not improved by that. Sheniang still could not find a place for herself and had to beg as a roamer. Because everyone was just appreciative of her appearance and many suspected that she was of humble origin. No one would take her in, let alone marrying① her. Sheniang was very aware of that. Even if she tried hard to show her once noble birth and impeccable pedigree through her singing, Sheniang did not really hope for anything.

---

① In ancient times, marriage among the Yi ethnic group centered on hierarchy. The Marriage System of Cousinship was strictly followed, supported by a whole special set of cruel punishments.

有一年春天，蛇娘途经一座大山时，看见山坡上荞花铺成毡，鲜花开满树，远处草地上，牧人哇呀哇呀地唱着，牛群哞哞地叫着，白色的羊群快速地往前涌着，心里激动得不得了。看着看着，蛇娘心里就悲哀起来了：天地虽然大，但谁也不理她；山水虽然美，但都不属于她。她东看看西望望，感到自己孤苦伶仃，像一个找不到神位的孤魂，像一条又瞎又聋的野狗。她想说很多很多的话，但没有倾诉的对象；她想唱很多很多的歌，但找不到一个听歌的伙伴。蛇娘的心乱了，苦水和酸水变成眼泪哗哗往外流，蛇的喉头颤抖了，不平和哀怨变成调子轻轻唱起来：

天下为什么要有路？
地上为什么要有草木？
可怜的孤儿为啥要长大？
长大了为啥无伙伴？
荞花忙着自结果，
树花忙着自开放，
牛羊只管自吃草，
孤苦的女儿无伙伴。

One spring, Sheniang went through a huge mountain where buckwheat flowers spread out like a thick blanket and trees were in full blossom. On the grassland in the distance, herdsmen were singing joyfully and herds of oxen also joined in, mooing when herds of shining white sheep wandered along briskly. At first, Sheniang found all those scenes thrilling but then she got a little sad, thinking that no one wanted her in this big world and no place was available for her to stay. Looking around, Sheniang was struck by the utmost loneliness. Even if she had a lot to say, she could not find a person to turn to; even if she wanted to sing a lot of songs, she could not be heard by a single living soul on earth. Sheniang was desperate and burst out into tears. Suddenly her larynx trembled a little, turning grievances into a humming tune. It went like this:

Why is there road in the world?
Why onto the earth floras hold?
Why do poor orphans grow up?
Why cant's grown-ups find anyone to play and hug?
Buckwheat flowers are busy at bearing fruits.
While blossom is all that a tree brews.
Flocks and herds just wanna eat.
Poor girl like me only wanna meet.

蛇娘唱着唱着，忽然听见山洼密林里传来猎人的喊狗声。狗叫起来了，铃响过来了，猎人的脚步声传来了。蛇娘刚慌慌张张地揩干眼泪，猎人已经来到了她的身边。猎人看了她一眼，又看她一眼，再看她一眼，从她的身边朝前跑去了。猎狗绕着姑娘转了三转，欢叫着跟去了。蛇娘被猎人火一样的眼光看得心跳血涌，头晕目眩。猎人英俊的面孔刻在了她的心上，猎人健壮的身姿留在了她的心中，猎人有力的脚步声像蜂蜜一样粘住了她的目光。她向着跑远的猎人看去，只见猎人站在一个大黑石头上，朝她侧着脸看什么；猎人的狗伸长了舌头，面向她而坐，用亲切的目光注视她。蛇娘的心里“噔”的一下，她忽然感到猎人会回来，于是撒开彩裙，手托下巴坐在花草地上，专等猎人回来。

等了一会，响起了猎人的唤狗声，狗叫起来了，铃响过来了，猎人的脚步声传来了。蛇娘转过头去，猎人已经来到了她的身边。猎人奔跑的姿势就像野猪窜山，叫她震惊；猎人奔跑的影子就像买的苍鹰，使她心慌。她以为猎人会开口和她讲话，以为猎人会停下脚步，可是猎人依然看她一眼，又看她一眼，再看她一眼，在她面前一闪而过，又跑到大黑石头上站着去了，还是那样的目光，还是那样的面孔。那一条猎狗，绕着她转了三转，又欢快地跑到石头边坐着，亲切地看她。

When she was singing, Sheniang suddenly heard a hunter shouting out to his hound in the deep forest. Then the hound barked. After a while, rings of hound' bells and footsteps of the hunter approached her. Sheniang wiped out her tears hastily and found the hunter standing just beside her. The hunter could not help but look at her three times and then ran away from her briskly. The hound circled around Sheniang and followed its master joyfully. Looked at by the hunter, Sheniang was set on fire, feeling so high as to faint. The hunter's handsome looks, stalwart figures and solid footsteps were engraved in her heart. So, she chased after him to take a look at him in the distance. She found that the hunter was watching something on a huge rock with his head facing the other direction. But the hound stuck its tongue out and sat facing her, watching her amiably. Having had this hint that the hunter might come back, Sheniang lifted up her colorful skirt and sat on the grass with her hand holding her chin, waiting for the hunter to come back.

After a while, hunter's shouting, hound's barking and rings of bells and solid footsteps were heard nearby. When she turned around, Sheniang found that the hunter was running towards her. The way the hunter ran brought many palpitations to Sheniang. And she thought the hunter would come to talk to her, only to find that he just took a look at her and scurried off. The hunter ran to the huge black rock and stood on it, watching something in the same way he did. And the hound circled around Sheniang again and rushed to the rock briskly and sat near it, watching Sheniang amiably.

蛇娘心慌意乱地想，猎人还会回来，还会装模作样地唤狗，然后又装模作样地从她面前走过。于是她一动不动地坐着，决心等猎人一出来，就站起来去迎。如果他不停步，就跟在后边追着去。果然过了不久，意料中的事发生了。猎人又在山洼密林里唤狗了。狗又叫起来了，铃又响起来了，猎人的脚步声又传来了。蛇娘慌忙起身迎上去。猎人看了她一眼，脚步停了停；又看她一眼，脚步停了停；再看她一眼，脚步停了停。蛇娘还没来得及开口，猎人又从她面前跑走了。猎人跑得很快，这次也没有在大黑石头上停留，一闪身跑下山坡不见了。但是猎狗这次在她身边绕了三转后，没有离开的意思，坐在猎人跑过的路上，回头等着蛇娘，直到蛇娘迈步跟上去，它才慢慢地走在前边引路。

猎狗带着蛇娘追着猎人在山路上走。走了一段路，蛇娘看见路边丢着猎人的弩箭，她把弩箭捡了起来。又走了一段路，看见路边丢着猎人的箭袋，她又把它捡起来。再走了一段路，看见路边丢着猎人的包头布，她又把它捡起来。聪明的姑娘知道小伙子已经失魂落魄，心里又温暖又甜蜜。继续往前走，来到一片小树林，蛇娘忽然惊呆了。

Sheniang could not decipher the hunter's move and got panic. But she still believed that he would come back, and then deliberately called out his hound and ran off again. So, she stayed where she was and sat waiting for the hunter. She also made up her mind to greet the hunter as soon as he came to her and chased after him if he did not stop. As expected, before long the hunter shouted out to his hound again in the deep forest, and then the hound barked, the bells rung and the hunter came. Sheniang hastily got up and went to greet him. The hunter looked at her and stopped for a moment. Then he looked at her again and stopped a while. He did it again and again. Before Sheniang could open her mouth, the hunter ran past her. This time, the hunter ran faster and did not stop at the rock. He ran down the hill in a blink of an eye. But the hound circled around Sheniang and showed no intention of leaving. It sat on the path where the hunter went and spun around to see Sheniang as if it were waiting for her. Then after Sheniang strode to catch up, it started walking and led the way ahead.

The hound led Sheniang and chased after its master. After a while, Sheniang saw some arrows beside the road and picked them up. Then after some time, she saw a quiver left by the hunter and picked it up again. Later she saw a piece of the hunter's headcloth and picked it up. The smart girl felt very warm and happy because she knew by then that the young lad had totally fallen for her. She walked on and reached a grove where she was so shocked by the scene in front of her.

在一棵大树面前，跪着一个可怜巴巴的小伙子，他头上没有包头布，英雄结①就像玉米苞垂挂在脸上；头发乱得就像反毛鸡；身上的黑披毡，被揉成一团夹在胳肢窝下。只见他脸色苍白，双眼紧闭，全身就像巫师跳神，抖成一瓢水。蛇娘又感动又心疼，轻轻走过去，把弩箭背在他背上，把箭袋挂在他腰上，把包头布包在他头上，为他拉开披毡披正，然后把他拉起来。面对着柔情的姑娘，小伙子不知怎么办好，忽然蹲下去说："让我背着你走吧。"

蛇娘知道猎人的心情，轻轻扑到了猎人的背上。高兴得发狂的猎人，大叫着，大笑着，背着蛇娘跑过山梁，跑过河水，跑过森林，跑过开满鲜花的荞山，跑过牧人放牧的草地。鲜花在他们后边乐得跳跃，牛羊在他们周围奔撞欢叫，猎狗在他们身边跑了一个又一个好看的圆圈。牧人们回家去说："猎人阿支疯了，背着一个姑娘在山上跑，就像发情的野猪。"

① 译者注：英雄结是一种彝族男子的头饰。

A poor young man keeled in front of a big tree with no headcloth on his head and his hero knot① hanging down over his face. His hair was unkempt and his black cape was huddled up and carried under his arm. With pale skin on his face, the young man closed his eyes and trembled greatly like a warlock dancing and performing a ritual. At the sight of it, Sheniang was deeply touched yet pitiful. So she walked softly towards him and put the arrows on his back, the quiver around his waist and a headcloth on his head. Then she helped him wear the cape properly and pulled him up. In the face of this soft and loving girl, the young man did not know how to respond but squatted down, saying, "Let me carry you."

Having read the hunter's mind like a book, Sheniang gently jumped on his back. The hunter became ecstatic, as was evidenced by constant fits of shouts and laughter. He carried Sheniang and ran through rivers and forests and mountains covered with buckwheat flowers and grasslands where herdsmen pastured, while his hound, flowers, and flocks and herds all joined in his joyful celebration. Even many herdsmen came back home, saying, "The hunter, Azhi, got crazy, carrying a girl on his back and running around in the mountain just like a wild pig in heat."

---

① Translators note: hero note is a kind of headwear for men of the Yi ethnic group.

猎人阿支跑啊跑，跑累了，便背着蛇娘回到第一次见面的地方，伸脚伸手地仰躺在草地上，像一个刚吃饱奶的婴儿，自足地呼呼大睡起来，一直睡到夕阳西下，雀鸟归巢。当他醒过来时，看见蛇娘笑吟吟地坐在面前，把撒开的彩裙盖在他身上。他就坐起来，故意问蛇娘说："你刚才为什么追我？"

蛇娘说："那你为啥跪在大树面前？"

猎人阿支说："谁叫你站在我经达的路上？"

蛇娘说："谁让你看了我九眼。"

两人越说越高兴，嘻嘻哈哈地打闹了一阵，亲热得不得了。猎狗见主人乐不可支，也兴奋得一下窜进猎人怀里一下窜进蛇娘怀里，好像是一个受父母宠爱的顽童。蛇娘和猎人的心，被它紧紧连在一起了。

Hunter Azhi ran and ran until he finally got tired. Then he carried Sheniang back to the place where they first met. He lied on the grassland, stretching his hands and legs. Then he fell asleep with satisfaction just like a well-fed baby. The hunter did not wake up until the sun set and birds returned to their nests. When he woke up, he saw Sheniang sitting in front of him, smiling, and spreading her skirt to cover him. So, he sat up and asked Sheniang deliberately, "Why did you chase after me then?"

Sheniang replied, "Why did you kneel before the tree?"

Hunter Azhi said, "If you hadn't stood on my path..."

Sheniang resumed, "If you hadn't looked at me nine times..."

The two people became more excited and messed around with each other cheerfully. The hound found that its master was happy with Sheniang, so it got very excited as well, sometimes jumping into the hunter's arms and sometimes Sheniang's. As the hound behaved like a spoiled child, the hunter and Sheniang were bound together by this cute being.

后来，猎人阿支对蛇娘说："美丽的姑娘，从此你就是我的媳妇了。"蛇娘听了，想起了自己的身世，悲哀地说："就怕你不敢要我。"猎人阿支说："把我砍成八大块，我也要要你。"蛇娘担心地问："你不怕你的家支惩罚你吗？你不怕你被家支歧视吗？你不怕我们的结合不会有好结果吗？"猎人阿支坚定地说："不怕！"可是蛇娘听了，一点也不高兴，她说："你不怕我怕，人是离不开亲友邻里的，交往是离不开名声的，这事得想想办法。"猎人阿支说："我们住到大山里去，永远不见人。"蛇娘说："不行，人又不是野兽，不能进山林。"阿支又说："那我们逃到远方去。"蛇娘还是摇着头："离开了家支的人，不管到哪里，都要受人欺负，遭人白眼，这办法不好。"

勇敢聪明的猎人阿支被难住了。他想呀想，想了很长时间，终于想出一个办法。阿支对蛇娘说："我有个最好的朋友，名叫力达。他原先是乃依大兹莫的跟班娃子，因为心眼聪明，被乃依大兹莫①提升为自由民②，刚领了块封地，住在附近呢，我们去找他帮忙。"

---

① 兹莫：古代彝族部落联盟的最高酋长。后世多被封为土司。

② 自由民：彝族社会中自食其力的阶层。

Then hunter Azhi said to Sheniang, "Beautiful girl, from now on I will take you as my wife." Thinking of her family background, Sheniang answered sadly, "I'm afraid you can't do that." Azhi said, "Nothing in the world can keep me from marrying you." But Sheniang was still worried and asked, "Aren't you afraid that your family will punish you and discriminate against you? Aren't you worried about our future?" Azhi was still determined and gave Sheniang a firm negative answer. But Sheniang was not very satisfied with his answer and said, "Well, if you are not afraid, then I am. How can I make friends and form ties with others if I have a bad reputation? You need to work that out." Then Azhi said, "Maybe we can live in the remote mountain where you don't need to meet anyone." But Sheniang rejected and said, "We can't. We are human not animals." Then Azhi proposed that they should flee far away. Sheniang shook her head again, saying, "Anyone without families will be bullied and discriminated wherever he goes. It's not a good idea."

The brave and smart hunter Azhi was cornered. After thinking for some time, he finally came up with a solution. He told Sheniang, "I have a best friend called Lida. He was once an attendant of Zimo① Naiyi. Because he was very smart, he was then promoted by Zimo to the independent class② and was granted land, just nearby. We can turn to him for help."

---

① Zimo: a high priest, and chief of a tribe among the Yi ethnic group in ancient times. It was called Tusi after.

② The independent class: a self-supporting class in the Yi society.

蛇娘担忧地劝说道："这种事，找人帮忙怕不好，我们还是自己想办法。"

猎人阿支说："你放心吧，力达可靠，我了解他。"说完，他把她领到一个岩洞里藏起来。不管蛇娘怎么劝告，他就是不听，留下猎狗给她做伴，就风风火火地找力达去了。他要找力达保媒，要找力达骗家支。

阿支把力达领进岩洞，力达见了美若天仙的蛇娘，两眼发直，一下惊呆了。阿支几次和他说话，他都不吭声；猎狗对他狂叫，他才回过神来。

左商量，右商量，阿支和力达想出了哄骗家支的办法。

当天晚上，阿支回到家里，对父母说："我的朋友力达决定到日浦索洛地方去走亲串戚说媳妇，我也想跟他去长长见识，请你们同意我去吧。"

阿支的父亲是个瞎子，母亲是个跛子。跛子没有主意，问瞎子怎么办。瞎子仰头看着天想了想，说："这事得问布布酋长，他是家支头人。"阿支跑去问布布酋长。老得像只猴子、瘦得只剩皮包骨头的布布酋长，板着从无血色的木板脸说："既然跟的是力达，那我同意你去。"阿支喜不自禁，第二天便跑到岩洞和蛇娘住在一起。

But Sheniang was not reassured and tried to persuade him out of it by saying, "It is not wise to ask others for help in such a matter. We should deal with it on our own." Azhi replied, "No worries. Lida is very reliable. I know him very well." Then he took Sheniang to a cave and hid her. No matter how hard she tried, hunter Azhi would not listen, leaving the hound to make a company, and went to Lida in a hurry. He asked Lida to make a match for Sheniang and himself, and lied to his families.

When he took Lida to the cave, Lida was so shocked to see the beautiful girl in front of him that his eyes were wide open and he did not come back to his mind and answered any of Azhi's questions until the hound barked at him.

After discussing for a while, Azhi and Lida came up with a plan.

At that night, Azhi returned home and said to his parents, "My friend Lida decided to go to Ripusuoluo to see his relatives and find a girl to marry. I want to go with him and see what will happen to me. Please let me go with him."

Azhi's father was blind and his mother was lame. Azhi's mother was foxed, so she asked his father what to do, who looked up and thought for a while. Then, he said, "We need to consult chief Bubu. He is the head of our clan." Then Azhi ran to chief Bubu and asked for his opinions. The withered old chief said with his always pale and serious face, "Since it's Lida you are going with, I have no objection." Azhi was thrilled and went to live with Sheniang the next day.

一个月过去，阿支装着出远门回来的样子，领着蛇娘回了家。家支里的大人小孩，见阿支带回一个比天仙还美丽的姑娘，全都惊奇地跑来看。阿支按照力达出的主意，对父母亲说：在去日浦索洛的路上，他碰见两个家支打冤家，有个家支打败了，剩下这个可怜的姑娘，因为喜欢她，想要她做媳妇，就请力达做了媒人，把她带回来了。他请求父母给他们举办婚礼。

阿支家很穷，瞎父跛母正愁无力给儿子娶媳妇，如今忽然飞来了个美丽的姑娘，他们巴不得马上给阿支成婚，但他们作不了主，得找酋长去商量。酋长布布老头找到蛇娘，把她的身世问了一遍又一遍。蛇娘只得用力达帮编的谎话来应付。

布布酋长眼睛翻了几翻，忽然又说："姑娘请你把你父亲的家谱①背来听听。"蛇娘背了父谱，又背了母谱，布布不再吭气了。不过力达是保媒人，他还得去问力达，由力达来证婚。布布酋长派人去请力达，可听说力达出远门去了。这事可麻烦啦。蛇娘发愁了，阿支也不高兴了。没有保媒人，布布酋长决定召开家支大会，要阿支当着祖灵位赌咒发誓，才准许他和蛇娘举行婚礼。

① 在彝族中，背不来家谱的人被视为奴隶，地位低下。

After a month, Azhi pretended to have had a long journey and took Sheniang to his home. When the news came that Azhi had brought home a fairy-like girl, adults and children in his clan all ran to have a look. Azhi told his parents the version advised by Lida, "On my way to Ripusuoluo, I came across two clans figh-ting each other. One clan was defeated, leaving this poor girl. I like her and want to marry her, so I ask Lida to be our matchmaker and bring her home. Please hold a wedding ceremony for us."

Azhi's parents could not wait to hold the wedding for his son and this pretty girl after learning the story. In fact, they had been worrying about whether their son could even find any girl willing to marry into such a poor family. But they were unqualified to make the decision and had to consult the chief. Chief Bubu went to Sheniang and asked about her family background again and again. Sheniang had to cope with it by telling a lie Lida fabricated.

Then chief Bubu rolled his eyes and tried to think of something else. He said, "Young girl, do you remember the genealogy of your father?" Sheniang recited to the chief the genealogy① of her father and then her mother. So, chief Bubu stopped questioning. But he still had to consult Lida and let Lida marry them since he was the matchmaker. So he sent a servant to invite Lida, only to find that Lida had gone on a long journey. What a troublesome coincidence! Both Sheniang and Azhi were very anxious. Without a matchmaker, chief Bubu decided to convene a meeting of his clan and asked Azhi to swear that everything he said was true in front of his ancestors' memorial tablets. Afterwards, he permitted the wedding.

---

① The Yi people traditionally believed that anyone who could not recite his family genealogy was a humble slave.

布布酋长端着一碗酒问：“阿支，你所说的这位姑娘的来历，都是实话吗？”

阿支说：“是！”

“如果不说实话呢？”布布酋长又问。

“用我的头担保！”阿支说着，转头去看蛇娘，只见她脸色苍白，全身发抖，好像要昏倒的样子。阿支知道她为这套不得不编的谎话感到难过。到了成亲那天晚上，他哀求说：“蛇娘，你好几天没有笑了，我看着真难过，你笑一笑吧。”蛇娘说：“布布酋长从来不露笑，这不是好兆头，我觉得灾难就在我们的面前。”阿支安慰说：“放心吧，不会出什么事的。”

但是不久，蛇娘的担心变成了事实。阿支的朋友力达出卖了阿支。蛇娘和阿支都落到他的圈套里去了。

力达那天在岩洞里见了蛇娘以后，回家去就病倒了。他十分嫉妒，他要把蛇娘从阿支手里抢过去。当阿支和蛇娘成亲时，他故意藏起来，不去证婚。等他们成亲后，他便来找布布酋长说：“啊，尊敬的酋长大人，我和阿支是最好的朋友，为什么他成亲时，你们不告诉我一声呢？”布布酋长听了，把嘴张得碗一样大，木板脸上的白眼仁也不会翻了，他

Chief Bubu held a bowl of liquor and asked, "Azhi, is everything you said true?"

Azhi replied firmly, "Yes!"

The chief asked again, "what if not?"

Azhi said, "Swear on my life!" Having said his piece, Azhi turned around to see Sheniang, only to find that she wore a pale face, trembling, and looked as if she was going to faint. Azhi knew that she felt bad about telling this lie. On their wedding night, Azhi begged, "Sheniang, you haven't smiled for days. It really makes me feel awful. Please have a smile." Sheniang answered, "Chief Bubu never smiles. It's not a good sign. I really think something bad is going to happen." Azhi tried to comfort her and said, "Be reassured. Nothing will go wrong."

But before long Sheniang's worries came true as Lida, the best friend of Azhi, betrayed Azhi. Sheniang and Azhi both fell into a trap set by Lida.

After meeting Sheniang in the cave that day, Lida got sick out of jealousy once he turned home. He swore to take Sheniang away from Azhi. When Azhi and Sheniang started their wedding ceremony, he hid himself deliberately in order not to marry them. After they finished the ceremony, he went to chief Bubu and said, "Your excellency, Azhi and I are best friends. Why didn't you tell me about his wedding?" Chief Bubu was so shocked at what he said that his mouth was wide open and his eyes became glazed. Then the chief asked, "Weren't you going out far?" Lida pretended to be very astonished and replied, "Excuse me? Who told you I went out? From the day when I was awarded with my

说："你不是出远门去了吗？"力达装作吃惊的样子说："什么，谁说我出远门了？自从我受到乃依大兹莫的恩封，直到如今，一天也没离开过封地哩。"布布酋长眼睛睁得茶杯大，跳了起来："前不久你不是到日浦索洛去了一个月？"力达笑道："我是个由娃子迁为自由民的人，天底下没一个亲戚，到日浦索洛去干什么呢？"酋长问："你真的没去？"力达笑道："布布酋长把我看成什么人啦！不信你可以去问我邻里嘛。"布布酋长听了，苦着脸叫道："坏了，坏了，这事全坏了。"等力达走后，布布酋长便派人把阿支偷偷叫来，骂道："阿支，你这欺宗灭祖的不肖子孙，你给我把你的罪行如实招来！"

阿支不知道力达已经出卖了他们，心里惊慌，嘴上却说："布布酋长，我不明白！"

布布酋长命人把阿支五花大绑起来。

布布酋长咬牙切齿地说："你媳妇到底是什么人？"

阿支说："我不是早说过了吗？"

布布酋长说："在你借口去远行的那天，放牧的人说你在山上疯了，背了一个女人满山乱跑，像一头发情的野猪，这是怎么说呢？"

阿支想不到那件事已让布布酋长知道，张口结舌，半天也说不出话来。

"先把他关进地牢里去。"布布酋长说。

land by Zimo Naizi, I have never left here for a single day." Chief Bubu was even more shocked and jumped on his feet. He said, "Not along ago, didn't you go to Ripusuoluo and stay there for a month?" Lida laughed and replied, "I was a servant and am now promoted to the independent class. Why on earth would I go to Ripusuoluo since I have no relative there." The chief then asked, "Are you sure?" Lida laughed at his question and said, "What do you take me for? If you don't believe me, you can ask my neighbors." Then chief Bubu shouted out with a grievance, "No, no, It's not a good thing." When Lida left, chief Bubu sent someone to bring Azhi here secretly and scolded him, "Azhi, you lying little bastard. You fooled us all. Now tell me everything!"

Azhi still did not know that his best friend Lida had already betrayed him. Panic as he may be, he replied calmly, "Chief Bubu, I'm afraid I don't understand what you mean!"

The chief asked a guy to tie Azhi up, and said champing with rage, "Who is your wife?" Azhi replied, "I have already told you."

Then the chief said, "On the day when you were supposed to set out your long journey, some herdsmen said you went out of your mind because you were carrying a woman and running around in the mountain like a wild pig in heat. How did that happen?"

Not knowing that the chief had already learned the story, Azhi was very shocked and could not say a word.

Then the chief said, "Put him into the dungeon."

阿支便被关进了地牢。这事除了执法的人和布布酋长，谁也不知道。后来布布酋长也只告诉了阿支的瞎父和跛母，瞎父和跛母被吓坏了，没想到一向正直恭顺的儿子会这么大胆。

是公开还是秘密处罚阿支和蛇娘呢？布布酋长想了好几天，也没拿定主意。这时，力达又来串门子了，布布酋长就把阿支的事告诉了他，向他讨主意："力达，你是乃依大兹莫最宠信的聪明人，你说，这事该怎么办？"

力达装作想了又想的样子，说："这事如果公开，进行五马分尸，那会变成一件丑闻；如果秘密对他们用极刑，使这么两个活人忽然失踪，必然引起各种猜测，对你们家支的名誉还是不利。"布布酋长说："我也正因此为难呢。"于是力达就说："我有一个最好的办法，你们把阿支送到乃依大兹莫那儿去管教几年，这样他说不定会改邪归正。至于那个来历不明的蛇娘，你们先把她关起来吧。"

Azhi was locked into the dungeon, which was known by no one except the chief and the man who executed it. Later, the chief told Azhi's parents. The two disabled old folks were terrified because they could not imagine that their obedient and honest boy would go this far.

Chief Bubu thought for days about whether to punish Azhi and Sheniang publicly or privately and still could not figure it out. Just at this moment, Lida called on the chief. So, the chief told Lida about Azhi and asked for his advice, "Lida, you are the most trusted person of Zimo Naiyi and also very smart. What do you think I should do?"

Lida pretended to think for a while, who actually already had plotted his plan, and said, "If you deal with it publicly and tear their bodies apart by horses, it will be a scandal for your clan. And if you torture them privately, it will sparkle some suspicion since two humans disappeared suddenly, which will still bring a bad influence to your clan." Chief Bubu said, "Yes, that's my concern." Then Lida continued, "I have a solution. Maybe you can send Azhi to Zimo Naiyi and let him serve him for some years. Maybe he'll change. As for the girl with an unknown family background, you can lock her up for now."

布布酋长觉得这办法很好，于是用派公差的名义，把阿支秘密押送到乃依大兹莫家去服役。然后装作不知道阿支去向的样子，三番五次派人去问蛇娘：“蛇娘，你的丈夫这几天到哪里去了？”蛇娘说：“前几天下午就不见了，我也不知道他去哪儿啦。”见蛇娘真的不知道，于是布布酋长便装模作样找阿支，他在本家支里弄个人装成假巫师陷害蛇娘，说是她谋害了阿支。蛇娘浑身有嘴难分辩，被折磨得死去活来。

布布酋长不知下一步怎么办，他把蛇娘关回地牢，去找力达讨主意。

布布酋长对力达说：“聪明人，再为我想个主意吧。”力达早知道布布还得找他。他假装想了想说：“蛇娘不能杀，杀了，她会变成冤魂复仇的。”布布酋长说：“我也这样想，但杀又杀不得，放又不能放，这事难办了。”力达说：“我看只有一个办法，让我装好人去把她救出来，这样你们可以对世人说，是我趁阿支不在家，把她拐跑啦。这样，阿支也就会对她死心了。”

The chief found the proposal very sensible. So he privately sent a man to escort Azhi to Zimo Naiyi's house and pretended not to know his whereabouts afterwards. Then, he deliberately sent someone to ask Sheniang for several times, inquiring, "Sheniang, where is your husband these days?" Sheniang always replied, "He was missing in an afternoon several days ago. I don't know where he is." As he found that Sheniang indeed had no clue, the chief then pretended to look for Azhi. He asked one of the members in his clan to pretend to be a witch and asked the fake witch to accuse Sheniang of murdering Azhi. Although knowing it a con, Sheniang could not defend herself properly.

The chief did not know what to do next, so he just threw Sheniang in the dungeon and turned to Lida for help.

Chief Bubu said to Lida, "Smart boy, come up with another solution, please." Lida had already predicted that the chief would come to him for advice. Still, he pretended to be thinking and said, "You can't kill Sheniang. If you did, she would become a ghost haunting you." The chief said, "I think so. But what should I do if I can't kill her or release her?" Lida said, "There is only one way. Let me pretend to be the good guy and save her. So you can tell everyone it is me who lure Sheniang away while Azhi was away. By doing so, you can also keep Azhi from returning to Sheniang."

布布酋长说："这怎么行呢，你一个清清白白的人，名誉不就全毁了吗？"

力达说："我不这么办，你们家支不就完了吗？再说，我一无家支，二无亲友，出身本来就低贱，这坏名声由我背，比由你们家支背轻松得多，而且，我以后的日子，还得靠你们这强大的家支帮助呀！"

布布酋长想了想，觉得也只好这么办了，不由得感激涕零，对力达说："唉，这可真是对不起你了，我们布布家支会永生永世铭记你的大恩大德的。"力达听了，长条脸上装出一副难为情的样子，心里却得意极了。这一来，他将成为蛇娘的救命恩人，并得到蛇娘。

第二天，正当布布家支又在折磨蛇娘时，力达出现了。他装腔作势，与布布酋长争斗一番后，把奄奄一息的蛇娘背走了。计谋得逞，力达高兴得不得了，心想：这下蛇娘该对布布家支恨之入骨了，我再施小计，不愁她不做我的妻子！于是他把蛇娘背回去后，又是杀鸡，又是熬药，一步不离地守着卧病在床的蛇娘，向她献殷勤。但蛇娘不吃他的鸡，不喝他的药，冷眼横眉地问他："你把我从布布家背出来，安的什么心？"

力达说："我不忍心看你被冤枉成这个样子，我怕他们毁了你。"蛇娘生气地说："这和你有什么关系？阿支不在了，我本就不想活了，死在他家，我心甘情愿。你明天就把我背回去！"

But the chief said, "How can I do this? It will ruin your reputation, for you are such an honest man."

Lida replied, "If I don't do this, your clan will be dishonored. Besides, I don't have a clan or family. I was born humbly. So, it is better for me to get this bad reputation than you. Besides, I still depend on your strong clan to live and I may need your help in the future."

The chief thought for a while and felt it was the only way. He felt very grateful and said to Lida, "We owe you a lot. Our clan will be eternally grateful for your help." Lida pretended to be very embarrassed at what the chief said, but he was actually satisfied inside secretly because he would naturally be Sheniang's savior and own her.

The next day, Lida showed up just when someone was torturing Sheniang. After fighting with the chief, seemingly, for a while, he carried away Sheniang who was almost dying by then. As his trick worked, Lida was overjoyed, thinking that Sheniang must have hated the clan so much that she would be willing to be his wife if he gave her a little nudge. So after carrying Sheniang back to his house, he cooked chicken for her and took a great care of her by her bedside. Though seriously injured, Sheniang refused to take his food or medicine but asked coldly, "What do you want from taking me out of Bubu's house?"

Lida replied, "I just could not bear to watch you framed like that and ruined by them."

Sheniang said in anger, "It's none of your business anyway. Azhi is gone and all I want is to follow him. I would rather die at the hands of his clan. Please carry me back there tomorrow!"

力达一听，心凉了半边。为了得到蛇娘，他想了想，说道：“蛇娘，你真憨，阿支只不过是失踪，说不定还活着呢。你如果被他们折磨死了，到时阿支回来，那不是害了他吗？”蛇娘听了，觉得这话也对，又犹豫起来。力达便进一步说：“你就住在我这里，我帮你再去找阿支。如果他活着，我一定把他找回来。”蛇娘想了想，点点头：“那真感谢你了，不过我还是要回布布家支去，我是他们家支的人，不能住在你这里。”力达听了，心里又气又恨，发了火：“好吧，你回去让布布家废了手脚舌头吧。到时如果阿支回来，可别怪我力达不够朋友。”蛇娘见他发了火，有点相信力达是真心的了，于是担心地问：“你以为，阿支真会活着吗？”力达火爆爆地说：“我不是说我去找吗？你既然不相信丈夫的朋友，那你走吧，我也不管这事了。”蛇娘听了，觉得错怪了力达，于是住了下来。力达想尽了办法讨好献殷勤，可是蛇娘什么事都自己动手，使得力达不敢急于对她下手，只得做出一副照顾朋友的样子，慢慢地试探。

Lida was very disappointed at what Sheniang said. To win Sheniang over, he thought for a while and said, "Sheniang, why are you so silly? Azhi is just missing. Maybe he is still alive. If you die from their torture, what will Azhi do when he comes back?" Sheniang found it sensible and began to hesitate. Then Lida continued, "Why don't you live in my house and I'll help you find Azhi. If he is alive, I will bring him back." After thinking for a while, Sheniang nodded and said, "Thank you. But I still need to go back to the chief. I'm a member of his clan." Pissed off by Sheniang's insistence, Lida replied angrily, "Alright. You can go back now so that they will have another chance to kill you. And if Azhi comes back, I will not owe him anything because I have already done my part." Sheniang started to believe him as he grew furious. So she asked with worry, "So you really think Azhi is still alive?" Lida replied with anger, "I said I'm going to find him. If you don't trust me as such, why don't you go? I don't want to help anymore." Then Sheniang felt very sorry for blaming Lida wrongly. Therefore, she stayed. Lida tried every possible way to win her favor but failed because Sheniang did everything on her own. So Lida wouldn't dare to possess her against her will and had to look after her as a friend.

这样的日子过了一个月，又过了一个月。力达借口说已请朋友四处去打听阿支的下落，他本人就是不去找阿支，这使蛇娘疑心又起。半年后，蛇娘已感到等待无望了，又提出要回布布家支去，力达这才无可奈何地装出一副去找阿支的样子，出门游荡去了。他东玩玩、西逛逛逛了三个多月，觉得这样下去不是办法，他要回家寻找机会占有蛇娘。回到家里，他告诉蛇娘，阿支被人杀死了。他以为蛇娘会昏厥在地，这样不愁蛇娘不属于他。不料蛇娘听了，只是呆了一呆，便平静地站起来，走到门外看太阳去了。这反使力达疑惑不定，不知蛇娘是对阿支死了心呢，还是她早有所料。他越想越糊涂，便试探地对蛇娘说："蛇娘，我在世上最知心的朋友，不明不白地去了，我心里也很难过。我和你一样，孤独地出生，又孤独地活着，将来孤独地死去。唉，我们的命一样苦啊！"蛇娘对他笑了笑，力达胆子一壮，又说："以后，我俩相依为命，一起过日子吧。我一定会把你保护好！"蛇娘说："谢谢你的好意。你能不能找到我丈夫的尸骨，把他埋到这附近来呢？"力达心中一喜，觉得事情有了眉目，于是点头答应说："我正这么想呢，明天我就去找。"第二天，他便动身出发，打算去找一架无人收的尸骨来骗蛇娘。

They lived like that month after month. Sheniang gradually became suspicious of Lida's words about having sent friends to find Azhi since he never thought of going out to find Azhi by himself. After six months, Sheniang finally got tired of waiting and proposed going back to the clan. By then, Lida had to go out unwillingly and pretended to look for Azhi. Having wandered around for three months, he thought he could not continue like this and made up his mind to forcefully possess her. When he went back home, he told Sheniang that Azhi was killed. He thought that Sheniang would pass out and be available to him at the news, so he was well prepared to own Sheniang forcefully. However, Sheniang was just a little dazed and then calmed herself and went outside to watch the sun. Sheniang's behaviors confused Lida who was not sure then whether Sheniang was already disillusioned with Azhi or had expected this very early. Then he asked Sheniang tentatively, "Sheniang, my best friend in the world died out of no reason. I am as sad as you are. Like you, I was alone when I was a child. And now I live alone just like you are. Maybe in the future we'll die alone. See what a miserable life we have?" Sheniang smiled at him. So, Lida emboldened himself to continue, "How about we spending the rest of our lives together? I swear I'll protect you." Sheniang replied, "Thanks. Can you find my husband's body and move it here?" Lida suddenly got very excited and thought he finally made a big progress. So he nodded and said, "That's what I'm thinking. Tomorrow I'll find him." The next day, he set off and planned to find a deserted body to fool Sheniang.

力达走以后，蛇娘到河边去，把衣裳洗得干干净净的，然后在河里洗净身子，梳好头发，等衣裳晒干后，又穿起来，打扮得比天仙还美。随后找了一棵弯腰树，把麻绳挂上去，打了一个活结套在脖子上。现在，只要她一脚蹬开垫脚的石头，就可以离开这个世界了。她的泪水像雨水，一串串滚出来。她揩干了泪水，最后一次抬头看看天，看看四周。忽然，她在通向力达家的小路上发现了阿支的猎狗。她飞快地解掉套在脖子上的麻绳，飞跑过去把猎狗抱在怀里。她伏在猎狗身上大声哭起来。

和阿支一同失踪的猎狗回来了。猎狗的身上伤痕累累，似乎被人毒打过。它的四脚跑得血迹斑斑，看样子已跑了很多路。蛇娘从猎狗的耳朵里找到了一封信，信上没有字，只画着一道宽大的石门和一顶兹莫的官帽。蛇娘狂喜得全身发抖，她知道阿支还活着。她对猎狗说：“谢谢你，好朋友，快带我去找阿支吧。”猎狗听了，便站起来，开始在前边引路。忽然蛇娘又改变了主意，她见猎狗又伤又累，心疼了，她要让猎狗休养一两天再走。她喊住了猎狗，猎狗叫着，绕着蛇娘转了一圈又一圈，想迫使她上路。但是蛇娘不上路，猎狗只得跟他回了力达家。

After Lida left, Sheniang went to the river. There she washed her clothes and then bathed herself. She combed her hair and put on her clothes when dried. She looked just like a nymph coming out of water. Then she found a bent tree to which she tied a rope, whose other end was wound around Sheniang's neck. Once she kicked off the rock down her feet, she could leave the world forever. At that moment, tears flooded from her eyes. She wiped her tears and looked up at the sky and looked around. Suddenly, she found Azhi's hound on the way to Lida's house. She instantly freed herself and ran to the hound and held it in her arms. She burst out crying on the hound.

The hound which was missing with Azhi returned. But Sheniang found that it was seriously injured. It seemed that the dog had been beaten viciously. Its four feet were bloody and chafed from a long run. Sheniang found a letter in the hound's ear with no word on it but a drawing of a large stone door and a hat of Zimo. Sheniang knew that Azhi must have been alive, so she trembled with joy. She said to the hound, "Thank you, old friend. Take me to Azhi." The hound stood up and led the way after hearing what Sheniang said. But Sheniang felt bad at the condition of the dog which was exhausted and seriously wounded, so she changed her mind as she wanted the hound to rest for a day or two. Then, she called out to the hound and signaled it to stop. But the hound was barking and circling around Sheniang, hoping to make her go. But since Sheniang did not want to move at all, it had to go with Sheniang to Lida's house.

第二天，力达回来了。他一见蛇娘，就骗她说："阿支的尸骨找到了。"蛇娘见他说假话不脸红，恨得牙痒痒的，心里十分厌恶他。于是她说："好呀，你留着它做伙伴吧。我问你，阿支真的死了吗？"力达心里有鬼，有点慌了。蛇娘接着问："我成亲时请你证婚，你为什么躲开了？"

力达说："我有急事呀！"

蛇娘又问："后来你去布布家支，为什么只去找布布酋长，却不见你的朋友？"

力达说："我忙不过来呀！"

这时，阿支的猎狗跑来站在蛇娘旁边，朝力达瞪着眼睛，龇牙咧嘴地哼起来。力达一见阿支的猎狗，不由得惊出一身冷汗。他已经明白事情不妙了。他不愿让到了嘴边的肥鸡飞掉，他的长条脸突然变得发绿，老鼠眼喷着火，朝蛇娘猛扑过去，和蛇娘扭打在一起。阿支的猎狗一蹿而上，一口咬住了力达的脖子。力达疼得大叫一声，放掉蛇娘，转身和猎狗搏斗，结果也被咬到了，昏了过去。猎狗也因为伤势过重而死了。蛇娘含泪埋了猎狗的尸体，便飞快地朝乃依兹莫衙门跑去。

乃依兹莫衙门的大门，和狗耳朵里那张画一模一样。蛇娘就要往里闯，守门的老人把她拦住了。老人告诉她阿支已跟乃依大兹莫到京城朝贡去了，要过一久才能回来。

The next day when Lida came home, he instantly told Sheniang that Azhi's body was found. Seeing Lida lying in her face, Sheniang was pissed off and began to loathe him. So she said, "Alright, it's your trophy, huh? Let me ask you, did Azhi really die?" Seized by a guilty conscience, Lida began to panic. Then Sheniang continued, "And why did you avoid us when we asked you to marry Azhi and me?"

Lida replied, "No, I was in emergency."

Sheniang asked again, "And why did you only go to chief Bubu instead of seeing your friends then?"

Lida answered, "Because I was too busy!"

Just at this moment, Azhi's hound ran forward and stood by Sheniang's side, glaring at Lida and barking at him with an intimidating face. Seeing the hound of Azhi, Lida was devastated and instantly knew things were out of his control. But he would still not give up what he planned so long to get. Burning with anger, Lida ran towards Sheniang and wrestled with her. And the hound jumped on Lida and bit his neck straight. Lida yelled and had to let Sheniang go to fight the hound. Eventually, he was knocked out and the hound died. Sheniang then buried the hound's body with tears and ran to Zimo's house to find her husband.

The door of Zimo's house was exactly what was depicted in the drawing hidden in the dog's ear. When Sheniang tried to get in, the guard, an old man, stopped her. The old man told Sheniang that Azhi went to the capital city to pay tribute with Zimo and would return later.

蛇娘一时没有了主意，不知怎样办。她把自己的遭遇向老人诉说了一遍。老人很受感动，非常同情，就把她领回家里住下。

但是，灾难还没有结束。被猎狗咬昏的力达没有死。他醒过来后，便跑到布布酋长家，告诉布布酋长说，阿支的猎狗跑回来了，蛇娘可能找阿支去了。布布酋长一听，吓得面无人色。如果让蛇娘找到阿支，天下人知道了布布家支娶了个下贱女人，那布布家支就没脸做人了。于是，布布酋长便暗暗派人，把蛇娘捉了回来，他要把蛇娘五马分尸。

行刑的日子到了。布布家支背后的山头上，布布家支远远近近的亲戚家支都来了，围成一个大大的圆圈。蛇娘和百匹大马被拖到圆圈中间。蛇娘心里喊着阿支的名字，痛苦地最后看了一眼天上的白云，闭上了泪水迸流的眼睛。

阿支跟随乃依兹莫去京城朝贡，恰好碰上一位大将带兵反皇帝。乃依兹莫不幸死于乱军阵里。阿支凭着他猎人的本事，用弩箭射死了一个又一个叛将，保护了皇帝。皇帝战胜叛军后就封阿支做了乃依兹莫，接管了老乃依兹莫的地盘。

今天，阿支乘着大轿，带着兹莫府的兵丁，向布布家支走来。他忘不了蛇娘，他听守门的老人说蛇娘被布布酋长派人拉走了，他急着要找蛇娘。

Not knowing what to do, Sheniang told the old man about her stories. The old man felt very sorry for her and agreed to let her stay in his house.

But Sheniang's disaster did not end. Lida was not dead. When he woke up, he ran to chief Bubu's house and told him that Azhi's hound went back and Sheniang must have gone to find Azhi. The chief was so shocked at what he said. His face turned pale and thought that if Sheniang did find Azhi, then everyone would know Bubu's clan took in a humble girl, which would be a humiliation. Therefore, the chief secretly sent a man to capture Sheniang and was ready to tear her body apart by horses.

The day of execution came. On the top of the mountain behind Bubu's clan, all members came to stand in a large circle to watch. Sheniang was dragged to the center by hundreds of horses. Calling out Azhi's name in her heart, Sheniang took a final look at the clouds painfully and closed her wet eyes.

As for Azhi, when he went to the capital city to pay tribute with Zimo, he came across a general who was rebelling with his army against the emperor. Zimo, unfortunately, was killed by rebel forces. But Azhi, a skillful hunter, killed rebels with his bow one after another and protected the emperor. When the emperor defeated rebel forces, he nominated Azhi as the new Zimo to take over the territory of his predecessor.

On the day of Sheniang's execution, Azhi was sitting on a glamorous palanquin, accompanied by his soldiers and servants, and marching towards Bubu's clan. He did not forget Sheniang. When he heard that Sheniang was seized by chief Bubu, he rushed to the chief.

这时，布布酋长正端着一杯酒祭天地，忽然听得人群骚动，转头看去，只见山下路上来了一群人，花花绿绿的，好像还抬着轿子。布布酋长派人前去打听，原来是新的兹莫大人来了。布布酋长一听，赶忙挤出人群迎接兹莫大人。兹莫府的兵丁已经抬着一乘大轿走了上来。布布酋长对轿内的兹莫行了按胸礼，说："布布酋长拜见兹莫大人。"兹莫掀帘，问道："你们这是干什么？"

"兹莫大人，我们正要请你主持，我们这是在处罚一个犯了灭祖欺宗乱伦之罪的人。"

阿支下轿，见到遭受不幸的正是蛇娘，便冲过去，把蛇娘紧紧抱在怀里。蛇娘定睛一看，来人正是自己的丈夫阿支，便放声哭了起来。布布酋长和众人见新兹莫原来是阿支，一时吓得目瞪口呆，不知如何是好。

Just when the chief held a cup of liquor to offer sacrifice, he suddenly heard the crowds moving in a tumult. He turned around and saw a group of people down the hill who were in a colorful parade and carrying a person on a palanquin. So, he sent a man to find out what was happening, only to be told the new Zimo came. The chief hurriedly made his way through his clansmen to greet the new Zimo. As soldiers and servants carried a palanquin forward, the chief gave a traditional and formal salute to Zimo in the palanquin, and said, "The chief of Bubu's clan hereby greets your excellency." The new Zimo lifted up the curtain and asked, "What's this about?"

"My lord, we ask you to preside. Now we are punishing a woman who has cheated our entire clan."

Azhi got off his palanquin and went to see the woman. Seeing Sheniang being tied up, he ran towards her and held her tightly in his arms. Sheniang opened her eyes and saw her husband. Then, she burst out crying. The chief and his clansmen were so shocked to see that the new Zimo turned out to be Azhi. They were all panic about what to do.

从此，蛇娘和阿支在兹莫府里过上了幸福的日子。据说后来蛇娘还协助阿支帮助皇帝平息了七十二兹莫的联合反叛，阿支因此又被皇帝封为尼威①。这都写在书里哩。蛇娘和阿支一起活到九十多岁，变成神仙，住到天宫里去了。

搜集整理者：乌者娜依热

① 尼威：旧时彝族的最高统治者，相当于诸侯国王。一般是皇封的为正一品。彝书载，兹莫阿支是彝族第一个皇封的尼威。

Ever since, Sheniang and Azhi lived a happy life in their house. It was said that later Sheniang also assisted Azhi in cracking down the united uprising of 72 Zimo for the emperor. Azhi was then given the title of Niwei① by the emperor, as recorded in history. Sheniang and Azhi lived until they were nineties. Then they ascended to the heaven and became immortals.

Collector and editor: Wuzhenayire

---

① Niwei: the supreme ruler of the Yi ethnic group in ancient times equal to a feudal lord and among the first class of officials. According to records of the Yi people, Zimo Azhi was the first to be given the title of Niwei.

红石岩

提起红石岩，着实叫人伤心。红石岩的故事，昆明彝家人十个有九个会讲，讲起来三天三夜扯不断。

红石岩是昆明城北三十里的一堵老岩子，岩子上的石头红彤彤的，像血染过一样，所以叫作红石岩。年年八月十六、十七、十八这三天，昆明城、安宁街、富民县、呈贡县和晋宁县的人，坐车赶马来这里唱调子，在那堵老石岩下，围着成山成海的人，你歇我唱，我歇你唱，一口气要唱三天三夜。唱着唱着，有情阿哥有情妹，就结成双配成对了。为什么人人爱来这里唱调子呢？因为最初来这里唱调子的一对情人，被逼死在岩子下面，现在大家来这里相聚唱调，就是为了纪念他俩。

他们原先是村里的撒梅姑娘和小伙子，一个住在山这边，一个住在山那边。箐鸡毛毛多，蜈蚣爪爪多，老古辈的规矩更多。古规规定：姑娘十八不上山，只怕山精地怪把魂拉去，所以他们“隔着竹林听鸟音，只听鸣(名)声不见影”，两个一处生、一处长，可惜不得见一眼。

Red-stone Rock

Speaking of the Red-stone Rock, one will certainly feel sad. Nine out of ten families of the Yi ethnic group in Kunming can tell stories about it for three days and nights on end.

The Red-stone Rock is an old rock 15 km north of the center of Kunming city. The stones on the rock are as red as having been stained with blood, thus making the name Red-stone Rock. On the 16th, 17th, and 18th day of the eighth lunar month every year, people in Kunming city, Anning Street, Fumin County, Chenggong County, and Jinning County come here on horses or vehicles to sing a tune. They circle around the Rock, singing antiphonal tunes for three days straight. In this way, those who fall in love can tie the knots. Why does everyone love to sing here? Because a couple who first came here to sing tunes were forced to jump off the rock. Now people sing tunes here to commemorate them.

The couple were villagers, living on the two sides of the mountain. While a pheasant has many feathers and a centipede has many claws, rules laid down by previous generations are even more numerous. According to the tradition, girls could not go up mountains at the age of eighteen for fear of being dragged away by monsters. That's why girls could only "listen to the chirping of birds from the bamboo forest", and people who grew up in the same place probably never had the chance to meet.

山这边的小伙子是出名的人，盘田、种地、撵山、探船，样样都数第一，人人敬他三分。

山那边的姑娘也非凡，纺线织布不消说，单说她一刀能剪十样布，一针能绣百样花，就晓得不是个弱手。

山不转路转，桥不转水转，太阳也有看见月亮的时间。有一日，他俩在一堵白花花的老岩下遇着了，小姑娘挑水过石岩，小伙子砍柴歇石岩，四只眼睛一相遇，两双脚就站住了。

小伙子看见面前站着个天仙样的姑娘，肤色嫩得像竹笋，脸儿秀得像月亮，一双眼睛像两点水雀，小伙子着迷啰。

姑娘的心比蜜蜂还聪明，看见前面站着个罗汉样的小伙子，要说力气，三条水牛不抵他，要说机灵，他一个胜过十只岩羊，进山虎王怕他三分，下水龙王怕他七分，姑娘也着迷啰。

The young man on one side of the mountain was a famous figure for his unrivalled skill of cultivating land, planting, climbing mountains and rowing boats. Everyone held him in high esteem.

The girl on the other side of the mountain was exceptional as well. Apart from spinning and weaving, she could make ten kinds of cloth with one scissors and embroider hundreds of flower patterns with one needle. Seen from these aspects, she was by no means ordinary.

A mountain never moved, but a path could wind its way around it. A bridge did not move, but water could flow freely beneath it. Even the sun had the chance to meet the moon. One day, these two young persons met near a white old rock. The girl passed by the rock while carrying water and the young man took a rest there after chopping wood. When they saw each other, their feet seemed to have stuck and frozen.

The girl in the eyes of the boy resembled a fairy, with skin as tender as bamboo shoots. Her face was as pretty as the moon, and her eyes were like two motacilla albas. The young man swooned over her charm.

The girl's mind was smarter than a bee. She could see that the strong, young man standing in front of her must have the physical power that could overwhelm three buffaloes combined. He must have the brain power that could rival ten blue sheep. The tiger king of the mountain feared him to some extent, while the dragon king in the sea did so to a larger extent. The young girl also swooned over him.

小伙子见了姑娘，不知怎样开口，心一动，摘片树叶“哔哔”地吹几声，放开嗓子唱起来：

今日来到半山腰，
两棵山茶一样高，
摘片青叶吹声哨，
哨声引得茶树摇。

听见他唱，姑娘害羞地转过脸去。小伙子吸口气壮壮胆，又唱一调：

阿妹是朵红山茶，
千里香风四处刮，
山茶香风吹得远，
阿哥今日来寻它。

他唱完，姑娘在那边也捂住脸搭腔了：

想吃嫩笋三月天，
莫等笋子生老茧。
想吃鲜鱼滇池钓，
快撒金钩手莫闲。

小伙子喜欢得跳三跳，又答道：

宽宽滇池白滩头，
小小鲤鱼水上游。
小小鲤鱼游水头，
阿哥滩头甩金钩。

When the guy saw the girl, he became speechless. Obviously, he fell in love with her. He picked up a leaf to blow a whistle. Then he let out his voice to sing:

Come to the mountainside,

And see two camellias of the same height;

Blow a green leaf I pick,

And cause the tea tree to shake.

Hearing this, the girl turned around shyly. The young man mustered up his courage by taking a deep breath, and sang again:

What a beautiful red camellia you are,

Thousand miles the fragrant winds blowing,

The camellia fragrance drifts afar,

Today I come here for a looking.

After he finished singing, the girl covered her face and started to sing:

Tender bamboo shoots wanna eat,

Never wait till it's old,

Fresh fish wanna eat,

Drop the hook before being told.

The guy was so overjoyed as to jump up three times and replied:

Riverside beach wide and wide,

Out of the water emerged little carp,

Jump and jump against the tide,

Golden hook from the beach I drop.

他还没收尾，姑娘转过身来，像画眉一样的声音接过去：

小小鲤鱼游水头，
阿哥滩头甩金钩，
鲤鱼偏偏不吃钩，
……

小伙子听了这句，像被雷劈的树，呆愣愣地不会动了。只听姑娘顿一顿，又唱：

鲤鱼偏偏不吃钩，
阿哥急得汗水流。
啊吱哟——依，
阿哥急得汗水流！

小伙子急啦，扯扯衣裳角，拉拉袖口，嘴倒是张得大，歌却不见唱出来。

姑娘咯咯地笑了，又唱起来：

只见风吹花落地，
哪见风吹花上枝？
阿哥有心来对调，
怎不开口接一支？

小伙子急得像热锅上的蚂蚁，抠抠耳朵，唱句“阿妹……”，不晓得下面要唱什么，又摸摸鼻子，唱句“阿哥……”又不晓得要唱什么好了。

姑娘老早笑弯了腰，张开口又接一调，声音软得像丝棉：

Hardly had he finished when the girl turned around and echoed in a thrush-like voice:

Jump and jump against the tide,

Golden hook from the beach I drop.

Not hooked is the Carp,

...

On hearing this, the young guy seemed to be dumbfounded like a thunder-struck tree. Then the girl paused for one or two seconds and went on singing:

Carp not eat hooks,

You are sweating in anxiety,

Ah zhi yo—yi,

Anxious you are sweating!

The young man was getting impatient. He pulled the corners of his clothes and cuffs. His mouth was wide open, but words failed him.

The girl giggled and sang again:

Onto the ground can flowers be blown by wind,

But can branches be blown away?

To have a antiphony you intend,

Why not have a try today?

The young man was as anxious as an ant on a hot pan. He picked his ears and sang "My lady..." and didn't know what to sing next. He touched his nose, singing, "My boy..." Then he got stuck again.

The girl guffawed to the extent that she had bent over. She continued singing again, with a voice as soft as silk cotton:

这个阿哥脸皮薄，
只听歌起不见落。
丢块石头壮你胆，
哥妹唱到太阳落。

两个对来对去，对到月亮升起才分手，后来他俩天天来这白石岩下面唱调子。两人一天不见想三回，三天不见想十回，一时一刻也离不开了。

哪晓得，他俩相好的事，被村里的一个觋波①知道了，他早就想讨姑娘做小老婆，只是姑娘望都不望他一眼，没法下手。

说起这个觋波，人人都说他的心比锅底黑，手比草乌毒。听说姑娘和小伙子相好，他鬼火冒齐屋檐头，用金银买通了官府，硬逼着姑娘嫁给他。姑娘的爹妈不敢不依，只好答应了，成亲的日子就定在八月十六。这下觋波高兴了，棺材钉②露出三尺长，一纵一纵地跑回去打酒割肉，缝衣裁裤，只等着做新郎。

---

① 觋波：祭师。
② 棺材钉：昆明话，形容又长又丑的门牙。

Thin-skinned is my gentleman,
You can hear the start but no end when he sang.
Throw a stone and come on,
Till sunset let's sing along.

The two chanted consecutively until the moon showed up. Later they would sing a tone under this white rock every day. They would miss each other for three times if they hadn't met for a day and missed each other for ten times if not seeing for three days. They could not part with each other for even a single moment.

Unluckily, the Xibo① in the village got the news of their affection towards each other. He had been longing to make the girl his concubine, but the girl didn't even look at him. So he could do nothing but wait.

Speaking of this Xibo, everyone agreed that his heart was dirtier and darker than the bottom of a wok, and his hands more poisonous than drugs. He was so enraged by the love of the couple that he bribed the government with gold and silver. In this way, he could force the girl to marry him. The girl's parents had no choice but to consent to their marriage on the 16th day of August in the Lunar calender. Filled with joy, the Xibo laughed, laying bare his coffin nail② as long as three chi. He rushed to buy wine and meat and make tailored clothes, waiting to be a groom.

---

① Xibo: a priest.

② coffin nail: Kunming dialect, long and ugly front teeth.

大风吹篱笆，总有一层透。小伙子听见这个消息，气都来不及喘，飞一样翻过山背，来到姑娘家，对姑娘说：“阿妹，我死也不让觋波讨着你，逃吧！”

姑娘说：“阿哥，我死也要跟你在一处！”

他俩就悄悄地逃上山去。

可惜这个消息被觋波知道了，他马上点起从官府借来的兵，遍山遍野地撵来，他俩朝东，就堵东，他俩朝西，就堵西，四处堵死，逼得两人只好爬上那堵白石岩。

白石老岩高悬悬，上面站着两个年轻人。白石岩脚黑漫漫，下面尽是官府兵。官府的兵像蚂蚁，一堆一团地爬上来。

姑娘站在石岩上，大叫一声：“看哪个敢爬，再爬，我就跳下岩子去！”

觋波听了忙说：“莫跳，莫跳，我们不爬了，你们赶紧下来，好说好商量！”

姑娘不理他，紧靠在小伙子身上，和他一问一答对起调子来。

The strong wind could blow through the fence, no matter how tightly-woven it was. When the young man heard what the Xibo had done, he immediately crossed the mountain and came to the girl's house. He said to the girl, "My sister, I won't let him marry you, even if I have to die. Let's run away!"

The girl said, "My brother, I will be with you even if I have to die!"

Then, they climbed up a mountain to escape secretly.

Unfortunately, their escape was known by the Xibo. He immediately called together the soldiers borrowed from the government. Marching here in great numbers, the soldiers set blockade in all directions to prevent the couple from fleeing. The couple were then cornered. They were obliged to climb up a white rock.

These two young people stood on the high-hanging white rock, under which, there were a mass of government soldiers, climbing up in groups like ants.

The girl stood on the rock and yelled, "You still wanna climb up? Listen, if anyone of you goes on climbing, I will plunge!"

At this, the Xibo said instantaneously, "No, don't jump. Stop! We are not climbing anymore. Come down and we can talk about it!"

觋波和官府兵不敢上去，只好听着他们唱。他俩一唱一和，把觋波的祖宗三代都骂尽了。觋波呢，骂又不能骂，打又不能打，只得眼巴巴地坐着听。

到了十八日的晚上，他俩唱道：

月亮变成黑炭团，
乌云遮住半边天，
觋波手毒心更毒，
毒蛇见他怕三分。

觋波在下面大叫："不许唱，不许唱！"

他俩望也不望，照样又唱：

风吹草动山不动，
水打浪摇岸不摇，
刀切藕断丝不断，
我俩生死不能分。

唱完，两人紧紧地抱在一起，跳下了白石岩！

白石岩，百丈高，两人一着地，两股鲜血像喷泉一样，"嘭"地飞到岩子上，把白石岩染成一堵红殷殷的红石岩。跟着，从岩子底下升起两朵红云，悠悠荡荡飘过觋波和官府兵的头顶，飘过两人住的村子，飘过滇池海子，飞到西山顶上去了。

The girl ignored him and leaned on the young man, starting their singing antiphony.

The Xibo and soldiers did not dare to go up, so they had to listen to their singing. The two echoed each other as a way to scold the Xibo and his ancestors. He could neither curse nor beat them, but sit there listening.

On the 18th day, they were singing:

Into a charcoal the moon turns,

Half the sky covered by dark clouds,

The priest's heart more cruel than his plot,

Even a viper fears him a lot.

The priest shouted from below, "Stop singing, stop!"

They went on irrespective of his shouting:

The hill stands still amid wind-tossing grass,

The bank remains firm against licking waves,

The lotus root can never be cut clean apart,

Life and death we don't part.

Afterwards, they hugged tightly and jumped off the white rock!

The white rock stood about 300 meters high. When the couple fell onto the ground, two fountain-like blood streams splashed onto the rocks with a loud sound. The white rock now was dyed red. Following that, two red clouds rose from under the rock, drifting leisurely over the heads of the Xibo, the soldiers, and over the village where they lived. Then the clouds floated over the Dianchi Lake all over to the top of the West Mountain.

从此以后，这堵岩子出名了。远远近近四州八县的姑娘小伙子，一到八月十六这天，就聚在岩下，学着他俩对起调子来。十六、十七、十八，一对就是三天三夜。这个冷落的地方，一下就变成最热闹的地方了。

他俩化成红云后，还忘不记这堵岩子。每隔二十年，到八月十六这天，人们就会看见两朵红云从西山顶上飘来。到了红石岩，他俩从云彩上走下来，和那些姑娘小伙子们对调子。他们见哪对年轻人真心相好，就帮人家说合，有些白胡子白头发的老人，当年就是他俩说合的。他们活着不能在一起，死了也希望别人能在一起，快快活活地过一辈子。

流传地区：昆明西山区

讲述者：杨湘

记录者：石涛

Since then, this rock became known to all. Young men and girls from other places both far and near would gather beneath the rocks on the 18th day of the 8th lunar month. They would sing antiphonal tunes as the couple did before. From the 16th to 18th day, they would sing for three days without a stop. The previous lonely place became the most lively place.

After becoming red clouds, the couple still remember this rock. Every 20 years, people could see two red clouds swirling from the top of the West Mountain to the Red-stone Rock. They would come down to join the singing with other boys and girls, and acted as a matchmaker for those who fell in love. Some elderly couple tied the knots thanks to their matchmaking. They couldn't be with each other when they were alive, but they hope others could and lived a happy life.

Spreading area: West Mountain Area of Kunming
Narrator: Yang Xiang
Recorder: Shi Tao

小白龙和彝家女

在草木葱茏的白竹山西麓，有一个彝族聚居的地方，这就是现在的双柏县雨龙公社所在地，公社下边有个村子叫碧庄。传说在古时候，碧庄村后冒着一股泉水，流过碧庄寨旁。有一个十分优美动人的故事，在这一带民间广为流传。

不知道那是什么年代的事了。那时候，白竹山比现在还要高，山顶上一年四季堆着雪；那时候，白竹山比现在还要美，山坡上一年四季开满了鲜花。碧庄村后的那股龙洞水，一年四季清悠悠的，喝起来甜，煮出的饭香，流到田地里，庄稼年年丰收。那时候，这一带彝家人的日子可好过了。据说，白竹山有一位美丽的仙女每年都从龙洞里生出许多金银宝贝来；并且龙洞水每月都会有三四天时间变成红色。村里还未成年的小伙子如果去那水里洗了澡，马上就会变成大人；成了年的伙子如果经常去那水中洗澡，一生都不想媳妇；如果女人去那龙洞水里洗了澡，十有八九要变成男人。自然，这是一股神水，四乡八岭的人都十分敬重它，每年都要杀牛宰羊祭祀它。

Little White Dragon and the Girl of Yi Nationality

At the luxuriant west foot of the Baizhu Mountain, there was a community inhabited by the Yi people, where Yulong Commune in Shuangbai county stands today. Down the commune is a village called Bizhuang. It was said that a stream of water originated from the Bizhuang village ran along the whole area in ancient times. There was also a very moving story widely spread among people in that area.

Long time ago, the Baizhu Mountain was higher than it is now. At that time, the mountain was covered with snow all year around. Also, it was more beautiful then than it is now since colorful flowers bloomed all year round on the hills. The stream of water behind the Bizhuang village was clear in four seasons and tasted sweet. Rice cooked with this water smelt pleasantly and fields irrigated with it had a good harvest every year. At that time, the Yi people enjoyed a happy life. It was said that a beautiful nymph in the Baizhu Mountain conjured a large amount of gold and silver in the Dragon cave every year, whose water turned red for 3 to 4 days every month. If an immature lad took a bath in the water, he would become a grown-up immediately; if a grown-up often did that, he would not be in any attempt to marry a girl; if a woman took a bath in the water, she would very likely become a man. The water was sacred and highly respected by everyone in the neighboring villages. So, people killed oxen and sheep to offer sacrifices to it every year.

不知过了多少代人，这水突然不会按月变成红色了，人们去洗澡也不会有什么变化了。虽然水仍然那么甜，山仍然开满了鲜花，可是白竹山却慢慢矮下来了，山上堆不起雪来了。人们感到十分奇怪，谁也不知道会出什么事情。就在这时候，碧庄村里有一户人家生了位漂亮的姑娘。姑娘生下来时，谁也没注意。姑娘长到十五岁时，大家才突然发现，碧庄寨子里出了位比仙女还美的姑娘。一时间，十天路程之内的地方都轰动了；十天路程之内的水无处不香甜；十天路程之内的山无处不鲜花怒放。

姑娘出了名，可把父母叔伯都乐坏了。四山八岭的人都沾了光，叫树开花树就开花，叫天下雨天就下雨，这一带地方所出现的那种繁荣富裕景象，简直是无法形容。

烧起香，就会有鬼神来；有了姑娘，就会有小伙子到来。那几年，姑娘家的房屋扩建过九次，可是来玩来访的客人还是挤不下；姑娘家的门槛换过九次，但九次都被客人踏损。来了这么多的小伙子，能说会道的，智勇双全的，能歌善舞的好小伙不知有多少，可是一个也得不到那姑娘。那是为什么呢？那是因为那姑娘刚生下地三天就被父母许给了舅舅家。彝家规矩：家水不肥外人田，姑舅开亲天经地义，谁敢说一个不字呢？当然谁也就不敢非分乱想要得到那姑娘为伴侣了。这样一来，可苦了那姑娘。她看上了东山上的打虎英雄，可是叔伯不允许他们见面；她又看上了西山的山歌好汉，可是舅家把他赶走了，姑娘再也见不到他；她又看上了南山上的捕龙大哥，可是捕龙大哥怕冒犯了祖祖辈辈的规矩，不敢来接近她。左一个如意的得不到，右一个称心的失

After many generations, the water suddenly stopped turning red and bringing changes to villagers who bathed in it. Although it still tasted sweet and flowers still blossomed all over, the Baizhu Mountain gradually lowered in height and was no longer capped with snow. Villagers there all felt strange and could not tell the reason. At that moment, a pretty girl was born in a family in the Bizhuang village. When she was born, she looked too common to draw any attention. But when she turned fifteen years old, everyone noticed that this girl was even more beautiful than the nymph. Very soon the news caused a sensation in places within ten days of walk. Suddenly, water within ten days of walk tasted sweet and smelled aromatic. Also, mountains in the same range were all covered with profuse flowers.

Her parents and uncles were all thrilled at having the girl who rose to fame overnight. In fact, everyone in her neighborhood benefited from it because an indescribably prosperous situation appeared in which trees would blossom and the sky would rain if told.

Whenever a stick of incense was lit, divine spirits would descend to answer to the prayer; whenever there was a beautiful girl, boys would come to seek for love. During those years, the house of the beautiful girl had been expanded for nine times but was still unable to hold all the guests. The threshold of her house had been repaired for nine times but was still impossible to remain intact. Of numerous young lads who came, no one managed to win her heart even if they were good at talking, or brave and resourceful, or talented in singing and dancing. The reason was that on the third day since she was born, her parents betrothed

去了，姑娘的眼泪滴进龙泉水，一条河都变苦了；姑娘的悲哭声随风飘到山上，山上的鲜花都纷纷扬扬地落了。姑娘长到十七岁时，舅家要来接亲了。舅家的儿子是个拐子、歪鼻头，半傻半聋的。姑娘死也不情愿嫁过去，可是姑娘不敢开口。她落一滴泪，父亲就用长烟锅头砸她额头一下；她叫一声苦，母亲就用针戳一次她的嘴巴；她摇一下头，叔伯就用皮鞭捆一次她的脖子；她叫一声不情愿，舅家就要过来打冤家。时间一天一天过去了，出嫁的日子就要到了。姑娘的命像马路边上的草，不嫁也得嫁，不去也得去了。姑娘越想越伤心，跑到龙洞口，想跳进龙洞自杀。正在这时，龙洞上边的山头上，传来一阵悦耳动人的笛声。姑娘不由得抬头看去，猛地惊呆了：山坡上，破败的花木忽然都迎风开放，盛

her to her cousin based on a rule among the Yi ethnic group that nourishing water should not be let out of one's own field. Besides, no one would stand against a marriage between cousins, which after all was the tradition. So, those young lads had to give up. But the girl lived in misery. When she had a crush on a hero who defeated a tiger in the eastern mountain, her uncles cut them off; when she fell for a talent in singing in the western mountain, her uncles drove him away; when she lost her heart to a dragon hunter in the southern mountain, the hunter dared not to break the rule and stayed away from her. As not a single beloved man was accessible, the girl couldn't help crying. Her tears dripped into the river and made it bitter, and her cries flew to the mountain and withered all the flowers on it. When she turned seventeen, her uncle came to pick her up for the marriage. And the man she was going to marry was lame, deaf and slow-witted with a crooked nose. Reluctant as she might be, she was afraid to say no. If she shed a drop of tears, her father would hit her forehand once with his smoke pipe; if she complained a bit, her mother would prick her mouth once with a needle; if she shook her head, her uncles would tie a leather whip around her neck tightly; if she showed any sign of reluctance, her maternal uncles would come to beat her. With time passing by, her wedding day drew nearer. The girl had no hold of her own life. Feeling devastated, she ran to the Dragon cave and attempted to commit suicide by jumping off the cave. Just at this moment, a flow of melodic sound of flute came from the mountain top above the cave. The girl looked up and was amazed at the scene. On the hills, withered flowers bloomed

开出五彩缤纷的鲜花，把天都辉映得像火一样红。在绿茵茵的草地上，悠悠放牧着一匹雪白的骏马，白马打着响鼻，不住地向山下张望。白马的后边，跟着一位身着雪白服装的小伙子，正悠然自得地呜呜横吹着一支金笛，顺着山坡慢慢走来。姑娘觉得这小伙子十分眼熟，但又想不起是在哪里见过，正在呆想，那小伙子已经来到了她面前。那小伙子也不看她，拉着马在她面前去饮水。小伙子让马去饮水，可又忘了松开手中的缰绳，因此马的嘴巴怎么也够不着水喝。姑娘看他那笨手笨脚的样子，忍不住"扑哧"一声笑了，连忙掉开头去，轻声说："缰绳松开，缰绳松开……"

马饮了水，小伙子十分感激地对姑娘说："你这位阿妹真仁义，我想到你家去做客，可不知门槛怎么进。"

姑娘受到了感动，轻声告诉他："爹生的是横眼，妈长的是侧眼，你莫横着进，你莫侧着进，只要弓着腰进就进去了，我住在最里边那间房！"

小伙子听了，更加激动了："我喝水的时候，喝到的是你的泪水，因此我知道你不愿出嫁，如果阿妹愿意的话，我在月圆星明的晚上，来你的枕头边吹笛子。"

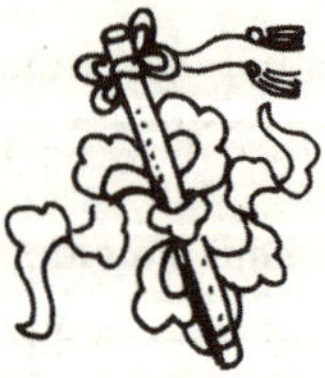

again in the face of wind and reddened the sky with its brilliance. On the verdant grassland, a handsome white horse grazed leisurely. It snorted and looked down the mountain. Behind the horse was a young lad in white costume who was playing a golden flute softly and walking slowly towards the girl down the hill. The girl found this lad very familiar in look but could not recall where they had met before. While she was pondering, the lad approached her and stood in front of her. However, without looking at her, the lad just hauled his horse to let it drink in front of her, but forgot to loosen the rein so the horse could not reach the water. The girl could not resist laughing out at this clumsy behaviour and turned around to him immediately, whispering, "loosen the rein..."

The horse finally had water. So, the young man felt grateful to the girl and said, "You are so kind-hearted. I want to visit your house but I don't know how to go over the threshold of your house."

The girl was touched and whispered to him, "My father sees things horizontally and my mother sees the sideways. Avoid these two directions. Just stoop and you'll get in. My room is at the end of the corridor!"

The young lad was thrilled at her advice and said, "When I drank water just now, I knew your tears were in it. So I can see that you don't want to marry. If you please, I can play flute on your bedside every night when the moon is high and stars are bright."

听了这话，姑娘可慌了："阿哥哟，我家的大门口，公狗有三只，母狗有三只，三双狗十二只眼，你进不来；我家的小门外边睡着爹，里边睡着妈，爹的枕头边有刺，妈的脚边有陷阱，我也进不来；我的住处在外边，十二道铁锁门，十二道铜锁门，我一睡着，十二道门用金铸起，十二道门用银铸起，你进不来。我的叔伯舅家，毒弩手有二十，大刀手有二十，你千万莫进来！"

小伙子笑了笑，拉着马慢慢走了，边说边留下话说："天下没有拦得住我的东西，阿妹哟，今晚上你就等着我！"

姑娘正要分辩，笛声响起来了。小伙子骑上白马，飞快地消失在远处的山林中。姑娘不知怎么办好，也晓不得那小伙子是哪方人，忘记了要寻短见，慌忙跑回家中，坐在床边着急地等起来。太阳落山了，月亮升起来了，大门外的狗睡着了，爹妈也睡着了。小伙子没有来，这可气坏了姑娘，她伏在床上痛哭起来。哭着哭着，忽然听见了笛声。姑娘连忙坐起来，睁开眼看时，果然见那小伙子手持金笛，含着甜甜的笑站在床边，对姑娘说："姑娘呀姑娘，等我等得泪水落，你真良心好！"姑娘说："大哥呀大哥，你怎么这样面熟？"小伙子说："姑娘呀姑娘，有情人都是面熟的。"于是他俩从此成了好朋友。每天晚上，当夜深人静的时候，那位小伙子就来了，直到公鸡叫了才离去。一来二去的，日子长久，当出嫁的日子就要到来的时候，父母发现，姑娘的肚子大起来了。

However, the girl felt panic and replied, "Three male dogs and three female ones guard our gate. You won't be able to get in. Outside my room are my dad and my mom. My dad has thorns beside his pillow and my mom sets a trap at her feet. Even I can't get in by myself. Worse still, there are twelve iron doors and twelve brass doors in my room. Whenever I go to bed, they are locked, twelve of which are locked with gold and the other twelve with silver. There is no way that you can get in. And my uncles have twenty archers with poisonous arrows and twenty hatchet men. Please don't break in!"

The young lad just smiled and walked away with his horse. Meanwhile, he said, "I can't be stopped. Just wait for me tonight!"

When the girl was about to explain, the sound of flute was heard. The young lad got on the horse and quickly disappeared into the deep forest. The girl did not know what to do or where the young man lived. Then, she ran back home in hurry and waited anxiously on her bed, without any thought of her suicide plan. When the sun went down and the moon rose, dogs fell asleep outside of her door. So were her parents. But the young lad was nowhere to found, so the girl went angry and cried heavily over her bed. Suddenly, she heard the familiar melody of the flute. She sat up quickly and opened her eyes. It turned out that the young lad was standing by her bedside with smile, holding a golden flute. The young man said, "Are you crying for me? How sweet of you." The girl replied, "Why do you look so familiar?" The man replied, "That's how lovers look at each other." Since then, they became close friends. Every night when it was quiet, the young lad showed up and did not leave until roosters crowed. After a long time, when her wedding day actually came, her parents found her pregnant.

姑娘的肚子大起来了，父母慌了手脚，偷偷去告诉舅舅家，大家共同来追查原因。

姑娘的肚子大起来了，心里很着急，那小伙子又总不告诉她他的地址。为了要知道他的下落，姑娘就偷来家里的羊毛，揉搓出一股又细又长的线，拴在小伙子的纽扣上。第二天，姑娘顺着线找去，只见线的另一头钻进龙洞里去了。姑娘这才明白，她的丈夫原来是龙。姑娘正要跳进水里去找，不巧被来接亲的舅家人看见了。接亲的舅家人看到这一情况很快知道姑娘肚子大起来的原因，于是打起了各种狠毒的鬼主意。本来，姑娘一直希望父母和舅家一发现了她出丑，便放弃她，她十分希望自己能被驱逐出家门去。可是她的美丽使得她的舅舅家舍不得丢开她。因此，在推迟了结婚日子后，舅舅家在背地里商量，先要暗暗打掉姑娘肚中的娃娃，然后把龙洞堵死掉，这样就断绝了姑娘逃走的路子和希望。就在那天晚上，姑娘的舅舅家拉了很多很多的猫狗，打死了丢进龙洞中，同时还把寨子里所有不干净的东西都丢进了龙洞中，大水顿时变得又腥又臭。那天晚上，姑娘刚要入睡，那位白衣小伙子面色惨白，遍身血迹地出现在姑娘面前，一见姑娘，便痛苦地呻吟着，伤心地哭着。他对姑娘说："阿妹哟，我是东海龙王家的第九千九百九十九个儿子，由于龙王父亲看见这里的彝家人可怜，特派我住在白竹山里，为彝家造福，可是这里的人杀猫杀狗丢脏物，把我的住处全部毁掉了。现在，我斗不赢山神了，山神把我赶出山，我不知要去什么地方才能安家。"说完就想走，姑娘一把拉住他，也哭了。

Her parents were panic at her pregnancy. They secretly went to her maternal uncles to figure out the reason together.

The girl was also very anxious because her lover would not tell her where he lived. To figure it out by herself, the girl stole wool from her family and rubbed it into a very long and thin strand to tie it to a button of the young man's clothes. The next day, she traced the strand which went all the way into the Dragon cave. Then she realized that her husband was a dragon. When she was about to jump into the water, her uncles, who came to pick her up for the marriage, saw it and immediately knew the reason why she got pregnant. So, they came up with various vicious plots. The girl had thought that once her parents and uncles found her pregnant, they would abandon and banish her, which she desired the most. But she was too pretty for anyone to give her up. So, her uncles postponed her wedding day and discussed behind how to abort her baby and block the cave to stop her from running away. At that night, her uncles dumped numerous dead cats and dogs into the cave, along with other filthy things, which instantly blurred the water and produced stink smell. Back in the house, when the girl was about to sleep, the young lad in white costume appeared in front of her with a pale face, covered with blood all over, moaning in great pain and crying with sadness. He said to the girl, "I'm the 9999th son of the dragon king in the East sea. I'm sent here by my father who felt sorry for the Yi people here. I'm supposed to bring benefit to your people. But they threw all those filthy things into my cave and now it's ruined. Now I can't beat the god of mountain and he drives me out. I don't know where to live now." Having said his piece, the poor dragon prince was ready to leave. The girl held his arm and cried.

第二天早上，人们都惊呆了：白竹山上看不见一朵鲜花，所有的树木都变得又枯又黄；碧庄村前后那些良田，泥土干裂，滴水不见，龙洞口堆着死猫烂狗。成群的蚊子苍蝇和蛆虫聚在那里过年过节。当舅舅家找来的堕胎的人赶到姑娘家里，姑娘也消失得无影无踪了……

从此，这一带穷了下来。时过不久，人们听说在易门界里，在一个十分干旱的寨子里，出现了一股桶大的龙洞水，这股水使得那一带的生活就像过去的碧庄一样好过极了。据说每当春雨潇潇或者是晚霞升起的时候，人们常看见一对白衣素着的彝家年轻夫妇，出没在龙洞边的花草地上……

人一过上好日子，就忘记了好日子是怎么来的，因此常常糟蹋了好日子，小白龙和彝家女的事情，我们都要记住啊！

讲述者：普德富
翻译者：普珠信，普有苟
搜集者：罗有能，罗有俊，毕继爱
整理者：罗有能

On the next morning, the villagers were astonished. There was not a single flower on the Baizhu Mountain. All the trees withered and all the once fertile fields were completely dried out. Dead cats and dogs were piled up in front of the dragon cave attracting millions of flies and maggots. And the witch sent by the girl's uncle for abortion could not find the girl anywhere in her house.

Ever since, poverty struck that area. And after some time, it was said that in Yimen county, there was a big stream of cave water in a once arid village. Since then, the village was nourished just like Bizhuang village was. The story went that whenever a rain fell or an afterglow appeared, people could see a young couple in white costumes playing on the grassland near the dragon cave...

Once people live a happy life, they can easily forget where it comes from and no longer cherish it. The story of the little white dragon and the Yi girl should always be kept in mind!

Narrator: Pu Defu

Translator: Pu Zhuxin, Pu Yougou

Collector: Luo Youneng, Luo Youjun, Bi Jiai

Editor: Luo Youneng

猎手和姑娘

很久以前，在美丽的梭罗山下，有一个勇敢、善良的猎手叫普阿扎。他射箭打猎远近闻名，而且还能吹一手好笛子。只要笛声一响，能把森林里的各种鸟儿引来。

时间一天一天过去，父亲看他已经是成人的年纪，劝他说："孩子，快成个家吧，你要哪位姑娘，我请人去说。"普阿扎不在意地回答："阿爹，暂且莫慌，我自己会找。"话虽这样说，可就是不见他去找。山寨里有许多长得像山茶花一样漂亮的姑娘，都用眼睛盯着他，对他表示爱慕之情，他也不理睬。父母对他的婚事很不放心。

有一天，普阿扎带上弓箭和笛子去撵山打猎，来到了一湾清泉边。一看芳草青青，一听流水潺潺，真像进了美丽如画的仙境。普阿扎坐在一块青石板上吹起了竹笛。清悠的笛声透过森林，飞向蓝天碧空，把森林里的各种鸟儿都引来了。鸟儿们各显神通，随着笛声翩翩起舞，千姿百态。突然，

A Hunter and a Girl

Once upon a time, under the beautiful Suoluo Mountain, there was a brave and kind-hearted hunter named Puaza. He was famous for archery and hunting, and he could also play a good flute. As long as there was sound of his flute, all kinds of birds in the forest would be attracted there.

As time went by, seeing the child had grown into adulthood, Puaza's father advised him by saying, "Dear child, it's time that you got married. Which girl do you want? I'll find a matchmaker for you." Puaza was absent-minded and said, "Dad, don't worry for the moment. I will find one myself." That said, he did not take any action. There were many girls as beautiful as camellia in the village, who kept their eyes on him and showed him their love, but he just ignored. His parents were very upset about his marriage.

One day, Puaza went hunting in the mountain with his bows, arrows and flute. He came to a clear spring, where there were fragrant grasses and a murmuring stream along side, like a picturesque fairyland. Puaza sat on a bluestone and played the bamboo flute. Its melodic sound could be heard in the forest and the sky, attracting all kinds of birds. The birds showed their special skills and danced with the sound of the flute. All of a

天空中一片阴影掠过，鸟儿们立刻慌乱起来。普阿扎向空中望去，只见一只巨大的恶鹰抓着一只白鸟在空中盘旋。他忙张弓搭箭，对着恶鹰“嗖”的一箭，正中恶鹰的脚杆。恶鹰丢掉白鸟，飞走了。普阿扎抱起白鸟，看着被恶鹰啄伤的地方，不觉有些难过。白鸟睁大眼睛望着他，像在说：“善良的猎手，再救救我吧！”普阿扎心想：“我怎么救你呢？身边一点药草也没有。”忽然，他想起从这里向北走，翻过一架山，在山箐里有间草房，里面住着一位老人，他有一种药草可以医百病。普阿扎抱着白鸟向北跑去，到草房门口，恰好深山老人走出来，他跪下哀求：“阿波，救救这只白鸟吧，它被恶鹰啄伤了。”深山老人打量了他一眼，用手把他扶起来，笑道：“年轻的猎手，别着急。”深山老人马上舀了一碗清泉替白鸟洗净伤口，又从草屋里取出一个葫芦，把葫芦里的仙药给白鸟敷上。

普阿扎又把白鸟抱回家。三天过去，白鸟的伤好了。普阿扎对白鸟说：“可爱的鸟儿，飞去吧！”白鸟扇动了一下翅膀，腾空而起，在普阿扎头上鸣叫一声，表示感谢，就飞向远方。

sudden, there was a shadow in the sky, which startled the birds. Puaza looked up into the air and saw a huge hawk circling in the middle holding a white bird. He quickly took up his bow and arrow, shooting at the hawk in its leg. The hawk dropped the white bird and flew away. Puaza picked up the white bird and looked at its wound pecked by the hawk. He felt sad. The white bird stared at him with eyes wide open, which seemed to say, "Kind-hearted hunter, help me again!" Puaza thought, "how can I help you? There is no herb around." Suddenly, he thought of an old man living in a thatched cottage in the mountain, who had a kind of herb that could cure all kinds of diseases. So he took the white bird in his arm and went north in the mountain. At the entrance of the cottage, he saw the old man who just came back from the deep forest. He knelt down and begged, "Abo, please help the white bird. It's pecked by the hawk." Looking at him, the old man helped him up with his hand and said with a smile, "Young hunter, don't worry." The old man immediately scooped up a bowl of clear spring to clean the wounds of the white bird and applied the elixir in the gourd he just took out from the cottage to the white bird.

Puazar took the white bird home. Three days later, the white bird's injury was cured. Puaza said to it, "Lovely bird, fly away!" The white bird fluttered its wings and rose to the sky. It tweeted on Puazar's head to express its gratitude and flew away.

普阿扎继续去撵山打猎。有一天，他到清泉边歇脚，正好有一个姑娘在泉水中洗澡，普阿扎忙向后回避。姑娘发现有人，也羞涩地上岸穿好洁白的羽毛衣服。啊，多么美丽的姑娘！她头发像柳丝一样柔软，她的眼睛像泉水一样清澈，她的脸庞像桃花一样娇艳……普阿扎不由动了情，拿出竹笛吹起调子。笛音打动了姑娘，姑娘和着笛音低声吟唱着向普阿扎走去，普阿扎向姑娘靠近。正在这时，来了一群毕摩，为首的一个喊：“捉妖！”其他的蜂拥而上，不由分说，抓住姑娘飞跑而去。普阿扎一时弄得不知所措，当他想去救姑娘的时候，姑娘的呼救声已经远去，最后消逝在旷野之中。

普阿扎后悔未能与毕摩们厮杀救出姑娘。而今到何处去找姑娘呢？他又想起了深山老人料事如神，说不定知道姑娘的下落。于是普阿扎匆匆赶到深山老人住地。深山老人告诉他：那姑娘就是他前次救下的白鸟，那为首的毕摩就是恶鹰。不听则已，一听更坚定了普阿扎救姑娘的决心。但深山老人告诉他：恶鹰住在黑风山，这座山山峰陡险，难攀难上，而且一片漆黑，不辨方向。普阿扎毫不畏惧，深山老人感动了，便说：“你一定要去救白鸟姑娘，那我送你两件东西，一是我的弓箭，它会帮助你战胜困难，二是我的这条狗，它会给你带路。”普阿扎告辞了深山老人上路了。

Puaza went hunting in the mountain as usual. One day, he stopped by the spring and saw a girl taking a bath in it. Puaza hurriedly avoided. At the sight of him, the girl went ashore shyly to wear white feather clothes. Oh, what a beautiful girl she is! Her hair was as soft as willow silk and her eyes were as clear as spring water and her face was as delicate as peach blossom. Puaza couldn't help feeling admired, so he took out the bamboo flute and played. The flute moved the girl. She softly sang with the melody and walked towards Puaza, who also approached the girl. Just then, a group of Bimo came, and the first one shouted, "catch the demon!" The others swarmed in, caught the girl and ran away. Puaza was totally at a loss for a moment. When he was about to save the girl, she was grabbed away and finally disappeared in the desert with only distant voices of cries heard.

Puaza regretted not having fought with Bimos and saved the girl. Where could he find the girl now? He thought of the old man in the deep mountain again, who might know the whereabouts of the girl. So Puazha hurried to the old man's residence, where he was told that the girl was the white bird he saved last time, and the first Bimo was the hawk. The old man's words just made him more determined to save the girl. But the old man told him that the hawks lived in the Heifeng Mountain, which was steep and difficult to climb; moreover, it was dark, so it was easy to lose direction. Puaza was not afraid. The old man was moved and said, "If you must go to save the white bird girl, I will give you two things, my bow and arrow which will help you overcome difficulties. Also, my dog will lead way for you." Puaza bid farewell to the old man in the deep mountain and set out.

翻过一架山又一架山，渡过了一条江又一条江。后来又来到一架大山前。山上狂风呼啸，乱石飞滚，人无法通过。普阿扎想起深山老人的弓箭，拉起弓向山尖射了一箭。山摇晃了一下，崩塌下来化为了平地。不知走了多少路，面前又出现一条宽阔的江水。江水滚滚沸腾，冒起一股股热气。普阿扎抽出剑来在水里一试，剑熔化了。狗也在旁边焦急起来："这样烫的水，我们怎么能过去呢？"普阿扎沉思片刻说："有方法了。"说着又一箭往江心射去。江里发出一声巨响，波浪一个接一个翻腾着，仿佛要把他吞没似的。忽然一条大鱼漂上水面，那鱼背像一座长桥，从这边搭到那边。普阿扎从鱼背上过了江。第三天，他来到一片茫茫无际的沼泽地，射箭也无济于事，急得满大汗。这时飞来了一只五彩巨鸟说："年轻的猎手，你要到哪里去？"普阿扎说："到黑风山救白鸟姑娘，她被恶鹰毕摩抓走了。你能帮助我吗？"巨鸟说："走吧，年轻的猎手，快骑到我身上。"巨鸟落在普阿扎身旁，带着他直飞黑风山去。

He climbed one mountain after another and went across numerous rivers. Then he arrived at a huge mountain. The wind was whistling with rocks rolling around, so it was impossible for people to go through. Puaza thought of the bow and arrow given by the old man, so he pulled up the bow and shot an arrow at the top of the mountain. The mountain rocked and collapsed to the ground. He continued his journey and could not count how many more roads he had taken until he arrived at a wide river. The river was boiling and steaming. Puaza took out his sword and tried it in the water, which melted instantly. The dog was also anxious and asked him, "How can we go over such hot water?" Puaza thought for a moment and said, "I have an idea." He shot another arrow to the heart of the river, which produced a loud noise in the river, making high waves one after another, as if he was to be engulfed. Suddenly a big fish floated up to the surface of the water. The fish's back was like a long bridge, linking the two sides, on the back of which, Puaza went across the river. On the third day, he came to a boundless swamp. As it was useless to shoot arrows, he grew worried and sweated all over. At that moment, a giant colorful bird came and said to him, "Young hunter, where are you going?" Puaza replied, "I am going to the Heifeng Mountain to save the white bird girl. She was captured by the hawk Bimo. Can you help me?" The giant bird said, "Let's go, young hunter. Ride on me." Then, the bird landed beside him and took him straight to the Heifeng Mountain.

黑风山上，有花花不开，有树树不茂，有鸟鸟不叫，死沉沉，阴森森，叫人不寒而栗。普阿扎上了黑风山，哪管这些，一心只想早早找到白鸟姑娘。但山上伸手不见五指，白鸟姑娘在何处呢？找呀找呀，找了很多地方，仍不见白鸟姑娘。他便用竹笛吹起了忧伤的调子。

再说，白鸟姑娘被恶鹰毕摩囚禁在一个山洞里，恶鹰毕摩限她三天内答应做他的妻子，不然就要害死她。今天是最后一天，姑娘伤心的眼泪像珍珠断线一样滴湿了羽毛裳。忽然笛声飘入山洞，姑娘知道猎手救她来了，又是欣喜又是焦急，也唱起了调子。普阿扎闻声急忙赶到洞前，但是巨石堵住了洞门。普阿扎使出浑身力气，拔箭射向巨石。轰隆一声，如天崩地裂，山洞门打开了。正在这时，恶鹰毕摩回来了，便与普阿扎厮杀开来。恶鹰一次又一次向普阿扎扑来，普阿扎都闪开了，然后沉住气，拉满弓，一箭射穿了恶鹰的胸膛。莽莽群山、漠漠林海豁然开朗，金色的太阳使黑风山增添了生气。

There were plants with no blossom, trees with few branches and leaves and birds daring not to tweet in the Heifeng Mountain. Everything was dark and gloomy, as dead as a doornail, making one tremble with fear. Now that he had arrived, Puaza had no mood to think about this and was single-minded to find the girl as soon as possible. But it was so dark and deep in the mountain. Where was the white bird girl? He looked for her everywhere but in vain. So he played a sad tune with his bamboo flute.

Actually, the white bird girl was imprisoned in a cave by the ferocious hawk Bimo, who demanded the girl to be his wife within three days; otherwise she would be killed. This was the last day. The girl's sad tears were like pearls dripping down from a broken line, making the feather clothes all wet through. Suddenly the sound of the flute drifted into the cave. The girl knew that the hunter had come to save her. She was both happy and anxious. She hummed a tune back. Puaza heard the sound and rushed to the front of the cave, which, however, was blocked by a huge stone. Puaza used all his strength to pull out the arrow and shot at the stone. The door of the cave opened with a thud like tearing the heaven and earth apart. Just then Bimo, the evil hawk, came and fought with Puaza. The hawk jumped on him for several time, which had all been skillfully dodged by Puaza. Then he calmed down, drew a full bow and shot straight to the chest of the hawk. All of a sudden, the vast mountains and forests became bright, with golden sunlight shedding, making it more lively.

白鸟姑娘又一次得救，感激之中深深爱上了普阿扎，默默无言许身给了普阿扎。当他们回到家中的时候，百鸟来庆贺，蝴蝶飞来起舞，溪水为之奏乐。普阿扎的父母更是乐得合不拢嘴。

讲述者：李开寿
整理者：姜仕英

The white bird girl was saved again. With deep gratitude, she fell in love with Puaza and gave herself to him. When they returned home, a hundred birds came to celebrate, butterflies came to dance, and streams played music for them. Puaza's parents grinned from ear to ear.

Narrator: Li Kaishou

Editor: Jiang Shiying

阿克和碧鸡姑娘

很久很久以前，撒梅人居住的坝子东面山头上，飞来了一头鹰怪。它蹲在怪石洞口，翻着绿眼珠，打起了破坏撒梅人幸福生活的鬼主意。

那年春天，栽秧的季节到了。可是沟底露出了泥沙，撒梅人日夜盼望着老天能够降下雨来。有几次，天边出现了几团乌云，人们向天祷告："老天老天快下雨，种出白米先供你。"哪知，一阵怪风吹过，乌云又散了。天上依然是火辣辣的太阳，烤得田里泥巴都裂开了。

撒梅人个个心如火烧，人人愁眉苦脸，可是却从东山石洞里传来了鹰怪哈哈的笑声。原来，天干地旱，就是这家伙捣的鬼。河水干涸，是因为天不下雨；天不下雨，是因为这鹰怪用翅膀扇散了乌云。这家伙为什么要把乌云扇散呢？原来它想让天下大旱，把人们活活饿死，然后它好胀饱肚皮。

Ake and a Girl Called Biji

Long time ago, a hawk flew on the hill east of the dam where the Samei people lived. It crouched at the entrance of a strange rock, rolled its green eyes, and came up with an evil thought to ruin the happy life of the Samei people.

In the spring of that year, when it was the season for planting seedlings, the sand was exposed at the bottom of the ditch, so the Samei people had to pray for rain day and night. On several occasions, when a few dark clouds appeared in the sky, people prayed to heaven, "God, please give us rainfalls, and the white rice will be offered to you first." However, at that moment, a strange wind would blow from nowhere, and scattered the dark clouds again. The scorching sun still hanged up in the sky, burning mud in the fields into cracks.

Torn with anxiety, the Samei people all wore a woebegone face. But a laughter of the hawk came from the Dongshan stone cave. It turned out that it was this monster that made the sky dry and the ground arid. The river dried up because there was no rain; it didn't rain because the hawk waved its wings and scattered the dark clouds. Why did it do this? The hawk wanted to dry up the land and starved people alive, so as to have a big feast.

一天，村民们聚集在一起，个个唉声叹气，正在商量如何找条活路。有的人说：“天这般旱，寸草难生，秋后怎能交得上官租?”有的说：“不如逃荒远走他乡去吧!”这时，人群中走出个名叫阿克的青年猎人。他安慰乡亲们说：“逃荒的路是不能走的。离开了生养我们的土地，更是没有活路。大家还是多想想办法吧。”人群中走出一位老大爹说：“办法只有一个，就是上山去找水源，只有找到泉水，才能消除旱灾。”阿克说：“到哪里去找水源呀?”老人说：“听老辈人讲，西边碧鸡山中有一股宝泉。这宝泉藏在密林丛中，只有诚实勇敢的人，才能找到它。”阿克听了，把嘴唇一咬，说：“只要有这样的宝泉，我一定去把它找到。”老大爹说：“你是个勇敢的猎人，一定能找到这股宝泉。我们大家在村里砍竹子，做涧槽，等着你找到这宝泉吧。”

阿克告别乡亲，进山找宝泉去了。一路上，他攀悬崖、钻刺树，射死了拦路的花豹、蟒蛇，历尽千辛，还没找到泉水。阿克刚想回头，忽又想起乡亲们的重托，他便又振作精神，继续向前走去。

One day, villagers gathered together, sighing, and discussed how to survive. One of them rumbled, "The land is so dry that it is difficult even to grow grasses. How can we pay the official rent after autumn?" Another one proposed, "It is better to run away and find another place to settle!" A young hunter called Ake stepped out from the crowd and comforted the villagers, "The road to flee cannot be taken. There is no way to live if we leave our homeland. Let's think of more ways." An old man walked out of the crowd and said, "There is only one way. We need to go up the mountain to find the source of water. Only by finding the spring can we eliminate the drought." Ake asked, "Where can I find the source of water?" The old man replied, "It is said that there is a spring hidden in the dense forest in the Biji Mountain in the West. Only the honest and brave people can find it." When Ake learned this, he bit his lips and said, "If such a treasured spring really exists, I will find it." The old man said, "You are a brave hunter. I believe you will find this spring. While waiting for the good news, we will cut bamboo in the village to make ravines for preparation."

Ake bid farewell to the villagers and set foot to the mountain. Along the way, he suffered from numerous hardships after climbing up steep cliffs, weaving through thorny trees, shooting leopards and boas that blocked the way to death, but still couldn't find any trace of spring water. However depressed, whenever Ake thought of the promise he had made to the villagers, he would pick himself up again and went onward.

走着走着，来到一块林中空地。由于又饥又渴，过分疲劳，阿克眼前一黑，昏倒在地。也不知道过了多长时间，阿克从昏迷中醒来，一睁眼，便见眼前闪着一片五彩虹光，虹光中站着一位美丽的姑娘。姑娘身穿彩衣，头上戴着一顶像鸡冠一样的帽子，手里拿着一束香喷喷的樱花。

姑娘见阿克瞪着眼睛直愣愣地盯着自己，便开口说："小伙子，你怎么跑到这里来睡觉，不怕老虎把你叼去吗？"

阿克听了，回答说："我们撒梅人的田地遭了干旱，我是来找宝泉水的。好心的小姑娘，你叫什么名字？你知道宝泉在什么地方吗？"

姑娘回答说："我名叫阿比吉，我也不晓得宝泉在什么地方，只听说一般人是找不到的，你还是赶紧下山回家去吧，免得碰上毒蛇猛兽，丢了性命！"

阿克说："没有水，乡亲们就不能活命。找不到水，我就不能回去。"说完，阿克转身向前方走去。

He continued his journey and went to an open ground in the forest. Being both hungry and thirsty, and over-exhausted, Ake fainted in the dark. Some time had passed until Ake finally woke up from his coma. When he opened his eyes, he saw a colorful iridescent light shining in front of him, in which a beautiful girl stood. The girl in a colorful clothes wore a hat like a cockscomb, and held a bunch of fragrant cherry flowers.

When the girl saw Ake staring at her, she said, "Young man, why do you sleep here? Aren't you afraid of being taken away by tigers?"

Ake replied, "Our Samei people are suffering from drought in the farmland. I am here to look for the treasured spring. Kind-hearted young girl, can you tell me your name? Do you know where the spring is?"

The girl answered, "My name is Abiji. I have no idea where the spring is, but I hear that ordinary people can not find it. Just go down the mountain and return home, in case you meet venomous serpents and wild beasts which can take your life!"

Ake said, "Villagers can not survive without water. So I will not return home unless I find it." Then, he turned back and headed forward right away.

青年猎人的身影在密林中消失了，阿比吉姑娘还一直呆呆地站在原地。她在想些什么呢？原来，她就是碧鸡山中的凤凰仙女。青年猎人为了搭救乡亲们活命，不畏艰难的勇敢精神使她敬佩。因此，姑娘下决心要帮助撒梅人解除干旱。只见她将身子旋转了几圈，一道金光闪过，姑娘变成了一只五彩绚丽的凤凰，昂首展翅，腾空飞起。接着，一声长鸣，山鸣答应。不一会儿，成千上万的鸟儿便纷纷聚拢来，围着凤凰翩翩飞舞。舞了一圈，天上出现了五彩祥云，遮住了火辣辣的太阳，又舞了一圈，四处刮起了清风，又舞了一圈，天上下起了蒙蒙细雨。百鸟不住地围着凤凰起舞，雨也不停地越下越大。霎时，河里沟里，田里地里，流水哗哗。

雨渐渐停了，猎人阿克在树林里浑身被淋得透湿，但他心里却比吃了蜜糖还甜。这时阿克忽然听空中传来了嘈杂的声音。他抬头一看，只见树林上空，一只美丽的凤凰率领着百鸟，正在与一头凶恶的巨鹰大战。

The young hunter disappeared in the dense forest. The girl stood still and looked at his back. What was she thinking? Actually, she was the phoenix fairy in the Biji Mountain. She admired the young man who would risk his life to save the villagers in his hometown in spite of grave difficulties. Therefore, she made up her mind to help Samei people out of the severe drought. She turned her body around for a few times and became a colorful phoenix after a flash of golden light, which flied up with her wings spreading. Then, she made a long cry, producing resonant echos in the mountain. In a short time, thousands of birds gathered and danced around the phoenix. After a round of dance, colorful auspicious clouds appeared in the sky, covering the scorching sun. When they danced again, a breeze blew everywhere. After the third round of dance, the sky started to drizzle. A hundred birds kept dancing around the phoenix, while the rain kept falling more and more heavily. In an instant, the river, ditches, and fields were flooded with water.

The rain gradually stopped, and the hunter Ake was drenched in the forest, but his heart was sweeter than honey. Suddenly Ake heard a noisy sound in the sky. He looked up and saw a hundred birds led by a beautiful phoenix fighting with a fierce giant hawk over the forest.

原来，这头巨鹰就是把旱灾降给撒梅人的鹰怪。它见凤凰和百鸟引来清风细雨，解除干旱，便气冲冲地飞来与凤凰恶战。

鹰怪施展它那凶恶的伎俩，用它那铁钩一样的嘴喙，狠狠地啄住了凤凰的翅膀。空中的情景，阿克看得清清楚楚。他立即拉满弩弓，搭上翎箭，“嗖”的一箭射去，鹰怪中箭坠落在地。

凤凰脱了险，向阿克身旁的树林落了下来。阿克忙向凤凰落下的地方奔去，走到跟前一看，并没有什么凤凰，只见草丛中躺着一位姑娘，肩膀上流着被鹰抓破的鲜血。

“阿比吉姑娘!”阿克惊叫起来。阿克赶紧从草丛中找来草药，用嘴嚼烂，敷在姑娘的伤口上。姑娘慢慢睁开了眼睛，然后把自己的身世和降雨战妖鹰的情况告诉了阿克。

阿克激动地说：“阿比吉姑娘，你为了我们撒梅人，才与妖鹰恶战，你受了伤，请你一同和我回村养伤吧!”

于是，阿克护送着姑娘回到村里。乡亲们见了姑娘，都来向她道谢。

不久，姑娘的伤好了，她和阿克彼此不忘患难之交，结为夫妻。从此两人过着幸福的生活。因为姑娘头上常戴一顶鸡冠形的帽子，所以人们称她为碧鸡姑娘。

讲述者：李树仁

搜集整理者：柳同

It turned out that the giant eagle was the monster that brought drought to Samei people. When it found that the phoenix and a hundred birds had removed the drought by introducing wind and rain, it angrily dashed out to fight with the phoenix.

The hawk monster used its ferocious trick to peck the wings of the phoenix with its hook-like beak. At the sight of it, Ake immediately pulled the arrow and shot down the hawk.

The Phoenix was finally out of danger and fell to the forest close to Ake. Aker hurriedly ran to it. When he arrived, he could not find the phoenix, but a girl lying in the grass, with blood on her shoulder scratched by the hawk.

"Abiji!" Ake exclaimed. He quickly looked for herbs in the grass, chewed them with his mouth and applied them to the girl's wound. Afterwards, the girl slowly opened her eyes, and then told him who she really was, how the rain was produced and the fight against the hawk.

Ake said enthusiastically, "Dear Abiji, you fought with the demon hawk and got injured for the sake of our Samei people. Please come back to the village with me to heal your wounds!"

So Ake escorted the girl back home. Villagers all came to express their gratitude to her.

Before long, the girl was recovered. In light of their friendship in adversity, they got married and lived a happy life ever after. As the girl usually wore a cockscomb-shaped hat, people all called her Biji girl.

Narrator: Li Shuren

Collector and editor: Liu Tong

神伞与宝葫芦

从前，有个姓艾的财主，他有三个儿子。

这年，艾财主眼看三个儿子都已长大成人，便把他们叫到面前，对他们说：“我给你们每人三驮货物，你们出去做生意，限你们一个月的时间，看哪个赚钱最多。赚了钱的，我给赏，亏了本的就休想进我的门。”三个儿子就各赶着自己的马匹出门去了。大儿子艾贵一心想当官，卖的货物价钱贵，卖了一个月才把三驮货物卖完，结果不赚不亏。二儿子艾财，平时就会做生意，能说会道，卖了三驮货物还买了三驮草药，赚钱最多。三儿子艾民，卖货价钱公道，遇到破衣烂裳的顾客，他就把货物索性送给了人家，不到半月就卖光了。卖来的钱，碰到穷苦人，他就这个送几文，那个给几块，不到一个月的时间，连本钱都已经用完。这天，艾民快到家了，身边只剩下三匹马了。他正走着，只见一对年老的夫妇，带着小男孩，从山箐里走来。突然“啪嗒”一声，小孩

The Magic Umbrella and the Precious Gourd

Long time ago, there was a moneybags named Ai, who had three sons.

One year, as his three sons had all grown up, this rich man Ai asked his sons to his side and said, "I will give each one of you three loads of cargoes to do business. The time limit is one month and I will see who makes the greatest profit during this time. I will reward those who make money; on the other hand, I will drive you out of this family if you lose any." Then, the three boys led the horses loaded with cargoes and left home. The eldest son Ai Gui set his mind to be an official, so he sold the goods at a high price. It took him one month to sell all the three cargoes and finally broke even. The second son Ai Cai had long learned business deals and had the gift of the gab. He earned a large sum of money, and not only sold three cargoes of goods but also bought three bags of herbal medicines. The third son Ai Min sold the goods at a reasonable price and even gave some for free if the customer wore shabby clothes. He sold out his goods in half a month. With the money he earned from the goods, he would give away a few cents or a few yuan whenever he met poor people. So in less than a month, all the money was used up, capital and profit.

失足滚下悬崖，老两口急得团团转。艾民见了，急忙跑上前，抓住一棵山藤，顺岩滑下，救起了小孩，但小孩左脚已跌断了。老妇人边哭边向艾民诉苦说：“我老两口五十岁才有这独生儿子，只望儿子长大能养活我们二老，现在脚断了叫我们怎样活呀！”艾民见老妇人越哭越伤心，便安慰说：“老人家，别哭了，快回家请医生医治吧！”二老说：“好心的年轻人呀，我们穷得家无隔夜粮，哪有钱请医生呀！”艾民听了，十分同情，便把自己的三匹马送给了他们。

艾民回到家时，他的两个哥哥也到家了。财主父亲问他们：“我的三个孩子，生意怎样？”老大说：“货物卖完，不亏不赚。”老二说：“货卖一半，赚钱三千；再卖一半，买得草药三担。”财主眼睛眯成一条线，夸赞老二说：“我的二心肝，能干呀，能干！”财主又问老三：“你呢？”艾民说，“爹呀，我货物卖完，银钱用干，骡马送人，只剩衣衫。”财主听了，火冒三丈，破口大骂：“你这不成器的败家子！你给我滚出去！”便把艾民赶出了家门。

One day, as Ai Min was about to reach home with three horses, he met an elderly couple, walking out from the bamboo forest in the mountain, with a little boy. Suddenly, the boy slipped and fell down the cliff. The couple was extremely anxious and helpless. At the sight of this, Ai Min hurried down the cliff with a vine in hand and saved the child. However, the child's left foot was broken. The old woman sobbed out her grievances to Ai Min, "We have this child, the only one, in our fifties and expect him to grow up and take care of us. Now his foot is broken, so how can we expect to live!" As the old woman grew more grievous as she cried, Ai Min comforted her, "Dear old lady, please stop crying. Hurry home and send for a doctor!" The elderly couple said, "Kind-hearted young man, we are so poor that we even do not have food stored for tomorrow. How can we afford a doctor!" Ai Min gave them his three horses out of great sympathy.

When Ai Min arrived at home, his two elderly brothers had come back as well. The moneybags father asked them, "My three boys, how is your business?" The eldest boy said, "I have sold out all the goods, without losing or gaining any money." The second boy said, "I have earned three thousand when half of the goods were sold; I have also bought three bags of herbal medicines with the money earned from the other half." The moneybags smiled and squinted, praising his second son, "My dearest second boy, well done, well done!" Then, he turned to his third son, "How about you?" Ai Min replied, "Dear father, I have sold out all the goods and used up the money. I have also sent away the horses. Now I have nothing but my clothes." The moneybags burst into a fury and shouted abuse, "You worthless rat! Get out!" Ai Min was then kicked out of the house.

艾民被父亲赶出了门，身上一文钱也没有，只好去当叫花子，乞讨过活。这天，艾民讨饭来到了蟒山村，只见家家关门闭户。后来他看到一位老头挑水，便跟了去，老人见他生得眉清目秀，十分可怜，就把他带到家里，准备给他点剩饭。再一看这青年有点面熟，便问艾民："你是哪里的？为什么年纪轻轻的就落到这步田地？"艾民把做生意亏了本，被父亲赶出门的事说了一遍。老头一听，眼泪顿时刷刷往下掉，弄得艾民莫名其妙。老头说："原来你是我的大恩人，要不是你救了我的儿子，又送了我三匹马，那我们咋个能活到现在？"接着老头又是烧火，又是做饭，热情地招呼艾民。

吃饭时，艾民问："大爹，为什么这村里家家关门闭户？"老人说："你不知道，我们这里蟒山上有座大庙，庙中有一尊大佛爷，佛肚中有条大蟒，经常爬出来伤害百姓和牲畜。我们村里的牲畜几乎都给它吃光了。因为它有一颗夜明珠，人们都说它是仙蟒，不敢惹它。大家怕仙蟒出来咬人，关门闭户，不敢出门。"艾民听了，对老人说："今晚我就到那庙里看看，如果有办法，我们就把它杀了，为民除掉这一害。"老人急忙说："一个都不敢进庙门，你怎么去得？"艾民说："大爹放心，只要给我一把刀，我自有办法。"老头说："我家有把祖传宝剑，倒是挺锋利的，只是好多年没有用了，可以试试。不过，我们不能让你去冒险。"艾民说："只要能为民除害，死也甘心。"两位老人劝阻不过，只好由他去了。

Ai Min was penniless when he was swept out like rubbish, so he had to beg for life. One day, Ai Min arrived at Mangshan Village, where he found that every household closed the door. Ai Min followed an old man who carried water. The old man felt pathetic at this young man with fine features, so he took Ai Min home and prepared some leftovers for him. When looking closer, the old man found that this young man actually looked quite familiar, so he asked Ai Min, "Where are you from? How are you reduced to such a misery at a young age?" Ai Min told the old man the whole story of losing money in business and being kicked out from family by his father. The old man immediately wept heavily, which confused Ai Min. The old man said, "You are my benefactor! If it had not been you who had saved my son and gave me three horses, how could we have lived till now?" Then, he lit the fires and cooked the food, treating Ai Min wholeheartedly.

During meal, Ai Min asked, "Why does every household shut the door in the village?" The old man replied, "You might not know, but up in the Mangshan Mountain, there is a Buddhist statue in the temple and a big boa lived in its belly. The boa always creeps out, hurting the villagers and killing animals. Nearly all the livestock in the village have been eaten by it. But, as it is said that the boa is celestial because of a luminous pearl in its mouth, no one dares to challenge it. So the villagers had to close their doors for fear of being bitten by it." Ai Min said to the old man, "I will go to the temple and have a look. If I can come up with an idea, I will kill it so that people can get rid of this evil thing." The old man said hurriedly, "No one dares to walk into the temple. How can you do it?" Ai Min replied, "Don't worry, just give me a knife and I will have my way." The old man said, "I have a sword, a hereditary treasure, very sharp, but I have not used it for years. You can have a try. But, we will not let you take this risk." Ai Min said, "As long as I can remove this devil for the people, then I shall have nothing to regret even if I die." Ai Min could not be persuaded by the old couple and went to the temple.

第二天清早，两位老人约上邻居猎手普旺，到蟒山庙前一棵大树背后等着艾民。直到太阳出山一竹竿高了，仍然不见艾民走出庙门。两位老人急得说不出话来，眼泪直流。猎手普旺也叹了一口气。他们正要往回走时，只听“嘎!”的一声庙门开了，三人吓了一跳，以为是仙蟒出来了。回头一看，只见艾民从庙中走出，三人又惊又喜。老婆子大叫：“哎呀！谢天谢地，恩人出来了!”艾民说：“大爹大妈难为你们了，让你们多操心了。”老头上前拉住艾民说：“走！快回家再说吧!”

回到老人家中，艾民说：“我昨晚躲在庙中大梁上的大匾背后，看清楚了大蟒的活动。它睡觉时间多，我决心把它除掉。”老人担心地说：“大蟒很凶，太危险了。”艾民说：“不要紧，你们给我打一个大木柜，安上阀销，抬上四扇磨，再给一盘大三脚，三十斤香油，一挑木炭，三只鸡，趁大蟒睡觉，把这些东西抬进庙去，我有办法治服。”老人一听，又惊又喜，很快去找村中几位长老商量，大家都很高兴。事情就这样定下了。

The next morning, the old couple asked the hunter, Puwang, living in the neighbourhood to come along and waited for Ai Min behind a tall tree in front of the Mangshan Mountain temple. Ai Min was not seen out of the temple even when the sun rose to the height of a bamboo pole. The couple grew too anxious to speak, with tears beginning to run down. Puwang, the hunter, also sighed. When they were about to leave, "Ga!", a sound came from the temple and its door opened. Startled, the three men thought it was the big boa. Turning back, in great surprise and joy, they found that Ai Min walked out of the temple. The old woman yelled in happiness, "Thank goodness! my benefactor is out!" Ai Min replied, "I am sorry to have worried you." The old man grabbed Ai Min and said, "Go, quickly! Let's talk when we are home!"

Returning to the old couple's house, Ai Min said, "Last night, I hid behind the inscribed board of the beam column and observed clearly the activities of the big boa. It slept for most of the time. I am determined to do away with it." The old couple began to worry, "The big boa is ferocious. It is too dangerous." Ai Min replied, "Don't worry. Give me a big wooden cabinet with a valve pin. Also, I need four mills, a big tripod, 15 kg of sesame oil, some coal and three chickens. Carry these stuffs to the temple while the big boa sleeps and I will have my way to kill it." The old man was astounded yet joyous. Immediately, he went to the head of the village to discuss the matter. They were all happy to hear the plan. Then, it was settled.

过了三天，一切都备齐了。猎手普旺选了几个胆大体壮的小伙子，趁着大蟒睡觉的时间，将艾民所要的东西悄悄地抬进了大庙，按艾民的要求摆下了。

这天夜晚，艾民身带宝剑轻手轻脚走进了大庙，在大火盆内生起炭火，放到大木柜里；火盆上面支上三脚，三脚上面支上大锅；大锅内放了三十斤香油，油内放进三只鸡；柜的盖子上拴了四扇大磨，柜盖开着，支撑了一个大阀销；阀销上拴了一根绳子，拉到大殿中梁大木匾后面。艾民一切安排好就爬上中梁，拉着绳子躲在大匾后面。到了三更时分，大蟒醒来，闻到油锅里的鸡香味，便从大佛爷嘴里钻了出来，一直冲进了大木柜。它围着火盆绕了三转，看见油锅里的鸡，猛向锅里插去，想一下吞下锅里的鸡。哪知它头一插进油锅，头就被油炸焦了。艾民见了，猛拉阀销，木柜盖子早已盖上，柜顶被四扇石磨紧紧压住了。艾民便从匾上跳下来，抽开木柜的一块活动板，举起锋利的宝剑，向大蟒猛力刺了几下，把它刺死在柜里了。

After three days' preparation, everything was ready. Puwang, the hunter, selected several courageous and strong young men to carry the things Ai Min needed to the temple at the time the big boa slept in secret and placed them according to Ai Min's instruction.

That night, Ai Min, carrying the precious sword, went to the temple cautiously without any noise. In the wooden cabinet, he burned the coal in the brazier, on which a big pan with 15 kg of sesame oil and three chickens supported by the tripod was placed. The cover of the cabinet, fastened with four mills, was opened and supported by a big valve pin, which was tied with a rope extending to the back of the inscribed board of the beam column in the hall. Fully prepared, Ai Min climbed up the beam column and held the rope behind the inscribed board. When it was around 12 o'clock at night, the big boa woke up. Having smelt the burning chicken in the frying pan, the boa got out of the mouth of the Buddhist statue and went straight into the big wooden cabinet. It circled the brazier for three times and saw the chicken in the frying pan. In the hope of getting the chicken in one breath, the boa went straight into the frying pan, only to have the head burned. At the sight of it, Ai Min pulled the valve pin, closing the cover of the cabinet, which had been pressed hard by the four heavy mills. Then, jumping from the inscribed board, Ai Min drew out a moving plate and stabbed the boa several times with a sharp sword, finally killing the boa in the cabinet.

艾民除掉了大蟒，取出夜明珠揣在身上。这时东方已经发白，艾民打开大庙出门，对等在门口的人群说：“大蟒已经死了，大家进去看吧！”众人拥进大庙，打开木柜一看，果然大蟒已经死在柜里了。人们把这除蟒英雄艾民用手抬了起来，一直抬进村里，摆上酒席，庆祝除蟒的胜利。

艾民为村民除了大害，人们都要求他留在村里。可艾民却说：“谢谢大家的好意，为民除害是应该的，现在我要回家乡去。”大家挽留不住，只好让他走了。

艾民走呀走，天黑时，他来到一个大海边，觉得十分困倦，很想休息一下。他四下一看，见海边有棵几围粗的空心大楂树，树根有个大洞，他便一头钻进树洞。不一会，便昏昏入睡了。到了半夜，巡海夜叉出海巡察，见树洞内宝光四射，就跑近树洞一看，原来是个青年的衣袋里有一颗海底夜明珠。巡海夜叉急忙潜入水晶宫禀报水母娘娘。

水母娘娘说：“这本是我家的宝贝，被一条水蛇盗去了，现在怎么会落到这个人手里，其中定有原因。你去拿回来，可不要伤害他。”巡海夜叉又来楂树洞前把艾民喊醒。艾民醒来见面前站着个怪人，有些害怕。夜叉说：“不要害怕，我是海里的巡海夜叉。我问你，你装的明珠是从哪里来的？”艾民把经过一五一十地讲了一遍。夜叉说：“这是我家水母娘娘的宝贝——海底夜明珠，你若能还给我家娘娘，娘娘定会酬谢你的。”艾民一听，说：“既然是娘娘的东西就还给她好了。”

After the death of the boa, Ai Min drew the luminous pearl from its mouth. At that time, it was already approaching the dawn. Ai Min opened the gate of the temple and informed the waiting crowd, "The boa is dead. You can come in and have a look!" The villagers flocked into the temple and saw the big boa really dead in the cabinet. The crowd lifted their hero Ai Min up together and carried him all the way to the village. They joyously put up a big feast to celebrate the successful removal of the hazardous boa.

As Ai Min successfully helped the villagers kill the boa, they all asked him to stay, but Ai Min replied, "Thanks for your kindness. This is what I should do. Now I am going back home." Unable to persuade him to stay, the villagers had to let him go.

Ai Min started off and went to a seaside when it was getting dark. He felt exhausted and desperately wanted to take a rest. Looking around, he found several fairly big but hollow hawthorn trees with a big hole in the root. He crept into it and fell asleep very soon. In the midnight, a patrol yecha went on duty from sea and saw radiant lights of some precious jewelry in the tree hole. It went closer and found that it was a legendary luminous sea pearl in the young man's pocket that gave out the light. The yecha immediately went back to the crystal palace under sea and reported it to the jellyfish queen. She replied, "This was our hereditary treasure, stolen by a water snake thief. How can this man get it? There must be some reasons. Go and get it back, but do not hurt him." The patrol yecha went back to the hole of the hawthorn tree and woke Ai Min up. At the sight of this strange-looking

说着便从袋里取出夜明珠交给了交叉。夜叉说："你要什么呢？"艾民回答说："我只要有吃有住就行了。"巡海夜叉又回到海里，禀报了水母娘娘。娘娘说："这真是一个好心人，你就把我的宝葫芦和那把八瓣破雨伞送给他，告诉他使用的口诀。"夜叉带了雨伞和葫芦来见艾民，说："这是娘娘酬谢你的东西。"艾民一看，心想："怎么会酬谢我这破雨伞和旧葫芦呢？"夜叉看出艾民的心思就说："啊！我还没告诉你，这是娘娘的两件宝物，你到了家乡，只要念诀，把这破雨伞撑开就是房子。你想吃饭或者请客摆席，只要把葫芦塞子打开，念念口诀，里边就会出来很多美女，帮你做饭待客，还会唱歌跳舞。但要注意，对这些仙女不能有丝毫邪念，吃完饭就送她们进葫芦，不然，娘娘就要收回。你千万要牢牢记住。"艾民说："请代我谢谢娘娘。"

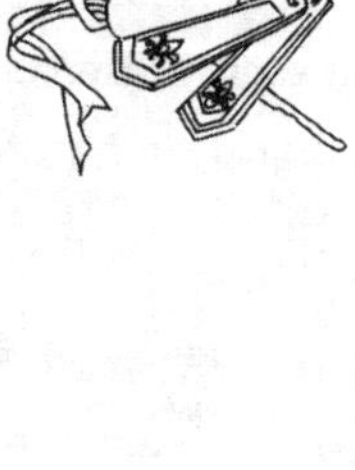

man, Ai Min was a little scared. The yecha comforted him and said, "Don't be afraid. I am the patrol yecha from sea. I want to know how you get this luminous pearl." Ai Min told him the story in detail. The yecha said, "This is actually a treasure belonged to my master, the jellyfish queen. If you return it to her, she will reward you." Ai Min replied, "If it belongs to the queen then I will just give it back." He took the pearl from his pocket and handed it to the yecha. "What do you want?" Asked the yecha. "As long as there is food to eat and a place to stay" Ai Min answered. The patrol yecha went back to the sea and reported back to the jellyfish queen. The queen said, "He is indeed a very kind-hearted man. Give him my magic gourd and the broken eight-petal umbrella. Tell him how to use them with the pithy formula." The yecha brought the umbrella and gourd to Ai Min and told him that these were the rewards from the queen. However, Ai Min was a little confused and thought to himself, "Why does she reward me with a broken umbrella and an old gourd?" The yecha knew what was in his mind and told him, "Oh! I haven't told you yet. These two are also treasures from the queen. When you reach your hometown. Read the pithy formula, the opened umbrella will turn out to be a house. If you want to treat your guests, beautiful fairies will come out of the gourd and help you treat your guests with singing and dancing, by pulling out the plug of the gourd and reading the pithy formula. Please take notice that do not have any evil thoughts on the fairies and always send them back after meal; otherwise, the jellyfish queen will get it back. Do remember it." Ai Min replied, "Please send my gratitude to the queen."

第二天天一亮，艾民拿着雨伞和葫芦，回到了自己的家乡。乡邻告诉财主：“老爷，你家三公子回来了。”财主问：“他带了些什么东西回来?”乡邻说：“只见他手提破雨伞，身背旧葫芦，别的不见有。”财主说：“还是个不成器的光棍，不准他进家来。”艾民回不了家，便走到村中一块空地上，口里念念有词：“破雨伞，破雨伞，快给我撑开八大院。”然后他把雨伞撑开，果然伞柄立即变成雕龙圆柱，八瓣伞面变成了八院大瓦房。房内家具什物，桌椅板凳，锅盘碗盏样样俱全。艾民十分高兴。从此，艾民每天两餐，味美菜香，蔬菜鱼肉不断，生活十分满意。他把母亲接来共享，只有那财主父亲无脸进他的门。

转眼过了几个月，艾民心想：“既然得了这样宝贝，也要请乡邻和兹莫来共享一次。”于是他决定摆一次酒席。他发了请帖，邀请他的父兄、亲朋和村中父老、兹莫来赴宴。一听说艾民大摆酒席，人们十分惊奇，说：“艾民被他父亲赶出家门，当了叫花子，今日咋个又会大摆酒席，倒要去看看。”这天，除了艾民的父亲艾财主不好意思来外，其他宾客都纷纷来到了。客人们一到门口就见门头上一块金匾，上面写着“艾民府”三个斗大的字样。进门一看那富丽的摆设，大家不禁啧啧称赞。

The next day, Ai Min set off to his hometown at dawn with the umbrella and the gourd. A neighbor in his hometown told the moneybags, "My lord, your third son is back." The moneybags replied, "What has he brought back?" The neighbour told him, "Only a broken umbrella in his hand and an old gourd at his back, nothing else." The moneybags said, "This good-for-nothing rat, don't let him step into the house." So, Ai Min could not return home. He walked to an open ground of the village and read the pithy formula, "Broken umbrella, broken umbrella, open up and make eight courtyards." Then, he opened up the umbrella. As expected, the handle was turned into columns curved with dragons and the eight-petal umbrella cover became a big tile-roofed house with eight courtyards, which was well furnished with tables, chairs, pans, plates, bowls, and all other things needed. Ai Min was very content. Since then, he enjoyed a satisfactory life with two hearty meals every day, which included abundant delicious fish and meat, and fresh vegetables and fruits. He invited his mother to live with him, but his father was too embarrassed to step into his house.

After several months, Ai Min thought to himself, "Now that I have this treasure, I need to treat villagers and Zimo." So he decided to entertain them with a feast. He sent invitation cards and invited his brothers, friends, neighbors and Zimo to the meal. People were all very surprised to learn that Ai Min was going to treat them with a splendid meal. They discussed, "Ai Min was banished from his house by his father and became a beggar. How could he treat us? We need to go and see." At that day, apart from Ai Min's father, the moneybags, all guests came. An inscribed board with Ai Min Mansion in gold hanged at the front door. The interiors were lavishly decorated, which marveled everyone.

艾民看客人到齐，便开葫芦盖念道："天灵灵，地灵灵，众家仙女请出葫芦门，帮我宴嘉宾。"瞬间，葫芦里面出来一群仙女，在客厅里摆上桌凳、碗筷，抬菜端酒，招待客人。大家正在吃喝着，众仙女翩翩起舞，笙、管、丝、竹、金五乐之声，十分动听。客人们赞不绝口。

客人中的兹莫，是个贪财好色之徒，他看到艾民家丫环侍女一个个长得像仙女，又都能歌善舞，口水淌了三尺长，心里打起坏主意。客人们酒足饭饱后，渐渐告辞走了。艾民又念口诀，请众仙女进了葫芦。唯有兹莫赖着不走，艾民只好陪他喝茶。兹莫盘根究底追问艾民，艾民被逼得无法，只好把实情告诉了他。

兹莫听了，忙对艾民说："我们交个朋友，我把官爵让给你，你就把这雨伞、葫芦换给我。"艾民说："这是水母娘娘送的东西，怎么能随便送给别人？再说，我单身一人，没有这两件宝贝怎么生活？"兹莫又说："我就连九个妻子也一齐换给你，空口无凭，立字为据。"说着就立即写了字据。字据上写道："本地方兹莫某某，自愿将官职及妻室调换艾民的雨伞葫芦，自换之日起，两厢情意，不得反悔。空口无

When Ai Min made sure that all the guests were here, he opened the gourd and read, "Spirit of sky and spirit of land, please ask all the fairies to go out of the gourd and treat my guests." In a moment, a group of fairies appeared and helped Ai Min with table setting, dish preparation and serving of wine. While everyone was enjoying the meal, the fairies began to dance following the melodic music of pipe instruments and stringed instruments. All the guests were full of praises.

Zimo was greedy and prurient. When he found that all the maids in Ai Min's house were as beautiful as fairies who could sing and dance so well, he was mouth-watering and came up with evil thoughts. After all the other guests left after a hearty meal, Ai Min read the pithy formula and all the fairies went into the gourd. Mozi was the only one who stayed, so Ai Min had to make a company and drink tea with him. During the talk, Mozi questioned him so closely that he was forced to tell him the truth.

After learning the truth, Mozi told Ai Min hurriedly, "Let us make friends. I will give you my official position and title; in return, you give me the umbrella and the gourd." Ai Min said, "These are gifts from the jellyfish queen. How can I give them away so carelessly? Besides, I am a single man. Without these two treasures, how can I survive?" Zimo replied, "I will also give you my nine wives. Words of mouth being no guarantee, a written statement is hereby given." Zimo immediately wrote a statement, "I, Zimo locally, voluntarily exchange the official post and wives with Ai Min for his umbrella and gourd. Since the date of the consensual exchange, there is no turning back. Words of mouth being no guarantee, a written statement is hereby

凭，立字为据。”兹莫把字据交给艾民。艾民不接，兹莫就威胁说：“你若不依，我带官兵砸了你的宝葫芦，撕碎你的雨伞！”艾民想：“与其让他损坏宝物，不如换给他吧！”于是艾民把雨伞、葫芦交给了他，拿上字据，随家丁到兹莫衙门上任去了。

兹莫得到神伞和宝葫芦，一心只想霸占那些仙女为妻。

于是他急不可待地念口诀，撑开了破雨伞，果然竖起一幢八个大院的大瓦房，和艾民家原先那幢一模一样。他高兴得手舞足蹈，又跳又唱，然后拉开葫芦的盖子大叫：“天灵灵，地灵灵，众家仙女快快出来给我做夫人，陪我逍遥到天明。”他说完，只见葫芦内飞出仙女，出来就向着他脸上吐唾沫，然后飞向天空，朝海面方向飞去。一个又一个都是这样，一连飞出九十九个仙女，吐了九十九口唾沫在兹莫脸上。最后一个仙女飞到天空，左手一招，葫芦便从兹莫手中飞到她手里。接着，她把右手一招，八院大瓦房不见了，只见一把破雨伞飞到仙女右手里。仙女一手拿葫芦，一手拿雨伞，飞向大海，回到水母娘娘那里去了。兹莫满脸唾沫，怎么也擦不掉。他走到哪里，人们围上来看他那满脸的唾沫，取笑说：“这才真正是被人唾弃的人呢！”

given." Zimo gave Ai Min the statement, but Ai Min refused to accept. Zimo threatened him, "If you dare to refuse me, I will lead my soldiers to smash your gourd and tear your umbrella apart!" Ai Min thought, "It's better to give him the treasures, which, otherwise, will be destroyed." So Ai Min handed in the umbrella and the gourd. In return, he carried the statement and took over the position in Yamen with his families.

With the magic umbrella and the precious gourd, Zimo just wanted to forcibly marry the fairies.

So he couldn't wait to read the pithy formula and open the umbrella. A big house with eight courtyards was erected as expected, exactly the same as Ai Min's, which made Mozi so happy that he danced and sang. Then, he pulled off the cover of the gourd and yelled, "Spirit of sky and spirit of land, please ask all the fairies to go out of the gourd and be my wives. Let's have leisure till dawn." When he finished, he saw fairies fly out of the gourd, spit on his face and fly up to the sky, towards the sea. One after another, there were altogether ninety-nine fairies who flew out of the gourd and spitted on Zimo's face. When the last fairy came out, with one move of the left hand, the gourd flew from Zimo's hand to hers. Then, with another wave of her right hand, the big house disappeared and the umbrella flew to her right hand. The fairy, carrying the gourd and umbrella, flew towards the sea and went back to the jellyfish queen. Zimo could not wipe off the spits as they were all over on his face. Wherever he went, people would gather around and laughed, "He is really the guy who deserves to be spitted!"

再说，艾民当上兹莫以后，人们都来争看这叫花子兹莫官，把兹莫衙门挤个水泄不通。艾民便乘机当着众百姓宣布：从此免除原有的苛捐杂税，放回兹莫抢来的民女，并禁止本兹莫辖地内的官员抢夺民女。人们听了，个个称赞。

后来，当地老百姓还编了这样一首歌："花子当兹莫，国泰又民安，自身受苦知人苦，减税又减捐，清正廉洁，人人都喜欢。"

流传地区：姚安县

讲述者：李玉才，李光明

搜集整理者：罗桂森

After learning that Ai Min was going to be the new Zimo, villagers all flocked to Yamen to see this beggar Zimo, which made Yamen fully occupied. In the presence of the public, Ai Min took the opportunity to announce that all the exorbitant taxes and levies would be exempted, all the women forcibly captured by the former Zimo would be returned back home and any robbing and forcible capture of girls and women by government officials within the jurisdiction would be strictly prohibited. Everyone thought highly of him.

Later, local people compiled a song, "When a beggar becomes Zimo, the country is prosperous and people are at peace. A person who has suffered from poverty understands it the best. He reduces taxes and duties, and remains honest and upright. Everyone adores him."

Spreading area: Yao'an County

Narrator: Li Yucai, Li Guangming

Collector and editor: Luo Guisen

阿勒喜和查尼诺

很多年以前，哀牢山里有一个勤劳的小伙子，名字叫阿勒喜。村里有个姑娘，名叫查尼诺。他们两个相爱，情投意合。

查尼诺家非常有钱，金银都用牲口驮。查尼诺长得漂亮、聪明，提亲的人来过几十个，她都不答应，一心爱着阿勒喜。阿勒喜也大着胆子请人去探过口气，可是，查尼诺的爹不肯答应，使劲摇头说："没门，吃了上顿没有下顿的人也想来要我姑娘，硬是饿老鹰想吃天鹅肉！趁早滚远些！"

村子后山上有一个像井一样的山洞，山洞里住着一只恶老鹰，它也爱上查尼诺了。这只恶老鹰，修炼了九万年，长了九个头，已经成精了。有一天，查尼诺在院场中做针线，忽然刮来一阵旋风，随着大风，九头鹰抓走了查尼诺。

Alexi and Chaninuo

Many years ago, a diligent young lad called Alexi lived in the Ailao Mountain. A girl called Chaninuo also lived in the village. The boy and the girl held a deep affection to each other.

Born in an affluent family in which its gold and silver flooded, Chaninuo grew up into a very pretty and intelligent girl who refused dozens of her pursuers and was only in love with Alexi. Alexi once emboldened himself to send a friend to discuss the proposal with her family, only to be refused by Chaninuo's father who said, "No way. A man who had to live from hand to mouth wants to marry my daughter. Is he out of his mind? Go away!"

There was a cave, deep as a well, in the mountain behind the village. An evil eagle lived there which also fell for Charninuo. Having practiced magic for ninety thousand years, it had grown nine heads as an evil spirit. One day, when Chaninuo was doing needlework, a gust of swirl wind roared all of a sudden, and the eagle came and took Chaninuo away.

这天，阿勒喜到山上砍柴。他正爬在一棵大树树枝上砍柴，九头鹰抓着查尼诺从树顶上经过。查尼诺一见阿勒喜，就大声喊叫：“阿勒喜哥哥，快快来救我！”阿勒喜眼明手快，用力把斧子对准九头鹰丢上去。斧子正正砍在九头鹰的头上，血流了下来。因为只伤着一个头，九头鹰照样飞掉了。

阿勒喜赶紧爬下树来，朝着九头鹰飞去的方向，顺着血迹找去。找着找着，终于找到了一个山洞，血迹一直滴进洞里。阿勒喜一看难住了，在洞边走过来走过去，想办法下洞去……

这时，来了一个白发苍苍的老人，看见阿勒喜一副焦急的样子，便问道：“小伙子，你在这里做什么？”

阿勒喜说：“阿波，我心爱的人被九头鹰抢进这个洞里去了，我想下去救她，但是无法下去，正着急呢。”

白发老人说：“我年幼的时候，听我的阿波讲过，这山洞有九十九丈深，要想下去，除非是去借一根九十九丈长的铁链子，才能下得到底。这么长的铁链子，只有左边村中的财主家才有啊！”

阿勒喜拜谢了白发老人，去财主家说明了来意。财主听说是救一个美丽的姑娘，心怀鬼胎，答应借铁链子给他，并愿意出人帮忙，阿勒喜很感激。

At that day, Alexi went to cut firewood in the mountain. Just when he climbed up a tree and sawed the branches, the evil eagle flew over the tree with Chaninuo held firmly in its claws. At the sight of Alexi, Chaninuo shouted out, "Alexi, help me!" Alexi responded quickly and threw his axe hard to the eagle which was hit right on one of its heads and bled. Because only head was hurt, the eagle still managed to escape.

Alexi climbed down the tree and went after the eagle hurriedly. He traced blood stains all the way to the cave. But when he arrived, he was caught out by a way in, so he wandered around the cave entrance in anxiety.

Just at this moment, a grey-haired old man came. Seeing his worried face, the old man asked, "Young lad. What are you doing here?"

Alexi replied, "Uncle, my beloved girl was taken in the cave by an evil eagle. I want to go down and save her. But I don't know how."

The old man said, "When I was young, my uncle told me that this cave was about nine hundred ninety feet deep. If you want to go down, you need to have an iron chain of the same length. And the only man I know who has such a chain is the rich man in the left side of the village."

Alexi extended his gratitude to the old man and went to the rich man's mansion and stated his intention. The rich man harbored indecent thoughts when he learned that it was about saving a beautiful girl. He agreed to let Alexi have the chain and several companions as helpers. Alexi was very grateful.

他们到了洞口，先在洞边栽了一棵大树桩，把链子的一头拴稳在树桩上，另一头拴在阿勒喜的腰杆上。阿勒喜手拿斧子，让财主派出的人把他慢慢地放下洞底。洞里伸手不见五指。阿勒喜解了链子，左右四周寻找，忽然发现侧面又有一个洞。他不顾一切顺洞摸了进去，洞道弯弯转转的，远处有一个蚕豆大的灯光。走近几步，借着灯光才看清楚，查尼诺正在为九头鹰被砍伤了的头部敷药、包扎。九头鹰疼得难过，没有发现有生人进来。查尼诺发现了他，向他比手势，叫他不要慌，等一下。

不多一会，九头鹰睡着了。查尼诺悄悄地过来对阿勒喜说："再等一下，等它睡熟时，我一招手，你再过来收拾它。"阿勒喜点头答应。不多时，九头鹰确实睡熟了。查尼诺一招手，阿勒喜就摸到九头鹰面前，举起斧子，对准一个脑袋使劲砍下去，九头鹰的一个头落下地。九头鹰梦中醒来，想起身和阿勒喜搏斗，哪知阿勒喜动作很利索，一眨眼，就把九头鹰的头全砍掉了。

阿勒喜和查尼诺赶紧往回走，但是到了洞底，一时没了主意，因为只有一根链子。查尼诺叫阿勒喜先爬上去，阿勒喜不肯，要叫查尼诺先爬上去，说万一有什么事情，他好抵挡。查尼诺同意了，阿勒喜帮助她把铁链子拴在腰杆上，洞口上的人慢慢地把她拉了上去。

When they set off and reached the cave, they fell a tree near the cave entrance and tied one end of the chain to the stump and the other end around Alexi's waist. With an axe in his hand, Alexi asked his companions, sent by the rich man, to send him down slowly. It was pitch dark in the cave. Alexi untied the chain and walked around. Suddenly, he noticed another cave at one side and found his way in bravely. Inside the cave was in twists and turns with a dot of bean-sized light in the distance. Alexi approached, with the help of the light, and finally saw clearly that Chaninuo was applying herbs to the eagle's wounded head and wrapped it up with gauze. The eagle was in so much pain that it did not notice Alexi nearby. But Chaninuo saw Alexi and signaled him to wait.

Before long, the eagle fell asleep. Chaninuo tiptoed towards Alexi and said to him, "Wait a little longer. When it sleeps on both ears, I will wave and you come to kill it." Alexi nodded. After a while, the eagle was in a deep sleep. No sooner did Chaninuo wave than Alexi rushed to the eagle and lifted up his axe and hacked its head. There being one head chopped off, the eagle woke up out of pain and attempted to stand up to fight. However, Alexi acted very swiftly and, in the blink of an eye, chopped off all the heads.

Alexi and Chaninuo turned back in haste. But as they stood under the cave entrance, they did not know what to do with only one chain. Chaninuo told Alexi to climb up first. But Alexi refused and asked Chaninuo to leave first because he could still fight back down here if anything happened. Chaninuo agreed. So, Alexi helped her tie the chain around her waist and went up slowly lifted by the companions at the entrance.

查尼诺一出洞口，财主家的人七手八脚就把查尼诺抢走了，把铁链子也抬回家去，不管查尼诺怎么样喊叫，财主家的人像没有听见似的。查尼诺到了财主家，不吃不喝，整天啼哭，心中恨死黑心的财主。

阿勒喜在洞底喊了半天，不见铁链子放下来，心中着急了，他只好四处寻找出井的地方。可是，井四周滑溜溜的，没有一点可以爬踩的洞眼。正在这时，忽然听见一个声音："哥哥，救救我的命吧！"阿勒喜顺着声音寻找过去，看见壁上有一条小白蛇，被铁钉钉在壁上，向他求救。

阿勒喜问："你怎么了？"

小白蛇说："哥哥，我是被九头鹰抓来的，他把我钉在壁上，我难过死了，你再不救我，过几天我就会死在这里呀！"

阿勒喜问："用什么办法可以救你呢？"

小白蛇说："只消把钉在我身上的铁钉拔掉就行了。"

于是阿勒喜拔掉了小白蛇身上的钉子，小白蛇得救了，并且摇身一变，变成一个小伙子。阿勒喜说："小弟弟，洞这么深，我两个怎么出得去呢？"

When Chaninuo went out of the cave, those helpers sent by the rich man took her away before she could realize it. They also retrieved the chain and carried it home. No matter how Chaninuo shouted out, they ignored her and carried her back to the house of the rich man. Chaninuo refused to eat or drink, and cried all day with hatred.

For Alexi down the cave, when he shouted out for a long time and saw no chain coming down, he grew panic and had to look around to find a way out. However, it was slick all around without any place to hold one's feet. Just at this moment, a voice came to him, "Brother, help me!" Alexi walked towards the direction where the voice came and saw a little white snake nailed on the wall and crying for help.

Alexi asked, "What happened?"

The snake answered, "Brother, I was taken by the eagle. It nailed me on the wall. I feel miserable. If you don't save me now, I will die soon."

Alexi then asked, "What can I do?"

The snake said, "Just pull out the nail."

So, Alexi pulled out the nail off the snake. The snake was saved, and turned into a young lad. Alexi asked, "Little brother, this cave is so deep. How can we escape?"

小白蛇说："不用怕，我有办法，你只消闭着眼睛，拉住我的衣裳角就得了。我不喊你，你不要睁眼。"

阿勒喜闭上眼睛，拉着小伙子的衣角，忽听耳边"呼呼"的风响，像在天上飞一样，不一会儿，便落在了地上。小白蛇说："哥哥，我是这个海里龙王的儿子，那天我出去山上游玩，半路上受害，若不是遇着了你，我的性命就没有了。今天，我要请你到我家坐坐，我要报答你的恩情。不过，你要先在这里等一等，我先去禀报，我要让我的父王来接你。"说罢便走入海里去了。

不到一锅烟的时间，忽听海水哗哗啦啦地作响，在响声中闪出一道大门，龙王爷出来了。

龙王说："小伙子，你救了我太子的命，我请你到我的宫殿里去住几天。走吧！"说毕，小白蛇走近阿勒喜，并让他闭着眼睛，拉住自己的衣角。不一会，他们就到了宫殿里。在龙宫中，龙王用上好的酒席招待他。小白蛇天天陪着阿勒喜到处游玩。

过了几天，阿勒喜思念查尼诺，便向小白蛇说出自己要回去的想法。小白蛇说："既然这样，也好，不过，我父王要送你一些金银财宝，这些你最好不要，你要向我父王要那个葫芦。那是一个宝贝，它能帮助你解决任何困难。还有，你向父王要一只小猫，那是保护小葫芦的，你要连猫一起要。"

第二天，龙王果然来见阿勒喜，并说："多谢你救了我儿子的命，我很感激你，你要回去了，我要送一些金银给你，走，这就同我一起去拿。"

The snake said, "Don't worry. I can help. Just close your eyes and grasp my clothes. Don't open your eyes until I say so."

Alexi did as told and felt the wind passing by like they were flying. Before long, they landed on earth. The snake said, "Brother, I'm a son of the Dragon King in the sea. One day, when I went out to play in the mountain, the eagle caught me halfway. If I didn't meet you, I would have died. So, I want to invite you to come to my house and repay you. But perhaps you need to wait here for a while because I need to report and ask my father to pick you up." Having said his piece, the snake walked into the sea.

Very soon sea water began to boil loudly in which a gate appeared. The Dragon King came out.

He said, "Young lad, you saved my son's life. I'd like to invite you to live in my palace for some days. Let's go." Then the white snake walked towards Alexi, telling him that he also needed to close his eyes and grasp his clothes. Before long, they arrived in the palace. Alexi was well-treated with feasts and was shown around by the snake every day.

After a few days, Alexi missed Chaninuo and said to the snake about leaving the palace. The snake answered, "Alright. But if my father wants to give you some gold and silver, refuse it. Ask him to give you the gourd instead. It's a magic object that can help you solve any problem. By the way, don't forget to ask for the kitten as well, which will protect the gourd."

The next day, the King came to see Alexi and said, "Thank you for saving my son. I'm very grateful. And since you are leaving, I want to give you some gold and silver. Come with me."

阿勒喜说："龙王爷，金子银子我不要，我想要你的宝葫芦和保护它的小猫。如果龙王不愿意送我，我也就走了，谢谢你对我的厚待。"

龙王一时答不上话来，心想，不给吧，自己说过要报答他；给吧，是自己的无价宝，有点舍不得。最后，龙王还是答应了阿勒喜的要求，把葫芦和猫给了他，并告诉了他葫芦的用法。

小白蛇送出阿勒喜，临别之时，又对阿勒喜说："哥哥，葫芦不能离开猫！"

阿勒喜回到地上来以后，到处打听查尼诺的下落，没有消息。忽然想起宝葫芦，于是他便对葫芦说："宝葫芦呀，我心爱的人现在在什么地方也不知道，请你帮帮我吧！"

这时，葫芦口里冒出一股白云，向天空飞走了。不多时，一股白云弯弯曲曲地又回来了。白云一散，查尼诺已经站在了阿勒喜的面前。他们又见面了。

阿勒喜原本就穷得没有房子，没有铺盖，没有田地，没有牲口。他们只好向宝葫芦要。宝葫芦都满足了他们的要求，他们过上了幸福的日子。

查尼诺突然消失，财主家的人都觉得奇怪，连看守的人也说不清楚。他们只知道起了一阵风，飘过一朵云，然后查尼诺就不见了。财主气得要死，只好派人到处打听。

Alexi replied, "My lord, please forgive me. I don't want any gold or silver. What I want is your gourd and the cat that protects it. But it's ok if you don't give it to me. I'm grateful for your treat anyway."

The King was caught out by Alexi's demand. For one thing, he did promise to repay Alexi. For another, the gourd was his priceless treasure which he was reluctant to give away. Finally, the King made up his mind to give Alexi the gourd, together with the cat, and the way to use it.

The white snake escorted Alexi out. Before they parted, the snake said, "Brother, the gourd has to be with the cat, remember it!"

When he went back to earth, Alexi asked around the whereabouts of Chaninuo, but in vain. Suddenly he thought of the gourd and said to it, "Gourd, I don't know where my beloved girl is now. Please help me!"

At that moment, a chink of cloud flowed out of the gourd's mouth and flew away to the sky. Before long, it returned with twists and turns. When the cloud dispersed, Alexi found Chaninuo standing right in front of him. They met again.

Alexi was very poor with no house, no belonging, no land, and no herd. So, they had to ask the gourd which granted them everything they asked for. Then they lived a happy life.

Everyone in the rich man's house felt so strange about Chaninuo's disappearance. The guards also couldn't tell. As far as they could remember, there was a gust of wind and a chink of cloud right before Chininuo was gone. The rich man was burning with rage and sent many people to figure it out.

过了不久，有人回来告诉财主，说找着查尼诺了，并把阿勒喜和查尼诺现在的情况一五一十地讲了出来。财主一听，知道阿勒喜遇着龙王太子，又得了龙王的宝葫芦，眼珠子骨碌骨碌地转，又在打鬼主意了。

有一天，财主的家丁来到阿勒喜家说："阿勒喜，财主老爷知道你回来了，明天要请你过去坐坐，顺便借你的宝葫芦看看，明天你带着来!"

家丁走了以后，阿勒喜和查尼诺可急了。他们知道这是阴谋诡计，可是人家有钱有势，又不敢不去。想来想去，阿勒喜想起小白蛇说过的话，便打算把小猫一同带着去保护宝葫芦。

第二天，阿勒喜拿着宝葫芦，抱着小猫，去到财主家。财主家的人早就在堂屋里等着了，他们坐在八仙桌周围。见阿勒喜一来，他们就叫阿勒喜把宝葫芦放在桌子上。还不等阿勒喜拿出宝葫芦，这个叫阿勒喜喊宝葫芦吐金，那个叫吐银，要求提了一大堆。

阿勒喜坐下以后，把宝葫芦拿出来放在桌子上，小猫也放掉。小猫一下地，在桌子周围转了一圈后就跑出堂屋去了。不大一会，小猫嘴里叼着一只老鼠回来，跳到桌子上，小猫就把老鼠放掉。老鼠在桌子上打了个转，用嘴咬着宝葫芦很快就跑进墙洞里去了。这一切，都发生在瞬间，等财主回过神来时，桌子上早已一样也不见了。

After a while, one of them returned and told the rich man Chaninuo's location and her life with Alexi. After learning the story, the rich man knew that Alexi had met the Dragon Prince and received the magic gourd from the King. Rolling his eyes, the rich man came up with a plot.

One day, servants of the rich man walked into Alexi's house and said, "Alexi, our master knows that you've come back. He invites you to his house tomorrow and also to have a look at your gourd. Please bring it along!"

After the servants left, Alexi and Chaninuo were anxious. They knew it was a plot, but they had no choice but to go because the rich man was very powerful. Alexi thought for a while and recalled what the snake said about the cat, so he decided to take it with him to protect the gourd.

The next day, Alexi went to the rich man's house with the gourd and the cat. The rich man and his men had long sat around a square table in the hall and waited for Alexi. Upon Alexi's arrival, they asked him to put the gourd on the table. Before Alexi took the gourd out, they bombarded him with a lot of requests of gold and silver from the gourd.

When Alexi sat down, he took out the gourd and put it on the table. He also dropped the cat which circled around the table and ran out of the hall. Before long, the cat came back with a mouse in its mouth. Then, it jumped on the table and released the mouse. The mouse held the gourd in its mouth after a circle on the table and ran off into a hole before anyone could realize it.

阿勒喜也感到奇怪，但又没有办法，只好愁眉苦脸地回家去。到了家中，查尼诺手中捧着宝葫芦，小猫也在一旁。原来是老鼠把宝葫芦拖进了洞里，又拖出房子外边，小猫在房子外边又将宝葫芦带回家。

眼睁睁地看着宝葫芦被老鼠拖进墙洞里去了，财主怎肯甘心，便叫家丁拿锄头来挖墙脚。墙脚挖了个大洞也不见宝葫芦，于是财主便命令所有的家丁都来挖。东挖西挖，左撬右撬，挖着挖着，墙壁倒下来，财主一家老小全部被埋在堂屋里了。

流传地区：楚雄市

讲述者：罗恩德，普连才

搜集整理者：者厚培，余立梁

Alexi also felt odd but had no idea what to do, so he went back home, frowning. However, when he walked in his house, he found Chaninuo holding the gourd with the cat standing nearby. It turned out that the mouse dragged the gourd into the hole and then out of the house, before the cat took it off its mouth and carried it back to Alexi's house.

The rich man refused to accept the fact that the magic gourd had been dragged into a hole by a mouse. So, he asked his servants to dig the hole with hoes. However, there was no trace of the gourd after digging a big hole in the corner of the wall. Then the rich man asked all his servants to continue to dig. Finally, the wall fell down and buried the rich man and all his families in the hall.

Spreading area: Chuxiong City

Narrator: Luo Ende, Pu Liancai

Collector and editor: Zhe Houpei, Yu Liliang

虎子[1]

从前，有母女二人上山去砍柴。柴捆好后，正要背回家，突然林中跳出一只大老虎把姑娘拖走了。母亲见女儿被老虎拖走，吓得昏死在地。等她醒过来时，找不着女儿，只好背着柴，一边哭一边往回走。

再说，老虎把年轻姑娘背到山洞里，强迫姑娘做了它的媳妇。姑娘在山洞里做了三年的老虎媳妇，生下了一个儿子，名字叫作里燕林提斯八库儿，妈妈叫他虎子。几年过去了，虎子长大了。一天，当他父亲外出时，他问妈妈："妈妈，你想家吗?"妈妈说："想啊，咋个不想！这几年我想你外婆，都快要想疯了。"虎子又问："妈妈，那你想不想回去看看外婆呢?"妈妈说："想是想，只是你父亲守得严，他出外时用三块巨石堵住洞口，我们没法去呀!"虎子说："妈妈，不要紧，我有办法。我背着你回家去吧！你闭着眼睛，不要睁开，不然头会晕的。"虎子三拳就打碎了三块堵住洞口的巨石，背着妈妈跑出了山洞。只听见后边山崩地塌似的一声虎

---

① 译者注：虎子意为老虎的儿子。

Huzi[1]

Once upon a time, a mother and daughter went up the mountain to cut firewood. When they were about to carry the bundle of wood home, a big tiger jumped out of the forest and took the girl away. Seeing her daughter dragged away, the mother passed out in despair. When she woke up, she could not find her daughter anywhere. So, she had to carry the bundle of wood back home and cried along the way.

The tiger, however, carried the young daughter back to his cave and forced her to be his wife. After three years of marriage, the girl gave birth to a son called Liyanlintisibakuer, or Huzi by his mother. A few years had passed and Huzi grew up. One day, when his father went out, he asked his mother, "Mama, do you miss home?" "Of course, I am. For the last few years, your grandmother has always been in my mind", his mother replied. Huzi asked again, "Then do you want to go home and see her?" His mother sighed and said, "I do. But your father had a close watch on us. When he went out, he blocked up the cave entrance with three huge rocks. There is no way out." Huzi did not share this pessimism and told his mother, "Don't worry, Mama. I know a way out. Let me carry you home. Just close

① Translator's note: Huzi means the son of a tiger in transliteration.

吼，一只猛虎怒吼着追上来了！虎子见父亲狂怒追来，就放下妈妈说：“你在这块石头上坐着等我，我去拦住爹爹。”说着就跑过去和猛虎扭打了起来。老虎被他咬死了，虎子背着妈妈来到了外婆家。外婆高兴得不得了。

外婆拿出两块银元，叫虎子到街上痛痛快快玩，饱饱地吃一顿。虎子在街上走了一转，来到大场上，见一群娃娃在玩皮球。他看得很出神，正想走过去玩一玩，突然皮球飞到他面前，他用手指一戳，皮球就飞到高高的天上去了。皮球落下来时，正好落在一个织火草布的老婆子跟前，把她的线打断了。这老婆子家有个小儿子，气力很大，他能三拳把人打死，脾气又怪，动不动就爱打人，所以没人敢惹他。虎子过去拿球，老婆子的小儿子上去就给虎子三拳头，却没有把虎子打死。虎子只轻轻给了他一巴掌，就把这个小儿子的脑袋打碎了。老婆子就跑去向兹莫报了案。

your eyes and do not open them. Otherwise you'll feel very dizzy." Afterwards, Huzi shattered three huge rocks against the entrance with three punches and carried his mother on his back. Then a deafening tiger roar came from behind and the tiger was catching up really fast. Seeing his father chasing after so furiously, he put down his mother and said to her, "Mom, wait on this rock. I'm going to stop father." Then he ran towards the tiger and tussled with it. Finally, the tiger was killed by Huzi with his bites. And Huzi carried his mother to his grandmother's place, who felt so happy to see both her daughter and her grandson.

The next day, the grandmother gave two silver coins to Huzi and told him to go out to the street to play and eat anything to his taste. Huzi walked around the street and saw a group of children playing a leather ball in a square. He watched it and found it very interesting. When he was about to go forward and play with them, suddenly the ball flied right to his face. He poked it with his fingers and the ball was deflected off to the sky. When the ball fell down, it happened to land in front of an old woman who was weaving cloth and broke her strings. The old woman had a little son with immense strength who could beat men to death with three punches. Also, he was very ill-tempered because he liked to beat others. So no one dared to argue with him. When Huzi went there to pick up his ball, the son of the old woman approached him and punched him three times. But instead of killing Huzi, he died with his skull smashed by Huzi's one gentle slap. Then the old woman ran to the Zimo and reported the case.

兹莫一听，着急了，他想，出了这么个怪人，我的地盘不好管了，这个祸根千万留不得，于是他派出两个大力士来抓虎子。虎子一拳头一个，将两个大力士打死了！兹莫越发觉得事情很不妙，于是找到虎子，对他说："龙潭里有一条恶龙，如果你真有本事，就去和他斗一斗看，如果能斗赢，我把我的地盘分一半给你。"虎子说："好吧！七天之内，我提着龙头回来。"

虎子高兴地跑回家去，把这事告诉了外婆和妈妈。妈妈很为虎子担心，外婆却说："他既然答应了，还是让他去吧！"又对虎子说："孩子，我告诉你，你要好好记住：这条恶龙有三套本事。第一套：它笑一笑，太阳就会辣得晒死人；第二套：它哭一哭，天就要下暴雨，地上就会起洪水淹死人；第三套：它还会吸人，它一对人吸气，就会把人吸进它的肚子里。你可要想法躲开它这三套绝招，这样就能够将它杀死。"

当天晚上，虎子睡到半夜，忽然看见一位老公公走到他床边，拍拍他说："虎子，我的好外孙儿，你是个勇敢而有志气的孩子。不过单凭勇敢还不够，恶龙可是个十分凶残狡猾的家伙，必须有吃苦耐劳的精神，练就一身好本事，才能制服它。你要去杀恶龙，我给你一件武器吧！家堂底下有一碗苦胆水，你要把它全喝下去。大门外那块大石板下放着两把大刀，你拿一把出来练习练习，舞得动，你才去，舞不动你就不要去。"老公公说完，便突然走开了。虎子揉揉眼睛原来是做了一个梦。

After learning this from the old woman, the Zimo felt a little anxious. He wondered how he could manage his territory well with this trouble here. Determined to remove this thorn in his flesh, he sent two strong hatchet men to get Huzi. But Huzi killed them each with a single punch. As the Zimo found that it was getting out of control, he personally came to Huzi and said to him, "There is a vicious dragon in a deep pool. If you are really powerful, fight with it. And if you win, I'll give you half of my territory." Huzi answered, "Alright. I'll come back within 7 days and bring you its head."

Huzi then ran back home happily and told his grandmother and mother about it. While his mother felt very worried, his grandmother said, "Since he took the job, let him try." Then she turned to Huzi and told him, "Child, you need to remember what I'm going to say. This dragon has three weapons. First, if it smiles, the sun will get scorching. Second, if it cries, the rain is going to pour down and flood the earth. Third, if it breathes, it can suck men into its belly. You need to find ways to avoid these three tricks, only then will you stand a chance of killing it."

At that night, when Huzi was in the middle of his sleep, he saw an old grandpa approaching to his bed and tapping him. The old man said, "Huzi, my dear grandson. You are a brave and ambitious boy. But courage is not enough. This dragon is very brutal and sly. It will not be defeated until you arm yourself with an indomitable spirit and a repertoire of combating skills. Now I teach you something! There is a bowl of bitter bile under our hall. Drink it all. There are two machetes beneath that huge stone slab outside our house. Take out one and practice with it. If you are able to wield it, you can go. If not, you should not take this risk." Then, the old grandpa left. Huzi rubbed his eyes and found out that it was just a dream.

早上起来，虎子到家堂下一看，果然有一碗苦胆水。他就端起来，咬着牙一口气喝完了。他又跑到大门外掀起大石板一看，果然放着两把大刀。他取出来练了练，大的一把还有点舞不动，小的一把能舞得像一团风。于是他就提着这把大刀去龙潭找恶龙。

虎子来到龙潭边探身向龙洞里一望，恶龙就伸出一只金甲利爪来抓他。他顺势一刀斩断了龙爪，恶龙便逞起威风来，施展它的第一招：笑一笑。天上的太阳晒得石头滚烫，山上的草木都冒出一缕缕青烟。虎子热得浑身像着了火，实在耐不住，他就跳进龙潭水里躲起来。恶龙见热不死他，又施展出第二招：哭一哭。天色突然变了，马上下起倾盆暴雨，山洪咆哮，洪水滔滔。这时虎子早已跳出龙潭，摸进了龙洞，悄悄躲在恶龙的下巴底下，恶龙看不见他，再大的洪水也淹不着他。过了一会，恶龙又向洞外长长地吸了一口气，想把虎子吸进肚里去，虎子早已防备着它这一招。趁恶龙吸人之时，他把大刀横担在身上，让恶龙一口连人带刀吸进肚里去。这一来，恶龙的嘴、喉咙、肚子被锋利的大刀割开了！恶龙抖动几下身子就死去了。虎子举起大刀砍下恶龙头，扛到兹莫家里来见兹莫。

When Huzi got up in the morning, he went to the hall and found that there was really a bowl of bitter bile. He held it up and drank it all without a break. Then he ran outside the door and lifted up the stone slab, under which there were truly two machetes. He took them out and practiced with them. For the bigger one, he could not handle it very well. But the smaller one was completely under his control. Still he took the bigger one and went to the vicious dragon in the deep pool.

When Huzi came to the pool and leaned forward over it, a sharp claw covered with golden scales broke through the surface and went after him. He wielded his machete and cut off the claw at one blow, which irritated the dragon. It started to use his powerful tricks. First, it smiled. The blazing sun burned rocks and withered all the grasses and trees in the mountain. Huzi felt scorching heat inside out and could hardly stand it anymore. So, he jumped into the pool and survived. As the first trick failed, the dragon unfolded his second one, crying. Soon the weather changed and a heavy rain poured down, followed by roaring flood. But by then, Huzi had already found his way to the dragon cave and hid himself under the jaw of the dragon. As the dragon could not see him, so it was not able to lead the flood to drown him. Later, the dragon took a deep breath facing the cave entrance in the hope of sucking Huzi into his belly. But Huzi had long already prepared for that and attached the machete to his body. So when the dragon breathed, the machete was also sucked in together with him. Then he wielded his machete and slit the mouth, throat, and belly of the dragon open. After quivering several times, the dragon died. Huzi cut off its head and carried it to the Zimo's house.

兹莫见虎子扛着恶龙进来，心里很害怕，越发感到虎子会和他抢地盘，于是他装模作样地说：“你杀死了恶龙，为民除了一害：功劳很大；但是现在并不太平，我们这地方还有一个妖怪，专门吃人，还特别爱吃小孩，闹得人心惶惶，夜不安眠。你若能杀死这个妖怪，天下太平了，我就封你做英雄。”

虎子听了这话，回到家里，把要除妖怪的事告诉了妈妈和外婆。外婆又告诉他说：“达个妖怪最会变化，很会迷惑人。它会七种变化，但是不管它怎么变化，它额头上的那颗黑痣是变不了的。你只要牢牢记住这一点，它就逃不脱你的眼睛，就会被你认出来。”当天晚上，睡到半夜的时候，他外公又托梦给他说：“勇敢聪明的孩子，你终于杀死了恶龙。但是那个吃人的妖怪更狡猾善变，你千万要多动脑子，切不可粗心大意，到时候我会帮助你的。在家堂底下有一罐苦胆水，你要把它喝完。你再把大门外大石板下那把大刀拿出来好好练练，舞得动你就去，舞不动你就莫去！”

The Zimo saw Huzi coming in with a dragon head on his shoulder and got very frightened. He had this strong feeling that Huzi would take his territory. So, he pretended to be very serious and said to Huzi, "You killed the dragon and did the villagers a big favor. You earn yourself some credits. But we can not have a life of peace now, because there is a monster here which feeds on villagers and especially the children. We are all jittery and too afraid to sleep well. If you can kill this monster, I'll honor you as a hero for the peace you've brought to us."

Then Huzi came back home and told his grandmother and mother about it. His grandmother said, "This monster is very good at shape-shifting which easily confuses us. Although it can shift into 72 forms, it always has a black mole in its forehand. Remember that and you'll be able to recognize it." At midnight, when Huzi fell asleep, his grandfather came to his dream again and said, "Brave young child. You've killed the dragon. But that monster is slier and very powerful for its shape-shifting ability. You need to be smart and more careful. I'll help you at a proper time. There is a jar of bitter bile under our hall. Drink it all. Also, practice with the machete beneath the stone slab. If you are able to wield it, you can go. If not, just give up!"

第二天一早起来，虎子去家堂底下端出那罐苦胆水，一口气将它喝光了。又去大石板下取出那把大刀来，试了试已经舞得动了。他就扛着大刀去找妖怪。走到半路上，碰着三个黑大汉挡住了去路。一问才知道是兹莫派来杀他的三个大力士，一个叫作上快羊巴，一个叫作中快羊巴，一个叫作下快羊巴。他来到上快羊巴面前，那个大力士就说："我两个来比一下看谁的力气大。"说着，上快羊巴就冲过来想把虎子一把抱起来。可是，他把眼珠都挣鼓了也抱不动。虎子上去轻轻一下就把上快羊巴高高地举了起来，然后掼在地下，把他砸死了。中快羊巴冲上来，也想抱起虎子，虎子又一把将他举过头顶，正要掼死他时，中快羊巴哀求说："你不要砸死我，我愿意当你的护兵，一起去杀妖怪。"下快羊巴见了也连忙跪下求饶，说他也愿意做帮手，一起去杀妖怪。虎子饶了他们，带着助手去杀妖怪。

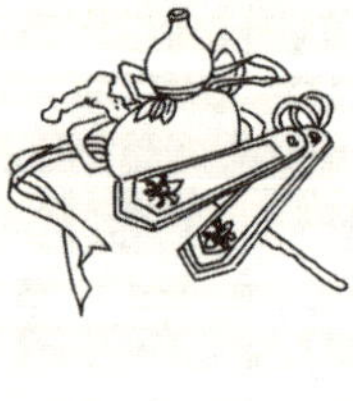

On the morning next day, Huzi took out that jar of bitter bile under his house and drank it all without a break. Then he went to get the machete and was able to wield it. So, he carried the machete to look for the monster. When he walked halfway, he was blocked by three dark-colored hunks. It turned out that they were the three hatchet men the the Zimo sent to kill Huzi. One guy was called Shangkuai yangba, and second one Zhongkuaiyangba, and the last one Xiakuaiyangba. When Huzi came forward to Shangkuaiyangba, Shangkuaiyangba said, "Let's see who's stronger." Then he ran fast towards Huzi and tried to hold him up. He exhausted himself but still failed. However, Huzi held him high without even trying and threw him hard down to the ground. Shangkuaiyangba was killed. Then Zhongkuaiyangba rushed at Huzi and also wanted to lift him up. But Huzi also outperformed him and held him over his head. When he was about to throw Zhongkuaiyangba, Zhongkuaiyangba begged, "Please do not kill me. I would like to be your guard and help you kill the monster." Seeing his companion giving in, Xiakuaiyangba also begged Huzi to spare him and expressed his will to help Huzi. So, Huzi showed mercy to those two men and went to kill the monster together.

虎子领着中快羊巴、下快羊巴一同去找妖怪，那个吃人的妖怪住在一座漂亮的大院子里。虎子走近院子里的第一道大门时，只见房子里熬着三大锅牛肉。虎子就对中快羊巴和下快羊巴说："你们饿了吧？饿了就把这三锅牛肉吃掉。妖怪来了，你们不要和他斗。你们斗不过他，你们只给我留心看着点，别让他逃走了，让我进去杀他。"虎子提着大刀跨进第二道院门，看见六七个年轻姑娘被妖怪用长长的头发吊在梁上，衣裙剥得精光，正准备杀了吃。虎子跑过去割断了头发，将她们一个个放了下来，把衣裙拿给她们穿上，叫她们都各自回家去。其中有一个最漂亮的姑娘，跪下哀求，说是已没有了家，要虎子把她留下做媳妇。虎子没法，只好答应了她。

正在这时，妖怪闯了进来，和虎子对打，虎子一刀砍掉他的头，妖怪又长出一个头来；虎子又砍掉他的头，他又长出一个头。就这样，虎子一共砍掉了妖怪的六个头，妖怪眼看抵挡不住就只好逃走了。

Headed by Huzi, the team followed the tracks all the way to the monster's den, an exceptionally splendid courtyard. When he approached the first door of the yard, Huzi found three cauldrons of beef in the house. Then he turned to his two companions and said, "Are you hungry? If you are, you can eat it. When the monster comes, stay away from it because you won't win. All you need to do is to keep an eye on it and don't let it escape. I'll kill it." Afterwards, Huzi carried his machete and passed the second door. Soon he found six or seven young girls stripped off clothes hung up on the beam with the monster's hair, clearly ready for slaughter. Huzi ran to them and cut off the binding hair. After the girls broke loose, Huzi helped them put on clothes and told them to go home. But one of the girls, the most beautiful one, begged that she be allowed to stay with him as his wife because she had no family or place to stay. Embarrassed as he may be, Huzi agreed.

Just at that moment, the monster broke in and fought with Huzi. When Huzi chopped off its head, another one grew back. After several rounds, Huzi cut six heads off the monster in total. Feeling unable to withstand, the monster ran away.

虎子领着姑娘和中快羊巴、下快羊巴刚走出庄院，只见迎面走来一个美貌的女子。虎子一眼看见了她额头上的那颗黑痣，便知道这是妖怪变的，冲上去举刀便砍。那个妖怪吓了一大跳，赶紧跑到半山腰的一个龙潭边，纵身跳下水里不见了。虎子追到龙潭边，对中快羊巴和下快羊巴说："你们守在这里，妖怪上来你们就把他推下去，我下去看看。"说罢取出一条牛皮条拴在龙潭边的一棵树桩上，就和姑娘一起拉着牛皮条下去了。下到龙潭底，他俩看见一座很大的院子，就走了进去。只见一只大白公鸡正站在檐下喔喔地叫，鸡冠旁有一颗大黑痣，虎子认出它是妖怪变的，就一刀砍过去。公鸡被砍倒在地，一滴血没有，妖怪又化作一道黑影逃到楼上去了。虎子紧追上楼，发现桌子上摆着一个木头盒子，里面装着一颗大白豌豆。再仔细一看，白豌豆上也有一颗黑痣。虎子知道它是妖怪变的，便赶紧把盒子紧紧盖起来，拿下楼去，将木盒子用铁钉钉死，架在柴堆上，点起大火来烧。一连烧了七天七夜，盒子烧化，妖怪也烧死了。

Then Huzi led the girl he saved, Zhongkuaiyangba and Xiakuaiyangba, leaving the courtyard. As soon as they left the yard, a beautiful girl came towards them. Seeing a black mole on her forehead, Huzi realized immediately that she was the monster and rushed to chop at her. The monster felt very shocked and ran to a deep pool halfway down the hill. Then it jumped into the pool and disappeared. Huzi chased after it to the pool. He said to Zhongkuaiyangba and Xiakuaiyangba, "You two stay here. If the monster comes up, you push it back into the water. I'll go." Then he took out a leather strap and tied it around a tree by the pool and descended to the pool with the girl. When they got to the bottom, they saw a splendid courtyard and walked in, only to find a large white rooster crowing under the roof. When he had a closer look, he found that it was the monster again because it had a mole besides its cockscomb. So Huzi gave it a heavy stroke and struck it down, but no blood spilled, because the monster had turned into a wisp of dark shadow and ran upstairs. Huzi followed it to the upstairs and only found a wooden box on the table containing a big white pea. Looking closer, Huzi saw a black mole on the pea. So he knew it was an incarnation of the monster and closed the box. He took the box downstairs and sealed it with nails. Then he put it over the woodpile and set the fire to it. The fire burned for seven days and nights and finally melted down the box. The monster was destroyed.

在龙潭边等着的中快羊巴和下快羊巴，等了七天七夜也不见虎子和姑娘上来，便一刀砍断伸下水去的牛皮条跑回去对兹莫说：“妖怪被我们杀死了，虎子也跌下龙潭里淹死了。”兹莫信以为真，大摆酒席为他俩庆功。

再说虎子将妖怪烧死以后，领着姑娘来到龙潭底，拉着牛皮条向上爬。刚刚爬到半口腰，听见“啪”一声，牛皮条断了。他俩就一直往下跌，最后跌到地上。虎子正急得没有办法，偶然见有一棵高耸入云的大松树，有一窝小乌鸦正在树上乱叫。他爬上树一看，只见一条大黑蛇盘在乌鸦窝里，张着大嘴恶凶凶地要吃掉那些小乌鸦，小乌鸦们吓得在树枝上乱跳乱叫。虎子挥起大刀，将那条大蛇砍死了。正在这时，只见一只老乌鸦叼着一条大水牛回来了。老乌鸦招呼小乌鸦说：“你们快来吃嘛！站得远远的怪叫些什么?”小乌鸦指指窝里的大死蛇说：“要不是这个人杀死大蛇，救了我们，我们早被大蛇吞吃了。他救了我们，我们应当报答才对!”于是虎子就请求它们帮助他出龙潭去。老乌鸦说：“等我去找七条水牛来做口粮，我就可以带你们飞出龙潭了。”

Having waited beside the pool for seven days and nights, Zhongkuaiyangba and Xiakuaiyangba still could not see any trace of Huzi and the girl coming out of the pool. So they cut off the strap and ran back to the Zimo and said, "We've killed the monster. And Huzi slipped into the pool and drowned." The Zimo fell for it and threw them a big celebration.

After burning the monster, Huzi led the girl and came to where the strap was hung. They held the strap and climbed up. But when they went halfway, the strap was broken with a clear crack. Then they fell and hit on the ground. While feeling very anxious and helpless, Huzi heard sharp cawing of little crows on a towering pine tree. He climbed up and found a big black snake coiling itself up in the crow's nest and opening its mouth to eat the scared crows. He took out his machete and killed the snake. At this moment, an old crow came back with an ox in its mouth and said to the little crows, "Come here for your dinner. Why are you standing this far and cawing oddly?" The little crows pointed at the big dead snake and replied, "Had he not been here, we would have been the snake's dinner. We should repay him for saving us!" So Huzi asked them to help him get out of the pool. The old crow said, "I can take you two out of here till I hunt seven oxen for food."

老乌鸦打来七条水牛，带在身边当口粮，又叫虎子和姑娘骑在它背上，然后用力往上飞。飞呀飞呀，飞了七天七夜，眼看快要飞出龙潭水面了，可是，七条水牛的口粮已吃光了，乌鸦再也飞不动了！虎子忙从腰上取下刀来，从自己腿上割下一块肉，喂给乌鸦吃了。乌鸦一下子就飞出了水面。虎子和姑娘从乌鸦背上下来站在龙潭岸边，感谢了乌鸦的帮助，乌鸦就飞回去了。

虎子来到岸边，找不着中快羊巴和下快羊巴，又见牛皮条是被刀劈断的，知道是那两个家伙存心要害死他们，气极了。他领着姑娘，一直找到兹莫家里，把中快羊巴和下快羊巴一刀一个砍死。兹莫为了保命，把自己掌管的土地财产让给了虎子，虎子便当了兹莫。据说后来虎子和他救回来的姑娘成了亲，夫妇活到一百岁那年，就一同上山隐居去了。

搜集整理者：潘广发等

Then the crow came back with seven oxen and asked Huzi and the girl to ride on its back. It exerted itself to fly up. After seven days and nights, when they were about to fly out of the pool, the seven oxen were eaten up and the crow ran out of strength. Huzi immediately took out the machete on his waist and cut off a piece of flesh on his leg to feed the crow, with which, the crow flied out of the pool at a stroke. Then Huzi and the girl got off its back and thanked the crow, which flied back later.

Huzi could not find Zhongkuaiyangba and Xiakuaiyangba anywhere by the pool. Instead, he found the strap cut off clearly by a knife. He got furious because he knew that they must have done it deliberately to kill him. Then he went straight to the Zimo's house with the girl and killed Zhongkuaiyangba and Xiakuaiyangba each with one blow. The Zimo was terrified. He gave up all his property and territory to Huzi out of a simple wish to survive. In this way, Huzi became the new Zimo. It was said that Huzi and the girl he saved got married and went up to a mountain to be hermits when they were 100 years old.

Collector and editor: Pan Guangfa, etc.

阿古与阿赊

古时候有两弟兄，哥哥叫阿赊，弟弟叫阿古。弟兄俩从小就没了父母，无依无靠，四处流浪度日，世间的酸甜苦辣，样样都尝够了。

熬过了十五个寒冬，送走了十五个春天，弟兄俩像两棵久经风霜的松树一样长大了。他们在一个长满绿树和翠竹的山头上，盖起了一幢三间两耳的茅草房安了家。弟兄两个在山坡上开了一块荒地，汗水换来了丰收；吃的有了，穿的有了，牛也养起来了，猪也养起来了，日子逐渐好过起来。

林中的雀鸟大了要寻伴，世上的男人大了要娶妻。哥哥阿赊讨了个媳妇，人长得倒可算是一枝花，只是好吃懒做，心肠像锅底一样黑。她整天在家收拾打扮不做活，还要阿赊留在家陪着她玩。这样一来，田地里的活计全都落到了阿古一个人身上。可怜的阿古，累死累活却不得吃顿饱饭，不得穿件新衣裳。跟着老鹰学着飞，跟着乌龟学着爬。起初，哥

Agu and Ashe

Once upon a time, there were two brothers, of whom the older one was called Ashe, the younger one was called Agu. The two brothers lost their parents in their childhood. With no family to turn to, they wandered around and couldn't be more familiar with bitterness in the world.

After struggling for 15 harsh winters, finally they grew up like two weather-beaten pine trees. Then, they built a thatched house with three principle rooms and two side rooms on the top of a mountain where green trees and bamboos were prosperous. On the slope of the mountain, a vast deserted land was also reclaimed by the two brothers. Finally, their hard work was paid off. They had enough food and clothes, and bred some cattle and pigs. A better life awaited.

Like birds in the forests in need of companions after growing up, grown men could not do without girls for marriage. Later, Ashe got married with a girl who was very good-looking but ugly inside. She was very lazy, dressing herself up all day without doing any work. She even asked Ashe to abandon work and play with her at home. Therefore, all the work in the fields fell on Agu's shoulder. The poor Agu could hardly earn a good meal or a piece of new clothes however hard he worked. To have more skills,

哥阿赊还心疼弟弟阿古，可到后来，他被黑心的媳妇教坏了，就像一头被穿了鼻索的公牛，牵到哪里就乖乖地跟到哪里，忘了骨肉之情。可怜的阿古尝尽了人间的苦难。

一天晚上，月亮升起来了。阿古借着月光从地里回来，一进家门，黑心肠的嫂嫂板着面孔对他说："一娘养的蜜蜂也有分离的时候，一母生的弟兄也有分家的日子。兄弟，你已长大成人，不能一辈子老守着哥嫂过日子，总有一天要分家，迟分不如早分，趁早你去立个家吧。"阿古听了，心里就像被一团乱麻裹住了。当他想起哥哥背着他四处流浪逃生的苦难生活，想到分家后自己要过的孤苦日子，想到嫂嫂的好吃懒做，分家后哥哥会受苦受累的情景，他不忍心和哥哥分家，便说："鱼儿和水不分离，我和哥哥不分家，要和哥哥在一起。"

嫂嫂听了，像香油泼进了火塘，一下子冒起了大火，说："你和我们一同过日子，福星永世不会照家门。自古弟兄兴分家，要分也得分，不分也得分。"

阿古知道嫂嫂心黑，不分也不行了，便横了心，说："要分就分，你说说东西咋个分？"

he even learned to fly from eagles and learned to crawl from turtles. At first, His elder brother Ashe still felt for him. But gradually, he was led astray by his heartless wife and became the puppet of his wife, going wherever she told him to. With no brotherly love anymore, poor Agu went back to the old miserable life.

One night, the moon was high in the sky. Agu went back home by the moonlight. Upon entering the house, his cold-hearted sister-in-law said to him with a grim face, "Bees born from the same mother shall get apart someday. So are men. Little brother, you have grown up. You can't always stay with us. Someday you'll have to leave us. It might as well be now. You need to settle down somewhere else on your own." Agu was utterly upset at it and went into deep thought, recalling old days when his brother carried him on his back and ran everywhere for a living and imagining a new life upon him when he would have to live alone and his brother would suffer from that lazy woman. He could not bear to leave, and said, "My brother is to me what water is to fish. I will not leave my brother."

Then his sister-in-law got furious all of a sudden and shouted, "If you live with us, luck will never come to us. Brothers are bound to fall apart. This is the old tradition! It's not your choice."

Agu knew that his sister-in-law was heartless, so there was no choice but to leave. He asked, "Alright. But how should we divide property?"

嫂嫂一听，立即鼓起螃蟹眼睛，说：“阿爸死时没留下一两银子，阿妈死时没留下一根线，只留下你们弟兄的两张嘴。房子是你哥哥亲手盖的，田地是你哥哥亲手开的，新布新衣是我从娘家带来的，蓑衣披在你身上，分家就是分张嘴，没有东西可以分。”

阿古一听，知道嫂嫂不是要和他分家，而是要把他赶出家门，气得立即要走。阿赊见了，便对媳妇说：“你今天不是答应分给弟弟一头牛吗？就让他牵走一头吧。”

嫂嫂恶狠狠地瞪了阿赊一眼，说：“我答应分给他的是三斤的一壶油①，没说过分给他一头牛，年纪小小的离死还远，不等着宰牛送葬，要牛整哪样？”

阿古听到嫂嫂狠毒的话，就像几十根绣花针往心里戳，实在忍受不了，便对阿赊叫了声哥哥，披着那件蓑衣，提着那壶香油转身出了门。

① 译者注：在汉语中“油”和“牛”的发音很相近。

His sister-in-law glared at him and said, "Papa left us no gold. Mama left us no cloth. They left you nothing. This house is built by your brother and the fields are developed by your brother. And those pieces of cloth are brought from my parents' home. Only a straw rain coat is yours and you are wearing it. So when you leave, don't take anything else."

By then, Agu knew that his sister-in-law was not planning a fair division but simply drove him away. So he got very angry and was about to leave. At the sight of it, Ashe asked his wife, "Didn't you promise to give him an ox? Let him have one." His wife gave him a murderous glance and said, "I promised to give him a bottle of oil① weighed three jin. Can't remember when I said about giving him an ox. He is so young. He doesn't need an ox to carry him to death!"

Those vicious words stung Agu's heart. He really could not stand it anymore. So he bid farewell to his brother and went out with the rain coat on his back and the bottle of oil in his hands.

---

① Translator's note: oil ("you" in pinyin) sounds very similar to ox ("niu" in pinyin) in Chinese.

再穷的鸟儿也有窝，可怜的阿古没有家，孤身走在黑咕隆咚的山路上，不知去哪里，不知走哪方，星星为他流下了伤心的眼泪，山林为他发出了悲恸的哭声。突然，透过层层乌云，一道闪电划破夜空。随着一声雷鸣，下起了瓢泼大雨。正当阿古顶着蓑衣艰难地在泥路上行走的时候，透过闪电的光亮，看见迎面走来一位全身湿淋淋的白胡子老爷爷。阿古立即迎了过去，拿蓑衣给白胡子老爷爷遮雨。可是雨越下越大，又刮起了大风，蓑衣不顶用。阿古想到这样下去不是个办法，便背起老爷爷往附近一座庙里跑去。到了庙里一看，静悄悄的没有一个人，灯也没点，香也没烧。阿古立即倒出香油，点亮了灯，然后铺好蓑衣，安顿老爷爷睡觉，他自己也靠在柱子上睡着了。

第二天，当阿古醒来时，天已经大亮了，太阳已经升起来了，白胡子老爷爷却不见了，只有那件蓑衣还留在原地。

While every bird had its nest, the poor Agu had no home. He walked alone in the mountain, surrounded by darkness. The stars and the forest shed tears for this man of misery. Suddenly, a lightning streaked through the gloomy sky. Then a thunder was heard, followed by a torrential downpour. When he was struggling to walk in the mud with his coat held over his head, Agu saw, in lightning, an old wet grandpa with white beards coming towards him. So, he immediately went forward and took his coat down to help the old man. But the rain went heavier and wind began to roar. The coat was not sturdy enough. So Agu carried the old man on his back and ran to a temple nearby to take shelter from the rain. It was a deserted temple with no trace of human, no light in the lamp and no lit incense. Agu poured out oil and lighted up a lamp. Then he rolled out his coat and helped the old man settle down. Afterwards, he leaned against the pillar and fell asleep.

The next day, when Agu was awake, the sun was high in the sky. He found that the old man had gone, only to see the coat in the same place.

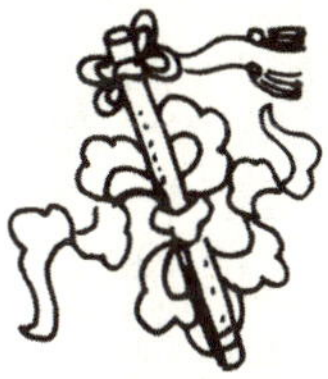

“老爷爷到哪里去了呢？会不会出事？”阿古翻过一道道山梁，跨过一条条箐沟，寻找白胡子老爷爷。他找遍了北边的高山，没见到老爷爷的脚印；找遍了西边的密林，没有见到老爷爷的影子；找遍了东边的箐沟，没听见老爷爷的声音。阿古来到了南山，那里，四周是密密的森林，一股清清的山泉，在绿树的掩盖下，悄悄流向遥远的地方；中间一块平坦坦的荒草地上，横卧着一块巨石。阿古走了过去，静静地坐在那块巨石上，遥望着挂在树梢的朵朵白云，心里挂念着那位白胡子老爷爷。突然，一只白鹤向他飞来，在阿古头顶上盘旋了一圈，然后站在一棵枝叶茂盛的苍松上，凝视着阿古。接着，只见白胡子老爷爷手拄一根龙头拐杖走出森林，一步步向他走来。阿古见了，很快迎了上去。没等他开口，白胡子老爷爷就问他：“孩子，你家住在哪里，家里还有些什么人？”

阿古把自己不幸的遭遇，一五一十地告诉了白胡子老爷爷，然后说：“老爷爷，我现在没有家，不知道该到哪里去。”

白胡子老爷爷用龙头拐杖指了指，说：“吃黄连长大的孩子，你的心像山中的泉水一样纯洁，你不要到其他地方，就在这里安家，开垦这块荒地，你会得到幸福。”

白胡子老爷爷说完要走，阿古又说：“老爷爷，我送你回家去吧！”

白胡子老爷爷回答说：“不用了，我有事还要到别处去，你快盖房子吧！”

"Where is the old grandpa? Is everything alright with him?" he thought. Then Agu climbed over numerous high mountain ridges and jumped over countless deep trenches to search for the old man. But he was nowhere to be found, not in the mountain in the north, the thick forest in the west or the deep trench in the east. Agu continued to head south and searched in the mountain where thick forests spread all around and a stream of clear spring, fringed on two sides, ran towards the distance. In the middle was a patch of flat withered grassland with a huge rock lying in between. Agu went towards it and sat on the rock quietly. He stared at clouds over the trees, thinking of the old man with white beards. Suddenly, a white crane flied towards him and circled above his head. It then stood at a robust pine tree, staring at Agu. Just then, the old man walked out of the forest assisted by a dragon-head crutch. Agu soon approached him. Before Agu said anything, the old man asked, "Son, where is your home? Do you have anyone in your family?"

Agu told his misfortune to the old man honestly and said, "Grandpa, I have no home. I don't know where to go."

The old man pointed to him with his crutch, saying, "Poor child, your heart is as pure as spring water. You shall go nowhere else. This is your home. You reclaim this patch of deserted land and you shall have your happiness."

Then, the old man left. Agu stopped him and said, "Grandpa, let me walk you home!"

"No, I have other business to attend to. You hurry up and build your house", the old man replied.

说完，白胡子老爷爷拄着龙头拐杖走了。接着，那只仙鹤也朝着白胡子老爷爷走去的方向飞去了。

阿古砍来栗木和竹子，割来茅草和长青藤，对着清清的流水，盖起了一间小小的草房。接着，阿古开出了荒地，种上了庄稼。庄稼长得一片葱绿，十分逗人喜爱，只是那块巨石占去了很大一片地，阿古觉得很可惜。他下决心搬掉那块石头，栽上庄稼。于是他砍来柴堆在那块巨石上面，然后，放火烧巨石。那熊熊烈火映红了半边天，几天几夜都不熄。烧到第七夜，巨石“嘭”的一声炸裂了，裂成许多簸箕大的石块。阿古高兴得不得了，忘记了吃饭，忘记了睡觉，不分白天黑夜地搬石头。他的脚掌磨破了，手心磨破了，鲜血、汗水润湿了土地。七七四十九天过去了，石头快搬完了。当他搬起最后一块石头的时候，突然，从石头下面射出一道耀眼的金光，定睛一看，原来是一大堆金子。他刚把金子取出来，下面又有一层银子，取完了银子，下面又有一层绫罗绸缎。发了财的阿古，想到没有白胡子老爷爷的指点，就不可能得到这么多的金银和绫罗绸缎，决心送一半给白胡子老爷爷。可是，阿古走遍了九村八寨也没见到白胡子老爷爷的影子，访遍了千家万户也不知道白胡子老爷爷的住处，他只得把金银和绫罗绸缎背回来放在草房里。

Then he walked off assisted by his crutch. And the crane followed.

Agu sawed bundles of chestnut and bamboo, and cut off some grasses and green vines. He built up a small thatched cottage facing the spring. Then he went to reclaim a patch of deserted land and planted some crops. The crop fields were joyously luxuriant. But a huge rock occupied a large patch of land, which was really a waste. So Agu decided to remove it, making space for the cropland. Then, he placed some firewood he cut on the rock and set them on fire, whose flames reddened most of the sky and thrived for several days. At the 7th night, following a deafening sound, the rock cracked open and shattered into lots of rocks as big as dustpans. Agu was so happy that he forgot to eat and sleep. So he began to remove those rubble day and night, regardless of any abrasion on his palms and sole, until the land was filled with his blood and sweats. After 49 days' hard work, Agu managed to remove all the rocks. When he lifted the last one, a chink of golden light projected from the bottom of thc rock. Looking closer, he found that it was a large pile of gold. When he took out all the gold, there was another pile of silver beneath. After he retrieved the silver, some pieces of luxurious cloth were hidden below. Agu didn't expect this fortune. He thought that he owed it to the guidance of that old man. So he was determined to give half of his wealth to the old man. However, after calling on numerous households in various stockades and villages, the old man was still nowhere to be found. Then, he had to carry gold, silver and fancy cloth back to his thatched cottages.

一天，一个癞头跛脚老人来到阿古家要饭，阿古听了老人的诉说，觉得他很可怜，便给了他一些金银和绫罗绸缎，并对老人说：“老爷爷，你先拿这点去用，用完了再来拿。”

癞头跛脚老人很受感动，说：“孩子，你心肠真好，给了我这么多的金银和绫罗绸缎，可我没有一样值钱的东西送给你，只有一颗桃子核，就当作礼物送给你吧！你栽在地里头，好好种植，等到第三年就会开花结果。”说完，取出桃子核递给阿古就走了。

再说阿赊和他的媳妇，自从把阿古赶走后，整天在家吃喝玩乐，很快把家当吃空了，田地也荒芜了，穷得没法，只好摘野菜充饥度日。不久，他们听到弟弟阿古发了财，自己也很想发发财。

一天，阿赊领着他的媳妇来找阿古，一进门，阿赊媳妇就对阿古说：“兄弟，你倒发了大财了，可你哥哥和我过得这么可怜，你看在爹娘的面上，教教我们你是怎样发财的吧！”

阿古自己也不知道为什么会发财，一时说不上来。

阿赊媳妇急着想发财，便说：“兄弟，你就从分家那天晚上说起。”

阿古说道：“那天晚上，我提着三斤香油……”

阿赊媳妇急忙打断阿古的话，问道：“啊，香油，三斤香油放到哪里去了？”

阿古说：“我拿到庙里去点了灯。”

One day, an old lame man in shabby clothes came to Agu's house, asking for food. Agu felt very sorry for his misfortune, so he gave some gold and silver and fancy cloth to him, saying, "Grandpa, take these. Come to me again if you need more."

The man was deeply touched and said, "Boy, you have such a good heart. You've given me so much but I have nothing valuable for you. I only have a peach kernel, so please take it as my gift. You can plant it in the field. If it's taken good care of, it will blossom and bear fruits in the third year." Then, he gave Agu this peach kernel and went away.

As for Ashe and his wife, they had been enjoying themselves by dissipation at home since they drove Agu away. Soon they lost all properties and was left nothing but a patch of deserted land. They were so poor that they had to live on picking wild grass for food. Before long, they heard that their brother became wealthy and wanted to make a fortune themselves.

One day, Ashe and his wife went to Agu. Upon arrival, Ashe's wife said, "Brother, you've got so much wealth, but your brother and I have been so poor. For the sake of our parents, please show us how to be rich!"

Agu actually had no idea how he got rich, so he couldn't come up with a particular reason.

But his sister-in-law was so eager to be rich that she reminded him, "Brother, let's start with the day you left."

Agu said, "At that night, I carried a bottle of oil..."

"Oh. Oil. Where did you put it?", his sister-in-law soon interrupted.

Agu replied, "I used it to light up the lamp in the temple."

阿赊媳妇一听，高兴起来："哟，原来是兄弟行善，菩萨爷爷让你发了财。"

说完，便拖起阿赊走了。来到路上，阿赊媳妇对阿赊说："阿古点了三斤香油就能发那么大的财，我们提九斤香油到庙里去点，要比他发更大的财。"

当天晚上，阿赊两口子提了九斤香油连夜赶路。当他们走到半路的时候，借着照明的火光，看见迎面走来一位白胡子老爷爷。老爷爷走近了拉住阿赊恳求说："孩子，我年老无力，天黑难走，送我回家吧。"

阿赊媳妇一心想早点发财，厌恶地对白胡子老爷爷说："死老倌，老虎豹子也嫌你人老皮硬，不会吃你的，你自己走吧，我们有急事赶着要去办。"

白胡子老爷爷又恳求说："求你们行行好，还是送送我。"

阿赊媳妇急了，走过去将白胡子老爷爷推下路边，嘴里骂道："真是树老心空，活着不如趁早死了好。"

阿赊两口子来到庙里，把九斤香油倒进灯盏点着灯。他们嫌灯芯小，不够亮，便撕破衣裳搓成大灯芯换上，等着金银财宝来。可是等到半夜也没有等得来，两口子便睡着了。不久，油灯烧热后燃起了大火，把大庙烧着了，阿赊和他的媳妇被烧死在庙里了。

His sister-in-law cheered up and said, "I see. It must have been the Buddha grandpa who bestowed him the wealth for his good deed."

After learning the truth she believed, she dragged Ashe away and left. On the way she told her husband Ashe that Agu got so wealthy by just offering three jin of oil and if they could offer nine jin, they would become much wealthier.

That night, they walked hurriedly to the temple, holding a bottle containing nine jin of oil. When they went halfway, they could see by the light an old man coming towards them. When he walked closer, he took Ashe's hand and begged, "Son, I'm old. And it's so dark. Can you walk me home?"

Preoccupied by the desire to make a fortune as soon as possible, Ashe's wife said to the old man with contempt, "Old goat, even tigers and leopards won't eat your aged meat! Why don't you walk by yourself? We have other business to do."

The old man begged again, "Please, have mercy. Walk me home."

Ashe's wife grew angry. She walked to the old man and pushed him down the road, swearing, "Old beggar. You might as well die earlier."

Then they reached the temple, and lighted the lamp by pouring in nine jin of oil. Not satisfied with a small wick, they tore apart their clothes and twisted them to make a big one. After putting the lamp on, the couple satisfactorily waited for wealth. But nothing came before midnight. So, they fell asleep. Soon after, the lamp was overheated and caught with fire which consumed the temple and the couple.

不久，阿古发财的消息很快传遍了三山五岭，穷人们都源源不断地赶来向阿古讨金要银。好心的阿古知道来的都是些穷人，每个人都给些金银和绫罗绸缎。不久，阿古得到的金银财宝和绫罗绸缎全部给完了，只剩下一间草房，一块地和那颗桃子核。但是，当他想到他让许多穷苦人得到了幸福的时候，心里有说不出的高兴。他仍在那块地上辛勤劳动，并按照老人的吩咐，把桃子核栽在那块地上。

第一个春天，刚下过头阵春雨，地上冒出了一棵碧绿晶莹的桃树苗，长出翠绿的叶片。

第二个春天，刚吹过阵春风，那棵桃树发出了一串串青枝绿叶，在雨露的滋润下茁壮成长。

第三个春天，刚照过头道春日，那桃树绽开了红艳艳的鲜花。

一天，阿古看见一对美丽的彩蝶双双从远处飞来，绕着他飞舞了一阵，又飞去绕着桃树飞舞了一阵，最后，双双飞到高高的蓝天上去了。阿古看了心里非常羡慕，心里想到，独自在深山，吃饭没有伴，做活没有伴，没个说话处，生活就像吃菜无油盐一样没有味，假若能有个姑娘作媳妇，做个伴，那该多好啊。可是，自己穷成这个样子，又有谁肯嫁自

Before long, the news that Agu made a fortune spread all over the mountains nearby. Poor men flocked towards Agu's house, asking for gold or silver. Good-natured Agu knew that those people were really poor, so he did not skimp on charitable handouts. And soon, gold, silver and fancy cloth he once owned were all given away. By then, he only had a thatched cottage, a patch of land and a peach kernel. However, he felt very content at having helped so many poor people. Since then, he worked hard in the field as in the old days and planted the kernel into the earth on the old man's advice.

In the first spring, after the first shower of rain, a green and translucent peach sprout popped out on the ground.

In the second spring, when a gust of wind blew, green leaves grew on the tree, thriving in the rain.

In the third spring, when the first beam of sunlight broke through clouds, red flowers blossomed on it.

One day, Agu saw a pair of beautiful butterflies flying from the distance, which circled around him and then the peach tree for a while, before finally flying back to the sky. He admired this pair and felt sad for his loneliness. He had no one in company by his side either in eating or working in this deep mountain. He was bored of this dull and lonely life, and prayed for a girl to be his wife so that at least he could have someone to talk to. "But which girl is willing to marry a poor guy like me?" he thought to himself. So, he decided to give up the idea of marriage. Instead, he would pick the most pleasing peach flower as his companion in the house. Then, he walked to the peach tree and began to select carefully. But it was hard to make a choice after

己呢？算了吧，娶不着媳妇来做伴，就摘枝最如意的桃花插在房里做伴好了。想到这里，他便走到桃树下挑选。他挑呀挑呀，从北边瞧到西边，从西边瞧到南边，总觉得满树桃花鲜艳夺目，枝枝都是一样美丽引人，挑不出哪枝多美，说不出哪枝多如意。当他走到东边时，脸上突然被一枝桃花碰了一下，凑近一看，哟，原来是一枚含苞欲放的桃花。就在这时，一个个花苞突然绽开了，开得非常鲜艳。奇怪的是，这枝桃花放出一阵阵奇异的花香，阿古闻着，心里像灌了蜜一样舒畅，眼睛像安了星星一样明亮有神，他便伸手摘了这一枝花。更奇怪的是，他刚把花摘到手，那枝桃花便带着他徐徐飞上高高的蓝天，最后落到一个遥远的地方。阿古人生地不熟，不知去哪里，不知走哪方，正当他拿不定主意的时候，看见一群人像蚂蚁一样抬一块条石。阿古走过去，一个人抬起一块条石跟在那帮人的后边。走不多远，一座金碧辉煌的宫殿出现在眼前。那群人把抬着的条石放在宫殿旁，阿古也跟着把条石丢在一旁。可是，当阿古丢下的条石一落地，立即响起一阵惊天动地的巨响，震得整个宫殿都摇晃起来，把阿古吓得呆在一旁。这时，从宫殿走出来一群彪形大汉，见了阿古，齐声喊道："就是他，就是他！"说着，一齐拥过来对阿古说："国王召见。"一边说，一边簇拥着阿古进王宫去了。

observing the flowers in the north side, east side and south side, as they all looked stunningly the same to him. When he walked to the east side, a flower touched his face. Looking closer, he found it was in bud. Then a bud suddenly blossomed in an eye-catching manner. Strangely, the flower emitted a stream of exotic fragrance which soothed Agu greatly. So Agu made up his mind to pick this one. But more strangely, when he touched it, he was taken up to the blue sky and finally a remote place where everything was new to him. Agu had no idea where he was and where he should go. While he was hesitating, a group of men carried a bar of rock past him. Then, he followed suit and joined the group. Before long, a splendid palace was seen in front of him. Then, the group of men put aside the bar of rock. So did Agu. But when Agu dropped the rock, a deafening sound occurred and the whole palace was shaking. He felt petrified. Afterwards, at the sight of Agu, a crowd of stalwart men came out of the palace and shouted, "That's him!" They approached Agu and said, "The king summons you, please." Agu was then escorted into the palace.

阿古以为自己闯了大祸，吓得面无人色。到了国王面前，阿古立即跪下，向国王求饶说："尊敬的国王，小人不懂事闯了祸，惊动了国王，请国王饶恕。"

国王笑呵呵地走过来，亲手扶起阿古，拉他坐在自己的身旁，然后对阿古说："年轻人，你救了我家公主，立下了大功，我要重重地奖赏你，你要什么我就给你什么，你说吧。"

阿古一听，弄懵了。他想，自己从没救过什么公主，也许是国王认错人了，便说："尊敬的国王，小人没救过公主，恐怕是你认错人了。"

国王非常自信地说："不会的，我家公主看得清清楚楚，不信，就叫公主来说。"说完便命人叫公主去了。

原来，国王只有一个公主，生得非常漂亮，非常聪明伶俐，是国王的掌上明珠。但后来不知为什么，公主的耳朵突然聋了，痛得非常厉害，整天哭得死去活来。国王请了天下最有名的神医，找来天下最好的神药，但公主的耳朵还是医不好。国王急得毫无办法，便向全国下了一道通告："谁能医好公主的耳朵，要什么就给什么。"

可是，三天过去了，不见一个人进宫殿来报告。三个月过去了，不见一个人来向国王献药。三年过去了，不见一个人来给公主医治。公主的耳朵聋得更厉害了，公主的耳朵痛得更加厉害了。

Agu thought that he must have made a big trouble, so he looked as pale as death. When he went to the king, he immediately knelt down and asked for mercy, "Honorable King, I did not mean to disturb you on purpose. Please have mercy."

The king laughed and walked towards him. He held Agu up and took him to sit beside him, saying, "Young man, you saved my daughter. You've done a great deed. I'm going to reward you handsomely. What do you want?"

Agu was confused at what the king said and thought that he must have mistaken him for someone else, as he had never saved any princess. So he replied, "Honorable king, I did not save the princess. I'm afraid that honor belongs to someone else."

The king was very confident and said, "No, my daughter is very sure. Servants, bring her here."

It turned out that the king had only one dearly beloved daughter who was very beautiful and intelligent. But then somehow, she got deaf and was in great pain every day. The king summoned every excellent doctor in the world and searched for all effective medicines. But the princess was still not cured. The king got very anxious and declared an announcement that anyone who cured the princess shall be rewarded with whatever was desired.

Three days passed, no one dared to try. Then three months passed, no medicine was found. And three years passed, nobody came to rescue. The princess suffered more from her aggravated disease.

这天，公主的耳朵比往常痛得更厉害了，她坐立不安，便倚在栏杆上呻吟。突然，她闻到一股奇异的花香，耳朵一点也不痛了。她便好奇地向四周打量，只见一位小伙子手拿一枝桃花，肩扛着一块条石走过来。小伙子一放下条石，只听得一阵惊天动地的巨响，公主的耳朵震好了，她连小伙子的心跳声也听到了，便高兴地把这件事告诉了父王。国王一听，高兴得不得了，立即命人找那小伙子来见。

不一会，公主来了，国王问道："我的好女儿，你瞧瞧是不是他？"

公主回答说："阿爸，我看见的就是他。"

阿古连忙说："不不不，我没有救过公主。"

国王又问公主："孩子，你是不是把人认错了？"

公主回答说："阿爸，我没有认错，你看，他手里还拿着桃花哩！"

公主说着，打量了阿古一眼，见他生得容貌英俊，肩阔腰圆，浓眉大眼，很是动心，又想到是他帮自己医好了病，心里顿时燃起了爱情的火焰，便暗暗向阿古投去一道爱慕的目光。

阿古一见，呆望着公主憨厚地笑了笑，然后将手里的桃花递了过去，说："公主，给你。"公主接过桃花，含羞地低着头一声不响。

On this day, the princess felt more pain than she ever had. When she was fidgeting and moaning by the handrail, suddenly, she smelled a gust of exotic fragrance, which miraculously cured her pain in the ears. She checked around curiously and found a young man who carried a bar of rock held a delicate peach flower in hand. When the young man dropped the rock, she heard the deafening sound and then recovered completely. Soon, she could even hear the heartbeat of the young man. Then she told her father about it. As soon as the king heard this, he was overjoyed and immediately sent for the young man to meet him.

After a while, the princess came. The king asked, "My daughter, have a look and tell me whether he is the man?"

"Yes, Papa. It's him." the princess replied.

Agu explained immediately, "No, that's not my doing."

The king asked the princess again, "Child, do you mistake him for someone else?"

The princess answered shortly, "No, Papa, he is the man. You see he's holding the flower!"

While speaking, the princess looked back at Agu, and saw that he was really handsome with a stalwart figure and heavy features. She found him very attractive and suddenly fell for him at the thought of his help to cure her disease. So, she glanced at him with affection.

When Agu found her look, Agu smiled timidly and passed his flowers to her, saying, "Princess, this is for you." The princes took it and remained silent out of shyness.

国王见了，高兴地笑了笑，说："好好，我看你们缘分好，就成全你们，今日就成亲。"说完，国王命人吹吹打打、热热闹闹地给阿古和公主办了婚事。从此，阿古成了驸马，过上了幸福美满的生活。

讲述者：普七鲁

翻译整理者：黄世荣

The king saw this and laughed. He said, "You two really meant for each other. I shall assist. You can get married today." Afterwards, he arranged a grand and festive marriage for the princess and Agu. Since then, Agu became the husband of the princess and lived a happy life.

Narrator: Pu Qilu

Translator and editor: Huang Shirong

阿依利里

从前，在瓦石觉落大森林的东边，住着一户姓阿布①的人家，这家人有两个女儿，姐姐叫利里，妹妹叫利尼。她们家住的地方，泉水漫地走，鲜花满坡开。利里和利尼天天跟着妈妈过着无忧无虑的日子。可是好景不长，利里满九岁时，妈妈难产死了。父亲便给她们娶了个人最漂亮、心肠最歹毒的继母。这继母让姐妹俩干最脏的活，做最累的事，吃最坏的饮食，还不满足，要把姐妹俩除掉才解恨。利里的父亲是一个毫无主见的人，当继母虐待女儿时，他不但不为亲生骨肉说话，反而帮着继母收拾他们。两个可怜的小姑娘上天无路，入地无门。睡在鸡窝里，眼看着父母吃香的喝辣的，她们却只能吃一点剩菜剩饭，过着比狗还不如的日子。

① 阿布：彝族没有这个姓，是故事中的杜撰。

Ayilili

Once upon a time, there were two sisters of the family of Abu①, of which the older one was called Lili, the younger one Lini. Spring water ran through in front of their house and flowers blossomed all over the hills nearby. The two sisters lived a joyful and easy life with their mother. But such a life did not sustain. Their mother died of hard labour when Lili was nine. Later, their father married a beautiful yet vicious woman to be their stepmother who set them to do the dirtiest and most tiring work while eating the worst food. But she was still not content until she had them killed. Sadly, their father was a nose of wax, and did not stop such brutality but encouraged it somehow. The two sisters could not turn to anyone for help. Living in a hen house, they had to watch how their father and stepmother feasted while they ate whatever was left.

① Abu: a family name only in a fairy tale because there was no such name in the Yi ethnic group.

母亲在世的时候，全家辛勤劳动，挣下了满楼的粮食，满山的牛羊。自从继母来了以后，她不劳动，父亲也就天天陪她躺着吃、睡着喝。姐妹俩一看见父亲杀羊，总是忍不住劝父亲少杀几只。有一天，当父亲又拉羊杀时，利尼伤心地对父亲说："阿爸，后妈是个妖精，她吃完我们的家产，会连我们也吃掉的。"利里也说："阿爸，你这样由着后妈，总有一天会后悔的。"谁知这话被父亲告诉了继母，继母一听，心想："看来不除掉这两个小妖精，我就吃不安，睡不宁。"于是，她又吵又闹，说如果不杀掉两个女儿，她就离开他。父亲舍不得继母，又不忍心杀死亲生骨肉，为难地说："难道就不能女儿也不杀，你也不走吗？我实在下不了手啊！"继母一听，哭哭啼啼地去收拾东西，她对丈夫说："要我，还是要女儿？随你的便！"父亲看继母真的要走，只得横下心说："我要你，不要女儿。杀又不忍心，还是把她们丢掉吧！"

When their mother still lived, the whole family lived in a house full of grain, on a mountain covered with countless flocks and herds because of their hard work. But ever since the lazy step mother was here, their father also indulged himself in idleness. Whenever the two sisters saw their father slaughtering sheep, they couldn't help but ask him to kill fewer ones. One day, when their father slaughtered sheep again, the desperate Lini told her father, "Father, that woman is a monster. She is going to consume our properties, and us eventually." Lili also joined her sister and said, "Papa, someday you will regret for not having stopped her." But their father repeated those remarks to his new wife. After learning it, the stepmother thought that she would not have a day of peace until the two sisters were removed. So, she made a big fuss about it and said to her husband, "You are going to kill your daughters or I shall leave you." Their father was in a dilemma because he did not want his new wife to go but also could not stand killing his own daughters. He had to say, "Isn't there a way I don't have to make such a hard choice? I really can't!" Then the woman went to pack her things, turning to her husband in tears, and said, "Me or your precious daughters. It is up to you!" Seeing his new wife really mean it, their father had to choose and said, "Of course I want you, not my daughters. But I really can't kill them. Let's toss them away!"

于是，父亲便和继母躲在家里谋划丢掉亲生女儿的办法，谋划了一整夜。

第二天早上，父亲谎称带姐妹俩去看江，把她们带到山脚下的金沙江边。他叫姐妹俩待在峡谷岩丛里，说自己有事，一下就回来，但一去就再也没有回来。姐妹俩等啊等啊，一直等到夕阳四下，眼看天快黑啦，江风吹在岩石上，发出可怕的啸声。姐妹俩害怕了，哭着叫着在峡谷里乱钻乱爬，大声呼叫："阿爸，你在哪里呀!"峡谷可怜她们，把她们的叫声传递得很远很远，可就是没有父亲的回答。

利尼说："姐姐，阿爸会不会丢下我们走了？为什么他不来找我们呢?"

利里说："不会的，阿爸可能有事先回去了，我们慢慢地找着回去吧。"

姐妹俩走了一会，可是忘记了家乡所在的方向，不知怎么走才好。利尼说："姐姐，我们找不回去了，家在哪一边呢?"利里也不知道。可她安慰妹妹说："妹妹，我们会找到的，不要怕，跟着姐姐什么也别怕。"姐妹俩走啊走啊，走着走着又回到了原地，怎么也走不出去。这时候，有一只岩鸡在她们头上的悬崖顶叫道："往左，找河，顺河走!"姐妹俩听了，照着岩鸡的话，果然找到了一条从山上流下来的河。河在江边形成一个大深潭，水上漂着一朵花。利尼一见花就叫道："姐姐，那就是昨天我掉进河里的花。"利里说："好啦，这是从我们门前流过的那条河，走吧，我们可以找到家啦。"

Therefore, the father and his new wife plotted the whole night about how to abandon his own daughters.

On the morning next day, he lied that he would take the two sisters to view the river and left them on the mountain feet, near the Jingsha River. Then he told them to stay among the rocks and bushes of the canyon and that he would return very soon after finishing his business. But he did not return. The two sisters waited and waited until the sun went down. It was getting dark. Wind roared past the rocks. The two sisters were so frightened that they cried and crawled in the canyon, calling out their father, "where are you, Papa?" The canyon pitied them and carried their voice far way. But no response came.

Lini said, "Sister, has Papa left us? Why won't he come back to us?"

Lili replied, "No way. Father might have gone home for other business. Let's find our way back home."

The two sisters kept walking for a while and got lost because they forgot the way back home. Lini said, "Sister, we'll never find the right way. Where is our home?" Lili did not know either, but out of a wish to comfort her sister, she said, "Don't be afraid. We will find our way home. I'll take care of you." The two sisters continued to walk. But it seemed that they always went back to the same spot, clearly trapped. At that time, a chicken cackled, saying, "Turn left, look for a river and walk along it!" So the two sisters followed the chicken's instructions and found a river running down from the mountain. The river flew to the ground and formed a deep pool where a flower floated on it. At the sight of the flower, Lini shouted, "Sister, this is the flower I dropped yesterday." Lili said, "Yes, it's the river in front of our house. We can go home now."

姐妹俩经过一夜的艰苦跋涉，第二天中午，终于找到了家。她们的父亲和继母，以为姐妹俩再回不来了，放心地大吃大喝，正吃得高兴，看见姐妹俩回来，惊得目瞪口呆。

姐妹俩回来后，继母气得瞪着眼，向她的丈夫吵闹着。父亲一计不成，又生一计。第二天早上，他用锥子在背水葫芦底上刺了很多小洞，然后交给姐妹俩，叫她们去河边背水。姐妹俩去了，无论水装得多满，回到半路上就漏光了。她们来回跑了好几趟，折腾了大半个早上，还是没能把水背回来。利里说："算了，妹妹，我们回去吧！"利尼害怕地说："不把水背回去，阿爸会打死我们的。"

正在姐妹俩左右为难的时候，一只乌鸦飞到她们头，大声叫道："呱、呱，补泥巴！"利尼说："姐姐，乌鸦好像在说话呢！"利里说："是呀，它叫我们用泥巴糊住葫芦底呢。"

利里和利尼，用胶泥糊住了葫芦底，把水打回去了。父亲和继母正收拾家屋，打算搬到远处去，把姐妹俩丢在这里。还来不及去，姐妹俩就打水回来了。这一回，父亲和继母都破例地没有打骂她俩。她们以为父亲变好了，心里高兴得不得了。实际上，父亲和继母背着她们，又打坏主意了。

After a tiring overnight trek, the two sisters finally went back home at noon next day. Their father and stepmother were having a feast very cheerfully, as they thought that they would not see the girls again. But such cheerfulness turned to pure astonishment when the two sisters came back.

The stepmother was shocked with her eyes wide open and went at her husband viciously. Not giving up, the father thought of another plan. Next morning, he drilled many small holes on the back of a gourd with an awl and asked the sisters to fetch water near the river with the gourd. But however hard they tried to fill up the gourd, the water in it just leaked out halfway home. The sisters went back and forth for several times the whole morning, but still could not carry any water home with the gourd. Lili said, "Forget it, Sister, let's go home." Lini was afraid and said, "If we do not fetch water home, father will beat us to death."

As they had no idea what to do next, a crow flied over their heads, cawing, "Gua. Gua. Plaster it with mud." Lini said, "Sister, the crow seems to be talking to us." Lili replied, "Yes, it told us to plaster the back of the gourd with mud."

So Lili and Lini did as told and successfully fetched water home. Their father and stepmother back home were busy packing things up with a plan to move far away and leave the sisters here. But before they left, the sisters came back. This time, neither their father nor stepmother scolded them. And the two sisters got very happy because they thought their father changed his mind and would be kind to them. But it was not true. Their father and stepmother were plotting something else.

又有一天，父亲对利里和利尼说：“我们家的房子已经破旧了，我打算砍些木头来翻修一下。今天你们俩就跟我到山上砍木头。”父亲把两个女儿带进瓦石觉落大森林，送进一个深箐里，叫她们走进去找藤子来抬木头，并告诉她们：“我就在山头上砍树，只要你们还听见我的砍树声，就不准到山头上来。”姐妹俩见山箐里阴森森的，长满青苔的藤子像蛇一样挂在荨麻林里的树上，只要脚一进去，头上的天就不见了。森林里毒蚊子很多，又不知什么地方会钻出一条蛇来。她俩非常害怕，又不敢违抗父亲的话，只得硬着头皮往里走。利尼一走进山箐，就被毒蚊子叮哭了。

父亲到山头上，把一个空葫芦挂在迎风的松树上，旁边再拴一块石头，风一吹来，石头打在葫芦上，发出“咚咚咚”的声音，远远听来，就像砍树一样。然后他就飞快地跑回去，带着继母，收拾家产，搬到了很远很远的地方。

One day, their father told Lili and Lini, "Our house is very shabby and I want to saw some wood for its redecoration. Today you two follow me to saw some wood in the mountain." So their father took them to the Washijueluo Forest and sent them to a deep thick grove. He asked their daughters to go inside and find vines to carry wood. He said to them, "I will be sawing wood on the top of the mountain. As long as you hear me sawing, don't come up here." The two sisters found the grove very gloomy. Vines covered with moss hung down from trees in the grove as if they were snakes about to be awakened. One foot set in the thick grove was enough to make a person not to see the sky. Numerous poisonous mosquito flied all over there and snakes lurked in the darkness. The two sisters were frightened but could not defy their father. They had to move on. Once she went in, Lini was stung by those mosquito and cried.

Meanwhile, their father went to the top of the mountain and hung an empty gourd tied with a rock beside on a tree in the face of the wind. So when the wind blew past, the rock would hit the gourd and made this rat-a-tat sound. When heard in the distance, it just sounded like someone sawing trees. The father ran home and packed up properties with his new wife. Then they moved far away.

再说姐妹俩不停地在箐里砍藤子，一直砍到天快黑，藤子砍了几大码，头脸也被毒蚊子叮得又红又肿，连眼睛都快睁不开了，砍树声还在响。利尼一边哭，一边叫饿，一边叫疼，可又不敢停下砍藤子的手。利里听见砍树声老在响，有点奇怪，于是停下手中的活计，听了听，顿时脸色苍白，她对利尼说："妹妹，别砍了，把刀丢掉！"利尼说："这……阿爸会打死我们的。"利里说："不，妹妹，我们受骗了，阿爸早走掉了，那响声根本就不是他在砍树！如果是砍树，为什么总没听见树倒下呢？"姐妹俩跑到山头上一看，只见树尖上风吹石头打着葫芦响，伤心地抱在一起哭了半天。

这时候，天黑了，大森林里伸手不见五指，远远近近的密林里，老虎叫、豹子哼、树林响、风乱吹，吓得姐妹俩找不到地方藏身，只得不停地走。她们谁也不敢说话，也不敢往树林密的地方钻，哪里有空处就往哪里走。天亮的时候，她们迷路了，再也不知道自己在什么地方，再也辨不出东西南北了。

"姐姐，现在我们怎么办？"利尼问。

利里说："密林走不通，我们就顺着山梁走，只要能走出森林，找到人烟，就好办了。"

The two sisters, in the deep forest, were still cutting vines till the sky began to darken. They had cut lots of vines and got stung by mosquito so badly that their faces and heads were swollen in redness and their eyes could barely open. But the sound of sawing trees was still heard. Lini felt hungry and painful. She couldn't help crying but still dared not to stop.

Lili thought it a little strange since the sound never stopped. So, she stopped and listened very carefully. Then her face turned pale and said to Lini, "Sister, stop. Drop the knife!" Lini said, "Why? Papa will kill us." Lili replied, "No, sister. We are fooled. Papa has already gone. That sound is not from his sawing trees. Because if it is, why can't we hear the trees falling down?" They ran to the top of the mountain only to see a rock hitting a gourd on a treetop. They hugged each other and cried for a while.

By then, it was pitch dark in the deep forest, where tigers and leopards roared and wind whistled past. The pair of sisters were frightened to death that they had to keep walking, not daring to find a place to shelter. They kept silent and only walked towards place with sparse woods. By daybreak, they got lost, not knowing where they were and where to go.

"Sister, what should we do now?" Lini asked.

Lili answered, "As we can't walk through the dense forest, we should go along the mountain ridge. As long as we can get out and find traces of human, we'll be fine."

姐妹俩走出密林，走到山头上，利尼担心地问：“姐姐，我们还回家吗?”利里说：“当然要回家，不回家我们去哪里?”利尼又问：“如果阿爸又把我们送出来呢?”利里说：“我们再找回去。”利尼想了想，气愤地说：“阿爸真坏，他为什么不要我们呢?”利里说：“不是阿爸不要我们，是后妈在使坏呢!”利尼说：“姐姐，阿爸那么听后妈的话，反正是不会要我们的，我们不要回去了吧!”利里说：“妹妹，不管怎么说，阿爸是我们的阿爸，我们不能离开他。继母不是个好东西，等吃完了我们家的粮肉，她会害死阿爸的。”姐姐说服了妹妹，姐妹俩决心找回家去，可是往山梁的哪一方走好呢?

姐妹俩正在犹豫，忽然从密林中跳出来一只老虎。老虎磨着牙说：“姑娘姑娘，我要吃掉你们。”利里请求道：“虎大叔，你是山林中最有名的英雄，英雄怎么能吃我们这两个可怜的小姑娘呢?”老虎说：“你们有什么可怜的，讲出来我听听，如果真的可怜，我就不吃你们。”于是姐妹俩哭着把一连串的遭遇诉说了一遍。老虎听得直流同情的泪水，愤愤不平地说：“你继母不是好东西，你父亲也不是个好东西，我带你们去找猴子毕摩卜个卦，看你家住在哪个方向，然后我带你们去找，教训教训这个无情无义的畜生。”

The two sisters walked out of the mid wood and went up to the top of the mountain. Lini asked her sister worriedly, "Sister, are we still going home?" Lili said, "Of course. Where else should we go?" Lini asked again, "What if our father sent us away?" Lili said, "We shall go back again." Lini thought for a while and said in anger, "Father is so cruel. How can he abandon us?" Lili replied, "It is not father but that woman who is behind all the plots." Lini said, "Sister, if father is so obedient to that woman, he will abandon us anyway. Let's not go back." Lili answered, "Sister, no matter what, he is still our father. We cannot walk away from him. That woman is evil. If she eats up our food someday, she will kill him." Lili finally talked her sister round. They made up their mind to go back home but did not know in which direction they should go along the mountain ridge.

When they were hesitating, a tiger jumped out of the mid wood, grinding its teeth, "Little girls. I'm going to eat you." Lili begged, "Uncle tiger, you are the most famous hero in the mountain. How can a hero eat us two poor little girls?" The tiger said, "Why do you call yourself poor girls? Tell me. If it's true, I will not eat you." So the sisters cried and told him what they had gone through. The tiger also cried out of sympathy. Then, it said furiously, "Your step mother is a scum. So is your father. I'll take you to the monkey Bimo to practice divination. We shall find out in which direction your house is located. And I'll lead you to find it and crucify those heartless monsters."

老虎带着姐妹俩去找猴子毕摩，猴子一见老虎来，惊叫一声，逃到树梢上去了。老虎坐在树脚下，对猴子哀求说："猴子猴子，今天我不吃你们，这里有两个可怜的姑娘，我决心帮助她们找到父母，请你们下来帮忙卜个卦。"猴子说："花言巧语的老虎，你用这种方法吃了我们多少伙伴，今天我们决不会再上当了。"老虎流着泪说："看来你们这些有灵性的猴子，还不如我这虎霸王仁慈。"接着，它把姐妹俩的遭遇复述了一遍，说："事情是这样，帮不帮忙由你们了。"

猴子坐在树上说："既然是这么回事，我就帮她们算一个卦。"猴子算了半天，说："这两个姑娘的父母，已经从山东边搬到山西边去了。往这座山的左边一直走，出了大森林，再走十天就到啦。记住，途中要过九十九个寨子，九十九条河，记错就找不到了。"

老虎说："知道啦!"领着姐妹俩就上路了。猴子又在后边补充说："喂，回来，你们现在不能去找，如果现在去找，个个都是死。等过六年再去找，到那时就没事啦！虎大王，你真心想救两个姑娘，就记住我的话吧!"

老虎对姐妹俩说："现在我只能把你们送到有人烟的地方去，你们找个地方住下来，过六年我再来帮助你们。"

The tiger took the sisters to the monkey Bimo. Upon seeing the tiger, all monkeys screamed and ran to treetops. The tiger sat near the tree root and begged, "Monkey, today I won't eat you. Here are two poor little girls. I make up my mind to help them find their parents. So I want you to come down and practice divination for us." The monkey said, "You canny tiger. How many of our companions have been eaten by you with the same trick? Today we won't be fooled." The tiger spoke with tears, "Intelligent you might be, but how can you be crueler than me?" Then he repeated stories of the girls to the monkeys and said, "This is the truth. Help them or not?"

The monkey sat on a tree and said, "If this is the case, I will practice divination for them." After a while, the monkey said, "Their father and stepmother have moved from the east of the mountain to the west. Walk on the left side of the mountain and out of the forest. Then, they will find the house within ten days. But remember, there are 99 stockaded villages and rivers on the way. If they make a mistake, they will never find it."

The tiger replied, "Get it." Then, he led the girls on their way. The monkey added, "Come back. Don't go for them now. If you do, you will all die. Look for them after six years. King tiger, if you really want to help the girls, mark my words."

The tiger said to the girls, "Now I will take you to places inhabited by people, where you can settle down. I will come back to help you after six years."

老虎把姐妹俩送出了密林，姐妹俩便依照猴子的嘱咐，找一家无儿无女的人家安下身来。六年后，那只老虎依约来帮助姐妹俩，不幸在路上落进了猎人的陷阱，猎人不管它怎么哀求，怎么讲述姐妹的遭遇，还是把它杀死了。姐妹俩只好自己去找父母。

姐妹俩从东往西一直走，穿过了九十九个寨子，跨过了九十九条河，在第一百条河边，有一个单村独户的寨子，就是父亲和继母的家。姐妹俩在河边遇见一个打水的小男孩，是继母把她姐妹俩赶出家门之前生的。姐妹俩一叫他的名字，他就知道了来人是谁，欢欢喜喜地把她们带回家去了。这男孩名叫阿各，他还有个六岁的妹妹阿妞。阿妞对姐妹俩也很亲热，先跑回家报了父亲。

父亲和继母以为搬得这么远，姐妹俩就算不死在山林，也永远不会找来了。现在一听她们又找着追了上来，真是吃惊不小。继母怒气冲天地对父亲说："当年你是怎么说的？这一次你如果不把这两个丧门星杀掉，我决饶不了你！"这时的父亲越来越怕继母，于是他讨好继母说："我这一次一定杀死她们，你叫怎么杀我就怎么杀，手软的不算汉子。"

于是两个人又商量了一下，定好了收拾姐妹俩的恶毒主意。

Then, the tiger escorted the girls out of the forest. They followed the monkey's instructions and lived with a family that had no son or daughter. Six years later, the tiger came to help the two girls as promised.

Unfortunately, he fell into the trap of a hunter on the way. No matter how he begged or told the hunter stories of the girls, he was still killed. So, the sisters had to go and find their father and stepmother by themselves.

They kept walking from the east to the west. After crossing 99 stockaded villages and 99 rivers, they finally arrived at a village that had only one family by the 100th river, which was the house of their father and stepmother. The sisters came across a boy who was fetching water. He was born before his mother drove the sisters away. At the sight of his half-sisters, he recognized them and took them home happily. The boy was named A'ge and had a six-year-old younger sister called Aniu who was also very kind to her half-sisters and ran home to tell her father.

The father and his wife had thought that even the sisters could survive in the forest, they would never find the way here. As soon as they learned that the sisters were coming here from Aniu, they felt shocked. The wife said furiously, "What did you tell me? This time I will never forgive you if you don't kill those two jinxes." As their father grew more fearful of his wife, he catered to her that, "I will definitely kill them this time. I'll do whatever you want me to do. See if I care!"

Therefore, they plotted again. A vicious idea came out.

阿各和阿妞各拉着姐妹俩的一只手，又笑又跳进了院子，大声说："阿爸阿妈，天大的喜事降临了，以前丢失了的两个姐姐回来了，快来迎接呀！"听到喊声，父亲从门里走了出来，阴沉着脸看也不看两个女儿，就去开猪圈门去了，顺手拿起两股麻绳。姐妹俩一见父亲，高兴地呼喊着"阿爸"亲热地跑了上去。谁知父亲板着面孔说："瞎了眼啦，谁是你们的阿爸？"

姐妹俩以为自己长成了大姑娘，父亲不认识了，连忙说："我们是利里和利尼呀！"

阿各和阿妞说："她们真是过去丢失了的两个姐姐吗？"

父亲吼道："瞎说，你们啥时丢过姐姐啦？"

姐妹俩见父亲不认自己了，不由得眼泪巴巴，哭了起来。阿各和阿妞在一旁呆了。

这时，继母从门里走了出来，见利里和利尼长成了比天仙还丰满漂亮的大姑娘，顿时感到又嫉妒又难受。心里说："你们长得越漂亮，老娘越要叫你们不得好死。老娘要吃掉你们的肉，喝掉你们的血才解恨！"于是她故作惊喜地说："哟，明天正是杀牲节，从哪里钻出这么一对胖胖的小嫩猪来，正好杀了过节。"

阿各和阿妞说："阿妈，你怎么啦？明明是两个大姐姐，你怎么说她们是小胖猪呢？"

A'ge and Aniu each took a hand of the sisters, laughed and jumped into the yard, shouting, "Papa, Mama. Let's see what an unexpected piece of good fortune is here. Our lost sisters come back. Come out and see them!" As soon as the father heard the shout, he walked out and went straight to the pigpen, taking up two strings of hemp ropes, without a look at his two daughters. At the sight of their father, the sisters were so happy that they called out their father and ran to him affectionately. The father, on the contrary, said with a grim face, "Look closer. Who's your father?"

The two sisters thought that their father could not recognize them as they had all grown up. So they explained immediately, "We are Lili and Lini."

A'ge and Aniu said, "Are they really the two lost sisters?"

Their father shouted, "Nonsense. What time did you lose sisters?"

The two sisters could not help crying as their father did not want to recognize them while A'ge and Aniu stood nearby in astonishment.

Then their stepmother came out. Seeing Lili and Lini having grown into two plump and beautiful girls, she suddenly felt envious and upset. She thought to herself, "The more beautiful you are, the more pain you will suffer! I'll eat your flesh and drink your blood." Then she pretended to be very surprised, mumbling, "Tomorrow is the livestock killing festival. Where are this pair of fat little pigs from? What a timely gift!"

A'ge and Aniu said, "Mother, what's the matter? They are our two elder sisters. Why did you say pigs?"

继母吼道："小娃娃知道什么，明天把她们杀了，你吃着肉就知道她们是人还是猪啦！"然后又阴险地冷笑着，对父亲说："喂，快把这两头小胖猪给我拴住关起来，明天好杀了过节！既然送上门来，可不能让她们跑了！"

父亲提着索子奔过来，把姐妹俩按倒捆住，拴到猪圈里关了起来。姐妹俩没想到父亲会这么残忍无情，竟把女儿当作猪关起来，真是又悔又恨。一想到刚才继母的话，料定明天必死无疑。她们恨死了继母，同时也互相埋怨起来。利尼说："过去我说不要回来了，你说为了父亲，死也得回来。这下，全完啦！"利里说："只要父亲能吃得下我的肉，就叫他吃吧。他吃下去了，总要屙出来的！"利尼说："我死也要变成一条虫，把他们的肚子咬穿！"

阿各和阿妞眼见父母真把两个姐姐当猪关了起来，心中愤愤不平。第二天早上，母亲找了两个背箩给兄妹俩说："去山上捋些松毛回来，我们要铺着松毛杀那两头小猪吃。"兄妹俩想，人怎么能当作猪杀来吃呢？父母真是疯了，这么好的两个姐姐，可不能真的叫他们杀了。兄妹俩心里这么想，又不能违抗父母之命，于是每人偷偷抓了一把麻子在腰包里。到了山上，他们把麻子嚼碎，吐在松毛上，直混到太阳当顶，才捋了几把回来，说："爹啊妈啊，山上的松毛到处都糊满了雀屎，我们找了一早上，连一把没有雀屎的松毛

Their mother shouted, "What do you kids know? Tomorrow when we kill them, you will taste their meat and find out whether they are pigs or human." She turned to her husband and said with a sneer, "You tie up this two little pigs so we can kill them tomorrow in the festival. We cannot let them go since they throw themselves in."

The father dashed to the two sisters with a rope in his hands, pinned them down, and tied them up in the pigpen. The two sisters felt very regretful because they did not expected that their father could be so brutal and heartless as to lock his own daughters like pigs. Recalling what their stepmother said, they knew they were going to die tomorrow. They cursed their stepmother and also complained to each other. Lini said, "I told you not to come. You said we should come here anyhow for our father. Now we are screwed." Lili replied, "As long as he bears to eat my flesh, let him eat." Lini said, "If I die, I will become a worm to bite through their stomachs."

A'ge and Aniu were indignant when they saw that their parents really locked up their two elder sisters as pigs. The next morning, their mother gave them two baskets and said, "Go to the mountain and pick some pine leaves. We are going to lay leaves on it and kill those two pigs." A'ge and Aniu thought, "How can human be killed and eaten like pigs? Our parents are crazy. Those two good-natured sisters can't be killed by them." Although they had such thoughts, they dared not to defy their parents. Therefore, they each grabbed a palm of seeds secretly and put them in the bags around their waists. When they reached the mountain, they chewed up the seeds and spat them on the

也找不着。"继母听后骂道："都长这么大了，连把松毛也找不来，真是白吃了饭。算啦，你们在家里守着这两个小母猪，我和你阿爸去捋松毛。"继母和父亲说着出门上山捋松毛去了，临走还再三嘱咐："如果放走了小猪，回来看我怎么收拾你们！"

父母走了以后，兄妹俩连忙把利里和利尼解开，从猪圈里放了出来，叫她们赶快逃命。姐妹俩感激不尽，千恩万谢告辞去了。阿各便叫妹妹打一土锅水支在火上，把家里那只大松鸡拿来杀了，故意把鸡血洒在墙上、地上和门上，还往门外的路上洒了一段，然后埋掉鸡肉，只洗了一截鸡肠子煮在锅里。

下午，继母和父亲捋了满满两背箩松毛回来，一见利里和利尼不见了，就去责问阿各和阿妞这是怎么回事。阿各装作生气的样子说："谁叫你们不快点回来，那两头小猪见大人不在，欺负我们是小孩，挣脱了绳子跑出来。我们兄妹俩打又打不赢，拉又拉不住，我拿着一把刀子追着杀，只杀出来一截肠子，正煮在锅里呢！"父亲和继母追着血迹看了一阵，又回来捞着鸡肠子分吃。继母问父亲："好吃啵？"父亲说："好吃！"继母叹道："只可惜让她们跑掉了。"

pine leaves. Until the sun was at its crest, they dragged their heels to go back home with a few bundles of pine leaves. "Father, mother, bird's shits were on the leaves everywhere. We have searched for the whole morning but still could not find a single bundle that has no bird's shit." Their mother scolded, "Grown up already, you could not even find me some pine leaves. Why did I raise you? Forget it, you two watch those two pigs. I'll go with your father." Then she went to the mountain with her husband. Before they left, they warned A'ge and Aniu, "If you let the pigs go, I'll know how to do with you."

After their parents left, A'ge and Aniu hurried to untie the two sisters, took them out of the pigpen and told them to run. The grateful sisters thanked their stepbrother and sister and ran away in haste. A'ge told his younger sister to pour water into a pot and suspended it over the fire. He killed the grouse in their house and spilled its blood on the walls, the floor and the door and even a small stretch of road outside the door. Then he buried the chicken meat, washed a section of its intestine and boiled it.

In the afternoon, his parents went back with two baskets of pine leaves. However, Lili and Lini were nowhere to be found. They questioned A'ge and Aniu about their whereabouts. A'ge pretended to be angry and said, "Why can't you come back earlier? When you were away, those pigs thought we were just two kids, so they broke loose from the ropes. But we were no match to them so we failed to hold them back however hard we tried. Then I took a knife to chase after them, only to cut a section of intestine off them which is now boiling in the pot." His father and mother followed and observed the blood stains for a while. Then, they came back to taste the intestine. His mother asked her husband, "Delicious?" "Very!", he answered. She signed and said, "But it's a pity to have let them escape."

利里和利尼逃命之后，在路上跑啊走啊，记不清走了多少天。有一天，她们来到一个开满了鲜花的地方，这地方美得叫人无法形容。只见甜甜的水在草地上一闪一闪地流，五彩的祥云在山林上一荡一荡地飘，一群蝴蝶飞过去，一群蜜蜂飞过来。她们一时兴起，在草地上跳起了舞，唱起了歌。她们的歌声飘啊飘，飘到了深山密林里，把两个正在打猎的小伙子吸引过来了。

两个小伙子先从东边看，看不清姐妹俩是仙女还是凡人；再绕到西边看，瞧不出姐妹俩是凡人还是仙女；从北边和南边瞧过来之后，两个小伙子就忍不住跪在了姐妹俩的面前。原来，这两个小伙子是山后阿呒土司的儿子，哥哥叫马马，弟弟叫俄俄。他们听了利里和利尼的自我介绍，非常同情她们的遭遇，加上心里又爱慕不已，就把利里和利尼带回家去了。阿呒土司知道利里和利尼的事后，也愤愤不平地说：“哼，天下竟然会有这样的父母，真是连猪狗都不如啊。姑娘，从今后你们就住我家，将来我一定替你们报仇。”

After running away from death, Lili and Lini kept travelling for countless days, until they reached an ineffably beautiful place where flowers blossomed everywhere. Sweet water tinkled through the grassland and sparkled as light called. Propitious colorful clouds wandered about the mountains and forests. A swarm of butterflies flied past, followed by their bee friends. The two sisters suddenly had a joyous mood, so they sang and danced happily on the grassland. Their voice drifted away to the deep forest in the mountain, which appealed to two hunting boys.

Looking in the east, the boys could not tell whether the two sisters were fairies or mortals. Then they went past to the west side to have a look and still could not have a clue. Afterwards, they did the same thing in the north and south. Finally, they went to the two sisters and couldn't help kneeling down before them. It turned out that the two young men were sons of chieftain Afu behind the mountain. The big brother was called Mahma and the younger one Ehe. Having heard stories of the two sisters, they felt very sorry. Then, they decided to take the girls home out of a mixed feeling of sympathy and affection. When the chieftain Afu was told the story, he was outrageous, "I can't believe such ill-minded parents really exist. I dare to say that they are worse than animals. Girls, from now on, you can stay with us and I'll help you revenge someday."

利里和利尼在土司家住了一年多，土司府上上下下无不交口称赞，说她们真是一对天下难找的贤惠姐妹。后来，马马、俄俄弟兄俩向父亲请求，要娶利里和利尼做妻，阿吪土司认为两个姑娘人品出众，高兴地答应了两个儿子的要求，并定在粮丰酒熟的十月举行婚礼。

阿吪土司认为，这场婚事是双龙配双凤，地地道道的双喜，应加倍庆贺，因而派出十二路使者，通告十天路程的所有黎民百姓，能来的都来参加婚礼。到正式举行婚礼那天，所有通向土司府的路上，都走满了前来贺喜的人；从有钱人到叫花子，从农户到商人，成千上万的人汇集在土司府门前的坝子里，庆贺利里、利尼和马马、俄俄的婚礼。

这场隆重异常的婚礼中，每天吃饭的时候，来参加婚礼的人都是沿路坐成两排，由土司兵赶着牛车分发饭食。头一天，分饭的人从排头把饭团和肉圆子分发到排尾去，当发到最末尾的叫花子时，没有饭和肉了。分饭的想，我们明天就从尾上发起吧。谁知头天排到末尾的叫花子第二天跑到排头去了，结果还是没有领到饭菜。分饭的又想："头两天，从头和尾发饭菜，都有一个没有发得，今天我们就从两头往中间发。"不料那叫花子在头尾都没领得饭，以为到中间去必然会得到，又跑到中间去了，结果饭菜发到他时，又没了他的份。

After living in the chieftain's mansion for one year, the two sisters won the favor of everyone for their rare virtue. Later, Mahma and Ehe asked their father's permission to marry Lili and Lini. The chieftain thought that these two girls were indeed of unexceptionable character and therefore happily agreed. A wedding ceremony was planned to take place in October, the time for harvest.

Chieftain Afu believed that the marriages should be celebrated with double efforts because the two couples were really a match. Therefore, he sent 12 envoys to inform every citizen to attend the wedding within ten days of walk. On the wedding day, the road to the chieftain's mansion was fully occupied by people who came to congratulate him from all walks of life, including rich men, beggars, farmers, tradesmen, etc. Tens of thousands of men crowded into the flat ground in front of the chieftain's mansion to celebrate marriages of the two couples.

In this exceedingly grand wedding, the participants sat in two rows along the road and were treated with food carried in ox-pulled carts by the chieftain's soldiers. On the first day, the soldiers handed out rice balls and meat balls from the front to the back of the rows. But when they approached the last man, a beggar, in the back, no rice or meat was left. The soldiers thought to themselves, "Tomorrow we'll hand out food from the back to the front." The next day, the beggar waited in the front of the row. However, when the food was served from the back to the front, none was left to the first man in the row. Again, this beggar got nothing to eat. On the third day, the servants thought, "In the first two days, there was still one man that got no food. Today we will hand out from the middle." This time, the beggar chose to wait in the middle as well, because he failed to get any when he was the first and the last in row. Ironically, when the cart went to the middle of the row, it ran out of food, so the beggar was left out again.

分饭的人感到奇怪，便告诉了管家大人，管家大人又告诉了阿吪土司。阿吪土司说："去，把他叫来，好好照顾他吃两顿。"于是管家就去把那人带了来。利里和利尼一看，惊呆了，这不明明是父亲吗？怎么两年不见就落到了这种田地？利里给利尼使了个眼色，等叫花子吃饱了把他带到金碧辉煌的府里。叫花子从没见过这么壮丽的殿堂，吓得路也不敢走，话也不敢说，哆哆嗦嗦地一个劲磕头谢恩。见无人吱声，他偷偷抬头一看，看见眼前站着两个比天仙还漂亮的姑娘。

他以为遇上了神仙，吓得惊慌失措，一下子跌跪在地上，口里乱叫着："神仙开恩，神仙救命……"

毕竟是骨肉亲啊，利里和利尼看着父亲的可怜相，含泪叫道："阿爸，我们是被你当作猪要杀了吃的利里和利尼呀！"

叫花子一听，吓得脑门着地，趴在地上，失声痛哭道："我该死，我该死，我不是人，做了那种伤天害理的事。如今年老体弱，被那妖精赶出家门，想活无力，想死无力。报应啊报应！"

土司见了，喊道："来人，把这老叫花拉出去，打三十大棍轰走！"

利里和利尼连忙阻止说："看在我们的面上，看他怪可怜的，饶了他吧，我们终究是他的骨肉呀！"

The soldiers were very confused and told the butler, who reported to chieftain Afu. The chieftain said, "Go and fetch him. Give him two hearty meals." So the butler brought him here. Upon seeing him, Lili and Lini were stunned, thinking, "Isn't he our father? How can he fell so slow after two years?" Lili tipped Lini a wink and asked him to go to the splendid mansion after a hearty meal. The beggar had never seen such a magnificent place before. He was so scared that he dared not walk or talk. All he did was mumbling and kowtowing. As no one responded, he looked secretly, only to see two girls more beautiful than fairies. He thought they were two goddesses and got panic. Then he fell to the ground and mumbled, "Have mercy. Have mercy..."

After all, he was their father. Feeling so pitiful, Lili and Lini said with tears, "Papa, we are Lili and Lini. Your daughters you wanted to kill and eat as pigs!"

When the beggar heard it, he collapsed and fell on the ground, crying, "I should go to hell. I'm a heartless beast. How could I have done such horrible things. Now I'm weak and old. So that wicked bitch drove me out. I'm too weak to live or die. It's my punishment. Yes, it must be!"

The chieftain saw it and shouted, "Guards, drag this old beggar out and beat him with a stick for 30 times. Then tell him to go!"

Lili and Lini stopped immediately, "Have mercy, please, for our sake. He is pathetic enough. No punishment please. After all, he is our father!"

土司说道：“你们的心这么好，你们请饶，就饶他吧。”顿时，父女三人抱头痛哭成团。

流传地区：永仁县
讲述者：陆洪英
搜集者：罗有芬
整理者：罗有能

The chieftain said, "You are so kind-hearted. Well, since you asked, I'll let him go."

Suddenly, Lili and Lini and their father hugged together and cried.

Spread area: Yongren County

Narrator: Lu Hongying

Collector: Luo Youfen

Editor: Luo Youneng